CW01507037

THE
DRAGON
AND THE
SUN
LOTUS

莲花出白夜

BOOKS BY AMÉLIE WEN ZHAO

THE THREE REALMS DUOLOGY
The Scorpion and the Night Blossom

SONG OF THE LAST KINGDOM DUOLOGY
Song of Silver, Flame Like Night
Dark Star Burning, Ash Falls White

THE BLOOD HEIR SERIES
Blood Heir
Red Tigress
Crimson Reign

AMÉLIE WEN ZHAO

THE DRAGON AND THE SUN LOTUS

莲花出白夜

HARPER
Voyager

Harper*Voyager*
An imprint of
HarperCollins*Publishers* Ltd
1 London Bridge Street
London SE1 9GF

www.harpercollins.co.uk

HarperCollins*Publishers*
Macken House,
39/40 Mayor Street Upper,
Dublin 1, D01 C9W8
Ireland

First published by HarperCollins*Publishers* Ltd 2026
1

A catalogue record for this book is available from the British Library.

ISBN: 978-0-00-867281-2 (HB)
ISBN: 978-0-00-867282-9 (TPB)

Printed and bound in the UK using 100% Renewable Electricity by
CPI Group (UK) Ltd

MIX
Paper | Supporting
responsible forestry
FSC™ C007454

This one is for Pete and Krista,
without whom my stories would not have reached so many.

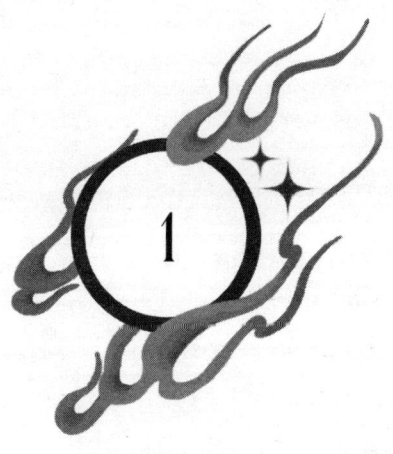

Àn'yīng

Xī'lín Village, Central Province,
Kingdom of Rivers

My mother always told me the sunrises were the most beautiful part of our realm. A sky on fire in shades of rose and persimmon, clouds streaked with flame, and the breath of a world waking to the light.

I remember Mā's words as I move through the pine forest on velvet tread. I hold a bow and arrow—but my crescent blades are tucked in the bodice and sleeves of my black gauze dress, like quiet companions in the predawn silence.

This morning, I am hunting.

Dew from pine needles wets my sleeves as I slip past, a trailing shadow. I hear a slight rustling, and a speckle-coated hare darts through the brush.

I squint through the foliage, following glimpses of the hare's coat as it skitters through the browning leaves, unaware of my pursuit. Méi'zi will cry that I've killed a rabbit, but Mā needs the nutrients as her body returns to full health.

Autumn has arrived, bringing a crisp bite to the morning air. The flowers are beginning to lose their bloom; soon, winter's snows will cover everything in white, and my realm will be made anew with the turn of a year. Yet ever since I've returned here to the mortal realm, its colors have seemed duller, the landscapes imperfect, compared with the ethereal beauty of the immortal realm.

Real, a voice in the back of my mind whispers. *It's real.*

The hare leaps into a small clearing and stops, nose twitching, as though scenting for danger. I, too, stop in my tracks. It's a long shot from here, but I might make it.

As I raise my bow and arrow and take aim, a sudden gust of wind stirs, shifting the clouds overhead. The clearing fills with the warm glow of dawn, and my mind conjures a dreamlike memory.

He stands in the clearing, turning toward me as though time has slowed.

Hair, billowing like swirls of ink.

Eyes, flashing like golden embers.

The phantom of a smile on his face as his gaze lifts to meet mine—

I take a swift step back. Blink and the vision's gone—there's only an empty clearing, leaves falling like the wings of dying butterflies.

The hare starts at my movement and shoots off into the brush again.

My heart is in my throat. I have the strangest feeling that I'm dreaming and that I've had this dream before. The setting changes: Sometimes it's a bamboo forest, sometimes a field of flowering cherry trees, other times a vast mountaintop . . . but the person I'm chasing is always the same.

The clearing before me blurs.

I hate him.

I miss him.

I hate myself for missing him.

Yù'chén is the son of the Kingdom of Night's demon queen, Sansiran—and the mortal emperor, as I found out a few days past. Half mó and half mortal, he tricked the wards of the immortal realm, sneaking in to compete in the Immortality Trials in the guise of a mortal . . . and enabling the Kingdom of Night's demonic army to cross into the previously impenetrable Kingdom of Sky.

He is also the man who saved my life more times than I can count.

And the man I thought myself in love with.

No. I release an arrow into the brush where the hare disappeared, imagining it to be Yù'chén's heart instead. "I hate him," I mutter, as though speaking the words aloud will render them true. "And I'll kill him."

"Admirable attitude, but your bow-handling skills leave much to be desired."

I whirl around. Hào'yáng strides toward me between the pines. He's shed the golden armor that once marked him a captain of the guard of the Kingdom of Sky, but light still wraps around him, teasing out the gold-stitched patterns on his pale shift. It catches on the silver hilt at his waist—the longsword named Azure Tide, gifted to his lineage by the dragons in a time long past.

Hào'yáng, my boy in the jade. Rightful heir to our realm, the Kingdom of Rivers.

And now, my betrothed.

He studies me as he approaches. "Nock your arrow and take aim again," he says coolly, and I obey, pivoting to face the clearing. My pulse is still racing, but in moments I feel a warm hand at my elbow.

"Lift it to be level with your chin." Hào'yáng's voice is low by my ear, and as his other hand comes to meet mine, steady and firm, the tumult of my memories dissolves. My mind clears, sharpens like a blade. "Draw . . . and release."

Swoosh. My arrow whizzes through the clearing, lodging firmly in the trunk of a pine.

Hào'yáng makes a satisfied hum. "Whoever your prior instructor was did not do you justice."

I turn to him and find his eyes narrowed, the corner of his mouth ghosting into a smile that I've seen only a handful of times. "It isn't the instructor who's at fault but the student who is lacking," I reply.

His gaze dances with light as it meets mine. "I find that difficult to believe," he says as he steps away, his hands coming to rest behind his back.

"You humor me."

It's been only two days since we arrived back at my village, Xī'lín—and less than a week since we escaped the battle between the demonic army and the immortals in the Kingdom of Sky that interrupted the Immortality Trials. Though the Kingdom of Night began its war against the Kingdom of Sky nearly ten years ago, the mortal realm is less safe than it's ever been.

Yet now, with Hào'yáng's return, we have a plan to take it back from the demons.

Before the Immortality Trials ended, I learned my true heritage. I am the daughter of Lady Shī'yǎ—one of the legendary

Eight Immortals—and as her sole surviving heir, I have the right to call upon an army of immortals pledged to her name.

Hào'yáng needs this army to defeat the Kingdom of Night and take back the Kingdom of Rivers from their clutches. And so we agreed to an alliance.

A marriage alliance. Political in nature.

I touch the broken jade pendant resting against my chest. My father gave me its other half when our kingdom fell to the demon realm, telling me there was a guardian at the other end of it; all I had to do was ask for their help. In the years after he died, my guardian in the jade was the person I turned to as war ravaged our land. Whether it was to treat my sick mother—who was slowly dying after an attack by a mó—or learning to care for and feed my baby sister, the guardian in the jade always had an answer.

I lost mine, but just weeks ago, I found the owner of its other half that I now wear: my guardian in the jade, Hào'yáng.

We have had little chance to be together in the past few days—me, focused on nursing my mother back to health; Hào'yáng, on strengthening the wards of our village with talismans.

Even so, we both know it's only a matter of time until Sansi-ran will realize that the heir to the Kingdom of Rivers is missing from the Kingdom of Sky, and she'll come searching—right into my village, I'm sure of it.

I glance up. Gold-tipped clouds are scattered across coral-hued skies—yet beyond them, storm clouds linger. The weather has been tempestuous since our return; there are whispers in my village that the gods are angry.

Only a handful of us know the truth: that war has arrived

at the immortal realm . . . and salvation for our world is more precarious than ever.

Hào'yáng follows my troubled gaze to the distant skies. The morning sunlight is a reminder of how little of it we have left— and how an eternal night awaits us should we fail.

"I have a better idea than hunting on land," he says lightly, but I know the time has come to take the first steps of our plan. He holds out his hand to me. "Besides, your sister wanted fish for her breakfast congee."

The sky over the river glows a luminous blush through the storm clouds, and a pale mist shrouds the silhouettes of the distant mountains. The Pearl's Claw is an offshoot of the river that runs through the mortal realm: the Long River, sprung from the bones of the Azure Dragon, who once upon a time lay down to slumber and birthed our land.

In the past, our village fishermen sailed the Pearl's Claw's abundant waters and returned with fresh fish, trading across the other villages and cities in the province. Bà, my father, brought me here once by horseback when I was small. I recall the wooden fishing boats with their webbed sails navigating the river's currents, the song of the fishermen as they cast their nets into the water and praised the dragons for their gift.

I never had the chance to return; the Pearl's Claw was farther from my village than I dared venture after my father died. But by dragonhorse, the journey takes less than an hour.

I know Hào'yáng deliberately selected this location for the two rites we are about to perform to begin our offensive. I slide off Meadowsweet's back after him. The dragonhorse whinnies as she leaps back into the air, kicking off into the skies. Her body lengthens and scales grow over her coat, and soon I watch her dragon form grow smaller until she's a tiny stitch of silver among the clouds.

I follow Hào'yáng to the river's bank. The rulers of the Kingdom of Rivers have always been tied to this land. Long ago, when our realm came to life from the springs of the Azure Dragon's bones, she gifted a drop of her blood to the first mortal empress. That divine dragon's blood bound the empress and her descendants to the land: to love it, to serve it, and to protect it. And in return, the land, too, would accept them and only them.

Hào'yáng told me that if the land of the Kingdom of Rivers was the blood and bones, then its emperor was its beating heart.

I watch him step into the river, and I have no doubt this is true. The waters rise in a whirl of blue ribbons, cradling him, as the sun gilds him in a halo of light. Only the true bloodline of our emperor, blessed with the blood of the dragons, has the power to control water. I have seen him call upon oceans, yet the sight never fails to steal my breath. Outlined against the turquoise, he is beautiful in a way poems cannot capture: a fairytale prince risen from the river. And in that moment, I have the sudden, hollow feeling that my boy in the jade is far away, the distance between us one that I can never close.

He turns to me and holds out his hand, and the feeling dissipates.

The river sweeps me up, and Hào'yáng draws me against him with the confident familiarity we developed throughout the weeks he trained me for the trials. The air is chill, though Hào'yáng is warm as he shields me.

"You told me once that you wanted to see the ocean," he

says. "Do you remember that day? It was when you shot your first quail. You were so proud, and it was the first time you told me that you thought you could hunt."

I close my eyes briefly. Yes, I remember my first kill—the first time I thought that my hands could be good for something other than sewing. Knives and blades, bows and arrows, had become the new keys to survival in our realm, and tasting the rich oil of the meat on my lips after months of foraging had felt like a new door opening.

One my boy in the jade had led me to.

That was the first time I'd felt like I could survive in a fallen land.

"I remember my first successful hunt," I say, opening my eyes and meeting his. "But I don't remember telling you about the ocean."

Hào'yáng studies me. Something in his tone softens when he continues: "That was the night you told me you would swap your needles and threads for your blades," he says. "It was after midnight. Méi'zi was asleep in the other room, and you sat by your father's bookshelf, holding the silk handkerchief you were sewing. You spoke to me then, and you said that you'd always dreamt of seeing the ocean. Of seeing the rest of the realm and capturing it in your sewing."

My lips part. I had forgotten about that dream until recently: the one I'd buried deep in my heart and left to dust and darkness. In the days that had followed and the nights that had befallen our realm, dreams had felt like a luxury when we were starving and dying. There had been only survival.

Hào'yáng watches me patiently. He's waiting for me to speak.

But I have nothing to say. And suddenly, the emptiness of that forgotten memory threatens to crack my heart.

"I don't remember," I whisper, blinking quickly.

Hào'yáng's hand is warm on my waist; he laces his fingers through mine, as though we are in a slow dance. "That's all right," he says. "I remember for you. I remember all of you, Àn'yīng. The girl you were when we first met, with dreams and a love of colors and silks."

I find that I cannot breathe.

"I wanted to let you know that—no matter who you become and what you choose to be." Hào'yáng's gaze shifts to the horizon. "Whether a mortal girl . . . or an immortal's heir."

My chest tightens. This is the first part we agreed upon: to secure our initial forces by calling upon the immortal army that once belonged to Lady Shī'yǎ.

My birth mother, who died to save my life.

Unlike mortals, immortals do not leave their corporeal forms behind when they pass. Yet Lady Shī'yǎ bequeathed one single item to me when she left this world, with only myself and Hào'yáng as witnesses.

Hào'yáng reaches into his storage pouch, where he has been keeping it safe for me.

Lady Shī'yǎ's lotus flower reflects the morning light with a sheen like magic. Blush-colored and framed by a jade-green leaf trailing a long, elegant stalk, it seems to pulse with a soft, dusky glow.

"You know the legends of the Eight Immortals Crossing the Sea," Hào'yáng says, and I nod. It is a fairy tale all mortal children have heard: the Eight Immortals using their vessels of power to tame an ocean during a storm as they crossed from the mortal to the immortal realm. "This lotus was the vessel of Lady Shī'yǎ's power. Some say the immortals' vessels hold a drop of their souls," Hào'yáng continues. He lowers his gaze and holds the lotus out to me as reverently as though it were a part of the woman who raised him for the last ten years. "It's yours, Àn'yīng."

The lotus shimmers between us. Even from here, I feel the magic energies spilling from it and sweetening the air. It's a fragrance so similar to Lady Shī'yǎ's that I half expect her to step from the river waters, that gentle half smile on her lips. The first time I set eyes upon her, having just qualified for the Immortality Trials, she was holding this lotus. I've seen her wield it as a sword as well as use it to heal the most terrible wounds, yet I know I've beheld only a fraction of the magic it holds.

This lotus, Hào'yáng and I have reasoned, is the way for me to legitimize my position as Lady Shī'yǎ's heir. And it may be the key to the one thing most important to Hào'yáng and this war: access to Lady Shī'yǎ's immortal army.

Today, I need to find out how to unlock its powers.

I slide my hands over his, our fingers clasping the lotus—the only thing left of the mother we shared: the one who gave me life, and the one who saved his. And when I look up, I see the heartbreak on Hào'yáng's face.

I press my palm to his cheek. He doesn't look at me, but there's a tension to the lines of his shoulders and his muscles. As though he's afraid of being touched like this.

"Hào'yáng," I say softly, and finally, he lifts his eyes to meet mine. And there, within, is an ocean of grief.

He doesn't speak—he doesn't have to. Though Lady Shī'yǎ

is my birth mother, it is Hào'yáng who was closest to her. She was his sole source of comfort during his time in the immortal realm; when his family was slaughtered in the war with the Kingdom of Night, she became all that he had.

I gained two mothers during my time in the Kingdom of Sky—and I found Hào'yáng. But he has lost all that he had of family.

Beneath his collected facade as the heir to our kingdom is a boy who is grieving.

Hào'yáng shuts his eyes briefly. When he looks at me again, his gaze is cool steel, a vast and unreachable ocean. He takes my hand from his cheek and presses it back to Lady Shī'yǎ's lotus. His palms are warm and firm against mine. "I'm going to let go now, Àn'yīng," he says.

I do not know if I am ready. I don't know if I ever will be—to fight in a war I wanted no part of, to put my life and my family's lives in danger again without the promise of a happy ending.

All I ever wanted was sunlit days sitting beneath my plum tree at my mother's feet, watching her and Méi'zi sew; evenings spent traveling the realms with my father along silvered rivers beneath pearl-dust stars in the night sky.

An ache rises in the back of my throat. In my dreams, my father's face is already fading.

But I know I will never see those days again if I do not choose to fight.

I nod.

Hào'yáng releases me and steps back. The river waters swirl, lifting me by his silent command, and the world seems to hold its breath to watch.

I'm not certain what I expected. In my hands, the lotus remains still. Yet as I watch, its glow seems to be dimming; its leaf is wilting, and the pink petals are curling at the edges, losing their blush. Faint sparks of light drift from its core.

A horrifying thought comes to me: Without Lady Shī'yǎ in this world, the lotus, too, is dying because I, her daughter and heir, am not strong enough to keep it alive.

I am not worthy of being her heir.

Please. I send a silent prayer to the vessel. *Please answer me. Give me a sign.*

At last, Hào'yáng approaches, gazing down at the flower, an inscrutable expression on his face. His hands wrap around mine. "Keep it safe," he says. "I may not be familiar with the magic of the immortals, but I do believe in destiny. The lotus is yours, Àn'yīng, and it will show its true powers when the time is right."

I can't meet his eyes. He's being kind, and I've just failed catastrophically in the first step of our plan. The lotus was meant to recognize me and allow me to summon Lady Shī'yǎ's immortal army.

Now we still have nothing.

I do as he says, tucking the precious flower into the innermost pocket of my dress, nestled against my heart. "I'm sorry," I mumble. "I'm so sorry, Hào'yáng."

Instead of answering, he cups my cheeks in his palms and presses a kiss to my forehead. The move is so swift, imbued with such familiarity, that I don't have time to react before he's drawing back, his dark brown eyes warmed by sunlight as he gazes into mine.

"I have something to show you," he says.

Then he tips back and falls into the waters, and without his magic holding me up, I go with him.

The plunge is a disorienting shock of cold at first. But

Hào'yáng's grip is strong against my waist and my back, and I hold on to him tightly, eyes squeezed shut.

A laugh sounds through the water. *Open your eyes, Àn'yīng.* Hào'yáng's voice echoes through the muted silence, just as it did when he saved my life in the frozen lake, and then again in the Four Seas, when I fell from the Immortals' Steps. *I'm here.*

I do.

It's more beautiful than I could ever have imagined. The surface of the river overhead has come alive with sunlight stitched through like gold threads upon a lapis-colored tapestry. Silver-bellied fish dart around us, scales glinting like crystals. And before me, drifting in the currents as though he belongs here, is Hào'yáng.

My surprise must show on my face, for his lips part in a rare, full smile. It's a distraction to take my mind off the lotus—but it's working. Ever since my near-drowning, being underwater has been a terrifying thought. But with him, I know that I'll be safe.

I stretch out a hand as a school of speckled carp swim by—only to have them dart away.

The currents come alive, pulling us in the direction of the carp, until we're swimming in their midst. Slowly we spin, sunlight sparkling overhead and the school of carp circling us, their scales the color of flower petals. I have the strangest feeling I have stepped into a fairy tale, one that has no place in the realm I live in.

That feeling swells as Hào'yáng takes my chin in his hand and tilts my face to his. His eyes flicker to my lips.

Then he lowers his face to mine and exhales.

Life energy springs from his mouth, golden and threaded through with bubbles. As it flows down my throat, his magic turns to breath. Fresh air fills my lungs, pure and sweet, tasting of pine and sunlight, the salty tang of the sea.

I inhale, leaning forward as I marvel at the sensation of breathing underwater. My fingers wind through his hair—and in the shift of the current, my lips brush his.

It's as though a whisper of wind touches my heart: rippling the surface of an ocean I didn't know I held within me. Hào'yáng's hand tightens almost imperceptibly against my waist; his eyes have fallen closed.

I blink and lean back slightly from the dizzying sensation that races through my head.

Hào'yáng moves back swiftly, and before I know it, we're rising back up through the depths of the river. We break through the surface and arc through the air, buoyed by waves, and he holds me as we land on the riverbank.

We are soaked. Water snakes down the hair that's escaped the golden pin he wears to pull it back. Our sleeves tangle in the soft morning light, his hands still tight around my waist.

And he doesn't let go. "Àn'yīng," he says quietly. "Can I ask you something?"

Again, that ripple in my heart, butterflies' wingbeats against a sunlit pond. "Of course."

Hào'yáng hesitates, his eyes searching mine. I imagine his brilliant mind forming the words, honing them to be as sharp and well-balanced as a blade. "How do you think of me?"

I am surprised by the heaviness to his question. I do not know what to make of his words, nor of the feeling of gentle currents threading through my chest. Shifting.

I smile teasingly to cover the warmth in my own cheeks as I select the most diplomatic response. "You are my . . . betrothed."

His face softens, and he returns my grin. Teasing in his own way, reminiscent of the days when I'd trained under him in the immortal realm. "Is that all?"

Hào'yáng is careful with his words, taught at a young age, I imagine, by the Imperial Court to speak only tactfully. Yet as I draw breath to answer, I'm aware of the sincerity in his gaze. I recall the terrible grief in his eyes when he gifted Lady Shī'yǎ's lotus to me, when he spoke his adopted mother's name.

He needs comfort. He needs family.

I reach up and place my hand on his cheek. "You are my guardian in the jade," I say, and I mean each word. "You are closest to my heart, and the one who understands me the most. I promised Lady Shī'yǎ that I would stay with you every step of the way, no matter how difficult the path."

Hào'yáng looks at me, and whatever is running through his mind snaps shut. "I see," he says. "Thank you."

Though I have, to the best of my ability, given the right answers, I feel as though they were not the ones he sought.

"And you," I finish, taking his hands, resolve steeling my voice, "are my realm's rightful heir. My emperor blessed with the blood of dragons, who belongs on the throne of the Kingdom of Rivers."

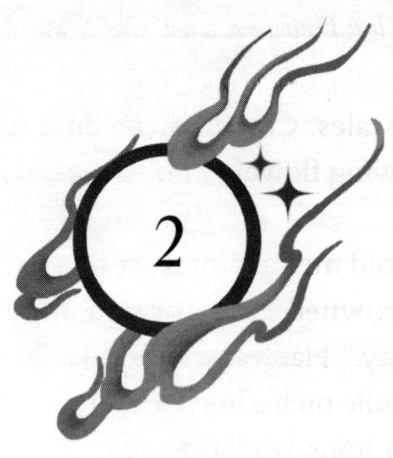

2

Àn'yīng

Xī'lín Village, Central Province,
Kingdom of Rivers

Hào'yáng's gaze sharpens, and I know my guardian in the jade is gone, replaced by the captain and heir. He traces a thumb over the back of my hand, the gesture almost reflexive, as he turns his gaze to the river. "You're right," he says quietly. "It's time for me to stop running and to face the realm's judgment as to whether or not I am worthy of ascending its throne."

"I've been waiting for this moment for nearly ten years," I say. "We all have. Claim your throne, Hào'yáng. Tell me what I need to do to help you."

The morning sun dances across his face as he turns to look at the water. "When I was eight years old, my father took me on a journey on the Long River, from where it runs past the Imperial Palace to where we believe the heart of the Azure Dragon pulses. The waters were the purest shade of blue, and the way sunlight refracted on the ripples gave the illusion of scales. Crowds were lined up as far as the eye could see, throwing flowers into the water to bless us and the dragons.

"My father told me that there, at that exact spot, was where he had been crowned emperor and where I would also be crowned one day." Hào'yáng speaks with a faraway look and the ghost of a smile on his lips. "The mortal emperor is selected when his blood joins with the waters of the Long River. His blood is an offering; the land will decide whether he is worthy of acceptance. If it does, he will be joined as one with the realm." He extends a hand toward the riverbanks. "As Pearl River is an offshoot of the Long River, here is where I'll offer my blood and face judgment today."

I've heard the legends, but none except the imperial bloodline know the secret to how the mortal realm conferred upon its emperors the divine right to rule. In the years when wars were fought between all the eligible heirs to the throne, the land grew unstable and tempestuous as harmony was broken. Those years were plagued with natural disasters; famine and disease swept through the people.

"How does the land choose?" I ask.

Hào'yáng laughs. "Had I the answer, I would not have waited so long to return. It's a divine decision, as mysterious as the Heavenly Order. Historians have tried to summarize the conditions: Typically, if the entire living bloodline declares allegiance to one ruler, that ruler is accepted. If there is only one with the dragons' bloodline left, the land will also accept. But those are guidelines; the exact choosing lies in the magic tying my bloodline to the realm. The land must believe the heir worthy to rule." Hào'yáng pauses. "That is why I remained in the

Kingdom of Sky all these years, why Lady Shī'yǎ trained me and pushed me so hard to become the best version of myself I could be. I needed to be worthy of the mortal realm's acceptance."

I imagine, as I often have, twelve-year-old Hào'yáng arriving on the steps of the Kingdom of Sky, having just lost everything: his family, his home, his kingdom. How well he'd hidden that part of him when he spoke to me through the jade pendant, guiding me and comforting me when he must have been going through so much pain of his own. I recall how he told me training with the immortals as a mortal was difficult; that because he was the weakest of them, he'd vowed to become the best.

And he had.

"I can't think of anyone more worthy," I tell him.

This coaxes another smile out of him. "Legends say that once the land chooses a new emperor, dragons will dance in the skies of our realm. If the land accepts me, Àn'yīng, the dragons will declare their allegiance to me. The tides of this war would turn."

To gain the allegiance of the Realm of Dragons would change everything. Gods of the rivers and oceans and every body of water across the realms, dragons are more ancient than even the Heavenly Order that governs all realms and living things, their powers uncontainable by the skies or seas.

"How would we get to the dragon realm to request their allegiance?" I ask. It had never occurred to me that this was a possibility, for growing up, the tales had portrayed the dragon realm as the most ancient and mythical of all.

"The Realm of Dragons is said to reside somewhere within the Four Seas—beyond the seams of the mortal realm. No mortal has entered it in a long, long time, and legend has it that to do so requires passing a test of sacrifice." Hào'yáng grins at my expression. "One thing at a time. If all goes according to plan and the land acknowledges me as emperor, the dragons will come to us; there will be no need to journey to them. The other realms, though, we'd need to seek out: the Clan of Phoenixes, the merfolk of the Southern Sea, the fox spirits of the Kingdom of Green Hills . . . They are not tied to the mortal realm as the dragons are."

"But if you're crowned emperor and the dragons accept you, we would have a formal title and banner under which to seek the others' allegiance in this war," I finish for him.

Hào'yáng nods and draws his longsword. Azure Tide gleams as he brings it to his side. "Only one way to find out." His smile turns grim. "When I offer my blood to the river waters and the land, I'm going to be vulnerable. I need my most trusted warrior to defend me should anything happen."

I draw my crescent blades. They clink gently as I tap them to his sword. "I'll be here," I say, "always, Hào'yáng. You need never ask."

He touches my cheek. "I know," he says, and straightens. "Let us hope this is the beginning of the end of this war."

As Hào'yáng turns and strides toward the river again, he sheds his pale shift. Sunlight sweeps across the hard planes of his stomach, the ridges of muscles on his arms and his broad shoulders. I catch sight of scars, so many scars, crisscrossing the golden tan of his skin and vanishing into the waistline of his pants. Scars, he once told me, accumulated from years of sparring and training, when the immortal instructors hit him for being weak and mortal and he was determined to prove them wrong.

This is my boy in the jade now: captain of the immortal

guard, heir to the mortal throne, and a man, tall and powerful and beautiful.

Again, I have the feeling of shifting currents in my chest as I watch Hào'yáng cast his shift onto the riverbank and stride into the water. Azure Tide glimmers as if it were made of the river itself.

Hào'yáng bows his head as though in prayer.

Then Azure Tide arcs sharply through the air as he plunges it down. Two slashes: one to each forearm, unlocking a flow of bright-red blood. As it trickles into the river, the river reacts.

Currents swirl in a circle around him, forming a whirlpool as the entire river pulls toward him, churning faster and faster, until all of a sudden—

Hào'yáng goes under.

I swallow a shout.

I'm running before I can think, my blades at my sides and my heart slamming against my ribs. I've survived too much to take anything lightly; I've lost too many people I love. Fear is an emotion stitched into my bones.

"Hào'yáng!" I gasp, but the tides are too strong and I'm forced to stop at the river's edge. "Hào'yáng!"

I scan the water for him, but they are frothy and it's impossible to see anything.

"Hào'yáng!" I call again, and then I hear it.

A high-pitched giggle sounds from somewhere near.

That's when I notice that the forest around us has grown eerily still. A shadow shifts between the trees as a lovely, singsong voice drifts toward me.

"O princeling, young princeling . . ."

The sun vanishes behind clouds, and I raise my crescent blades to greet the mó approaching through the pines.

★ ★ ★

It's a female. I'm struck by how much she resembles a fairy from mortal paintings, all billowing silks and black hair and porcelain skin, and she's holding a lyre. The only thing that gives her away as a demon is her eerie stillness as she watches me—and the purple horn protruding from her forehead.

A demon who can no longer hold the camouflage of her mortal appearance is weakened—starving, perhaps—and reliant upon the strength of her dark magic.

"*O sweetling, O sweetling,*" the mó sings softly, strumming her lyre.

She pauses and breaks into a sudden smile. The muscles of her face are out of sync: One eye falls shut, and only half her mouth lifts while the other half sags, like a broken puppet. "I smell blood."

I don't dare to move from the river where Hào'yáng remains underwater. I cock my head at the mó. "Come closer and I can give you a taste," I say.

The mó stares at me, still attempting that gruesome half smile. But for the wind stirring her clothes and her hair, she might have been carved of stone. Then, slowly, she tilts her head.

"*Blood, bright and sweet as nectar, O, imbued with a drop of . . . the other.*"

Her song lyrics send a shiver through me.

"*Two princelings were born, sun and moon brothers,*" the mó croons, plucking the strings of her instrument. "*Neither can be emperor without killing the other.*"

"What is that song?" My voice roars loudly in my ears, and I'm breathing fast.

The mó smiles suddenly. "Do you like it, sweetling? It is common knowledge in our realm. There are two heirs—one mortal and one halfling—so neither can triumph. And now we will be handsomely rewarded to bring the mortal princeling to the Empress of Fallen Darkness."

A halfling, she speaks of. *Yù'chén.*

Yù'chén, illegitimate child of the demon queen and the late emperor of our land, and half brother to Hào'yáng . . . could also be a contender for the mortal throne.

Hào'yáng and I discussed this possibility, yet there is no precedent for a demon halfling taking the mortal throne. Still, the mó's eerie song and words give me pause.

If the demon queen Sansiran has issued a reward on Hào'yáng's head, then the news this mó brings must be fresh from the Kingdom of Night. That means Sansiran, at least, believes there are two heirs—and that her own son is one.

I can't help it: I glance back at the churning river where the waters swallowed Hào'yáng, my certainty dissolving in the morning air. Hào'yáng said the entire bloodline needed to be aligned with one ruler. If there are two living heirs, will the land hold off on selecting its rightful emperor?

"Blood, bright and sweet as nectar, O . . . imbued with a drop of . . . the dragons," the mó finishes singing, her voice deepening as her smile shows her canines. "I can smell it, sweetling. That same strange scent that runs through the veins of our prince. The fabled blood of the dragons. Reveal him, and I may let you live."

I angle my daggers. "Over my dead body."

She laughs, a sound high-pitched and jarring. In half a blink, she's vanished and reappeared a half step from me. Up close, I can see the cracks of her camouflage: fingers strangely curved and nails sharp like claws, eyes that flash between silver and black as though she bears an affliction. A trail of saliva glistens down her chin as she tips her head back and inhales deeply.

I lash out. Fleet enhances my speed as I plunge Striker down into her chest where, instead of a heart, a demon's core pulses—with enough strength to crack open stone.

Except Striker arcs through empty air where the mó was. And I know I'm in trouble when I hear a soft giggle at my ear.

The mó's razor-sharp teeth sink into my shoulder.

As pain sears through my bones, I grit my teeth.

Then I turn and I stab her.

The mó hisses and leaps, impossibly far and fast, to the tree line, where she nurses her wound as I nurse mine.

Spirit energy flows to my fingertips as I trace the talisman for healing upon my skin. I learned this from my father's engraving on Healer, one of the eight crescent blades he gave me. Over the past days, I've been practicing my magic beyond using the blades. During the Immortality Trials, when I lost two of my weapons, I realized that there may come a day when all I have are my own two hands and my practitioning abilities.

Warmth infuses my shoulder as the talisman takes effect. My bleeding slows; the pain subsides.

The sound of rushing water comes from the direction of the river, and I turn just as a wave rushes up onto the bank, leaving behind a familiar figure.

Hào'yáng lies motionless, his dark hair fanning out under him. Next to him, Azure Tide gleams.

A scuffling noise sounds from behind me. I turn just in time to catch the glimmer of the mó's pale skin as she springs for Hào'yáng.

I throw myself forward, pivoting in midair. My vision sharpens as though time has slowed, and there, as I drive Striker upward, it happens.

Light blooms from beneath my skin, spiraling up Striker's handle and pooling in the blade. It's that same glow that saved me before, when I slew the beast Áo'yīn during the Immortality Trials. A glow that I cannot explain.

But with the wound in my shoulder, my aim is just off.

The mó screams, a strangled noise that sounds neither human nor animal, as I open another gash in her abdomen—just a handbreadth below where her core should sit. She leaps back again. A trail of ichor dissolves like smoke from a gash in her side, and it is with grim satisfaction that I catch the dark substance staining Striker's blade.

The mó's form is changing: Webbed wings sprout from her back, and violet veins begin to darken her skin. Her face has warped: an animalistic snout, thick cords on her neck, and muscles bulging on elongated limbs. She must be severely weakened to be morphing back into her true form like this.

The mó turns and vanishes into the thicket.

I send a pulse of spirit energy into Fleet, preparing to give chase, for I cannot have her bring news of Hào'yáng's whereabouts to the Kingdom of Night.

I have taken several steps forward when a thought stops me abruptly.

Hào'yáng. I can't leave him here, defenseless.

He's stirring slightly as I run to him and kneel by his side. His skin is hot, almost feverish to the touch, his chest bare and corded with raw power. A long white scar runs up each of his arms where he cut himself to join his blood with the water—healed already, perhaps by the magic of his ties with the river.

Hào'yáng's eyes flutter open, and within their familiar brown, I find my boy in the jade. The tightness to my chest dissipates, replaced by a sinking stone of trepidation in my stomach as he speaks the words I most dreaded.

"The land rejected me."

3

Àn'yīng

*Xī'lín Village, Central Province,
Kingdom of Rivers*

We are silent as we wing our way back to Xī'lín astride Meadowsweet. The wind makes it difficult to speak, but the weight we carry at our failures this morning is a shared feeling. The sun glides through gray clouds, their shadows drifting across the pine forests and silver rivers beneath us—a reminder of the darkness into which our realm continues to fall. It is still morning, and Mā and Méi'zi will be making breakfast at home, but we have only a handful of hours of sunlight left before the long night of the demon realm swallows our day.

We land in the forest near my village. Here, at least, near the warded walls of Xī'lín, we're safer—though the concept of safety is fraught.

"Àn'yīng." Hào'yáng's fingers slip easily through mine. I turn to face him, recalling the raw power of his arms and chest. He's looking at my shoulder. My wound has healed with the help of my talisman, but the blood remains. "I'm sorry," he says.

"What for? I'm all right."

"For putting you in danger." Hào'yáng exhales slowly. "My father told me once that my duty would come into conflict with my personal will—and that I should always choose my duty to the realm and the people."

Lifting my gaze to his, I lay it bare between us and speak the truth. "It would have been my duty to defend you with my life," I whisper, "but above that, Hào'yáng, I did it out of *my* personal will."

His grip tightens on mine. "That's not what I wanted. I don't wish to be the reason you're in danger, Àn'yīng. Ever."

"Hào'yáng, you're the only hope for our realm. You're the only way for me to save Mā and Méi'zi and my village and everything I've loved in this life. I can't lose you."

Something like sorrow flickers over his face before hardening into sharp-edged resolve. "You're right," Hào'yáng says, and he lets go of my hand. "We cannot stay here much longer. We need to move forward with the next steps of our strategy." He tilts his head, his gaze faraway, and I recognize the calculating look that slides over his brows. "Àn'yīng, I believe we need to go to the immortal realm. The answers to how you will go about inheriting Lady Shī'yǎ's powers and army lie there. We need to focus on that part of our plan while I resolve . . . mine."

I draw a deep breath. "I know why the land couldn't accept you," I tell him.

Hào'yáng's eyes cut to mine. "Because of Yù'chén," he says, and everything in me tightens. "You told me he was the halfling child of my father and the demon queen. I wasn't certain before whether he would be eligible for the mortal throne, but it seems he is." Hào'yáng's hand goes to the hilt of Azure Tide.

"It seems the land will not accept me with him still as a contender for the throne. So either I kill him . . . or he kills me."

His words crack through the air, shattering the illusion of the idyllic, golden morning I'd dreamt of: bringing fresh meat back to Xī'lín for breakfast with Méi'zi, quiet moments with Mā catching sunlight through our plum blossom tree.

I'd wanted just one more day like that, away from the inevitability of war, of kingdoms, of realms.

But the mó in the forest served as the clearest reminder of the danger we're in. I recall her song and ominous words: *There are two heirs—one mortal and one halfling—so neither can triumph.*

"Then we leave for the Kingdom of Sky tomorrow," I say. "It's only a matter of time before Sansiran and her army know we're here. Before they come after you." I touch a palm to my chest, where the lotus hides beneath the folds of my dress. "I'll find a way for the lotus to recognize me and to summon Lady Shī'yǎ's army. Then . . ." I find that I can't finish, so Hào'yáng does for me.

"Then we strike the mó at our Imperial City when their forces are busy with the war in the Kingdom of Sky," he says. "We break their stronghold on the mortal realm and deal them a critical blow. Next, in order to ascend the mortal throne and push the Kingdom of Night out of our realm once and for all . . . I must kill my half brother."

Ice has frozen over my heart. Yù'chén's eyes, so earnest and dark and wide, are in my mind, the echo of his whisper—*real . . . it's real*—in my ears. I hear my voice, as though from a distance, say: "Yes."

Hào'yáng is silent for a long while. There is something of

regret to his tone when he finally speaks again. "In that case, I'd like to seek your mother's permission for our betrothal today."

I'd known this was coming; after all, I'd agreed to this alliance between us. But for some reason, the detachment in his tone sinks like a weight into my stomach.

I'm to be married.

I'd never thought myself destined for any great romance like those our epics sang of. But as I think of love and the closest I have come to knowing it, my traitorous heart unfurls a memory I'd tried to banish to the back of my mind.

I want you, more than anything in my life. More than anything I have ever felt. I . . . want you.

I inhale sharply and twist my head to push the voice away. A part of me wants to dig out everything I ever felt for Yù'chén, every memory I have of him, and fling them into the ocean.

"Àn'yīng?"

Hào'yáng's voice pulls me back to the present. My pulse is racing; I wonder if he senses my guilt.

Selfish, I berate myself. *While you were dreaming up foolish fantasies of your heart, Hào'yáng has been thinking of the ongoing war, of his duty as heir to the Kingdom of Rivers.*

"Yes," I blurt out. My voice is loud to my own ears, but I would do anything to forget the image of that crimson cloak, those ink-black eyes and soft grin. I reach for Hào'yáng's arm, as though to anchor myself. I chase the feeling of familiarity in his warm brown eyes, and my heart settles slightly. "Yes," I repeat, more gently this time. "Let us be married by nightfall, then."

This way, at least Mā and Méi'zi can attend my wedding— before we ask them to leave the village and go into hiding.

Hào'yáng nods. In that moment, his expression is not so dissimilar from those of the immortals who raised him: utterly devoid of emotion or empathy, as cold and immovable as the mountains of our realm.

"Good," he says. "I'll speak with your mother."

He turns and makes for Xī'lín, tension in the lines of his shoulders. And as I follow, I feel that my boy in the jade is slipping away from me with every passing moment.

Xī'lín is waking when we arrive. Zhū'zhū and Shēn'ní stand watch at the pái'fāng. Survivors of the Immortality Trials, they are from the Northern Province, where their families perished in the war against the Kingdom of Night. With nothing to return to, they elected to stay behind and fight with us when we escaped the Kingdom of Sky, along with many others. The rest of the surviving candidates chose to get far away from the dangers of the demon-plagued Central Province, returning to their families and loved ones in the outer provinces, where mó presence is scarce.

Hào'yáng stops to fill the warriors in on our encounter with the rogue mó and asks them to rally the villagers for a meeting at my house.

I enter the village first, making for my home at a run. The close brush with the mó has brought back familiar nightmares that used to spin in my head. Mā, lying prone on the ground with Bà's body next to her as the Higher One—whom I now know to be Sansiran—drinks her soul. The same thing happening to Méi'zi, like that vision the monster known as a painted skin once taunted me with in the Immortality Trials.

A peal of laughter rings through the bright morning air.

I round the corner of Fú'yí's house, with its stack of firewood for the winter and a fresh vase of yellow dandelions—the last flowers her late husband planted for her before perishing in the war.

Then there is my house, marked by bright plum blossoms.

My front yard is alive with motion. A little white fox darts around our flowering plum tree, letting out yips of glee. Chasing the fox and squealing with joy is my little sister. As I watch, she lunges and snatches the tip of the fox's tail. The next moment, the fox is gone and my sister and a young woman dressed in white wrestle on the ground, their laughter ringing in the sweet morning air.

Beneath the plum blossom tree next to the house, reclining in an old bamboo chair, is my mother. Autumn sunlight dapples her complexion as she watches all this with a faint smile.

My steps slow; my heartbeat settles. Suddenly, my panic seems outsized.

"Méi'zi! I thought you were washing the rice," says an older woman who rounds the house from our backyard with a washcloth and a pail of water. Fú'yí, our widowed neighbor who helped take care of my family in the years of the war, sets the pail by Mā   and catches sight of me. "Ah, Àn'yīng! You're back."

Méi'zi glances up. "Jiě'jie!" she shouts, and erupts into giggles as Lì'líng—our fox spirit halfling friend from the Trials—tickles her.

"They've been at it for the past half hour." A tall figure peels away from the wall of my house. Tán'mù's eye bags are darker than ever, but her normally somber expression has softened over the past few days. Her nostrils flare and her eyes narrow as she scents the blood on my shoulder—which is now hidden beneath a cloak. "What happened?"

I lower my voice so that Méi'zi and Lì'líng's play fighting washes over my words. "Mó."

Fú'yí is crossing the yard to greet me; her expression tightens as she overhears our quiet conversation. "Where?" she asks in an undertone.

"The Pearl's Claw River." I turn to Tán'mù, who is less familiar with our geography, and explain: "A half day's journey by foot—but we flew."

"Dead?" she asks calmly.

"Gone." I can't bear to look at Méi'zi, Lì'líng, and my mother in the yard as I say, "It's not safe to stay here much longer." *It never was. Never will be, unless we win this war.* "We've called for a meeting with the villagers now, to discuss an evacuation plan."

"Jiě'jie!" A small figure barrels into me, nearly knocking the breath from my lungs.

I find myself smiling as I hug my little sister, burying my face in her hair. She smells of sunlight, of blossoms and earth and everything good in this world.

I wonder how many more times I will hold her like this.

A sharp yipping bark sounds at my heels, and I laugh as Lì'líng nips at my thigh. She and Méi'zi have become practically inseparable since we arrived back at the village.

My sister draws back, taking in my face with her ever-observant eyes. I pull my cloak a little tighter around myself, but thankfully, she sees only my windswept appearance and damp hair. "Jiě'jie," she says, a sly grin lifting one corner of her mouth. "You were gone a long time with— Oh, Your Highness!"

I turn.

Hào'yáng strides toward us. A smile lights up his face as he pats Lì'líng on her furry head and greets Méi'zi, who accosts him, demanding an explanation for the missing fish he'd promised to bring back for her this morning.

"Forgive me that I wasn't able to bring back your fish," the heir to this realm replies with a hint of bashfulness. "We ran into a little inconvenience."

"What kind of an inconvenience keeps you and my sister in a river for an entire morning?" Méi'zi asks, glancing pointedly at me with an evil little smirk. I glare at her and drag a finger across my throat.

But Hào'yáng counters with a sweetly innocent smile. "Grown-up inconveniences," he says, and pinches her nose.

"That's enough!" I snap. My cheeks are burning. "No fish for you, Méi'zi!"

"Oh, well," Méi'zi sniffs. By her side, Lì'líng lets out a sad little whine. "I suppose I'll have to make do with plain congee for breakfast."

"My favorite," Hào'yáng says, and the way he ruffles my sister's hair stirs my heart. He glances up at me, and I quickly shift my gaze away.

The villagers are beginning to trickle in, summoned by our warriors—the beginnings of Hào'yáng's and my small mortal army. Only twelve of us, fighting to liberate the Kingdom of Rivers.

That's not many fewer than the remaining villagers. Our numbers dwindled steadily throughout the years as more and more packed up and sought the relative safety of the distant provinces. Now there are barely forty of us left.

"All right, that's enough foxing around," Tán'mù growls, snatching Lì'líng by the scruff of her neck. "We have important things to do."

In a blink, the squirming white fox has transformed into a diminutive young woman with a heart-shaped face and two buns in her snowy hair almost shaped like ears. Her amber eyes are bright and her cheeks flushed as she ducks and escapes Tán'mù's grasp.

"You *bore*." Lì'líng giggles, poking out her tongue. "Games of hide-and-seek *are* important." She pecks Tán'mù with a kiss before flouncing off, weaving nimbly through the oncoming crowd.

Tán'mù sighs and rolls her eyes as she hurries after Lì'líng, but there's a hint of a smile on her lips.

"Méi'zi," I begin, intending to tell my sister to go back to the house, but she fixes me with a stern glare.

"I'm staying for the meeting, Àn'yīng." She uses my name as opposed to referring to me as her *jiě'jie*, "older sister." All traces of teasing are gone from her face. "I'm fourteen years old—I'm not a child anymore."

I open my mouth to argue, but I'm interrupted when Fú'yí comes and places her hand on Méi'zi's shoulder. The two of them are almost the same height now.

"She's right, Àn'yīng," my neighbor says. "We'll go bring your mother from the yard for this meeting."

I watch them leave with an odd sense of having lost control over something I can't name. For as long as I can remember, my purpose in life has been to protect my mother and sister from the Kingdom of Night—the mission my father left me with before he died.

"If there's anything I learned, it's that you can't shield the ones you love from danger forever," Hào'yáng says. I turn to find him watching Méi'zi and Fú'yí, an unreadable expression on his face. His gaze shifts to me—and there it is again, the ripple of waves in my chest as our eyes meet.

I duck my head to hide the heat rising to my cheeks. "Of all the dishes of the mortal realm you've been able to choose from since birth," I say, "plain congee is your favorite?"

Hào'yáng folds his arms and smiles almost lazily at me. "At the risk of sounding extremely privileged, all they ever did in the immortal realm was hold banquets and feasts."

I snort. "How utterly atrocious of them."

Hào'yáng laughs, a clear, bright sound. "Congee was my mother's favorite," he says at last. A faraway look crosses his face. "She was a noblewoman from the Southern Province. Sweet congee—congee with a sprinkle of cane sugar—is a southern specialty. My mother used to make it for me on nights when I had trouble falling asleep. Of everything I left behind when the mó took my home, it was sweet congee I missed most in the Kingdom of Sky."

I'm holding my breath, hanging on his every word. In most of the time I've known him in person, Hào'yáng has worn his armor as either the distant captain of the guard or the calculating heir to our kingdom. Rare are the moments in which he sheds that armor and I catch a glimpse of who he is beneath it. Younger. More vulnerable. With his own hopes and dreams and fears of failure.

Glimpses of the boy in the jade I came to know and love.

That all vanishes as he turns to the crowd gathered around us. It's both incredible and disconcerting to watch him step seamlessly into the role of the imperial heir. The effect is not lost on the crowd, either; they lean into him as though he has a magnetic pull. Over the past two days, Hào'yáng has spent time with every single villager, revealing his identity and learning about their backgrounds, of how their husbands or sons or fathers fought in the war against the Kingdom of Night. When he returned each evening, his hands and knees were dusty from kneeling before them to apologize for their losses.

He has earned their complete loyalty and their trust.

"Residents of Xī'lín," Hào'yáng begins, his voice as clear and precise as the strike of a sword. "My fellow warriors."

He holds nearly nothing back of the events from the morning, of the rogue mó and the certainty that the Kingdom of Night will descend upon this village to kill him.

A few of the widowed older women gasp. My mother's face pales, and Méi'zi claps her hands to her mouth. Fú'yí's mouth sets in a grim line.

Then Hào'yáng begins to lay out his strategy. Eight of our warriors will lead a caravan of Xī'lín residents to the Western Province, where the strong sun and heat of the Golden Desert makes it the least accessible for the night-loving mó—and therefore safest for humans.

"Ān'yīng and I will go with a small group to the Kingdom of Sky, where we'll continue to build an army and seek out alliances for war," Hào'yáng finishes. "We aim to leave today, before the long night begins to fall. Pack only what is essential, and gather here by the hour of the monkey."

With the meeting adjourned, the villagers hurry back to their homes, murmuring amongst themselves. My heart breaks for them as I watch them go, all familiar faces I've known my entire life. The butcher's wife, who took it upon herself to teach us all to skin rabbits and pluck quails, to cure meats and preserve them for the winters. The carpenter's daughter, who helped patch crumbling roofs and broken doors; the silk trader's wife and her son, who was too young to join the war when it began; the fishermen's wives and daughters, who turned to raising chickens and would spare an egg or two every so often when my family was hungry.

If this is all that is left of our humanity, I will fight for them with every last breath.

"Àn'yīng?" My mother's voice drifts to me.

"Mā." My gaze lands on her, reclining in her favorite chair at the edge of the gathering place, with Méi'zi and Fú'yí by her side.

She's still thin, too thin, but she no longer has the appearance of bones wrapped in skin. Her cheeks are beginning to fill out, and her brown eyes catch the light.

My chest tightens when I think of the evacuation. My mother is in no state to travel; she can't even walk.

But we have no choice.

As I run to her, my resolve hardens into steel. *This* is why I fight. To drive those mó bastards out of my home, *our* home. To kill them all, so that my sick mother and my baby sister won't ever again have to flee the home they've known and loved for their entire lives.

"Mā." I wrap my arms around her, savoring the fresh soap smell of her hair, the warmth of her body. As her fingers come to stroke my hair, I realize I would go through a thousand trials again for her, for this. "How are you feeling this morning?"

"Yīng'zi." She uses my nickname. Her voice is frail, but there is a spark of energy in her tone now. In the few days since she took the pill of immortality Lady Shī'yǎ gave me before she died, she has spent most of her time sleeping in the sun and eating to regain her strength. Méi'zi and I have been making her favorite chicken ginseng soup each night, replenishing her life energy with nutrients from the meat—meat that Hào'yáng hunts for us. "Your shoulder. What happened?"

"I fought off a mó." I beam and stretch my arms to show her I'm fine. "Bà would be proud, wouldn't he?"

Pride blazes in her eyes. "So damn proud," my mother says. My smile is so wide, it hurts.

Slowly, in her waking moments over the past few days, I've told Mā of my journey to the immortal realm, of the Trials and the pill that brought her back. I've filled her in on the war between the realms, and the candidates from the Trials who returned with us to fight in this war. But I've held back from going into too much detail, afraid that her heart and mind were still too frail to take in the full story—that of my birth mother, my father, and Hào'yáng.

"Mā," I say softly. "Hào'yáng wishes to speak with you."

My mother's eyes spark with mischief. "Oh, he's so hand-some, Yīng'zi," she whispers so that only I can hear. "I know I'm recovering, but I haven't missed how close you two seem and how his eyes follow you around." She taps my nose in a conspiratorial way. "Has a cherry blossom love found my prick-liest daughter after all?"

She's only teasing, but she has no idea both how close and how far she is from the truth. My smile now feels frozen. "Cherry blossom love"—the age-old poetic adage of romance and mar-riage, of the red thread of fate binding two partners together across lifetimes.

Mine is a marriage, but not one born out of romance.

My mother's teasing smile falls as Hào'yáng approaches. He's gentle, his movements infinitely graceful, as he draws to a stop before her. Then, to my astonishment, the late son and the heir to our kingdom sinks to his knees and presses his palms and forehead to the ground.

"Hào'yáng," I whisper.

My mother leans forward and places a hand on his shoulder. "Your Highness, please," Mā says. "I am not worthy of such a heavy gesture."

Slowly, so slowly, Hào'yáng lifts his head. He remains kneeling as he replies quietly, "Lady Hé, without the sacrifice your family made, I would not be here today."

My mother gazes at him in silence, and I wonder what she sees as she takes in his steady, brilliant beauty, his strong brows and sharp-cut jaw, the steel to his gaze and softness to his mouth. Does she think of what might have happened had my father never given him the place our family was promised in the immortal realm? Or is she grateful that her husband's ward has returned, so healthy and alive?

"You have suffered greatly," my mother says gently. "The past nine years cannot have been easy on you, Your Highness."

Surprise blanches Hào'yáng's face. "Lady," he says haltingly, "I could spend the rest of my life repaying you and your family for what you have done for me, and it would not be enough."

"My daughter tells me that you have watched over our family from afar all these years," my mother answers. "And you have brought my Àn'yīng safely back from the immortal realm. We have gained a guardian in you, Your Highness. Please, rise."

"I cannot yet, Lady," he says quietly, "for I have another favor to ask of you." Hào'yáng turns to look at me as he draws a deep breath and says, "I would like to ask for your daughter's hand in marriage."

Méi'zi claps her hands to her mouth again, her eyes darting

to me. Fú'yí's lips part in one of the few expressions of surprise I've ever seen her wear.

My mother is silent for a long while. A wind stirs the branches of our flowering plum tree, petals scattering between snatches of sunlight and blue sky. It couldn't be a more beautiful day to be married.

But my heart is sinking with each passing moment that my mother does not speak. Her gaze is lifted skyward, and I catch plum blossoms reflected in her soft brown eyes. In that moment, she seems to be very far away.

Then, finally, she blinks and looks at Hào'yáng. "Might we speak inside the house, Your Highness?" she asks, then glances at me. "Alone, please."

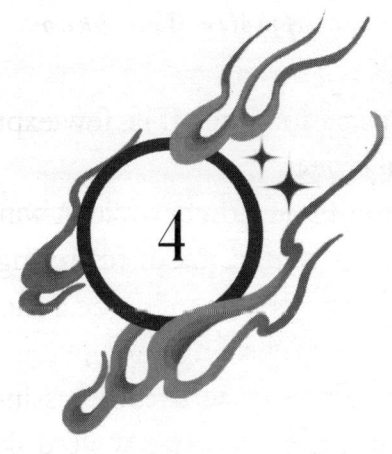

4

Àn'yīng

*Xī'lín Village, Central Province,
Kingdom of Rivers*

I leave my mother in the kitchen with Hào'yáng and two steaming mugs of tea. I make sure to tuck her into her bamboo chair just right, wrapping the old cotton blanket she sewed with peonies around her shoulders and placing another over her knees. She doesn't like to spend her waking hours on the couch; perhaps her body remembers the years she lay there, prone and half-alive, a shell of a person.

I blink the memories away and glance back one more time. I, too, love seeing my mother upright and alert, seated at the kitchen table where she and my father once made meals for Méi'zi and me.

Sunlight streams through our paper shutters, bathing Mā and Hào'yáng in a lambent light. The sight of them should warm my heart—my future husband and my mother, taking tea together. But as I slide the wooden door closed behind me and make for Fú'yí's to find Méi'zi, the only thing I feel is cold disappointment.

A hand darts out of nowhere, and before I know it, I'm yanked behind our plum blossom tree, facing a set of large, stern-looking brown eyes.

Méi'zi presses her index finger to her lips. I clamp my mouth shut and run a narrow gaze over her. I recognize that look. "You're up to something," I whisper. "You should be packing."

She rolls her eyes and swats me. "I'm here to help you take charge of your own cherry blossom destiny," she replies. "Jiě'jie, you can't just walk away from one of the most important discussions pertaining to *your* life."

I sigh. "Méi'zi—"

"Listen to me! What harm does it do? It won't change the fact that you're marrying him." Méi'zi tucks a hand beneath her chin in the manner of a scheming philosopher. "The heir to our kingdom is restrained, careful, and noble. I have good instincts, but even I can't tell his true intentions."

"His intentions are to win this war and take back our realm," I say firmly. "He's noble, pure, and selfless above all—"

"He's a *man*," my sister says with another roll of her eyes. "I've seen the way he looks at you, jiě'jie, when you're not paying attention."

I cross my arms, even as my stomach does a small flip. "It's not like that," I begin, but I'm swept away by a memory from the morning.

How do you think of me?

The answer had always been straightforward but twofold. My boy in the jade—gentle, kind, and caring—was my confidant, the guardian I came to think of as a part of my heart. And then there was Hào'yáng: captain of the immortal guard, my trainer, teacher, and now political ally. Stoic and cold and distant—but with glimpses of warmth that are worth all the light in this world.

Now he is both.

I do not know how to reconcile the two. So I lied to him this morning. I took the easy way out rather than try to decipher the complicated feelings inside me.

Méi'zi takes my hands in hers. "Jiě'jie, you deserve a love of a lifetime and more happiness than anyone else I can think of. You've lived your life making choices that benefit others, protecting me and Mā and chasing after the shadows of Bà's wishes. But Mā is safe now, and I've grown up." Her gaze holds mine, and I realize my baby sister and I stand nearly eye to eye. "You can let go of us now, Àn'yīng. You can let go and start living for yourself. I want you to step away from the path Bà carved for you and to choose your own destiny. Don't be afraid to ask yourself what it is *you* really want."

I hate the way my eyes are warm and my throat aches. Méi'zi wears her heart on her sleeve, but I've always held mine close.

My sister's eyes soften as she seems to read this all on my face. "Go back there, Àn'yīng. This is one of the most important decisions of your life, and I refuse to believe it should be made without you present." She gives me a little shove. "Go."

Then she's gone, scampering down the path to Fú'yí's cottage, where she was meant to be making congee.

I turn, glancing at my house, gilded by the slanted autumn sun. A few plum blossoms drift off in an errant breeze.

One of the most important conversations of my life is taking place inside—without me.

Méi'zi's right.

Before I can think twice, I round the plum blossom tree and make my way back to the house. The shutters to my bedroom are open, and voices drift out as I draw near.

". . . tried to seek you and your family out in the mortal realm." It's Hào'yáng. His tone is quiet, like the clear surface of a stream—yet beneath, I sense undercurrents of emotion. "Lady Shī'yǎ caught me and gave me a talking-to."

I hesitate, slowing my steps. I'd fully intended to walk to the front door and knock. But something in Hào'yáng's words, in the vulnerability threaded through his voice, tells me that the conversation would flow very differently with me there.

"What did she tell you?" My mother's voice is muted but warm. I picture her leaning forward, cup of tea forgotten, as she listens to his story. While Bà was the practical one in our family, Mā was always the one who made magic out of the ordinary.

"She said that I must not behave like a child my age but like an emperor. That if I was to take back the Kingdom of Rivers, I must bide my time and grow strong. That I must view my life as not mine but the kingdom's and the people's, and that each of my choices must be made with them in mind."

I smile as I imagine Hào'yáng as a child, sitting as straight as a rod, brows creased in solemn concentration as he listened to his tutors or spoke with Lady Shī'yǎ. My hand goes to the jade pendant at my neck. Strange to think that though we existed in different realms, our lives were always intertwined.

"Lady Shī'yǎ is wise," my mother says.

"Was." Hào'yáng's tone grows smooth, flat, diplomatic— the tone of the heir, of the guard. Of the mold I imagine he has shaped himself into over the years.

A pause. My heart aches for him; I should be there, next to him. This is a choice we made together, and he should not have to discuss our strategy alone with my mother.

I draw a deep breath and step out of my hiding spot. Through my window, I catch sight of them in our kitchen. My mother is leaning forward, her back to me as she covers Hào'yáng's hand with her own. "I'm so sorry," she says.

Hào'yáng's face might have been carved of stone, but I have come to learn that this is when he is most vulnerable. When he needs the full strength of his armor. He parts his lips to respond—and that is when he sees me. His eyes widen nearly imperceptibly with shock.

Then my mother asks him, "Does Àn'yīng know the true story of her birth . . . and her blood?"

I freeze. This is a subject I have not yet broached with Mā: the fact that I am not her child but Lady Shī'yǎ's.

Quickly, I press a finger to my lips. Hào'yáng blinks, then his features smooth seamlessly as he pulls his hand back. I give him a slight nod.

"She knows. She knows everything, Lady Hé." Hào'yáng's gaze slides back to my mother. Clearly, he is trying very hard not to look at me. "That is why I've come to ask for Àn'yīng's hand in marriage. She is Yī'lín Shī'yǎ's blood; she alone can claim Lady Shī'yǎ's title, her position, and the army that comes with it." He exhales sharply. "I need your daughter in order to take back the Kingdom of Rivers, Lady Hé. I can't win this war without her."

I lean against the wall so Hào'yáng can see me through my open bedroom door.

He doesn't look at me, but the corners of his lips curve slightly.

My mother is silent, her outline glowing in the morning

light. Though her hair remains white, the sun brings color to her cheeks. "Is that all, Your Highness?"

Hào'yáng's brows crease. "Pardon?"

My mother does not relent. "Is that all you'd ask? For my daughter's hand in marriage in order to win this war?"

Hào'yáng blinks, and I have the strangest impression that he and my mother are engaged in a silent game. One I am not privy to. "I would promise her the freedom to love as she wishes throughout our marriage," he says quietly, and I have the sense that though he gazes at my mother, he speaks directly to me. "I would not hold her to anything she doesn't wish for. And once the war is won, she is free to annul the marriage, and I will see to it that she and your family want for nothing for the rest of your lives."

"You are generous, Your Highness. Is there no part of you that wishes to keep my daughter for yourself?"

Something in my chest clenches; the encouraging smile I'd been wearing for Hào'yáng slips.

I pull myself back from the window frame, my heart pounding. Though I can no longer see them, I can still hear them— the pause, the strain in Hào'yáng's voice when he replies. "Even if I did, I would not deserve her, Lady Hé. Your family has been through the Ten Hells and back because of me. I could spend the rest of my life atoning for that and still, it would not be enough."

"You are harsh on yourself, Your Highness."

"I am truthful, Lady Hé."

"Truthful," Mā echoes. "Very well, Your Highness. I have only three questions. Answer them *truthfully*, and I will grant you my daughter's hand."

"Anything, Lady." Hào'yáng's voice is warm with sincerity.

Before I can think twice about it, I've taken Shadow in my hand and activated the blade's talisman. Now hidden from sight to most mortal eyes, I peer back through the window just as my mother asks a question that tips my world.

"Do you love my daughter?"

I inhale so quickly, I'm afraid they might hear me. Hào'yáng freezes, yet there is a bewilderment to his gaze that has replaced his regular steady calculation, the cleverness and cunning of his court-taught negotiation skills.

An ache rises in my throat. I suddenly regret coming here, regret listening in, because the truth unspoken between us is better than the truth exposed with finality from Hào'yáng's own lips.

That he doesn't love me in a romantic sense. That he only needs me as part of a political alliance. That he cherished me as part of the strange bond we fostered through the jade pendant as children out of necessity. Only he's been too kind to say it all to my face.

At last, so quietly that I strain to hear him, Hào'yáng replies: "Lady Hé, I do not deserve to love your daughter."

I should leave. I should never have come.

Yet I find that I am rooted to the spot. *Why do you care whether he loves you or not?* a small voice whispers in my mind, and the question is the answer I have been searching for all along.

I care because I *want* him to love me.

A ridiculous notion, one that has no place in our relationship. One that I can quash right now, when I hear the answer from Hào'yáng's own mouth.

"Whether or not you deserve her is what others believe," my mother replies. "It's a simple question, Your Highness."

Hào'yáng presses his lips together. His gaze drifts toward

the window, and it feels as though he's looking directly at me, though I know I cannot be seen. "I would love her, Lady Hé, as is the duty of a husband to love his wife. If that is what you and Àn'yīng would wish."

"Whatever we discuss stays between us today," Mā adds gently. "It is not my place to reveal matters of the heart nor secrets one wishes to keep, Hào'yáng. And no matter your answer, you need not fear that I will stop you from what you need to win this war." She leans forward. "I do not wish to hear what your duty would be. I wish to hear the truth from your heart." Her voice grows soft. "Tell me, Your Highness. Do you love Àn'yīng?"

Hào'yáng's jaw tightens; his face is drawn. He stares at a spot on the table for several moments, his throat bobbing as he works through any tricks and traps to her question, the best and most diplomatic way to respond.

Then he exhales and closes his eyes. When he opens them again, there is a sorrow on his face that I have seen before. It's an expression I have seen when he's looked at *me*.

One I didn't know how to read until I hear his next words.

"Yes, Lady Hé," Hào'yáng says quietly. "I love Àn'yīng. I love her more than anything else in this world. More than my own life. I have for all of nine years."

The world slows. The sunlight and shadows of my plum blossom tree imprinted against my walls blur, and suddenly, I am ten years old again, curled against my door with a dead father, a near-lifeless mother, and a baby sister not five years of age, and the only thing holding me together is my jade pendant and the guardian within, writing to me one golden stroke at a time. I can't breathe, can't think, as I stare at him now, seated in my kitchen, heir and captain and my boy in the jade.

For all of nine years.

The river in my chest surges to a roar.

I only catch the barest glimpse of my mother's profile and cannot make out her expression as she says, "And have you expressed this to my daughter?"

Hào'yáng doesn't look up. Won't look up, perhaps because he knows I am standing here, invisible in the shadows, watching him confess a truth he has held to himself until now. "No," he says at last. "I wished to give her time and her own choice. I promised your daughter the freedom to love as she wishes in this marriage alliance. All I care about is her happiness, whether it is with me or someone else."

Someone else.

My chest burns. He knows about Yù'chén—of course he would. He was the captain of the immortal guard, tasked to protect the candidates of the Immortality Trials. I begged him, the night all hells broke loose, to let me see Yù'chén.

I recall the emotion that had crossed his face as I made that ask. I didn't understand it then, but I understand it now, the deep sorrow that lines Hào'yáng's expression in moments when he thinks I do not notice.

My mother listens in silence. "You are an honorable man, Your Highness," she says softly. "You will make a fine emperor one day."

Hào'yáng doesn't lift his gaze. "You praise me too highly, Lady Hé."

"Here is my second question: Do you love your kingdom?"

This time, Hào'yáng's answer comes as straight and true as

the strike of a sword. "Of course. My kingdom and my people are my duty."

"Then, my third question," my mother says. "Which would you choose, were you allowed to choose only one?"

Hào'yáng's face is smooth, but I catch the tightening of his eyes as he realizes, as I do, what my mother means. "You speak as if they are mutually exclusive, Lady Hé."

My mother sighs and leans back, turning to look out through the shutters of our living room. From the way her gaze shifts and the age-old grief that seeps in, I know she is gazing at our plum blossom tree.

I know she is thinking of my father.

And I have a chilling premonition of what might come next: fate, run in a circle across two lifetimes, returned to where it all began.

A cold breeze rises, stirring the wild silvergrasses that have grown on our village footpaths. The sun is bright in the sky, but the air is cold; winter will be upon us soon.

"I do not mean my words as a trap for you, Your Highness," my mother says quietly. "It is only that . . . Àn'yīng has been through more than most of us in this world. She was ten years old when she lost her father, and the task of being sole care-taker of me and her sister fell upon her. She has lived her life in service to others, never for herself."

You've lived your life making choices that benefit others, protecting me and Mā and chasing after the shadows of Bà's wishes. Mā's words are an echo of Méi'zi's.

"I don't want her to live for anyone but herself after this war," my mother continues. "I don't want her to suffer a day more. And if there is anything she deserves in this life, it is someone who will love her first and foremost, irrevocably. Who, when it comes down to it, will choose her over a kingdom.

"You, the imperial heir and, one day, emperor of our kingdom, will hold the weight of our people, of our realm. Each and every day, you will need to choose between kingdom and love. And I don't wish my daughter to love someone who would choose his kingdom over her. Àn'yīng deserves to see the oceans. She deserves a life of freedom, of laughter, of love. Not shackled to a cold throne and a colder bed."

My eyes heat. I understand, so well, so deeply, the words my mother speaks. My father chose kingdom over love. And I was left to pick up the broken pieces after his death, to live in the aftermath and consequences of that choice.

Mā doesn't want me to live the same story.

"You say you love her more than your own life," Mā continues, "and it is my deepest honor to know that, Hào'yáng. But once the war is won and you step onto the throne, your life will no longer be yours. You will no longer be Hào'yáng but emperor of our realm and sovereign of our people. Your life will be a vessel through which the good of the people and the good of the Kingdom of Rivers is governed. Your heart and your soul will be buried under this vast decree beneath the Heavens, child—and there will be no space for love or a life for you. Less so for my daughter." Her voice softens. "Can you understand that?"

For the first time since I met him, Hào'yáng seems at a loss for words; he has no clever retort nor diplomatic response. He only sits there, gazing at my mother. Like this, he looks young and lost, like a boy not two decades old with the weight of an entire kingdom upon his shoulders—and I suddenly see the way he must have been the night he arrived in the Kingdom of Sky, having just had his life upended. The most vulnerable parts of my boy in the jade, I realize, he has never shown to me before.

"Your Highness," Mā says gently. "Hào'yáng. Please do not misunderstand me. I would never seek to dictate the course of your life, nor to take my daughter's choices away from her. I only speak to you as someone who has walked this line of fate and reached its other side. Your path was charted for you long before you were even born. The fates have brought you and my daughter together; I only ask that you consider from her perspective before joining your paths for the rest of this lifetime."

Hào'yáng's face is bowed. The silence stretches until, at last, he looks up. Any traces of emotion are now gone; he is a blank slate. Cold and austere, the guard and the heir.

"I understand, Lady Hé," he says. "Forgive me that I must continue to ask for more sacrifices from your family when you have already given me so much." His gaze does not waver. "Should you give your blessings, I will ask Ǎn'yīng for her hand as a political alliance only. She has agreed to fight with me and grant me access to the Heavenly Army that her birth mother was entitled to. I will care for her, but once the war is over, I will annul the marriage so that she may choose the life and the love she wishes. This I promise you."

My mother watches him, and to my surprise, she covers his hand with hers. "You are honorable, Your Highness," she says gently. "You will always have my blessings, and my gratitude."

Hào'yáng sets his knee to the ground and bends until his

forehead presses the floor. He does this three times, then turns to leave.

The front door slams open; by the time I reach it, it has already closed, and there is only a trail of settling dust and fallen petals by our steps, colorless in the late autumn light.

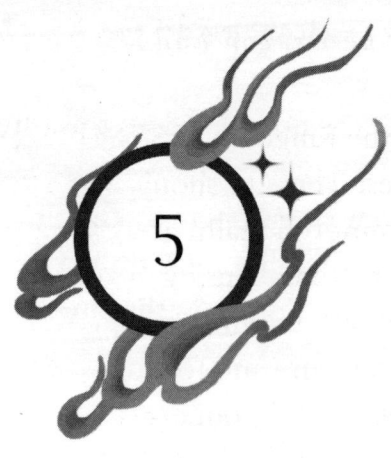

5

Yù'chén

Temple of Dawn, Kingdom of Sky

*I'm dreaming the same dream. It's one I've had many times before.
The setting changes: Sometimes it's a pine forest, sometimes by a
murmuring river of silvergrasses, other times in a clearing at sunset.
In this dream, there is someone chasing me, calling out my name. And
each time I turn, about to see their face—*

I wake.

In the dark, in those moments between sleep and wakeful-
ness, I always reach to my side. I know what I'm looking for:
soft black hair, pale white shift hiding daggers, and the shape of
her curled by my side.

Always, my fingers close on empty air, and I finally open my
eyes to the living nightmare of my reality.

I push up into a sitting position on this stranger's bed in this
stranger's room I have come to occupy at the Temple of Dawn.
There is no moon—there hasn't been since the Kingdom of

Night invaded the Kingdom of Sky—but a few cold stars shimmer in the skies. The sun should have risen already, but the nights in the immortal realm are growing longer as my kingdom's hold on it strengthens by the day.

Beyond the half drawn curtains, flashes of lightning sear across the skies from time to time—clashes of battles being fought, lives being lost, as our army advances through the Kingdom of Sky.

A pounding at my doors draws my attention—the sound that must have woken me in the first place.

"Not now," I snarl, but the guards stationed outside control access to my chambers. They do not heed my command—they never do.

I throw my robes on, tightening the sash at my waist to hide the sword at my hip.

The cherrywood doors swing open. In the dim moonlight, I make out the silhouette of the Higher One known as Niefuzan as he enters. One of the most powerful mó ever to have come into existence, he is my mother's faithful general and her second-in-command . . . and the one who sired the halfling Yán'lù, killed in the Trials.

As always, Niefuzan is trailed by a harem of lesser mó: newly formed creatures with insatiable hunger and only basic needs, there to serve him as he wills. One of them sniffs the air in my direction, catching the scent of my mortal blood.

My vision in the dark is better than a regular mortal's but weak compared to a purebred mó's. I catch only the flash of red eyes, a flick of a tongue, a glimmer of saliva.

Danger tightens a noose around my neck. I press a hand over my left wrist, where one of these newborn specimens attacked me just the other day. The wound is gone, but I can still feel her tongue tracing over my skin as she drank my blood, hear her high-pitched laughter as I struggled against her.

"Niefuzan." I twirl my fingers, and red scorpion lilies bloom on the walls as my magic fills the chamber. A teapot appears in my hands—but it's not tea inside.

I take a swig, smacking my lips as the plum blossom liquor drips down my chin. Instantly, my stomach burns, but the tension in my chest uncoils slightly.

I fix Niefuzan with an indolent grin. "To what do I owe this . . . pleasure?"

The general chuckles. His voice is deep, rough, matching his considerable bulk. Like his dead halfling son, there is nothing he loves more than playing with his food. "Someone has been hiding secrets."

"Oh? Do enlighten me."

Niefuzan's smile widens. With a flick of his hand, the doors slam shut; I hear the snap of a bolt lock sliding into place.

Dull dread blooms in my stomach. My expression schooled to reveal nothing, I smile back at him.

"Go on, my lovelies," Niefuzan croons to his companions. "You must be hungry."

I've been expecting this.

My teapot catches the first one squarely in the face. The mó reels back with a shriek, but I follow; my sword plunges through her chest, and she dissipates in a puff of smoke. Another slice, and a second staggers back. I whirl as a third springs at me from behind, impaling it on my blade, but the fourth I only manage to catch by its thigh. Then a fifth slams into my back and a sixth grabs my ankles. The world tilts sharply, and my head cracks against the floor.

I'm dazed, unable to move or breathe for several heartbeats. But I'm acutely aware of the red eyes watching me in the dark, of the creatures emerging from the shadows as they crawl toward me.

I twist and aim for one with my sword, but it's knocked from my hand; with my other, I unleash the magic I've been gathering in my palm. Ribbons of red unfurl from my fingers, shifting into twisted crimson petals of my scorpion lilies, their petals razor-sharp. I shoot them toward these creatures' chests, aiming for their cores—for the killing blow.

Except they have their own magic, and it's stronger than mine.

My scorpion lilies dissolve into shadows and dust. And then it's all that I can do not to scream as the creatures plunge their teeth into my flesh, as my blood pools on the marble beneath me.

I fall very still. It hurts more when I struggle. A sound escapes my throat—ragged, animalistic even to my own ears—but I refuse to look away from Niefuzan.

I refuse to stop grinning at him even as his lowest mó feed on me.

He watches with a sick gleam in his eyes. He knows I can't and won't say anything to anyone; the guards standing watch outside my doors know this, too. I have no allies in the Council of the Kingdom of Night. Growing up, the mó at court tolerated me as a tool to take the mortal throne.

Now I am denigrated and disdained as the traitor son, fallen out of favor with their empress. The halfling who gave in to his weak mortal instincts and betrayed his kingdom—all for a girl.

Though I'm kept alive as the Kingdom of Night's way to

take the mortal throne, a few, like Niefuzan, have grown bolder in their mockery of me.

My smile slips for a moment as one of his mó's teeth scrapes against my bone.

I won't beg. They could drink me dry, and I'd never beg for my life.

Except they can't kill me, and that's the worst part—*they can't kill me*, because my magic will continue trying to knit my flesh together and pump blood through my heart, my human heart.

And they can't kill me because I am heir to the Kingdom of Rivers. Without me, the Kingdom of Night loses its grasp on the mortal realm.

Niefuzan chortles. "Ah, always so proud, weren't you, halfling? Even as nothing more than a feeding bag and a body to warm the mortal throne, you've looked down on us, haven't you?"

I want to respond, but I can't think of any of the clever retorts I prepared. Can't think of anything beyond the pain. By my ear, one of the creatures moans in drunken ecstasy over my flesh and blood.

Niefuzan watches me for several moments more. Then he leans back, disappointed at my lack of reaction. "You're a stubborn one, I'll give you that," he says. "Well. As much as I enjoy watching you being put in your place, halfling, I didn't come just for this.

"The empress is back. She's called for the council to assemble—and for you to appear as our special guest." He claps his hands. The newborns tear their teeth from me to look to their master, and I fight against the black spots filling my vision. "Come, lovelies. The empress has requested his appearance in an hour, so we can't drain him *completely*."

As the mó reluctantly slink back to their master, Niefuzan grins at me in a nearly apologetic fashion. "Oh, come. You can't blame me for allowing them a treat. Thanks to your mother's war, we've been in the Kingdom of Sky for nearly a week now, and the immortals we capture just don't bleed like mortals do."

As soon as the doors close behind them, I shut my eyes and let my smile fall.

I don't know how much longer I remain lying on the floor, unmoving. The room blurs before me, and I feel a strange warmth on my face. Gingerly, I test my right arm—the flesh has mostly knitted back together, though the ache is not yet gone from my bones—before reaching into the folds of my robes. My fingers close around a small hilt, and I retrieve it.

The crescent blade sits in my palm. From this angle, it catches the moonlight just right, rendering the entire thing silver.

It's one of Àn'yīng's blades. Each, I've observed, bears a different practitioning talisman carved into its peachwood hilt. This one is strange; I'm not able to decipher it, but the part I *can* read of it suggests that it obeys the heart's desire.

It's the blade she tried to kill me with the night everything ended, only she missed.

She never misses.

I draw my knees to my chest and curl around the blade, pressing it to my cheek. If I inhale deeply, I think I can make out her scent on its hilt: the faint tang of blossoms mixed with something sweet and sharp. And if I close my eyes, I can take myself back through every single memory I have of her, indelibly seared into my mind. I can see her pale shift, her long hair braided through with that ribbon, the blades in her hands and cautious, tight lines at the corners of her eyes as she beholds me.

My life changed the moment I met her in that clearing. For

so long, all I'd known was war, hunger, and desire; the cruel necessities of the Kingdom of Night, the hierarchy of power and cycles of bloodshed.

Àn'yīng showed me kindness when she saved that halfling fox spirit in the clearing. She showed me courage, and most of all, she showed me love, in the relentless way she fought for her family. Before her, I didn't think a creature like me—half demon, half mortal—was capable of being loved.

I still don't. But she gave me hope. Perhaps that is the cruelest affliction of them all.

Slowly, I draw the crescent blade to my chest. Feel its tip against the beat of my heart.

Something sparks between my fingers and the hilt of the blade. A flash of heat, and then a vision blooms, white, into my mind. Àn'yīng holds me, her hair falling over her shoulders, her outline haloed by the sun—and she's smiling. She's smiling as she gazes at me, as she's never smiled at me before.

"Yù'chén . . ."

The blade clatters to the floor as though it has leapt away from me. I blink in the darkness, disoriented, reaching for the empty space before me where she was just moments ago.

"Àn'yīng?" My voice is raw with disbelief. What was that? It wasn't a memory; it looked so real, it felt like a vision, but I don't know how my mind could have conjured that. "Àn'yīng—"

But she isn't here, and I'm alone again in the dark.

Loving her was like drawing a blade deeper into my heart. Now she is gone, and so is the pain in my heart.

Now I find that I no longer feel much of anything at all.

★　★　★

The Temple of Dawn is a flurry of motion when I depart my chambers. Since the mó captured it as their stronghold, the place has undergone a transformation, so that it is barely recognizable from the ethereal, sunlit structure I first set foot in when I arrived for the Immortality Trials. The gauze curtains have been enchanted with scenes of the night, of a sickle moon hung lone and cold in a black sky. Any fires that burned and lanterns that once lit the halls have been smothered, for the mó are creatures of darkness.

All the strongholds the Kingdom of Night has managed to capture in the Kingdom of Sky have gone through similar changes. When I look out between the gauze-draped pillars, the skies of the immortal realm are now peppered with patches of night.

My sword is strapped to my hip, and the long black robes my mother had made for me billow behind me as I walk. The silk is stitched with patterns of stars that form the shapes of dragons—a joining of the symbols of the Kingdom of Night and the Kingdom of Rivers, a reminder of my position as heir to the mortal throne.

I trace the familiar path down to the great hall, where candidates once gathered in anticipation of the next trial. Back then, my greatest concern was to follow Àn'yīng and learn the identity of the mortal heir to the Kingdom of Rivers through her.

The identity of my half brother.

Hào'yáng.

She let it slip in the healing chamber, right before everything fell apart. I recall the sorrow bright in her eyes, the feel of her hand against my heart, as she whispered, *I'm going to make a safer world, for mortals and for halflings alike. For you.*

And I betrayed her. I tricked her, did everything in my power to get close to her, all the while knowing I was the reason she had lost her family and her kingdom.

An old pain flares in my chest. My steps falter, and I press a hand to it briefly. Then I straighten as I approach the hall. Voices—loud, heated, accompanied by snarls and growls—drift to me.

Immediately, I sense the presence of my mother amongst the loitering courtiers. There is no way to explain it, this bond between mó and their offspring. While mortals can turn against their own blood and their history is riddled with such familial betrayals, the mó have seen less turmoil within their own lineages. We are flowers blooming from the same tree, roots inextricably intertwined. It is an age-old magic unique to our kind.

No matter how many times I try to run, my path always turns back to her.

My mother lounges on a seat on the dais, one I recognize as that of Dòng'bīn, the highest-ranking member of the Eight Immortals. Behind her is a hulking shadow the size of a small hill. I sense it stirring as I draw closer. Two eye slits crack open, blood red.

Drifting on enchanted vines are golden cups of wine; the mó wasted no time in raiding the immortals' cellars for their finest peach blossom liquors and honey meads.

I snag a cup and toss its contents down my throat.

Sansiran notices me. Our realm's finest blood garnets glitter on her pale neck and in her black hair as she turns to face me. Her eyes burn with a crimson glow, her magic rampant and stirred by the heat of battle.

She ought to be resplendent in her gown—a red so dark it looks nearly black—but the sight of it raises bile in my throat.

A few of her generals have returned, and even several of the Higher Ones, but most are still away—spread throughout the immortal realm, waging battles against an immortal army that has proven exceedingly difficult to defeat. The skies are their home domain, and they have drawn our forces thin.

Sansiran's court officials stop their conversation and turn to look at me as I pass. Several are accompanied by lower-level mó as servants, escorts, prey, or all three. Among them is Niefuzan and his harem. He smiles at me, baring sharp teeth. Some of his group still have my blood on their chins.

I look away sharply. The sound of my steps gives way to silence as I stop before the dais.

My mother's eyes glitter.

Sansiran has very little use for me, other than the fact that I am the key to the mortal throne. Interacting with her is like lying down in a pit of vipers.

I'm trying to guess at the reason she wants me here today as I sink to one knee and bow my head in my customary greeting. A matter related to the mortal realm, perhaps, or for a few sentences of mockery before she relegates me to the back of her court to listen to her strategy sessions.

I try not to think of the third possibility.

"Oh," my mother purrs, a smile baring her sharp teeth as she watches me through her long lashes. "How filial and loyal my son appears in front of me."

I remain kneeling, my every nerve tensed. Listening between the lines for the moment she reveals her intent today.

"I wonder," Sansiran continues, "how he behaves *behind my back?*"

And there it is.

I lift my head to meet her gaze. I'm well practiced by now in keeping my face pleasant, dissociating any of my true emotions from the masks I wear. "Whether I am in front of you or behind your back does not change how I behave, Empress." The lie slides smoothly from my tongue.

Sansiran's smile widens. It doesn't reach her eyes. Never does. "Just an hour ago, I received a report," she says idly. "News, from the mortal realm."

I keep silent. This, I've found, is the best response to any of my mother's goading.

Holding my gaze, my mother stretches out a hand in an elegant twirl. I glimpse a dark, pearl-like object between her fingers. As the entire hall watches, it begins to dissolve, shifting to smoke and shadows.

In those shadows, a scene forms. Sunlight, golden and bright, crisp as morning. A forest of pines in the background. A singsong voice drifts into the hall, as real as if its owner is here with us. But I know what this is: a memory captured in demonic magic, like the feathers my shadowcrane can send me, or the spike Yán'lù used.

The memory crystallizes, focusing on a figure in a clearing—and the world falls away as I catch sight of her face.

Àn'yīng.

It's her, it's truly her. She's holding two crescent blades, her jaw tight and her eyes bright with caution and fury as she gazes at a mó. Through the memory, she might have been looking at us. At me.

I drink in the sight of her, taking in every detail. She's wearing a black gauze dress in this memory, but her hair is bound in exactly the same way as the day we met.

My heart slams against my rib cage. *Safe*, it beats out. *She's safe. She's safe. She's safe.*

Behind her, the rivers shift, and a figure rises in the midst of the currents.

I can't make out his face, but I know it's him. Hào'yáng, the man I once knew as captain of the guard at the Temple of Dawn . . . and Àn'yīng told me is the heir to the Kingdom of Rivers.

My half brother.

The tides carry him like a throne of water. Sunlight gilds him, and even from here, I can make out the aura, elegance, and power that spills from him.

He is every bit the heir I am not.

Àn'yīng raises her blade to defend him. Protectiveness tightens her features in an expression I have seen her wear when she speaks of her mother and her sister. Her loved ones.

As I watch, the ache flares again, hot and strong, like a blade slicing through my heart.

I want to call out to her. I want to step into that memory and hold her to me. I want to promise her everything I can't and he can.

Most of all, I want to be on the other side of that expression she wears. I want to be someone she loves so much and so fiercely.

The words, the ache, build in my chest, burn up my throat. I swallow them all, hold myself very still in this hall I'm trapped in, gazing at an illusion I can never reach.

The memory vanishes like a flame flickering out, and then

I'm looking into my mother's face. I know I'm no longer smiling, but I can't summon the strength in this moment.

My mother's expression has twisted into a snarl, her eyes colder than the depths of our kingdom.

"Tell me, my *son*," she says, and suddenly, her voice is low and terrible, "how the mortal heir and the girl you love ended up in the *mortal realm*?"

Shit.

I shrug. "Perhaps your defenses aren't as impenetrable as you thought?"

Pain slams into me like white-hot lightning in my bones. I gasp and pitch forward, arms trembling as I try to hold myself up, to retain some semblance of dignity. Spots bloom before my eyes. What Niefuzan's newborn mó did to me earlier feels like nothing compared to this.

It's gone as suddenly as it came, and I'm left on all fours before the dais, panting and sweat-drenched. I hear titters around me as my mother's most powerful generals and Higher Ones watch.

This is nothing new to them, but they relish it each and every time. Watching me, heir to the mortal throne, be denigrated at their empress's feet satisfies an ancient anger they hold toward the other realms and the hierarchy that the Heavenly Order dictates. The hierarchy that puts the mó and the Kingdom of Night at the very bottom.

I push myself to my feet. There is no way out, no escaping this but to endure it until it is over. I'm breathing hard—and the strength it takes to lift the corners of my lips into a grin again feels like moving mountains.

My mother stands now. "The periphery of this training temple was completely guarded and sealed," she hisses, her power coiling like a gathering storm in her palms. The room darkens, charges with lightning. "Which means the *only* way out for them was *through your gates.*"

Her fury hits me again, like a tide this time, pounding into me with the sensation of all my bones shattering and my skin tearing. My mother's magic morphs, and she is endlessly creative in her cruelty, always seeking a new method of torture. This time, it mimics the feeling of water filling my lungs, that acute, burning sensation of drowning in thin air.

I choke, clawing at my throat, but I can't breathe. My chest is on fire. Dimly, I hear jeers and howls of approval from my mother's court as, finally, my body gives out and I crash to the floor. I'm curled up on myself, but I can't scream, can't make a single sound.

Darkness envelops my vision.

When I come to, I'm lying on the marble floor. *Get up*, I tell myself. *Get up.*

I bear no physical injuries—I never do, for my mother's magic is too sophisticated for that—but every nerve in my body protests as I push myself up into a kneeling position. This time, I do not have the strength to stand.

But my mother does, her hand outstretched to something behind her. The taunting and mockery in the hall has given way to silence. All the generals have backed away a respectable step, and even the Higher Ones stand straighter, more alert.

Behind my mother, the mass of shadows *moves*, splits. As another set of crimson eyes flares open, I realize I'm looking into the faces of two of the Four Perils. It takes me a moment to recognize Táo'wú, with its boarlike tusks and gold-tinged mane. Yet as the other emerges, I'm filled with a cold premonition of what my mother means to do.

Qióng'qí's growl rumbles like thunder through the hall. The last time I came across it was in the mortal realm, at the beginning of the Immortality Trials. Àn'yīng tried to save me from this beast, not knowing that my mother had sent it to keep the other hellbeasts in the Way of Ghosts from tearing me apart before I completed my mission.

Now my mother is going to send them after her.

"No." The word breaks from my lips. Too soft for most to hear. The vision the monster of nightmares taunted me with on Péng'lái Island flashes in my mind: Àn'yīng, lying prone on the grass in her white dress, eyes glassy and stomach torn open.

And I know, without a doubt, that this is the worst kind of torture my mother can inflict upon me.

Sansiran's lips curl. "Oh, *yes*," she breathes as the two beasts flank her. "I think we'll send a lovely surprise to them, don't you agree?"

"Let me go." I'm reeling, grasping at straws, but I no longer care. I have no more cards to play, no walls to put up—not when it comes to her. "I'll find her and the mortal heir, and I'll bring them back to you. I won't fail you again, I swear on my life."

"Unfortunately, your promises aren't worth very much anymore, my *son*."

"Don't hurt her." The crowd titters, no doubt murmuring at my mortal weakness, my foolish human heart, but I ignore them all. "Your Majesty. I have never asked anything of you—"

"And you have no right to." My mother raises an eyebrow. "Surely you aren't deluded enough to believe you have the right to bargain with me, especially after your miserable failure in letting the heir to the mortal realm slip through your fingers?"

She's right. I have no goodwill in this court. Nothing to give in exchange.

I hesitate only for a fraction of a second. "A covenant, then."

A stillness falls across our court as soon as my words ring out.

"A covenant," Sansiran repeats softly, but I sense intrigue in the way her tongue caresses the word. Beneath us, the mó are whispering. Said to derive from the same ancient magic of our realm that constitutes the bond between a mó and their offspring, a covenant is a binding agreement between two mó and can be invoked outside of familial relationships. So long as one side completes a bargain, the other is held to their service for eternity. It is a way for Higher Ones to gain loyalty of lesser mó: By sparing their lives through a covenant, the lesser mó are forced into a lifetime of servitude. Often, demons at war would rather die by their own sword than be forced into a covenant with their enemies.

The only requirement is that it must be given willingly.

My heart begins a drumroll. I stare at the monster who calls herself my mother, and suddenly any lingering hope, no matter how faint—for escape, for rebellion, for ways to subvert my mother's plans—dissolves before my eyes. The world narrows into this hallway, the jeering crowd, and Sansiran leering at me from the dais.

An eternity of this—in exchange for Àn'yīng's life.

I hold my icy stare. "A covenant. Spare her life and ensure that no harm comes to her, and I pledge myself completely to you. No more disobedience, no more betrayals; my life would be yours to command." I pause, then add, to seal it: "For as long as I live, I live to serve you."

Sansiran's ruby lips curve in the truest smile I have seen my mother display. "I accept," she says, and sweeps down the dais, impossibly fast and elegant. *"A covenant."* Magic trembles in the air as her words invoke this ancient rite. *"With this covenant, I bind you, under the condition that I spare the life of the woman you love and protect her from harm."* Vines of red oleander bloom from her chest where her core rests, twining around her arms down to her palms as she speaks. *"Should I fulfill my end of the covenant, hear your terms: So long as you live, you shall not use your magic to harm our kingdom. You shall not hurt me. You shall not disobey me. So long as you live, your life shall be mine to keep and mine to command. Do you accept?"*

I stare at the flowers pulsing on her palm, the color so similar to the hue of my own magic.

Àn'yīng's face comes to me, through wisps of memories, and more often these days, through remnants of my dreams. In my dreams, she's half-turned to me, sunlight limning the angles of her face, the shine of her braid, the curve of her lips. And I'm chasing her, chasing a life in which she might look at me and smile.

I extend my hand to my mother's. Her cloying scent of blood and flowers chokes me as I say, *"I accept."*

Ancient shadows and a whispering wind rise between us as soon as the words fall from my lips. Scorpion lilies blossom on my open palm, snaking toward the oleander, faster and faster, the two flowers twining around each other, encircling me and my mother in a blood-red light. I grit my teeth as the power of the bond burns into me, characters glowing like embers on my skin with all the vows I have made, all the conditions of my servitude burning, bleeding, into my bones.

Then it ends, as suddenly as it began. The ancient, bodiless voices fade. The shadows around us dissolve. And I'm kneeling before my mother at the dais of the Temple of Dawn, the court watching us in stunned silence.

The world settles again as if it never changed.

As though from very far away, I hear my mother speak: "Let us test it, shall we?" Sansiran holds out her hands to her council as if this is a show, and she receives the adequate roars of approval. "Let us see what happens when he uses his magic against me. Niefuzan, command him to harm me."

Her second-in-command steps forward and utters a command: *"Rise and draw your blade."* The power of his magic twines around me, suffocating and impossible to escape.

I do as he bids.

Niefuzan hesitates only a half second before he utters, *"Cut the empress."*

I move forward, sword raised, compelled by the overwhelming power of his command.

A searing pain tears through my chest as the ancient bonds of my covenant knife into me. My sword hand shakes. Remains frozen in place.

"Cut the empress," Niefuzan repeats, his magic pushing against me like an immutable wall, somehow stronger and more insistent than the last command.

I've taken one step forward before the covenant strikes again. Pain blazes through me, white-hot, like a thousand burning blades running through my bones. A red glow lights the hall as I fall to the floor. The taste of blood fills my mouth.

Slowly, it subsides. And this time, I do not have the strength to get up again. I lie there, drawing ragged breath after ragged breath, fighting the dark that crowds the corners of my vision. The cold marble floor beneath me is wet with the blood I coughed up; my robes are soaked with sweat.

Something sharp digs into my cheeks, shifts my face so that I am gazing up into my mother's cruel beauty. Her nails dig into my flesh, hard enough to hurt but not enough to break skin.

"Good," she says softly. "Very good." Her fingers glide across my jaw in a cold caress as she lowers her lips to my ear. "Your life is worth more to me than this realm, now, for I have a new plan for you, my darling son."

Then she thrusts my face back to the floor and straightens to address the court. Dimly, I hear her voice echoing in the throne room:

"Find them. Kill the heir and bring me the girl."

6

Àn'yīng

Xī'lín Village, Central Province,
Kingdom of Rivers

We have only hours before the sun vanishes and the long night takes over.

I can't recall seeing this much activity in the village since the early days of the war. There are provisions to be packed: dried meats and salted vegetables that will keep for weeks on the road. The weapons left behind by the soldiers and practitioners from our village who once fought against the Kingdom of Night—their daggers, longswords, and armor—must be distributed among the villagers.

Hào'yáng and I, along with Lì'líng, Tán'mù, and three more of our most trusted warriors, will make for the Kingdom of Sky—or whatever is left of it.

I'm grateful for the constant action that keeps my mind moving, distracted from the revelation I overheard earlier.

One I do not know how to approach.

What I do know, with certainty: Hào'yáng is avoiding me. I catch glimpses of him speaking to our soldiers, yet he is always gone before I can reach him.

I focus on packing the most important items in my room. I run a hand over the shelves of practitioning tomes from which my father learned his arts, and through which he taught me in the early days of the war before he died. How many days and nights did I spend curled up against these books as my mother and sister slept, yearning and yearning for his return—to hear the whistle of his sword outside in dawn's light as he practiced his fighting and realize this was all simply a long nightmare?

And when the nightmare did not relent and you realized this was the new normal, whispers a small voice in my mind, *who did you turn to?*

Even touching the jade pendant—*Hào'yáng's* jade pendant—sends a jolt through my fingers. I turn the stone over, careful and hardly daring to breathe as I examine its smooth surface; the jagged edges from when it was broken off from mine. I imagine him sitting in the Temple of Dawn, writing to the mortal girl a realm away.

For all of nine years.

". . . Àn'yīng?"

I startle and scramble to my feet as my mother appears in my doorway. She's swaying, leaning heavily on the walking canes the carpenter's daughter fashioned for her as she regained use of her legs.

"Mā!" I exclaim, rushing to her. She trembles as I lower her into a chair; her clothes and forehead are sticky with perspiration. She holds up a hand as I grab a cloth to clean her face with.

"I'm fine," she says. She looks up at me and beams, her

winter-tinged cheeks flushing pink. "I just wanted a few mo-ments alone with my daughter. Come here, Àn'yīng."

She opens her arms, and suddenly I'm a child again, folding myself into her hug after a long day at the village school. I close my eyes and breathe in her scent of soap and chrysanthemums, and the faint, homey smell of cooking lingering in her hair.

"Àn'yīng. Àn'yīng?" Mā strokes my hair. "Don't cry."

"I'm not," I whisper, but my cheeks are warm and wet, and my voice shakes. "I just . . . I don't want to leave you again." I swallow, but the words pour out, the most shameful and selfish and vulnerable truths I have hidden away all these long years. "I don't want this. I just want to be with you and Méi'zi and Bà, right here, in our home."

"Oh. Oh, my heart, shh." My mother caresses my hair in the way she did when I was little and had trouble sleeping. Her voice washes over me in waves as she murmurs, "I won't cod-dle you with any promises, Àn'yīng. But if you have made the choice to fight in this war, then I need you to honor that, and I need you to be brave." She pauses. "If you find you cannot live up to the promise you made, you need to let Hào'yáng know now."

"No!" I shake my head. I've made my choice already; so much of this war depends on me and my ability to claim Lady Shī'yǎ's title and army.

The lotus weighs heavy in my dress bodice.

"It's not that, Mā," I say. "It's just . . . I don't know what will happen in the after, when all this is over." I lean back, holding my mother's hands as if they are anchors, gazing into her eyes as if she will have the answer for me. "Everything will have changed. I'm marrying the future emperor of this realm, and I . . ." I swallow, and I finally speak the truth aloud between us.

"I am Lady Shī'yǎ's heir; I hold a piece of her legacy in the immortal realm." My grip tightens. "I don't know that anything can go back to how it once was."

My mother tips my face up to hers. Her thumb, rough with her seamstress's callouses, strokes my cheek. "Such is life," she says softly. "Àn'yīng, you cannot live your life chasing the shadows of the past—whether it's your father's dying wishes or the days in the sun with me and Méi'zi. You must look to the future, my daughter, and choose how you wish to shape it. Your sister and I will always be here, and we will always be a part of you." She gathers me in her arms again, holding me so, so tightly. "No matter what you choose, who you become, and where you are in these realms, Àn'yīng, you will *always* be my daughter."

I hear the words she does not speak; I feel, then, a strange untethering, an ending and a beginning, and a revelation of the hints Méi'zi has given me over the past few days.

I have been fighting for so long to return to those golden, hazy afternoons with my family beneath our plum blossom tree. But that past is long gone.

You can let go of us now, Àn'yīng. Méi'zi's wide eyes come back to me.

"There is one thing," my mother says softly, drawing back, "that I would like to ask of you."

"Anything, Mā."

My mother's face lights up. "It is the wish of every mother in this world to see their daughter be married in a beautiful wedding gown," she says and turns toward the door. "Chūn'méi!"

My sister appears, holding a bundle in her arms. When she shakes it out, a traditional wedding gown unfurls—the brightest spot of color in all the village, gleaming as if it holds fire.

Gold embroidery laces the red brocade bodice in intricate patterns of cherry blossoms and peonies. A pleated tulip skirt spills from the waist, layered with shimmering tassels and silk bands.

"I sewed it for a bride just before the war," Mā says, beaming at me. "We never had a chance to deliver it, but I worked on it in the days after to keep myself sane, knowing there would be a future when each of my daughters would wear a dress like it. The cherry blossoms are for you."

"And I spent my day tailoring it!" Méi'zi bursts out proudly, lifting the brocade to reveal a strap. "It's got the same eight hiding spots to store your daggers as the white dress I made you." She holds it out. "Will you wear it, oh please, oh please?"

"Of course." I'm too overwhelmed to say much else.

Méi'zi helps me as I step into this new gown. It fits perfectly, sliding over my body like a second skin. She does the ribbons at the back, clasps the mother-of-pearl buttons, and when she steps away, my mother lets out a soft sigh.

"It's beautiful," Méi'zi squeals, and throws her arms around me. Then Mā comes and wraps us all together in an embrace, and in that moment, *everything* is suddenly perfect.

Eventually, Mā draws back and pats Méi'zi's shoulders. "I believe we have a groom to find," my mother says. "I hear he has been with his forces out by the gates all day. Méi'zi, would you—"

"I'll go." I stand, surprising even myself with this declaration. Yet as I slide my crescent blades into my gown and pat down my skirts, I feel a calm certainty settle in my chest.

You must look to the future, my daughter, and choose how you wish to shape it.

I tuck Lady Shī'yǎ's lotus into the most secure folds of the bodice. Its soft petals brush against my heart. For a moment, I think I feel a spark of . . . something. Yet when I look down at the lotus, it remains unchanged, its jade-green leaves gleaming.

It is nearing twilight when I step outside.

News of my wedding has spread without my knowing, and preparations are in full swing. Throngs of my neighbors are arranging wooden tables and bamboo chairs along the dusty road near my house, chattering and laughing amongst themselves as they work. Red banners and ribbons hang from nearby houses; lanterns and paper fish for luck decorate our plum blossom tree and shutters and eaves. The air smells of good food, and I hear a few of the aunties singing a folk tune about jasmine flowers in Fú'yí's kitchen.

For the first time in nearly ten years, there is song and movement and life in our village.

An ache rises in my throat at this touching gesture. I'll marry tonight and make this the most joyous occasion—one to remember our lives here by. One without regrets.

But first, I must sort out the tangle in my own heart.

I activate the talismans on Shadow and Fleet, slipping unseen past the villagers along the dusty road.

A group of warriors are gathered at the pái'fāng; the rest are dispersed around the periphery of the village as patrols. Tán'mù's gaze slides to me for a split second as I pass by them, and she tips her head nearly imperceptibly in the direction of the little stream just outside the village. Then she turns away and leans forward to listen to something Lì'líng's saying, giving no indication that she has seen me.

I head toward the clearing near the stream where I was hunting this morning.

Just as Tán'mù hinted, he is there.

Hào'yáng stands by the flowing water. He is back in his Kingdom of Sky armor again, fully suited, Azure Tide at his hip. His face is turned to the skies, the last glow of sunset catching against the gold of his armor and the silver of his brocade robes beneath. His hair is neatly drawn up and pinned. Like this, he looks every bit the heir he was born to be.

He turns his head sharply as I near, and I marvel that even with the protection of my talismans, he can sense my approach. I slide Shadow and Fleet back into their sheaths in my new sleeves and step out from beneath the treeline.

"Àn'yīng?" Hào'yáng spins around; the guarded surprise to his expression dissipates into something else, something entirely *un*guarded, as his eyes fall on me. He inhales sharply as he takes me in, gaze roaming down my dress, his hand tightening on the hilt of his sword. Desire surges across his face, and I wonder how I could ever have missed it.

Just as quickly, it's gone, schooled into the careful, distant expression of the captain and heir.

Hào'yáng glances away toward the water again. "I didn't mean for you to have to come out here to find me. The festivities start in a half hour, and I thought—"

"I came to talk to you," I interrupt, "about the conversation you had with my mother."

His jaw flexes. "You already know the strategy we laid out. There is nothing more we need to discuss."

"I disagree." I start toward him, and his head snaps up. He looks almost afraid of me. And though my heart is pounding against my rib cage, I find that I am no longer frightened to face the truth, as messy and complicated and unresolvable as it is.

Hào'yáng makes as if to step back, but the water is behind

him, and he has nowhere to go. He looks at me helplessly. "Àn'yīng, I don't wish to discuss this now," he says.

I stop before him, an arm's reach away. "Why didn't you tell me?" I try to keep my voice steady, but something inside me is loose, unmoored. "All this time. Why didn't you?"

"Because your mother is right. I cannot offer you the life you deserve."

"And you're the one to decide that?"

"No," he says. "No, of course not."

"Then—"

"Because I knew it would be fruitless," Hào'yáng says at last, and his expression breaks open with that familiar sorrow. "Because your heart is taken already, Àn'yīng. And I have no right to use our alliance to get in the way of that."

I draw a tight breath.

A memory hangs in the air between us. Him, facing me in the dusk light of the immortal realm. Watching me beg him to save Yù'chén's life.

"You say his name sometimes when you dream," Hào'yáng continues quietly. The last rays of sunlight limn his profile. "I had no wish to burden you with feelings you cannot return."

I think of those nine years I spent in my house crying over the shadow of my father, when I still had my home, my sister, a part of my mother, and my neighbors—when Hào'yáng had witnessed the death of his entire family and been spirited away to another realm. All those times I spoke to my guardian in the jade of my grief and he wrote back to me words of comfort and care when he was the one with nothing. I think of him watching me through the jade, perhaps waiting for me to speak to him of the pieces of his heart he'd kept hidden from me for half a lifetime.

I've seen the way he looks at you, jiě'jie, when you're not paying attention.

"Tell me." My voice is soft, so soft. "I would like to hear it from you."

He draws a sharp breath. "Àn'yīng," he says. "I know you see me as your friend, your guardian, your trainer . . . but I am a man, too, and I have my pride."

I'm not sure what gives me the courage to close the gap between us, to reach out and tip his chin toward me, forcing him to meet my eyes.

Within, I find grief and broken dignity—and unmistakable desire as he gazes back at me.

I surge up on my toes and brush my lips against his.

Hào'yáng inhales sharply, and I feel the muscles of his shoulders tense. He catches my arm as I draw back. A hundred thoughts seem to race through his eyes, the intricate calculations of his brilliant mind.

Then it all clears. Hào'yáng cups my cheek, his touch gentler than anything I have felt before.

And kisses me.

His lips are soft, his palm steady and warm against my waist, his other hand cradling my chin. He tastes of salt and spun sugar, and as his eyes flutter shut, a wind stirs flower petals from the trees around us. They drift in the fading glow of sunset, showering over my wedding gown and Hào'yáng's golden armor, and I find myself thinking that this is the type of kiss befitting fairy tales.

Slowly, he pulls back. Blinks away the haze in his eyes. "Àn'yīng." He speaks my name in a way that sends shivers across my skin.

Reaching to close the distance between us, I kiss him again.

Hào'yáng thaws—and this time, the kiss is no longer a fairy-tale one.

He grips my waist and pulls me against him, the movement sudden and hard. His grasp tightens, and he makes a noise low in his throat as his mouth caresses mine. And I'm drowning in sensation as the dam in my chest finally breaks open, those whispering waters swelling into the waves of oceans.

Hào'yáng draws back sharply—and there it is again: the conflict in his eyes, the sadness that shadows his face.

"I made a promise to your mother, Àn'yīng, and I will not be a man to break the promises I make," he says haltingly, as though each word costs him a great effort. "But most of all, your mother is right. I will not be the man to hold you back from the life and the love you deserve."

The words take flight in the soft dusk air. Beyond us, the last light of sunset fades from the surface of the river and drains from the sky, and I imagine the distant horizon, a place where sea and sky meet, forever reaching yet never touching.

Hào'yáng steps away. Cold air seeps in between us; the blossoms litter the ground like dying butterflies. His hand goes to the hilt of Azure Tide. In the moments that follow, his lips move, and the words he speaks might have been something like *I love you too much to be selfish*—had I heard them.

But I don't.

A great tremor rolls through the ground, and the setting sun seems to vanish completely from the sky. Hào'yáng's gaze snaps to the east, where Xī'lín lies. His hand tightens against my waist.

I turn, and what I see nearly sweeps my legs out from under me.

In the sky above my village, a fracture has appeared. It

widens and shadows spill from it: amorphous at first, and then I make out claws, jutting bones and ribs, wings . . . and two deep, crimson flames burning with the light of the Ten Hells.

Hào'yáng draws his sword; the sound of the metal slicing through the clearing. He utters a word that breaks open my world, draws me from the sunlit, golden afternoon back into my old nightmares:

"Hellbeast."

7

Àn'yīng

Xī'lín Village, Central Province,
Kingdom of Rivers

My blades are in my hands, and the world blurs around me as we run. The sky has begun to bleed into night, the gash between realms exposing a familiar bone-white moon. There, the periwinkle dusk is gone, eclipsed by the monstrous creature clawing its way into our mortal kingdom.

Distant screams rend the air as we draw close to Xī'lín. The fear in my chest is so thick that I can't breathe, can't think.

Hào'yáng tips his head to the skies and lets out a high-pitched whistle. From afar comes a whinny as a silver light streaks toward us across the darkening night. Meadowsweet canters through the air in her equine form, landing before us with unnatural grace. Her eyes, normally a liquid brown, now churn like an ocean in a storm.

Hào'yáng swings up onto her back and pulls me in front of him. I hold tightly on to Meadowsweet's neck as we gallop through the gates into the village.

It's a cacophony of noise and activity. People run past us, crying, and suddenly, I'm ten years old again, the Imperial Palace has just fallen, the emperor and his family have been killed— and the mó have reached our village.

Except this time, there are no village practitioners here to fight them off and to raise wards around our borders. There is no Bà to draw me into his arms, the reassurance of his large hands covering my small ones as he pressed my blades into my palms.

This time, there is only me and Hào'yáng—and the hellbeast.

There is a familiarity to the way its ribs protrude from its shadowy mass, the wings that spread over rooftops. I realize that I *know* this beast. It is one of the Four Perils of the Kingdom of Night, the same one that hunted me when I'd been traversing the most treacherous parts of the mortal realm in hopes of reaching the Kingdom of Sky for the Trials.

The one Yù'chén saved me from.

Qióng'qí.

I grip the hilts of my crescent blades so tightly that the grooves of the talismans dig into my palms. We're racing down the dusty road that leads straight through the village to my home, and I'm craning my neck to catch a glimpse of my house when the earth before us splits open. Meadowsweet screams, the world tilts, and I'm only aware of Hào'yáng's arms around my waist as we're thrown. He breaks my fall, but there is nothing to break his.

He slams into the ground.

We scramble upright as a colossal shadow falls over us. In a blink, Hào'yáng is on his feet. He thrusts me behind him with one hand as he lifts his sword with his other.

Before us, where the carpenter's house once stood, is now

a gaping hole. Earth crumbles into it, vanishing into utter darkness—a darkness that *moves*. It ripples over the talismans my father and the village practitioners drew as protections before they died, which I have been reinforcing year after year, now broken and scattered.

Talismans that are nowhere near strong enough to hold back one of the Four Perils.

Claws appear from the writhing mass of shadows and gouge into the soil as the opening in the sky widens and another hellbeast emerges into our realm. Its tusks gleam bone-white from a dripping maw; horns the length of spears protrude from a mane of shadows. I recognize it from the myths: Táo'wù, another of the Four Perils.

Outlined against pitch-black skies, second Peril lifts its tusked head over the rooftops of our village and lets out a snarl that sends tremors across the ground.

Hào'yáng turns to me. "Go to your family," he says, and then calls to Meadowsweet. "Go with her. Hold off Qióng'qí."

"Hào'yáng," I begin, catching his hand. The words at the tip of my tongue turn to ash, for it is now that the true meaning of my mother's words to him hit me with full force:

Each and every day, you will need to choose between kingdom and love.

She spoke not just of Hào'yáng—but of me, and my life were I to be with him.

The heir to my kingdom, the man who can liberate my realm, stands before me. The logical thing would be to flee with him, let his dragonhorse carry us swiftly out of here to safety.

But choosing that means leaving my entire village behind to die. And in this moment, all I can think of is saving Mā and Méi'zi and my home.

Hào'yáng's gaze does not leave mine. "Go," he repeats. "Meadowsweet, with her—"

"No!" I steady my voice. "No, Meadowsweet, take him and run."

"Meadowsweet," Hào'yáng repeats. "Stay with her. If anything happens to her, then I—"

But the rest of what he says is drowned out by an earth-shattering roar. The second Peril's crimson eyes sweep over us. Pin Hào'yáng.

Hào'yáng spins and kicks off, and his fingers slip through mine as he arcs through the air, an image I will never forget: a golden streak against the overwhelming darkness of the other realm—and Táo'wù.

Àn'yīng. The dragonhorse's familiar voice sounds in my mind like rushing currents of a river. *Your house.*

I turn, and my knees weaken.

Over the gentle curve of gray-tiled roofs, my plum blossom tree has vanished, swallowed by the night pouring from the gash in the skies. *A gate*, I think, recalling the openings Yù'chén once made in the Kingdom of Sky's wards, enabling us passage between realms despite the immortals' magic. No one knows for sure how the Kingdom of Night first gained access to the Kingdom of Rivers, but the rumors whisper of a gate opening between realms.

I have never seen anything on this scale: a gate large enough to envelop half my village.

And I can no longer see my house.

A scream dies in my throat as I run toward it.

The scene on my street unfolds in chaos and terror. The tables and chairs meant for our wedding banquet are overturned, some splintered into pieces. The lanterns and decor are trampled and torn, strewn like entrails in the dirt. A fire has started; flames lick up Fú'yí's wooden shed, illuminating the battle waging before me.

A small white fox darts through the wreckage of our wedding banquet. It turns back to bare its teeth as the entire *sky* seems to shift.

Overhead, Qióng'qí's tangle of razor-sharp bones and skeletal form is cast into sharp relief by the firelight.

As it lunges toward Lì'líng, a shape rises between them: the silhouette of a monster I have never seen before. Slate-gray scales and webbed wings that shift like smoke as they uncoil from a serpent's body with a woman's torso and arms. Bloody light limns the monster's face, and I nearly stop in my tracks. It's a yāo'jīng—a halfling child of a human and a spirit—and it takes me a moment to recognize her as someone I know very well.

Tán'mù's features are longer, sharper, and more terrible than her mortal form as she rises to meet Qióng'qí. Her tail whips out, catching the hellbeast square in the shoulder and sending it stumbling back.

By my side, Meadowsweet, too, is shifting. Her snowy coat morphs into rippling silver scales; her hooves lengthen into claws, and then it's no longer Meadowsweet cantering by my side but the full dragon form of She of the Moon-Frosted Sea. As she leaps forward to join the battle, I swap my crescent blade Shadow for Striker and lunge.

My weapon barely scrapes the thigh of Qióng'qí before the monster pivots and vanishes from my sight. I feel a huff of fiery breath against my back, catch a glimpse of shadows in my peripheral vision, but I can't turn fast enough . . .

She of the Moon-Frosted Sea lunges between us, jaws open. Mist pours from her mouth, forming a tide of ice. Qióng'qí rams into it with enough force to shatter city walls. Specks of ice tumble from the shield, and as the Peril's tail whips out, I catch sight of something that draws a scream from me.

"Lì'líng!"

The small white fox looks up just as the shadow of the hell-beast's tail smashes toward her—

A spark of spirit energy; a resounding *crack* echoes in the night as Qióng'qí's spiked tail strikes an invisible barrier. As it recoils, I spot Lì'líng, now in her human form as a young girl—and before her, holding a very familiar crescent blade I gifted her, stands my little sister.

Méi'zi smirks as she lowers Shield. She's in a pink silk dress, the shape of which mimics the white one she made for me. She's woven her hair into two braids, and as she lifts her chin, the firelight catches in her eyes.

Tán'mù lets out an inhuman scream as she slices her claws at Qióng'qí. Behind her, Méi'zi pulls Lì'líng to her feet. The fox spirit bares her teeth and with a leap, she joins the fight by her lover's side.

I race to my sister.

"Jiě'jie!" She folds herself into my arms. "Mā's safe, sheltering with Fú'yí. We were waiting for you."

"Méi'zi," I begin, and that's when Táo'wù, several streets down, lets out an earsplitting roar. I look up, and there, in the shadows, a streak of golden armor plummets from the skies like a shooting star.

Hào'yáng.

Suddenly, I recall the memory of Lady Shī'yǎ falling from

Sansiran's death blow, her spirit energy trailing ashes in the night.

Realize the consequences of the choice I am to make.

I take my baby sister's face in my hands. Hold her tightly, so tightly, so that she knows in my heart, I wish to never let go.

"Find Fú'yí and get Mā out of here," I tell her.

Her eyes widen as the meaning of my words sinks in. "Jiě'jie," Méi'zi whispers, a tremor cracking her voice as she searches my gaze.

I take her hands in mine. Prise open her fingers. And slip into them two more blades. "Healer," I manage, squeezing her left hand, "to cure flesh wounds with life energy. And Shadow, to keep you hidden from prying eyes." I swallow, my vision blurring as warmth pools in my eyes. "Bà would be proud" are the last words I say to my sister as I turn away from her.

"Lì'líng! Tán'mù!" I call, and they're both there, Tán'mù shielding us with the powerful wings of her full spirit form.

I meet Tán'mù's gaze, her pupils turned to slits like those of a snake. Understanding flickers in the space between us, and with every fiber of hope and conviction in my body, I entrust the most important parts of my life to her. "Take care of my family."

She nods once, and that's all I need.

I turn away, my heart hardening against Méi'zi's sobs as Tán'mù gathers her in her arms, those great wings shielding Méi'zi from harm as she turns and starts for the village gates.

Lì'líng darts up to me. She stops before me and holds out something cupped in her palms.

"My tail," she says. "When separated from my body, no matter how far away, it emits a jingling sound that only I can hear." She places it around my wrist, where the thing—white and fluffy like a hare—wriggles once and nestles around my forearm like a bracelet.

"I can't take your tail," I begin, but Lì'líng giggles.

"You look so disturbed," she says, but her smile slips as one of the hellbeasts lets out an earsplitting scream again. My friend holds my hand between hers and lifts her large, amber eyes to me, unblinking. "Take it. This way, no matter where you are, Tán'mù and I can find our way back to you." She slips her arms around me in a quick hug. "Besides, one tail means nothing to me. Haven't you heard the myths?" She wriggles her hips as she turns. "I have nine."

With a leap, the young woman is gone and the version of my friend looking back at me is the little white fox. She lifts her tail—a second one, I suppose—in a cheeky parting gesture, and then she's off, darting between the trees faster than I can track.

On my wrist, her tail taps me in what seems like a reassuring gesture . . . and then vanishes.

Another roar rips through the air. Overhead, She of the Moon-Frosted Sea dances before Qióng'qí, engaging the beast in battle, her silver, serpentine form cutting against its mass of darkness.

Suddenly, the dragon lets out an anguished cry—one so foreign and yet so human in its heartbreak. As she lifts her head in the direction of the battle waging behind me, a terrifying pain sears across my chest. My hand darts to the jade pendant at my collarbone.

Hào'yáng.

Fleet and Striker are in my hands, their power becoming an

extension of me as I pivot, adrenaline and spirit energy thrumming through my blood, my hands and feet in a harmonious weave.

Táo'wù towers over a patch of rubble. Amidst wood splinters and stones and tile is a figure in gold.

Hào'yáng is kneeling, which strikes me as horribly wrong, yet as I close the distance, I make out his hand clutched to his side—and how his gold armor and white shift are stained red.

Táo'wù lets out a roar of triumph. It rears on its hind legs, swordlike claws heavy enough to crush entire houses, and leaps for Hào'yáng.

Something cool and hard presses against my collarbone. I stumble, momentarily thrown off-balance. Then I reach into the folds of my wedding gown and draw out a sword.

It's more slight than other longswords, made of a metal I cannot place: one that glows a soft blush, the color of sunrises. Its hilt, a deep-green woven through with veins like a leaf, warms beneath my fingers as I lift it. Somehow, in my hands, it is as light as a feather . . . and it rests in my palms as though it has always belonged there.

I have seen this blade, on many occasions. I know with a bone-deep recognition, what it is:

It's Lady Shī'yǎ's lotus, transformed into its sword form.

My skin begins to dance with light, pouring into the weapon, as I leap into the air and lift it over my head.

Then I plunge it through Táo'wù's tusked, open maw.

The hellbeast's scream fractures the ground as it reels back, crashing into a nearby house. Overhead, the seam splitting the skies trembles, the scythe moon and night stars within rippling like the surface of a lake.

I land by Hào'yáng's side. He kneels, sword driven into the

ground before him, other hand clutching his side to stem the flow of blood.

"Àn'yīng?" he rasps as I kneel before him, patting him down to check for more injuries.

"I'm here," I tell him. "I'm here, Hào'yáng."

He blinks rapidly, and I'm close enough to see my reflection in his eyes—the lotus's light dancing over my skin and radiating from me. "You're . . . *beautiful*."

A sob bubbles in my chest, which I turn into a laugh. "You tell me this now? When my wedding gown is ruined and our banquet destroyed?"

He slumps against me. His breathing is shallow, fast, and I am suddenly more terrified than words can describe as I hold him.

I press my fingers to my lips and whistle.

From somewhere nearby comes a responding whinny—followed by a roar.

Hào'yáng's grip tightens against my back. "Go," he breathes. "They're after me. Go, Àn'yīng."

Beyond us, Táo'wù is stirring from the wreckage of a house. Behind us, the ground shakes as Qióng'qí closes in. Yet the world seems to slow and fall away as I hold my boy in the jade.

There are a handful of moments in life when the meaning of destiny becomes clear. As Hào'yáng's blood warms me and his life energy ebbs away, my mother's words to him come back to me:

Your life will be a vessel through which the good of the Kingdom of Rivers is governed. Your heart and your soul will be buried under this vast decree beneath the Heavens, child.

There will be no space for love or a life for you.

And yet, Hào'yáng is here with me, so alive and so human.

To most, he is the heir and the captain, cold and distant and powerful—yet to me, he is so much more. He is my guardian in the jade, with the warmth in his eyes reserved only for me, the rare smiles I've come to love coaxing from him, lighting my skies like a glimpse of the sun. He is my political ally: When his brows crease, his gaze goes unfocused and a calculating look appears in his eyes, a look I've come to recognize when his brilliant mind is at work.

And then there are the parts of him that have threaded into my heart like the currents of a sunlit river. The Hào'yáng whose touch stirs those tides, whose gaze sets my world on fire like the sun burning flames into the sea.

The one whose kiss slammed the waves of an entire ocean into my chest.

If he must hold the weight of realms on his shoulders now and for the rest of his life, I will not let him do so alone.

As She of the Moon-Frosted Sea stops before us, I clasp his chin between my hands, forcing his eyes to meet mine. "I'm not going anywhere without you," I tell him, and without waiting for a response, I hoist him onto the dragonhorse's scaly back. I loop my brocade belt around her and strap Hào'yáng down. Then I slide on behind him and we're off, gaining speed as we rise into the air. Behind us, roars of the two hellbeasts follow us into the night.

Red seeps from Hào'yáng onto the dragonhorse's scales.

I brush a thumb along the hilt of my birth mother's lotus sword, feeling the grooves of its etchings against my skin, an ancient calling that might have been the start of my destiny.

"We make for the immortal realm tonight," I say, glancing to the distant horizon. She of the Moon-Frosted Sea's ears twitch back to me; her scales ripple dimly in the cloud-swathed night as she gallops. I grip my lotus sword tightly, its blade trailing an aurora glow through the darkness. "My mother's lotus vessel has recognized me. It's time I declare myself as Yǐ'lín Shī'yǎ's heir and summon her army."

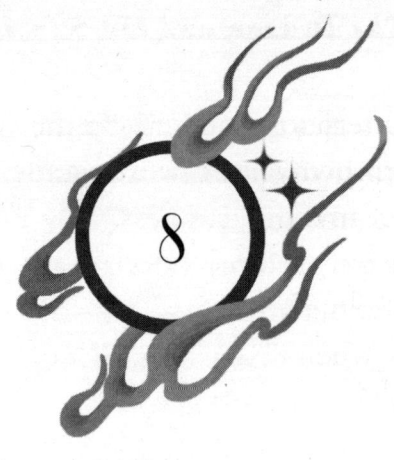

8

Àn'yīng

Kingdom of Rivers

I glance back as we fly. Xī'lín is falling away from us, a speck of jagged lights emanating from lamps in windows and the lanterns at the ruins of our banquet that never was. A fire has spread, illuminating two great, shadowy figures that prowl the streets. One spreads its wings to take flight.

Desperately, I search the vanishing realm for traces of my mother and sister. I must have bought them enough time to escape. Mā had already gone with Fú'yí, and Méi'zi was with Tán'mù and Lì'líng—they'll be all right.

They'll be all right.

Adrenaline yields to waves of fear and helplessness that threaten to drown me. Méi'zi's tear-streaked face, lips forming the shape of my name as she reaches for me, surfaces again and again in my mind's eye.

When was the last time we were all together as a family? I

recall the early afternoon, sunlight slanting through our house's paper shutters, thrown open to the fragrance of plum blossoms. Mā and Méi'zi beaming at me as I twirl in my wedding gown. The memory is only a few hours old but feels as though it is from another lifetime.

I don't know when I'll see them again.

"Àn'yīng." Hào'yáng's voice is quieter than I have ever heard it.

I avert my gaze, preoccupying myself with fashioning a makeshift saddle out of the brocades and satins of my wedding gown to strap us in more tightly. Hào'yáng's breaths are hitched; his face is ashen and lips are bloodless in a way that frightens me.

I slide my lotus sword into my belt, making sure it's secured, before turning back to him. "I'm going to take a look at your wound," I tell him, my hand hovering over the buckles of his armor. "May I?"

Hào'yáng's lips curve in a weak smile. His lashes flutter, and I see his eyes rolling as he fights to stay conscious. "I've imagined this ten thousand times for our wedding night," he mutters, "only never with me bleeding out."

Heat warms my cheeks, but my embarrassment falls away when I peel back his golden lamellar armor to reveal the blood-soaked shift underneath.

It's worse than I thought. On the left side of his powerful, corded chest, the skin is shredded by a giant puncture wound. Blood glistens and oozes out with each of his breaths.

"It'll be all right," Hào'yáng says, catching my expression. "I'll be all right, Àn'yīng."

I press my fingers to either side of the wound and begin weaving the talisman I learned from Healer.

Spirit energy flows from me, shimmering gently in the night. *A talisman is only as powerful as the strength of your will*, my father once told me in the early days of my training.

I bare my heart now, opening all I have been through with my boy in the jade and letting it flow into the rhythm of my hands as I trace this healing talisman to save his life.

But his blood continues to leak between my fingers. I feel him slipping away.

Help me. I speak into the echoes of my mind. My vision blurs; the flow of my spirit energy falters. *Meadowsweet, help me.*

The dragonhorse's familiar presence enters my mind in a swirl of silver and waves. Her voice is quiet as she replies:

I do not possess the ability to pull someone back from the Nine Fountains as the ancients of my realm do, she says. *But there is something I'd like to show you, Àn'yīng. Hào'yáng will never be selfish enough to express any of this to you, and so I will in his place.*

The waves in my mind grow louder; the dragonhorse's eyes begin to glow the color of the sea, and the clouds and skies of the mortal realm fade as I'm pulled into the tide of her memories.

It's bright, clear, the sun pouring through puffs of clouds, gilding everything. I recognize the ethereal perfection of the immortal realm, the way everything gleams as though wrought from paintings. A white dragonhorse dozes beneath a familiar-looking osmanthus tree; plumes of clouds curl over distant mountains, and a river sparkles as if it holds stars.

It's Hào'yáng's residence at the Temple of Dawn. I try to make out the year of this memory, but it proves impossible: The immortal realm is as unchanged as ever, eternally beautiful.

Footsteps sound from inside the cliffside house. The wooden doors slide open, and a boy emerges from beneath the curved eaves—a boy I would recognize anywhere.

This Hào'yáng must be twelve or thirteen years old; I make out traces of him like a sketch superimposed over the memory. His hair is tied in an austere bun, and he wears plain white silks. A golden tassel hanging from his waist marks him as a student. He's cradling something in his hands.

"She spoke." His voice is calm, yet there is an undercurrent of excitement. His eyes spark in a way that lights up his entire face as he kneels by Meadowsweet and holds out his hands. As the jade pendant glimmers in the sun, something in my heart shifts. "She was telling me about her day."

Meadowsweet blinks slowly. *You are meant to be practicing your skills with the longsword, and yet you spend all day waiting on a piece of stone.*

"That isn't true," Hào'yáng replies, but the ghost of a smile curls his lips as he settles beneath the tree, leaning against the dragonhorse and holding the pendant up to the sun. "Besides, I have a duty to take care of the girl in the jade." He pauses, and the smile slides from his face, yielding to that familiar crease between his brows. "The man who saved my life and brought me here is—was—her father. He gave me her place in this realm." His face holds that practiced, careful blankness; his thumb trails an involuntary stroke across the smooth surface of the pendant as he stares at it, lost in thought.

The scene shifts, and this time, I recognize Lady Shī'yǎ's home drifting in the skies of the immortal realm, with the cherry blossom tree in the courtyard, for which my father named me. My breath catches at the sight of her, well and alive, plucking at the strings of a lute as she sits by a stream flowing through her garden. The music tangles with the fall of cherry blossoms and the sound of rushing water in the soft evening air; there is a certain melancholy to it all.

Hào'yáng stands before her. A year, maybe more, seems to have passed since the last memory; he has grown taller, his shoulders and chest broadening and his jawline sharpening. His head is bowed, his hand on the hilt of Azure Tide.

The music stops. Lady Shī'yǎ looks up.

"You directly disobeyed me." There is no anger in her voice, only disappointment.

Hào'yáng lifts his gaze. His jaw is clenched, but there is a storm in his eyes, too. "Was I meant to watch her drown?" he asks, and I suddenly know what memory this is. It was after my first excursion in search of the light lotuses for Mā, when I'd fallen through the ice of a pond.

The first time I dreamt of the boy in the sea.

Lady Shī'yǎ's expression is calm as she gazes back at her protégée. "Hào'yáng," she says gently. "You must make your own choices in life. Yet if you commit to the path of heir, if you desire to one day take back your kingdom from the mó, there are sacrifices you must make. Going to the mortal realm put everything we have been working toward at stake."

"But I'm here and well and alive, aren't I?" There is a touch of anger to Hào'yáng's words. I have never seen this side of him: younger, more tempestuous, emotions sharper.

"You could have been killed—"

"Àn'yīng's father was killed! And if she'd died tonight, it would have been because of *me*, and I can't—" Hào'yáng blinks rapidly, breathing fast. "I can't live with the guilt of that, Lady. Can you at least understand that?"

The immortal remains as stoic as though carved from stone. It is several heartbeats before she speaks again. "If you choose the path of heir, you must cast aside all else. Love, family, friendship . . . you must shed everything in pursuit of your duty to your realm, to your people, and to your kingdom. You would exist not for yourself but as a vessel to serve the Kingdom of Rivers. Can you understand that?"

Hào'yáng's fists are clenched, his knuckles white in the moonlight. He swallows, and when he looks back up, his eyes glisten with tears. "I can," he whispers, and it is a hollow sound. "But, Lady, it hurts."

The scene blurs again, and this time, it is one that I recognize: the rosewood pillars, the gauze drapes, and the soft chirps of cicadas. Dusk at the Temple of Tranquil Longevity, in the immortal realm.

I recognize this scene—or what happened moments before it.

Hào'yáng, now in his present-day age, leans against a pillar as we approach through Meadowsweet's memory. His forehead rests against his arms, but every line in him is drawn tightly.

How did it go? Meadowsweet's voice rings in my mind.

Slowly, he tips his face up. Tries and fails to meet Meadowsweet's gaze. "She went to him," he says, so quietly that I barely catch it.

Meadowsweet approaches him. Gently, she touches his hand with her snout. It is all the comfort she knows to offer him.

Hào'yáng squeezes his eyes shut, reining in his expression. The pain on his face is gone, and there is only a shattering grief.

I dream, sometimes, of a lifetime in which I am not destined to be emperor. His voice rings in Meadowsweet's memory as he speaks to her through their minds, and I hear it as though he speaks to me. *I dream of not being shackled to my duty, Meadowsweet, free to live and love as I please. I dream of a life where I did not take her family away from her. A life where I deserve to love her.*

The last of the sunset rays have drained from the immortal skies, and the memory fades from my mind. Night of the mortal realm sweeps in as the present returns. Hào'yáng lies before me, his life bleeding out with every passing moment.

Tears roll down my face. I take his palm and press it to my cheek, knowing that these hands wrote those careful, golden words that helped me live, day by agonizing day, through all of nine years.

"Àn'yīng?" He opens his eyes. They reflect the light of Meadowsweet's glow, of my talisman's spirit energy working to heal his impossible wound. His fingers cup my cheek, his thumb tracing a caress across my skin. Wiping away my tears. "Àn'yīng, don't cry. Don't cry for me."

I can't move on from Meadowsweet's memories. All these years, I've had his comfort in my solitude, his encouragement in my grief. Yet when it came down to it, there was no one by his side to take away his tears.

I know instinctively what to do as I lean forward, pressing my fingers to my heart, where my life energies thrum with the pulse of my blood. I guide them up as I lean down, place my palm to his cheek, and kiss him.

He inhales as I exhale, my life energy streaming into him with my breath. Hào'yáng's eyes fall shut, his lashes fluttering against his cheeks. I exhale again, following the rhythm of his breaths as they grow steadier. By contrast, my heartbeat slows as my life energy continues to drain from me into him.

"Àn'yīng." His voice sounds distant to my ears even as he folds me into his arms. I lean into him, too tired to hold myself up any longer, yet all I'm aware of is my own overwhelming relief as I listen to the song of his heart.

"Stay," I whisper. "Please, stay with me." For half my life, Hào'yáng has been the steady presence by my side, a warmth like sunlight. And now, finally, possibly too late, a realization spills from my lips, falling like teardrops: "I can't bear the thought of a world without you, Hào'yáng."

His eyes shine, the corners softening until all his masks fall away. He's smiling at me as he parts his lips to speak.

The hellbeast comes out of nowhere. I feel only a rush of cold wind, sense a darkness denser than night pressing at my back, and then—

Impact.

My head's ringing. The world is spinning, a kaleidoscope of stars and clouds and the deep, deep sea beneath. Dimly, I hear Meadowsweet's scream, feel Hào'yáng's hands slipping through my fingers . . .

"No," I gasp, reaching for him as I orient myself again. I'm not falling—I'm *rising*, there's pressure around my midriff.

When I look down, I realize why.

A pair of giant claws hold me, tightly enough that I can't move but not enough to hurt me. A shadow envelops me; from above comes the beat of wings.

Qióng'qí.

Beneath us, hanging between me and the deadly drop to the sea, is Hào'yáng. He grips my fingers with one hand, his other reaching for Azure Tide at his hip. But with each wingbeat of the hellbeast, Hào'yáng's grip slips farther and farther down.

I draw my lotus sword and slash at Qióng'qí's talons.

The first swing falls on empty air.

The second is when it happens: As the blade arcs, it slows, and the surface of the blade brightens. I catch my reflection on the ancient metal the sword is forged from, catch the way my eyes widen in horror as, with a streak of light, the blade shatters into a million glittering pieces. For a heartbeat, they linger in the air, fractals in a kaleidoscope of motion and soft light.

Then, they fall. Pieces drift onto Hào'yáng's and my skin so that, for a few heartbeats, the two of us are aglow in the remnants of the sword. Light threads through Hào'yáng wrists, his fingers, his cheeks, the curves of his throat, dissolving into his veins. When he looks up at me, his eyes shine with the color that once ran through the lotus sword.

Àn'yīng, he mouths, and I realize that I, too, am illuminated in the sword's light.

But the light is dimming. Night rushes in, the wingbeats of the great hellbeast carrying me higher in its claws as Hào'yáng continues to slip down.

I seize Hào'yáng's arm with my other hand. My fingers are stiff with cold, and his wrist guard cuts into my palm with his weight—but I can't let go, I can't.

Hào'yáng gazes up at me. His face is serene.

Àn'yīng. His mouth moves in the shape of my name, and I

hear his voice as though he speaks in my ears, as though I am once again eleven years old and lost and alone, drowning in the depths of a frozen pond. Yet this time, the words that come are different.

Àn'yīng, he says. *Let me go.*

"No." His wrist slides farther down my grasp, the metal of his lamellar armor tearing my flesh. My blood drips on his armor. "No, Hào'yáng, you promised me—"

Even as I speak, I catch the growing shadow behind him. I lift my gaze to find two pinpricks of hellfire red burning through the night, the massive shape eclipsing half the sky.

As Táo'wù slams into us, Hào'yáng's hand jerks in mine. I don't comprehend the blood trickling down his chin, nor the dark patch spreading across his armor, until I see the claw protruding from his midriff like a curved sword.

A scream tears through the night as a silver streak rams into the hellbeast: She of the Moon-Frosted Sea, scales flashing and talons out. Táo'wù's great claw rips from Hào'yáng's chest as it turns to fight the dragonhorse, blood arcing like crimson beads through the night.

Together, dragon and hellbeast hurl down through the night into the dark.

But the damage is done.

Hào'yáng's lashes flutter. He lets out a sigh that might have echoed through the realms. His grip loosens in mine even as I dig my nails into his wrist, then his palm, then the tips of his fingers—

And he falls.

Through the night, illuminated by the cold light of stars.

I'm left with only the wind between my fingers, screaming his name until he's swallowed by the sea of clouds, screaming until my throat is hoarse and my chest is on fire and my heart feels as though it has torn from my rib cage and plummeted into the deep, cold sea with him.

Àn'yīng

Kingdom of Night

We fly. Onward, rising through the skies, the air around us growing colder, my breath pluming in front of me. We fly, bursting through the layer of clouds to a clear night. Stars reel overhead, and the moon casts all in monochrome.

The moon begins to warp. The full circle shrinks; an invisible darkness eats away at its light, spreading to the skies all around. The shadow grows, black enough to consume the stars, and all that's left is a hollow crescent, pale as bone, gleaming in the depths—a scythe-like moon I recognize, have seen in all my visions of the demon queen watching me from my nightmares.

That is how I know when we enter the Kingdom of Night.

Yù'chén

Palace of the Aurora, Kingdom of Night

The revelry is particularly intolerable tonight.

Since Sansiran and I returned to our realm, the mó at the Court of the Aurora have been throwing a lavish banquet in honor of our progress into the Kingdom of Sky. Sansiran wasted no time parading me around in a magnificent new outfit—one unmarked by the teeth and tongues of the mó that feasted on me back in the Temple of Dawn. My new circlet gleams gold on my forehead: *A crown,* my mother had crowed, to the roaring approval of her entire court, *for the future emperor of the Kingdom of Rivers and heir to the Kingdom of Night!*

The Palace of the Aurora is an ancient thing made of night-glass, rock, and old magic. Its main ceremony hall perches on cliffs yawning into shadows, and the rest of it—wings, temples, courtyards, and gardens—is connected by passages formed of demonic magic. Beyond, our realm is a world of jagged mountains and plunging clifftops wreathed in silver fog. Brightly colored trees choke the landscape, luminous in the eternal night and illuminated by the aurora snaking through the skies.

Moonlight streams into the great banquet hall that opens to worship the night sky, spilling on scenes of debauchery before me. Mortal prisoners, drunk on oleander nectar, follow mó around the dance floor or into shadowy alcoves, where, in the dim lighting, I make out flashes of flesh . . . and often, dark liquid dripping onto the floor.

I always look away before I can see more.

Behind my throne, a gate arcs high into the sky. A magnificent hallway stretches within, its blue silk banners and warm cherrywood pillars threaded through with gold and silver engravings incongruous with the decor of our realm.

This is the gateway to the Kingdom of Rivers. It's the one Sansiran opened with my blood ten years ago; the entire reason she keeps me alive. The gate refuses to remain, fading over the course of a day or a few—a source of irritation for my mother. It isn't the fact that she needs to use my blood to reopen it each time that bothers her. It's that she hasn't found a way to permanently cement her power across the mortal realm.

A phantom ache throbs in the heart of my palm, where my mother drew my blood earlier this evening—as soon as she returned from whichever battlefield she had been off to. Tonight, like so many nights before, she'd reopened the gates and led me into the mortal realm, then shoved me onto the mortal throne in hopes that the Kingdom of Rivers would finally accept me as emperor. She'd learned from my father, the late emperor, that there is a divine selection process by which the land of the mortal realm crowns its emperor. It is said that the land itself will join with the chosen emperor and that there will be signs. Sansiran believes that when I am finally selected by the Kingdom of Rivers, the land will fall into eternal night, the gate between our realms will expand to merge the two, and mó will be free to roam between the realms.

My mother's eyes had been blazing with renewed fervor tonight when I sat on the throne. But when nothing happened, like all the other times, she'd taken out her rage on me right there for all to see.

If the mortal throne ever chooses to accept me as its emperor by whatever divine selection it runs on, all I will remember when I sit upon it is pain.

Several mó have come up to the dais to proffer me toasts of oleander nectar, which I decline. I know what the sparkling fuchsia liquid swirling about their bronze cups will do to me. Oleander nectar has the effect of strong alcohol for the mó—but for mortals, it behaves like a drug. One sip and your judgment weakens; another, and your memory goes. A third, and you're at the mercy of whoever and whatever is around you—a vessel made to please. The mó love using it to command mortals to do their bidding: crawl like a dog, lick their feet, and whatever other depraved acts they find amusing.

I would know.

My mother bade me to drink wine instead, and I obliged. Toast after toast, I sipped from bronze goblets that servants swapped in and out of my hands until the banquet hall began to blur and the music began to swell and I couldn't remember why in the realms I was so worried in the first place.

It is in this state that I notice the surge in cheers and hollers somewhere beyond our banquet hall. A group of our soldiers seems to have returned. Lower-class mó rush to them immediately, plying them with wine and nectar and cold cuts of meat, scrambling to see if they've brought back young, beautiful mortals for entertainment.

My mother rises to greet them, but I remain seated on the starlit throne next to hers. My head is starting to pound in an unpleasant way.

The procession of soldiers is beginning to make its way down the hall.

I frown, straightening slightly. There's a palpable air of excitement spreading through the crowd; they all turn to the new arrivals. I make out a figure slumped in their midst, catch the whites of my mother's smile, and suddenly I'm sitting forward, my heart in my throat, unable to breathe.

The floor tilts beneath me as two of the generals approach the dais, half carrying the figure between them. From here, I make out the locks of her black hair against her pale shoulders, the spill of her deep red gown—but my heart, my *soul*, knows who it is even before my mother reaches her and tips her chin up.

Àn'yīng.

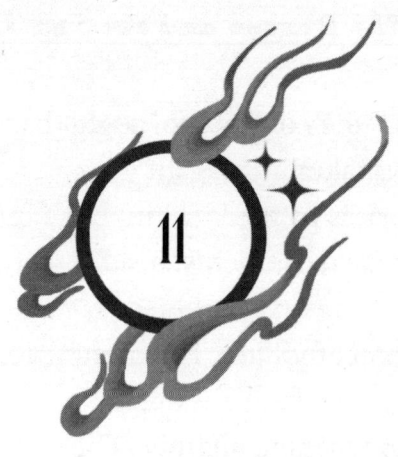

11

Àn'yīng

Palace of the Aurora, Kingdom of Night

I don't remember anything but the taste of the nectar, warm and honey-sweet as it lingers on my tongue. A bliss I haven't known in so long crashes into me like a wave. The world sways, and overhead, a kaleidoscope of stars spin like I'm gazing at a celestial river.

Wherever I am, it's beautiful.

So is the woman who steps before me and smiles at me with blood-red lips. She wears a black gown covered in diamonds, giving the illusion that she is draped in the night sky and all its stars. Garnets flash in her elaborately styled hair. The sight of them stirs something inside me, a memory drifting just beyond my grasp.

"Hello, Àn'yīng," she purrs. "We have all been waiting for this day."

I beam at her, because I want her to like me. I want to please her.

"Some of us," she continues, "more than others."

The woman makes an elegant gesture with her fingers, and I rise, feeling like a paper kite tugged along on a string. She leads me up onto a dais, then steps to one side.

Before me, sitting on a throne of silver, is the most beautiful man I have ever set eyes on. His hair tumbles like ink over his broad shoulders. His features are sharp enough to cut, brows rising like raven wings beneath a gold circlet, soft lips stained and swollen with wine.

I meet his eyes, and that gives me pause. They're wide; he's staring at me as though he's seen a ghost.

A momentary pain blazes through my mind—a streak of a memory, too quick for me to catch. Yet as I stare back at him, I'm filled with a strange intuition that I *know* him.

He swallows, and then that expression is gone, replaced with a cool gaze as he turns to the woman. "I'm honored. You went to great lengths to find me a mortal offering." His voice, low and rich, twines around me like an intimate velvet caress.

The woman smiles at him in a way that does not reach her eyes. She stands before her own throne, larger and darker and writhing with shadows. "You will see, my son, that I do indeed care for your desires." She turns to address the rest of the crowd gathered before us. "My loyal subjects! We have fought hard, and we have made sacrifices—but not without rewards.

"The heir to the Kingdom of Rivers is dead!"

Raucous, deafening cheers break out. I blink, the bliss slipping from me for a heartbeat. *The heir to the Kingdom of Rivers.* The words should mean something to me; I feel an insistent tugging at the back of my mind. Then, an image.

A face. Eyes as steady and warm as the earth, a smile like the sun.

Slipping through my fingers, vanishing into the clouds, into the sea.

The nectar's cloying sweetness intensifies on my tongue. The images vanish, and I can't quite remember why I was ever unhappy in the first place. The crowd is chanting *Empress, Empress, Empress.*

The woman—the *empress*—continues to speak. "We cannot forget that this victory would not have come without the pivotal role my *darling* son played in this war. Mistakes can be made, especially when it comes to the foolishness of his mortal instincts—but he has proven his loyalty by pledging his life in service of me and our kingdom. Therefore, I honor his covenant and reward him with that which he most desires. Let it be remembered that I am merciful." She turns to me. "I hereby announce that my son, Yù'chén, heir to the Kingdom of Rivers, shall take this girl as his betrothed." She waves a hand, and her voice pitches low: *"Go to him."*

I look from the empress to the man seated before me. Something feels off, but those invisible strings tug at me again.

I smile blithely as I gaze up at the man—it is easy to smile at his beauty—and slowly, clumsily, I lower myself to my hands and feet.

Behind me, the crowd goes wild, and my heart surges. I am doing this right. I am pleasing them.

Warm hands encircle my wrists and my shoulders, stopping me as I fold myself onto the floor. I'm lifted again, and when I look up, it is into the devastatingly beautiful face of that man. *My betrothed,* I think in happy disbelief.

Except he doesn't look pleased. He looks *furious.* He's breathing hard, trying to hold me up and at arm's length, but my body pitches forward unsteadily.

Yet his expression shifts into boredom when he faces the woman—his mother—again. "You'll have me take as a wife someone who resents our kind for destroying her home?" he asks petulantly. "She would never agree, were she not drunk on oleander nectar. This won't pass as a marriage under the Heavenly Order."

"Then you'll convince her until she wishes to, of her own volition," the empress replies. "You were persuasive enough last time. I'm certain you can do it again."

The crowd is turning away already, their voices rising as the celebration resumes and goblets clink together in toasts.

The man remains very still. His voice is quiet when he replies. "She won't make the mistake of falling for me again. You made sure of that."

"And you'll make sure that she does," the empress replies with a wave of her hand. "For both of your lives' sakes." A razor-sharp smile with those gleaming red lips. "Or shall I show her *my* methods of persuasion?"

Only I am close enough to hear the man's sharp inhale. He stares at the woman again for several heartbeats.

"Why?" he asks tonelessly. "Don't expect me to believe that you went through all this effort just to please me."

The empress flicks me a glance. "Of course I didn't," she purrs, and leans close to him. "You and I both know the mortal throne has yet to accept you. There must be another secret to it, a method to completely and wholly take that realm, which the imperial bloodline guards closely. Certainly, you'd expect your father to have passed on the secrets to claiming the mortal throne to his most legitimate heir, son of the late mortal empress. Now he is dead, yet the land still does not accept you."

The man's jaw tightens. "Have you considered the possibility that I cannot take the mortal throne because I am half mó?"

The empress's eyes narrow to slits. "The very reason you exist," she hisses with sudden venom, "is to claim that mortal throne for our realm. The girl was close to the mortal heir, who confided in her through that jade pendant for years. She may be our only chance to understand why the mortal land does not accept you, and the secrets to claiming that throne. Find out from her, or you'll discover that my patience for your existence runs to its end."

I try to pay attention to their conversation, but their words drift through my mind like fog. My attention pulls to the man by my side, who listens to all this without expression.

The empress draws back and smiles. "Be a good boy," she croons, and stalks away to join the revelry.

The man stands there for several moments, seemingly lost in thought, before he turns to me. He appears drunk, his cheeks and lips flushed, his hair wild and his collar askance. Yet his movements are gentle as he draws me into his arms and lifts me.

The sounds of celebration fall away from us, replaced by the rhythmic sound of his boots as he carries me from the banquet hall. It's dark here, dark everywhere, the entire building lit only by starlight.

Everywhere around us, flowers bloom, bright in a way that makes my head spin. *Red scorpion lilies*, I think, and another memory brushes against the edge of my consciousness. *I know them.*

Their light drapes my companion in a beautiful wash of crimson. His eyes, most of all, catch their glow. Transfixed, I reach up and touch a finger to the man's jaw. He flinches, then turns his head away.

I quickly draw my hand back. "Did I do something to displease you?" I ask.

"No," he says.

"Tell me what it is, and I'll make it up to you. Anything you want."

"It's nothing to do with you."

The warmth of the bliss in my veins turns cold, the honey-sweetness on my tongue growing bitter. "You don't want me?"

His gaze slides to me again, and his lips part in a breath. "You're very intoxicated right now, Àn'yīng," he says softly.

It's growing brighter. At the end of this passageway of flowers, a screen of smoke swirls.

We step through it into a vast chamber awash in gentle candlelight. A great rosewood bed sits in one corner, draped in dark velvet and silver sheets. Gauze curtains drift in a serene breeze through doorways that lead to a pavilion outside.

Behind us, the smoky screen hardens into doors that gleam like black glass.

My companion carries me over to a silk-covered futon perched before the pavilion.

"Are you hurt?" The question is so gentle.

Something stirs in my chest. An old, familiar ache. "I don't think so," I whisper. I'm suddenly tired, so tired that I cannot fathom moving from this futon again.

"Whose blood is this?" He touches my midriff, my hands, and that's the first time I notice the sticky sensation between my fingers, the darkness coating my dress.

I frown. "I don't remember."

My host leans forward, studying me with urgency. "Do you know what happened?" he asks.

Something in his tone cuts through the fog in my mind. A

primal instinct whispers that something is wrong, so devastatingly wrong, but my head begins to pound whenever I try to latch onto that thought. The sweetness on my tongue turns cloying, as though I've bitten into a fruit only to discover the rot within.

"No," I whisper, and I reach out, because I feel a little lost and I want someone to hold on to in this moment. My fingers close around the collar of his robes, and I tip forward, curling against his chest. There, I hear a familiar *thump, thump, thump* of his heart, feel the tick of his pulse against my cheek.

My host exhales slowly, and then he sweeps his arms over me, gathering me to him with an intimacy that feels almost familiar.

"Àn'yīng," he murmurs.

I know him. I know him with my heart, a deep sense of familiarity that feels engraved into my bones—but my mind is filled with fog, and I cannot for the life of me reconcile this echo in my soul with the blankness in my head.

"You're shivering," he observes. His hands are warm against my bare shoulders. "I'll draw you a bath outside."

For some reason, I feel safer than I can remember as his arms close around me and he lifts me once again.

We step beyond the silks and gauzes, and the world opens to me: one that feels utterly new. The moon is a scythe, bone-white and gleaming. In the distance, at the edge of the realm, colored lights weave amidst stars.

The ground of soft grass opens into a crystal spring surrounded by barren trees, their branches cutting jagged shadows in the night. My companion deposits me by the spring. The water is so clear that I reach for it, believing I can grasp a fistful of the shifting stars reflected within it.

It's ice-cold and draws a yelp from me.

"I have to heat it for you," my host says, his lip twitching in amusement. He bends and presses his palms to the surface of the spring.

The water begins to ripple. And all around us, the barren trees begin to change. Small red buds that resemble glittering rubies appear—and as the spring starts to steam, they bloom.

I reach out to the nearest flower. At my touch, it drifts into my hand, the petals curling like claws. A wave of warmth and healing washes over me, chasing away my cold and fatigue. The dread in my chest fades, and I can't ever remember feeling anything but this spiraling bliss. *A flower made for a tragic fate,* I think, and I glance up at my host. His eyes are glowing the same color as the scorpion lilies.

He catches me staring at him and smiles. I like the way it softens his features, transforms his entire face. "The water is warm now."

Gently, I reach for him and tip his chin toward me.

His shoulders tense. Quickly, he looks away. "They're red from my magic," he explains. It takes me a moment to realize he's talking about his eyes. "To heat the water. Don't . . . don't be frightened."

"It's beautiful." The taste of honey nectar intensifies on my tongue, and those invisible strings tug at me again. "You're beautiful," I tell him, because it's true.

He draws a sharp breath. "You're not in your right mind," he says, and stands swiftly. "The water is ready."

Before I can reply, he strides through the gauze curtains and vanishes into the chambers.

It takes me a while to get out of my dress—a wedding gown, torn and shredded in places, that I don't remember putting on.

The spring water is hot, vaguely fragrant with the sharp, spicy tang of a flower I can't place. I close my eyes and let myself sink into the heat, the ache of my muscles and my fatigue setting in, the fog in my mind darkening with the steam that envelops me.

When I climb out of the spring, a small silver-lined tray has appeared next to me. It sits in a patch of red oleander that wasn't there before. Folded atop it are a towel and a beautiful silk shift, a steaming cup of tea, and a delicate little platter of cakes and sliced fruit.

I dry myself and slip on the nightgown. It falls to my ankles, a gorgeous deep violet that yields to corals at the bottom, reminiscent of dawn or dusk. Small silver stars are stitched into the bodice.

The heat of the spring bath has left me parched, so I reach for the tea. As soon as it coats my tongue, a feeling of wrongness strikes me—before it's hidden by the cloying sweetness of the drink. As it swirls down my throat, that hot, euphoric bliss surges again in my chest. The moon and stars overhead seem to enlarge, and the glow of the scorpion lilies expands.

The world tilts as I make my way inside. It's dark beyond the gauze curtains, and the uneven stone smooths into obsidian beneath my feet. It's only by the red light of the flowers inside that I can see anything at all.

"Ān'yīng?" My host spins from a futon at the foot of his tall, curtained bed. He freezes as he catches sight of me.

"Who gave you that?" he asks sharply, but I can't answer, because the entire chamber is spinning and I can no longer move forward. It feels as though I'm stuck in a dream. When I'm next aware, I'm in his arms, and he's carrying me across the room. As he places me gently on the bed, I'm seized by a sense that something terrible will happen when I wake—if I don't hold on to him now.

I reach for his hand. He tenses in surprise, but he doesn't pull back.

Instead, he sits down next to me. With his other hand, he brushes aside a lock of my hair. That faint crimson glow—traces of his magic, I find myself thinking—is draining from his eyes, like a sunset turning to night.

I have the feeling I am falling into those eyes.

Slowly, I sit up and lift my hands to his cheeks. His skin is made of the same warmth as mine, yet I marvel at the way the faint moonlight worships him. He holds very still as I explore his face. His eyes, too, roam my face, yet when he raises them to meet mine, I am unprepared for the wave of emotion that crashes into me.

Because I can't have you, but I can't stop wanting you.

I draw back, my heart thundering against my chest. "I know you," I whisper.

He stares at me. A hundred emotions flicker across his face. "You're drugged with oleander nectar," he says quietly. "You don't know what you're saying."

"I know you," I repeat, with more conviction.

It takes several breaths before he responds. "You know me," he echoes. His fingers dig into the sheets of the bed.

I take his face in my hands. Focus on a single image, the red of his gaze burning into my mind. Close my eyes, trying to catch the fleeting, shattered memories through the fog in my head.

Red. *Red.*

A wedding gown. A banquet, paper lanterns . . . *my betrothed.*

The name comes to me in a rush, all at once.

"Hào'yáng." Yet even as I speak it, a different set of memories surface. The shimmer of dragon scales. A prince beneath the sea. A lotus in the sun.

My eyes fly open. The face before me is not the one in my memories of sunlight, water, and laughter. No—the face before me is bathed in half darkness, lit only by the cold light of the moon, eyes tainted with that eerie, otherworldly crimson.

For the first time tonight, my host's composure shatters. He reels back sharply, but I don't miss the devastation in his expression as he turns away from me.

"I'm sorry," I begin. "I'm so sorry—"

"Don't," he says. He grips the bedpost, his knuckles white, his back to me. Only the rise and fall of his shoulders tells me that he is breathing.

"I'm so sorry," I try again, but he cuts me off.

"Please, Àn'yīng." He won't turn to look at me. "Please, stop." Then his voice changes. It pitches low, magnifies, filling the chamber and my mind. *"Rest, Àn'yīng."*

Darkness fills my consciousness. I try to fight it, try to call out to him—a name on the tip of my tongue—but my thoughts are blurring, my eyelids too heavy. As the world fades, my dreams rush by in a torrent of crimson flowers and soft whispers and the gentlest of red gazes, swallowed by the dark.

12

Yù'chén

Palace of the Aurora, Kingdom of Night

I manage to stumble out onto the balcony. I've spent my entire life building walls around myself, so high and so thick that no one and nothing can hurt me. It was necessary for survival as a halfling in the Kingdom of Night.

One word from her, and the walls fell.

Hào'yáng. Her voice echoes in my mind. A hot knife through my chest.

I lean over the cold spring, my reflection perfectly captured by the scythe moon, my eyes burning that damning red of demonic energies, my lips and cheeks flushed in a way no mortal's can be.

You're beautiful. Her words, laced with the impossible sweetness of oleander nectar, drift through the wind to me.

I choke out a sob and slash my hand through the spring water.

I'd imagined her in a gown like that, in my most farfetched dreams. I'd imagined, a thousand times over, a lifetime in which she might wear a smile and a dress for me. Tonight, those dreams were willed into existence, yet I hadn't realized just how cruel the irony would taste.

Because tonight, smiling up at me from the dais, she looked beautiful in the gown she wore to wed another man.

I extend my hand, and where scorpion lilies bloom, a carafe of liquor appears. I toss the contents down my throat, again and again as it magically refills, the oleander nectar hot and cloying against my tongue. Just this once, I wish to forget everything, so the ache in my chest will go away.

As I down another cup of the poison, I sense the air shift. Red oleander begins to bloom, a trail flowering from beneath my feet to the trees around. Magic gathers in the air like shadows. The wind picks up, and as my head begins to rush, whispers fill my mind.

Hào'yáng, Hào'yáng, Hào'yáng . . .

Faint laughter swirls in the air. As the shadows behind me thicken, I know it's Sansiran.

A cold hand slides over my back. "Poor little halfling. Intended to give up his life and his kingdom for a girl, only to have her run off with another man."

She steps out in front of me, shaking off her cloak of night. She gazes down at me, and tonight, I truly don't have the strength to act like I care nothing for what is happening around me.

"My pitiful son," my mother says gently, leaning forward and tracing her fingers across my cheeks.

"Why are you doing this?" I demand. No more pretending.

She's won, and she knows it; I'm laid bare to the bone in front of her. "I've let you denigrate me every day before your court. I've endured your torture, I've said nothing as your generals use me and let their subordinates abuse me. Haven't you had enough?"

My mother examines the wetness on her fingertips, her face inscrutable. "Why?" she repeats softly. "I could ask the same of you, Yù'chén."

I glance at her sharply, and she sighs.

"I loved you," she says. "The Heavenly Order would say we mó are incapable of love, but I loved you as best I could, as best I knew how. I gave you everything: a life, a throne, the promise of a future where you hold the realms in your palms. And you threw it all away—for what?"

I'm too stunned to say anything. To hear the woman who is my mother tell me she loved me when all I've known at her hands has been pain and terror simply feels inconceivable. I'm convinced this is another one of her tricks, that at any point, she's going to hurt me in some new way.

"You betrayed me," she hisses, the sudden vehemence in her tone making me flinch. "I gave you everything—I *loved* you— and you still chose to betray me." A pause, and her crimson eyes go dark and empty. "Just like your father."

The pain comes, sharp and sudden as always. This time, it's the sensation that all my bones are snapping, over and over and over again.

When my mother's anger ebbs, I'm sprawled on the ground, my clothes soaked through, slipping in and out of consciousness. Sansiran's voice resounds in my mind: *I wanted your father to feel the pain I felt. I wanted him to watch as his entire family was slaughtered, his people were fed on, and his realm was burned to ashes.*

Now I want you to feel the same.

"That's not love." My voice is ragged.

My vision filters back slowly. My mother stands beneath a tree of red oleander, watching me. "And you think you know, because of a girl who's so disgusted by you that she can't even stand to look at you?"

I think of Àn'yīng, limned by the light of the moon and my magic, her cheeks flushed and eyes dark with the nectar. *You're beautiful.*

The pain in my chest returns.

"One day, my son, you will understand," my mother continues. "Love is nothing like all the mortal poems describe, all peach blossoms and sunshine and beautiful things. Love can grow dark and twisted and sharp, can hurt you like nothing you have felt before. One day, your love will hurt you so much that you will understand why I would burn down kingdoms for it."

I press a hand to my ribs, willing the ache to go away. And I think, in this moment, that I understand a little of what my mother means.

Maybe this is how love is meant to be for the likes of me. Maybe this is the only kind of love I deserve.

Sansiran kneels by me and grasps my chin. Her fingers are cold, so unlike the heat of my mortal skin. "Let it be known that I am never unmerciful to my son," she whispers. "I have given you the woman you want. I will bind her to you through marriage. Coax the secrets to the mortal throne from her, my son, and you will become the ruler of all the realms." Her lips curve, and I believe she actually means it when she says, "I am giving you everything that you desire, Yù'chén."

Everything my mother is saying makes sense; it's all that I could dream of, as though she's pried open my chest and clawed out my deepest, most desperate desires.

I want to be accepted by both realms I come from.

I want to be with the girl I love.

But somehow, it's all wrong.

Sansiran's nostrils flare, and her eyes narrow. Her grip on my face tightens painfully. "I give you everything you want," she says, her voice dangerously soft, "yet still, you are dissatisfied."

I should return to my mask, to the performance of drunken indifference I've put on over the past few weeks. Yet as I gaze into her face, I recall the woman who saved me from the wrath of the man who fathered me; who pulled me from the clutches of death as the mortal imperial army came for us that fateful day.

I think of the mother who did not know how to raise a mortal halfling like me—but who tried, nevertheless.

She had no one to show her the kind of fiery, blazing love I'd found in Àn'yīng. She'd only learned of love's cruelty, its sharp edges made to hurt.

"Because it's not right," I say. This conversation—with me prostrated on the ground before her, her nails piercing my flesh—is the most intimate one I've had with my mother in a while. "Taking everything you want like this isn't right."

My mother's lips curl in disgust. "Again, you show your mortal weakness," she says. "Mortals are so concerned with right and wrong. A set of arbitrary rules, as defined by the Heavenly Order, of what constitutes good and evil. The world is made of pain and cruelty, Yù'chén. Even if you satisfy all their arbitrary rules, the Heavenly Order will still mark you as less-than because of what you are."

"What does it matter?" I demand, pushing myself into a kneeling position. I face Sansiran. "Isn't our realm enough? Growing up, I never thought of our kingdom and our way of life as lesser. We live on the energies of darkness and night. Our realm is beautiful beneath the moon. I was never ashamed of what I was until we began the war against the mortal realm."

My mother is silent, unblinking as she watches me. I've spent half my life around pure mó, and still, I find myself thrown by their thoughts, their expressions. Like the immortals, they possess their own codes of behavior, their own traditions and thought processes, which feel so different from mine. It is hard for me to fathom that Sansiran birthed me of her flesh and ichor, that we share a bond stronger and older than any other magic in this realm. The pure mó do not feel love, loyalty, and most other emotions as the mortals do. To them, the world runs on power, pain, and cruelty.

And I have no doubt that, in my mother's mind, she believes she is doing the right thing for me, for us, for our bloodline.

Sansiran blinks at last. "In this world, no matter which realm you are born into, power is the only thing that matters. Whether you are made immortal, mortal, demon, or anything else, the only rule that holds true is that the strong will vanquish the weak." She rises like a serpent uncoiling, impossibly graceful. "If I ruled all the realms, even the Heavenly Order could be remade by me. You see, it does not matter how one goes about attaining power. Once you have it, you can rewrite the entire world." She smiles at me, and it is dazzling. "The realms will be ours soon, my son. You can choose to come willingly and take all that you desire in this life and bask in the glory of our power. Or I can force you to by invoking the terms of our covenant. You will always belong to me. And if I find you succumbing to any weaknesses and foolishness of your heart, then I shall have to break it until you no longer feel anything at all."

Àn'yīng

Palace of the Aurora, Kingdom of Night

A gentle blush light pulses before me in the dark. I cannot see, but all around me is a rushing sound and the distant echo of voices, as though I am submerged beneath water. I can't make out the words—like the speakers linger just beyond and I listen through a veil.

Then I hear a name. A familiar voice, one that conjures the sun and the sea. Calling to me.

Àn'yīng, wake.

When I open my eyes, it is dark. Above me, a silken drape hangs between four bedposts—and beyond that, a ceiling enchanted to resemble a night sky. I lie frozen, unable to place where I am and how I got here.

Yet when I inhale, the unfamiliar bed yields a familiar scent.

Soft, dark sheets cool against my skin, smelling of midnight and sharp pine, petals on a breeze.

"Àn'yīng." A most beautiful voice from both my dreams and nightmares speaks.

I'm on my feet in a heartbeat, reaching for my crescent blades—but they're not there, and I'm not in my normal white dress.

The shadows rearrange themselves into the figure of a man. He steps out into a pool of moonlight filtering in from an open-air pavilion. It takes a moment for my eyes to adjust, another for me to recognize him without his red cloak.

Yù'chén watches me from across the room. He's in a set of black robes, stitched through with small silver stars that form the shapes of dragons. It's transformed him into someone new. Someone I barely recognize.

In a sudden and violent rush, my memories filter back.

The wedding. The hellbeasts. My lotus sword, shattering into a million pieces.

Hào'yáng, slipping through my fingers.

I make a choked sound, stumbling back until my shoulders hit the bedpost. "You," I gasp. "How—what did you—"

Yù'chén is silent, eerily still in that mó way of his. His expression is inscrutable.

Fear kicks my old instincts into high gear. But when I flex my fingers, my hands draw up empty instead of grasping the familiar grooves of my crescent blades' hilts.

I feel naked. Violated.

"Give me my blades." My voice shakes.

Yù'chén blinks slowly. "I'm afraid I can't do that."

Realization after realization hits me, knocking the breath from my lungs.

Hào'yáng is dead.

My village is burned.

I don't know if my family, the villagers, and Lì'líng and Tán'mù and the rest of our allies are alive. Even if they are, I don't know where they would be or how to reach them. And as I turn to take in my surroundings—this unnatural night, the cold obsidian floor and gnarled trees out on the pavilion, all imbued with a twisted and terrifying foreignness . . . I realize with a bone-deep knowing that this can't be anywhere in the mortal realm.

Which means . . .

I'm in the Kingdom of Night.

"Àn'yīng," Yù'chén begins, but I've fallen to my knees, the floor before me spinning. When I blink again, he's kneeling by my side, his hands on my shoulders to steady me.

I strike out. The slap echoes across the chamber; the force of it sends him sprawling backward.

Slowly, Yù'chén straightens and looks at me again. Three vivid slashes of red streak across his cheek. When I look down, my nails are coated in his blood.

"Get away from me," I gasp.

Yù'chén wipes at the blood dripping down his face. Then he inclines his head. "As you wish."

Without a word, he turns and walks away, vanishing into the dark.

I wait until I'm certain he is gone before I slump against the wall, drawing my knees to my chest. Everything that happened over the past day hits me like a tidal wave: the insurmountable weight and irreparable cost of my failures.

I press my palms over my mouth to silence any sounds I might make as my tears come.

*　*　*

It's been minutes, or hours—I can't tell, for there is no sun here, only an eternal night. I'm alone in the dark, the cold beginning to settle into my bones and making me shiver.

I've thought through endless ways out, and each plan I've discarded. The chamber is sprawling, the pavilion outside like a maze of eerie, barren trees and a cold spring. Yet the rocky crags of the pavilion end at a sharp drop. Beneath is only darkness, with mist clinging to sharp cliffs and jutting mountains. When I reached a hand out toward the ledge, I encountered pressure, as though the air itself resisted me. It eased when I backed away.

Wards. I'm being kept here as a prisoner.

I look everywhere, but my three remaining blades are gone. They must have been removed along with my wedding dress. *A scorpion without a stinger*, I think—but there is a chance they haven't been discarded yet.

A chance I can still get to them.

My lotus, though, is a different story.

In the dark, the memory of its last moments flashes through my mind. Its glow as, in the form of a sword, it arced through the air toward the hellbeast, the shock on my face reflected in its blade as it shattered. Glimmering fragments, flickering like embers, swirling onto my skin.

I hold my hand out before me, turning it to examine my skin. There is no remaining trace of the lotus's glow, and I have no answer to the question of how an immortal's vessel could simply shatter and vanish without a trace.

I sense his presence before he appears: a shift in the shadows, a knowing in my bones. He stands in the corner of my vision, halfway across the vast chamber. I don't know where he has come from—I've searched every corner of this room, but the doors have remained locked and warded and there are no other exits.

Yù'chén approaches, stopping far enough from me that I can't strike him again. He sets something on the floor before me. "Drink it," he says, and then with a touch of wryness: "And before you say anything, one: no, it's not poisoned—if I wanted you dead I wouldn't have gone through all this effort—and two: if you want me to poison-test it anyway, you only have to ask. Nicely."

It's a cup of dandelion tea. The smell is a painful reminder of home. Of the time I made him this exact tea in my kitchen. Allowed him near Méi'zi and Mā.

I hurl the cup at him with all my strength. He reacts too fast, making a sharp gesture with his hand, and the teacup explodes in midair, hot liquid and shards of porcelain clattering to the gleaming obsidian floor in a violent mess.

Yù'chén raises an eyebrow as he surveys the damage. "Good thing I didn't use my favorite cup."

I activate the talisman for swiftness I'd drawn during this moment of distraction. In a spurt of spirit energy, I charge him, snatching up one of the jagged pieces of teacup from the floor. I swipe at his throat—

His fingers close around my wrists. It's disconcerting how effortless he makes it seem to hold me off. His eyes are blazing crimson, his jaw tight, as he studies my face.

"Would it please you to hurt me, Àn'yīng?" he says. "Would you feel better if you cut me and drew enough blood to turn my floors red?" His hands slide away from mine, and he opens his arms. "Go ahead."

I'm too surprised to react for several heartbeats. But my

anger returns at the hint of a smile playing on his lips, the cocky way in which he tips his head back, baring his throat for me. He can't die from being cut by a piece of teacup, and he knows I know this. I've seen the way his skin stitches itself back together with his dark magic, leaving no scars behind.

I curl my hands into fists. "I won't be satisfied until I watch you die before my eyes," I snap, driving every ounce of vehemence I feel into those words.

Yù'chén laughs. "You break my heart," he says, pressing a palm over his chest in a way that makes me wish I'd tried to slit his throat after all. He clears his throat, fixing me with an inscrutable gaze. "But I didn't come only to ask to be stabbed by you. I bring news." His tone prompts me to look up at him. I'd thought him impossibly beautiful once, in the mortal realm—but here, the shadows *worship* him. Darkness pools at his feet, kissing his black cloak, the silver threads on the fabric gleaming like constellations. "Your family is well."

Instantly, the fight drains from me. Every nerve in me stretches taut as I say, "You can have your way with me, but please"—my voice cracks—"don't play with me on this."

"Always assuming the worst of me," Yù'chén says, and twirls his fingers. A familiar black feather appears as though he plucked it from the shadows, its edges shifting from light to dark. An illusory memory from his shadowcrane.

He releases it. Like before, the feather dissolves, reshaping itself into a rippling surface, so that I have the impression that I gaze at a scene on the other side of a clear spring.

Sunlight pours through, as golden as syrup. In a forest of red-and-gold camphor trees, a small group of people cluster around a fire and a girl serving broth.

Méi'zi.

The fight goes out of me as I watch her chatter with Fú'yí. My mother is seated just several steps behind her, a weary but hopeful smile on her face. Then there's Lì'líng, slurping merrily from a bowl, steam wafting in her face. Leaning against a tree just beyond, Tán'mù stands with her arms folded.

"Méi'zi," I whisper. "Mā—"

Tán'mù straightens suddenly, her gaze snapping toward me. For a giddy moment, I think she's heard me—but as she draws her two-pronged spear, I remember that this is a memory, perhaps from earlier in the day when Yù'chén's shadowcrane happened upon them.

The vision shifts as the shadowcrane turns to take flight, and then the scene fades until all I'm left with is the echo of laughter and their faces seared into my mind.

"This was near the border to the Western Province," Yù'chén says. But instead of giving me comfort, fury surges in me as I remember whose forces attacked my village and tore my loved ones away from me.

"What are you going to do to them?" My voice shakes.

He blinks. "Nothing—"

"Don't lie to me," I spit, "you *monster*."

I relish the flicker of his easy grin. "My tenure here forbids me from doing anything to harm my kingdom. But I am not obligated to report to my mother everything I do, either."

"Don't tell me you showed me out of the *goodness of your heart*."

"Ah, I forget how hard that is for you to believe."

I let out a cold laugh. "Harder now that I know you *used* me to let the Kingdom of Night infiltrate the immortal realm."

He's silent at this, looking at a spot on the wall instead of at me.

"Please don't hurt them," I say into the silence after a while. "Please. I'll do anything you want."

Yù'chén sighs and drags a hand down his face. "How swiftly you forget that I once risked my life to save your sister," he says. His eyes glint through the spaces between his fingers. "Did that mean nothing to you, Àn'yīng?"

I'm quiet, if only because I remember all too clearly, and it had meant *everything* to me then, and I will never tell him that now.

Seeing that I won't speak, Yù'chén continues: "I have no reason to hurt your family. You assume many illogical things about my actions, Àn'yīng, merely based on what I am."

"Then why are you keeping me here?" I ask instead. "Why not just kill me?"

Yù'chén folds his arms and straightens, turning to me. "Àn'yīng. Please have some tea. Your body won't last long without sustenance."

"Why do you care?" I demand, but he's already calling upon his magic. The chamber lightens and warms. Scorpion lilies blossom on the bedposts, heat pouring from them, and I realize that I was shivering.

Yù'chén approaches with a tray laden with a teapot, a teacup, and several platters of delicacies. He stops a few steps away. "Will you throw this at me again?"

The question is so incongruously innocent that I have the urge to laugh. Seeing my family alive and well has filled me with hope, fury, and, most of all, renewed resolve.

I don't wish to feel anything anymore, I once wrote Hào'yáng through my jade pendant, when my father died. *If this is how much it hurts to love and lose someone, I never wish to love again.*

Love is the most powerful magic in our realms, he replied. *Take what you feel and hone it into a blade. Even when all else fails, you will have love to guide you.*

My mind sharpens. Yù'chén is the only resource I have access to in the Kingdom of Night—which means I can start by finding out information from him.

I accept the tray, aware of his gaze upon me as I drink the tea. It warms me instantly, and I find myself reaching for more. After several refills, I pause to study the cup. It is different from the artistic style of the Kingdom of Night: obsidian inlaid with bursts of silver with bright glazing. This one is also porcelain, but with butterflies soaring amidst peonies and willows, reminiscent of the motifs and art style of the Eastern Province.

"This is from the mortal realm," I observe, running a thumb over the little blue glazings.

He nods. "My father gifted it to me when I was a child. I always had a pot of hot water or tea on my desk as I studied with the mortal tutors. When my father destroyed the private residence he had built for my mother and me, this is one of the few pieces I managed to salvage."

I focus on the cup, imagining Yù'chén as a young child being cast away and hunted for the circumstances of his birth. I imagine the emperor—his father of flesh and blood—speaking the command for his and Sansiran's heads.

I set the cup down with a loud *thunk*. "So, do the mó keep mortals here for food or pleasure?" I ask.

He raises his eyebrows but offers me an answer anyway. "Both. But mortals don't last long here. There's no sun or heat. The makeup of mó is very different. They—we—derive our energy from the night, from the darkness."

"What about you?" I'm making conversation, hoping for

anything he might let slip that could be useful to me—yet with this question, I'm genuinely curious, too.

Yù'chén studies the destiny lines on his palms. "I need both," he says at last. "My vision in the dark isn't as good as the mó's, and I need heat to survive. But I gain power from both darkness and light."

He sounds almost hesitant. It suddenly occurs to me that perhaps no one has ever asked him this question. I recall the brutal way his mother treated him that night in the immortal realm, and I suddenly wonder what his childhood was like.

I wonder if he cared for me because I was the first person in this world to treat him like a human being.

"How did I end up here?" I crane my neck at the starlit ceiling, the flowers blooming softly against dark walls. "I have no memory of it."

"Oleander nectar. In the future, should anyone offer it to you, do *not* accept."

Oleander nectar. The words don't trigger any memories, yet bile rises on my tongue, tasting of honey. "You fed it to me?"

Yù'chén glances at me. "No."

"And what exactly does it do? Make you lose your memory?"

"It makes you forget who you are. It makes you pliant. Drink enough of it, and you'll do anything to please whomever you happen upon." He says all this as though through a recitation. "It works like our magic; it's how the mó lure mortals into their traps."

My heart is beating faster and faster in my chest. The black hole of the past day—night—however long I've been here—expands into a new fear as I brush a hand against the bodice of my new nightgown. "And you changed me into this?"

His gaze slides to where I touch my waist. "No. You did. It was gifted to you."

"For you to enjoy?" I don't know if I manage to keep the fear from my voice.

Yù'chén is no longer smiling. "I may be your villain, Àn'yīng," he says, "but I'm not a monster."

The seconds tick away between us.

"And what do you want with me now?" I ask again. "Why keep me here, alive, when they could have just killed me as they did—" I draw a sharp breath. I can't say his name out loud, can't think about it yet without breaking.

I press the heels of my hands into my eyes, willing my breathing to steady. For the feeling of drowning to subside as I pull in lungfuls of air.

When I look up again, Yù'chén is still watching me, his expression inscrutable, his eyes dark. "I don't want anything from you," he says.

"Then why am I here?"

It takes a long time for him to reply. "Because I asked my mother to spare your life." The words rush from him. He studies a spot on the floor between us.

I open and close my mouth several times. "Why?"

A muscle clenches in his jaw.

"Do you plan to imprison me in your palace for the rest of my life?" I'm suddenly furious, if only to hide my fear at the prospect of an eternity here, trapped in darkness as my realm falls into night and everyone I love dies. "Am I to . . . to service you and please you and—"

"Is it so terrible," he says, his tone suddenly harsh, "to be here and alive with me rather than dead, Àn'yīng?" When Yù'chén finally looks up at me, anger brims in his eyes, his voice.

I can't do it. I can't be civil, can't be logical or clinical, not when everything that happened is still so fresh in my mind, my heart left blazing and broken into a million pieces.

I hold his gaze and reply in a low tone, "I would rather die than be trapped here for a lifetime with you, a monster who is actively destroying my kingdom, my home, and all that I love." I pack as much vehemence into my next words as I can. "I *hate* you."

His hands have fisted over the little teacup. "I know," he says quietly. Something dark passes over his face, then it's gone— a fleeting cloud in the skies.

Yù'chén stands, spinning the teacup between his fingers. "Eat, Àn'yīng," he says with a casual wave at the food. "If you're going to spend eternity with a monster like me, might as well do it on a full stomach."

He melts into the shadows, vanishing before I can reply.

14

Àn'yīng

Palace of the Aurora, Kingdom of Night

I don't know how much time passes until I next see him. As the sun never rises here, I'm only guided by the turn of stars, which seem to shift with a fluidity vastly different from the fixed constellations of the mortal realm.

Every few hours, red scorpion lilies bloom and a tray of food and drink appears in the chamber. The platters are delicately arranged, the dishes cooked to perfection in a way that reminds me of the food I consumed in the Kingdom of Sky.

I pace around the chamber, yet no matter how much I press against the walls or test the invisible wards on the terrace, I can't find a single point of weakness I can leverage. No access to the outside . . . except through *him*.

When Yù'chén reappears from the shadows through whatever entryway he's been using, I stand immediately. "Where have you been?" I demand.

He raises an eyebrow. "I don't see how that concerns you," he says, and a corner of his mouth lifts in that smirk. "Unless . . . Did you miss me after all? Is eternity with a monster starting to sound more palatable?"

He has always known how to draw a response from me. But this time, I only frown. "I want to know how you're able to do that. Just . . . appear and vanish at will."

In the near-unbearable stretch of time that has passed since our last interaction, I've been able to think things through. I've held on to the memory of Mā and Méi'zi and Lì'líng and Tán'mù in that sunlit forest—and I've known that I will do whatever it takes to find a way out and back to them again.

I need to focus. Gain his trust.

"I told you before," Yù'chén replies, still looking bemused, "we mó have the ability to fold distances and travel through passages of our own making. Only this time, I'm merely making a passage to a different part of my own wing in this palace. It's how the Palace of the Aurora works."

I straighten slightly at that. "Can you show me the rest of your wing?"

He cocks his head, studying me. "No feral cup-throwing this time? No cursing at me or furious demands for me to leave you alone? Why, keep this up, and I may mistake it for a declaration of love, little scorpion."

Just like that, I want to discard the strategy I've come up with. "Are you here for any reason other than to goad me?"

"It may surprise you that I am," Yù'chén replies steadily, and holds out a palm. The sight of the shimmering dark feather drives every other thought from my mind. "Your family has crossed into the Western Province. Would you like to see?"

"Yes," I say quickly, and he obliges. This time, the feather shifts into a landscape of rolling sand dunes, golden sun, and fierce blue skies. A line of travelers casts long shadows over the undulating desert. I make out Méi'zi and Tán'mù leading a camel, upon which my mother sits. Bounding by their side is a small white streak: Lǐ'líng in her fox form.

I stare at the memory until it flickers and the illusion ends. The image of blazing sands and blue skies and sun is seared into my vision as I blink, readjusting to the darkness.

"They're safe," Yù'chén says. "I'll return when my shadow-crane sends word." He turns to leave.

"Thank you." The words slip past my lips; I don't even catch them until I've spoken aloud.

Yù'chén pauses. Slowly, he glances back at me. "You're welcome, Àn'yīng," he says.

"Wait." I take a step forward, grappling for an excuse to keep him here. I need information on where my blades might be. I need to see more of this palace to devise an escape plan.

Yù'chén is staring at me, one eyebrow cocked. "Yes?"

I open and close my mouth as I try to come up with something that doesn't sound too obvious.

He smiles suddenly, disarmingly. "Either you ask me to leave, Àn'yīng, or you ask me to stay. Which is it?"

I swallow. "Stay."

Yù'chén turns to face me. His eyes are bright as he approaches, then stops at a comfortable distance. "Is there any reason you've requested the pleasure of my company tonight, little scorpion?"

Precisely because I'm scheming your timely demise, I think, but outwardly I only reply, "How long have I been here?"

"A little under two weeks."

That chills me. Two weeks, and while my family is safe . . . Hào'yáng is still dead. And I have no plan of escape, no chance of turning this war around to save my realm.

"Please don't leave me alone for that long again," I say quietly.

"I'll stay for as long as you like, Àn'yīng," Yù'chén says with a shrug. "You need only ask."

I wrap my arms around myself, only just remembering that I am in that thin, sheer nightgown. "Could I have a proper dress?" I ask.

Yù'chén's gaze flickers over me. "It would take at least a few days to tailor a new one for you. But I can alter your clothes with my magic. Would that be all right with you?"

What I really want is a weapon. But I have to start small. Begin by gaining his trust. "All right," I echo.

Yù'chén leads me onto the pavilion. I haven't ventured outside in a while. Fresh night air caresses my cheeks, and I could weep for the way the wind moves over me after having spent so long in the suffocating darkness of his chambers. Overhead, the aurora dances and the jagged mountains and shifting clouds come alive with colors. I catch myself admiring the eerie beauty of this world, at once frightening and breathtaking.

I look sharply away. I can't think of them without thinking of the invisible wards at the edges of this terrace, imprisoning me here.

Yù'chén turns to face me. His eyes glow crimson as magic pools in his palms. I hear him draw a quiet breath, as though to steel himself, and then he begins. The fabric stretches where he coaxes, his hand brushing featherlight against my skin as he guides an iridescent thread to weave sleeves over my bare shoulders and arms.

He moves to my bodice next. I suppress a shiver as the heat of his hands roams up my waist, the tips of his fingers grazing the sheer fabric.

When he reaches the top of my rib cage, Yù'chén pauses. He glances at the soft silk over my breasts before quickly averting his gaze.

"Bear with me," he says, and then his hands move up. I close my eyes, waiting for nausea or disgust to rise in my throat.

Only it doesn't.

Yù'chén's fingers barely skim against the sensitive parts of my skin before they move to my collarbone.

When I open my eyes, he is already stepping away. A chill replaces the heat of his body. "I can change anything you don't like."

I step to the edge of the cold spring to peer at my reflection.

Yù'chén has completely changed my nightgown. It holds the original structure, hugging my body and kissing my waist before spilling down in a sheath . . . but he has enhanced it beautifully into a proper dress. Silver twines with the black silk like a celestial river, cascading down to my feet. My bodice glimmers and ripples like an ocean at midnight. And my hair falls in waves down my back, pinned only by a glowing red scorpion lily.

Like this, fully dressed, I feel settled in a way I haven't since I arrived.

And I feel powerful.

"I didn't know your magic could do this," I say.

"It's stronger here," he replies.

"You have an eye for design. I thought I was the seamstress."

His lips curve at the corners. He's still staring at me, and he seems to realize this, for he quickly looks away. "Is there anything else you need, Àn'yīng?"

I take a step toward him. Something has eased in the dynamic between us, and I feel emboldened to ask, "Can I go outside of these chambers with you?"

He hesitates, and I wonder if I've pushed too far. But Yù'chén says, "The Palace of the Aurora is heavily guarded. My wing in particular has limited exit and entry. I'm not exactly popular in my kingdom right now after . . . well, after some of the choices I made back in the Kingdom of Sky. We would need a reason to leave."

I know exactly what choices he's referencing. An image flashes in my mind: me, standing at the edge of the waterfall leading to the mortal realm, hand in hand with Hào'yáng as we prepare to escape. Yù'chén, stepping out from the shadows behind us, the red of his eyes burning into me.

He let me go.

"I have an idea," Yù'chén says now, drawing my attention back to the present. He proffers his hand.

And because I have nothing more to lose by trusting him this once, I take it.

Caution tightens my throat as we step into his chambers and near those obsidian doors. I don't know what might be waiting for me on the other side. By instinct, I keep flicking my wrists, grasping for my crescent blades.

Gain his trust, I repeat to myself firmly—the mantra that is at once keeping me moving and holding me together. I touch the bodice of my gown, where I've pocketed that shard of the porcelain teacup I broke several days ago. With it and a proper dress, I'm already in a better position than I was when I arrived.

The obsidian doors shimmer with a luster I thought to be

mother-of-pearl, yet as we approach, I realize that it resembles stardust. When Yù'chén raps on the doors, the stardust ripples, revealing two silhouettes on the other side, like shadows through a screen.

Guards.

"Open the passageway," Yù'chén demands, every bit the petulant prince of this realm. "I'm going to a moonsong revelry."

A sly female voice responds, echoing as though she speaks to us through a long tunnel, "You and your mortal pet, halfling prince?"

"Need you even ask?" he drawls.

There's faint laughter; he seems to have passed the test, for the doors open like drapes parting. Flowers bloom, their stems weaving into an archway: silver narcissuses, their petals like pale butterflies.

Yù'chén draws me close to him in the semblance of an embrace. "You know the rules," he says to me, his breath grazing the shell of my ear. "Stay close to me. Don't touch the flowers. And don't believe anything you see or hear."

The last time I went through a demonic passageway, it was formed of *his* magic. He'd been leading me home.

I never thought I'd miss the sight of the red scorpion lilies.

Cold brushes my shoulders when we step into the narcissus passageway, as though I step through a sheet of frost. I hear whispers and strange chittering in the distance, but when I turn my head sharply, there's nothing—only walls of pale flowers everywhere, glowing unnaturally.

The passageway branches off, like a great underground tunnel. The walls are nearly translucent, like smoke screens filtering through light . . . and I have the strangest sensation we're being watched. Ghostly shapes move on the other side at the corners of my eyes; when I look at them directly, they're gone in that swirling mass of gray.

As much as I try to resist it, the dark magic affects me. My senses slow, and I catch my attention sliding no matter how I try to focus on observing their magic, deriving any new information from the passageway or finding any weaknesses in their snares.

Yù'chén's hand tightens around my waist, as though he can sense me slipping. His sword is out, and he walks with a predatory grace, his eyes glinting red as he surveys our surroundings. "Almost there," he says to me, and suddenly something pounces at us.

I swallow a scream as a hellbeast forms out of the mist, claws and fangs flashing. Yù'chén lashes out; there's a burst of red, and then we're standing in a cocoon of scorpion lilies. Their glow lights the dark . . . and the air begins to shift with the familiar taste of his dark magic.

The hellbeast is gone as quickly as it appeared. The passageway fills with faint, feminine laughter—and I realize this was merely a demon's illusory trick.

"Come on," Yù'chén says, and as his scorpion lilies brighten like fire, the passageway releases us.

Wind, stars, sea. We're plummeting through the night in a whirl of magic and blossoms. Overhead, the tunnel vanishes, replaced by the crescent moon—so close and so bright that I almost reach out, thinking I can skim my fingers along its surface.

Yù'chén's body is warm, shielding me from the cold of the night, his chest and arms locking me in a hard grip. Great shadows spread like wings beneath us, interlaced with flowers, and Yù'chén rights us.

We slow, and I step onto the ground. The grass is as soft as carpet beneath my bare feet; the air is crisp with the scent of pines, flowers, and water. The dullness in my head induced by the dark magic of the flower passage clears.

I'm in a village or a town—but it's unlike any I've seen in the mortal or immortal realms. We've landed in a valley drifting in the night sky, mist woven through its glades and clouds threaded through its gullies. Pagodas and temples and houses with curved eaves are tucked in between, as though they are part of the landscape; unlike the mortal realm, they have no lanterns. Sheer drapes flutter in the wind like gossamer wings, and the moonlight pouring down upon them seems to weave into their fabric so that they glow.

It's eerie and foreign and wild, yet a part of me can't help but admit that it's also beautiful.

And all around us, shimmering softly beneath the aurora, are blossoming trees. Even from a distance, I feel their lure: soft pulls, like a lover's caress, drawing me toward them.

A sharp tug against my wrist. I find Yù'chén frowning at me, and I realize I've wandered several steps from him without noticing. As he draws me back to him, I'm reminded of just how much danger pulses beneath the beauty surrounding me.

"This way," he says, and I follow.

"Where are we?" I ask. The footpaths here are of white stone, tucked into the long grasses.

"One of the many enclaves of this kingdom. Those outside our realm tend to think the Kingdom of Night comprises only our court and the Palace of the Aurora, but they forget there is so much beyond that."

Yù'chén leads me into an open-air temple perched on a sloping hilltop. Tangled vines of wisteria drape down like curtains, hiding us from sight while framing the landscape beyond.

A glade of silvergrasses stretches beneath us, sprinkled with little white starflowers. At its heart is a lake, reflecting the night sky like a looking glass.

And around it, dancing, are mó unlike any I've seen. They resemble humans, yet unlike those I have come across in the mortal realm, these mó all retain characteristics of their true form: a horn here, a tail here, a glint of scales and a sheen of green skin. I catch glimpses of liquid black eyes or yellow slits; forked tongues and sharp ears.

Faint, sourceless music echoes as though the wind and grasses and trees sing. Pure and clear, the melody undulates to the rhythm of their steps and the pulses of dark magic weaving around them. Moonlight pours down, intertwining with their hair and flowing into their skin.

"Moonsong." Yù'chén's voice startles me; I'd almost forgotten he was there. I find him watching the scene below us with a strange, almost wistful, expression. "Dark magic meeting the energies of the moon creates something akin to music. We call it moonsong."

I shake off the stir of longing that the music invokes in me. We are close enough for the mó to smell us, to notice our presence—indeed, several close by glance our way between the trees—but none of them appear interested.

"A moonsong is how the mó replenish their energies," Yù'chén continues. "Much like how mortals sustain ourselves through food, mó sustain themselves through night, shadows, and moonlight. Partaking in moonsong together is like sharing a meal. Mó do not understand love as mortals do, just as the immortals and the gods have different views as well in this aspect. But companionship and pleasure are a part of their essence. Many mó are born during moonsong and grow up in their enclaves as one with the land across this realm."

As he speaks, two mó break away from the lake: a young woman with catlike eyes and talons and a man with golden skin. I hear their laughter as they dart through the flowering trees in a semblance of a dance, she leading and he chasing.

I glance at Yù'chén. "What about you?" The question is open-ended, and I'm not even certain what I'm asking. Whether he partakes in the moonsong. Whether he sustains himself on shadows and moonlight. Whether he shares the essence of the mó.

A wry smile. "Me? I'm too mortal for this. The moon and darkness make me stronger, which is why my magic is more powerful here in this realm. But I need sunlight, food, and water, just like all other humans."

I start as the darkness between two overhanging wisteria vines melts away to reveal a small figure. A child, I think incredulously, for it had never occurred to me that the mó had young. The being stares at us from between the flowers, unnaturally still, eyes glinting. There is something birdlike to her appearance: Iridescent white feathers sprout from her arms and rustle on her bodice.

Yù'chén's hand touches my elbow as reassurance, and I don't pull away. "She won't harm you," he says. "Most mó did not grow up feasting on mortals. Not until my mother created a gate between our realms and launched the war."

The child vanishes in a rustle of flowers and silvergrass.

I realize I've been holding my breath. "What do you mean, the mó did not feast on mortals until your mother began the war?" Having spent half my lifetime fearing these creatures that were known to us as monsters who would consume our flesh, blood, and souls, I didn't know it had ever been otherwise.

"Very long ago," Yù'chén says, "before the Heavenly Order imposed wards between our realms and banished the mó to the lowest-ranking creatures in all realms, there were occasional humans who wandered into this realm—and met tragic fates. Similarly, some mó crossed into the mortal realm, where they were corrupted by the taste of human blood and flesh." He gestures at the moonlit figures by the lake. "This is the natural way of mó. Mortal bodies and souls are not sustenance for them. Merely intense pleasure—like a drug or an addiction. One taste and you'll be left craving more."

His own mother told me as much nearly a decade ago, when she drank my father's soul. *Like honey, like sunlight, like sweet morning dew.*

In the cold and dark recesses of my heart, something sparks: Anger.

They destroyed our home and have been hunting us, hurting us, not out of necessity . . . but for pleasure.

I turn to Yù'chén. "Is that true for you?"

His jaw tightens. "I've only had mortal blood once, and I taste both what humans would as well as what mó would. But I do not crave it." His smile is dark. "Worrying that I'll develop a sudden hunger for your flesh in the night?"

My fury grows, and I cut my next words to hurt: "Just trying to understand how much of a monster you are."

Yù'chén blinks. The teasing vanishes from his expression as

he lifts his gaze toward the revelry. "To be honest, Àn'yīng," he says, "I don't even know."

My anger dissipates at the rawness of his tone. He wears a thoughtful expression as he observes the revelry, and again, I wonder if he has ever discussed this with anyone else. I recall the way Sansiran treated him back in the Kingdom of Sky, the way she hurt him without batting an eyelash . . . and I think I know the answer.

Yù'chén continues, his tone flat and distant, as though reciting a story: "My mother pushed for me to be raised in the mortal realm, perhaps in hopes that my father would see my value and name me his heir—or at least, legitimize my title and hers. But my father sent me to a private palace away from the Imperial City, where I saw him once a season, if even then. I grew up around mortal servants, educated by tutors of the Kingdom of Rivers, but I knew I was different.

"When my father found out about my mother's true identity—and therefore what I was—Sansiran stole me back into the Kingdom of Night. Suddenly, my world changed, and everything I'd known was no more. I was a halfling from a different realm, an aberration to the rest of the mó, needing sunlight and sustenance to survive, physically weaker, my magic stunted by my mortal blood. I experienced emotions the mó do not, and I craved things they did not understand and could not give me.

"I learned to protect myself, of course; I needed to, to survive. But when my mother sent me back to the mortal realm to find you before the Immortality Trials, it felt like coming home." Yù'chén draws a deep breath, as though waking from a dream—or perhaps a long nightmare. His gaze falls on me, and I hear the words he does not speak aloud.

And then we met.

The air between us grows taut. I think of Yù'chén, lonely and cold and deprived of human contact for so long, stepping back into a world of sunlight. Of me, being the first human he's interacted with in ten long years.

I am in dangerous waters. The last thing I want to feel for him is sympathy; I can't afford to think of him as anything other than the villain in my world.

I need to think of him only as someone I can use to escape this realm.

"And the gate that your mother created," I say. "Where is it now?"

But Yù'chén tenses, his gaze flitting to something behind me. "Don't move," he says. "We have company."

15

Àn'yīng

Palace of the Aurora, Kingdom of Night

It takes every ounce of restraint I have to stay still. I feel it then, the way prey can feel a predator closing in on them. A slight stir of wisteria petals, a shift in the air behind me. The presence of danger that lifts the hairs on the back of my neck. Something, or someone, watching me. Prowling closer.

Yù'chén reaches for me, and this time I don't protest as he draws me close to him. His arms fall against the small of my back. "Don't be frightened," he whispers. "Don't react; don't do or say anything. Follow my lead."

I hope I haven't made yet another mistake in trusting him.

As he begins swaying to the tune of the moonsong, I place my hands on his shoulders. All I can think of is how exposed my back is and how the only excuse for a weapon I have is that jagged shard of porcelain tucked into the bodice of my dress.

A voice speaks behind me, low and guttural. "Enjoying the spoils of our victory, are we, Princeling?"

Yù'chén's steps fall still. When he looks up over my shoulder, he has entirely transformed: eyes half-lidded, mouth curled with displeasure.

"I *was*," he drawls irritably, "until you showed your ugly face and ruined my night, Niefuzan."

A peal of delighted laughter tears through the dark. "Then let us see what kind of a pretty face has captivated your attention, Princeling," comes a woman's voice, coy and lilting. *"Turn around, mortal darling."*

Her magic encircles me at her command, and it feels like ice sinking into my bones. I'm wrenched from Yù'chén's grasp and spun around to face the mó.

There are two of them, as different as ice and fire. Power radiates from them in an almost careless manner, the air and flowers trembling from the sheer magnitude of their dark magic. Immediately, I know these are not the same as the mó dancing to the moonsong below us.

These are mó from the Court of the Aurora.

Higher Ones, my instinct screams.

My gaze is drawn to the woman. Her hair has the sheen of freshly fallen snow; her eyes are fully white, her lips the palest, most delicate shade of blue. She wears a finely-made dress that looks woven of frost, as if she has draped a winter forest over herself.

Her breath plumes as she leans forward. *"Oh,"* she breathes. "What a lovely mortal face. What do you think, Niefuzan? Was she worth the extra effort?"

The mó next to her is one of the biggest I have ever encountered, yet his bulk does not diminish his grace. He holds himself with a predatory sharpness, and when he grins down at me, his elongated teeth gleam. Behind him, emerging from the footpaths leading from town, are more mó. Their glittering attire suggests they also hail from court, yet they lack the sophistication and power the two Higher Ones hold. Their red eyes flash as they settle on me, noses twitching as they no doubt scent the blood thrumming in my veins.

The one named Niefuzan steps toward me in an elegant, deliberate move. "I wouldn't know, Xisenyin." His voice rumbles like thunder. "Perhaps I should have a taste of her myself."

But I'm staring at his face, struck with a sense of familiarity and fear. Memories resurface in my mind: the taste of black water, of numbness poisoning my body. The image of my friend Fán'xuān, green eyes open and blank.

"*You,*" I whisper, and I can't help the tremor in my voice.

Yù'chén tugs me sharply back to his side. "I'm not in the mood for games tonight, Niefuzan." I flinch at how cold his voice is. "You want to play, come back later and I'll entertain you and yours for as long as you like."

The Higher One's lips pull back in a grin. His pupils are permanent black slits, the rest of his eyes completely red. "No need for hostility tonight, *Your Highness.*" The title sounds like a mockery on his tongue. "We only came to see that you were adequately enjoying what you so desperately bargained for." His gaze slides to mine, and I suppress a shudder. "Besides, it seems as though she recognizes me." Niefuzan's smile splits his face. He wears vaguely mortal features, yet threaded through them are what must be his true form. Dark veins filled with his demon's ichor bulge from his taut muscles; his hands end in claws tipped with familiar-looking black spikes. "Or perhaps," he continues, "she finds me familiar because she has come across the halfling I sired."

The realization hits me: *Yán'lù*. The other halfling who by-passed the Kingdom of Sky's wards and participated in the Im-mortality Trials. He'd been tasked with finding the identity of the mortal realm's heir.

And he'd killed five candidates—including Fán'xuān.

Hatred surges in me as I stare down his father, bigger and crueler and more beautiful than Yán'lù ever was. "I relished hunting your son," I spit, but Niefuzan only laughs.

"I do not think of that pathetic halfling as my *son*. Merely a creature I bred and raised to be of use to me. I would not de-base my lineage by mixing my ichor with the mud of mortals."

"This is all rather dull, Niefuzan," Yù'chén drawls. "If you're intent on ruining my fun tonight, then we'll take our leave."

"Is she not drugged, Princeling?" the female with the white hair—Xisenyin—says suddenly. Her gaze is sharp on me, like a cat scenting prey.

"I don't see how that's any concern of yours," Yù'chén re-plies after a nearly imperceptible pause.

Xisenyin laughs again, a soft, beautiful sound. "Oh, it isn't. It just makes playing with them so much more fun. Worry not, Princeling," she adds as Yù'chén moves toward me suddenly. *"Just stay there and watch."*

The words are spoken like a casual invitation, but I *feel* the tremor of power to her command. Yù'chén freezes in place, his hand at the hilt of his sword, his muscles straining against her magic.

"Come to me, mortal girl," Xisenyin says lazily, and her power twines around me like iron, bending my body and legs into action.

She smiles at me as I approach, and I am certain she can

hear my racing pulse, scent the sweat beading on my scalp as I try and fail to resist her magic. Her fingers are ice-cold as she takes my wrist and, with her other hand, she pulls something from the glittering folds of her winter gown. I recognize the hilt engraved with the talisman and the curved blade before she presses it into my palm.

It's my crescent blade Fleet—I can immediately tell by the grooves in the wooden hilt, the shine of the metal.

My blade. She has my blade.

"Cut open your throat for me," Xisenyin sings.

Yù'chén makes a sound, but Fleet is at my neck before I can blink. A hot flash of pain, then warm liquid spills down my collarbone, seeping into my dress.

My mind blanks.

Xisenyin shifts, reappearing behind me. Her hand envelops mine, and my blade vanishes into her grasp again. I feel the scrape of her teeth against my skin, the softness of her tongue as she traces one long, languorous lick up the curve of my neck.

Trapped in my own body, I'm reliving the nightmare of nine years past, when I sat beneath my kitchen table and watched a mó drink my father's blood. Sansiran had held him as tenderly as a lover as he'd struggled, and I'd recalled seeing, in the forest once, a deer caught in the claws of a mountain lion.

"Mmm." Xisenyin makes a satisfied sound as she draws back. Her pupils are dilated, her mouth and chin smeared with my blood, and her teeth red as she says, "Lovely. *Now walk off the edge of the cliff.*"

The world grows mute but for the shrill screaming in my head as I pivot toward the open night and the sharp drop into the valley below. My legs move of their own accord: one step, then another. Mercilessly bringing me to the edge.

I raise a foot into empty air.

Dark energies erupt behind me. Scorpion lilies burst from the soil at the cliff's edge, their vines and leaves twining around my ankles and thighs, rooting me to the spot. A hand wraps around my waist, tugging me backward. Xisenyin's command surges through me, and I fight until a voice says in my ear, *"Àn'yīng, stop."*

The present filters back in fragments. The glint of a garnet on a sword pommel, pointed at the two mó facing me. Someone's fingers digging into my waist, a solid chest behind my back, rising and falling rapidly. And when I turn to look back, Yù'chén's eyes match the jewel, burning crimson with his power. His canines have lengthened; the skin on his hands and neck has shifted to scales of black and red—an indication of just how much energy he exerted to defy Xisenyin's command.

"You forget your place, Xisenyin," he says calmly, but his voice is laced with threat. "Touch another hair on her head and I'll call in my mother's bargain."

My head is light from the efforts of resisting the dark magic earlier, but I latch onto this piece of information. "What bargain?" I whisper, glancing up at Yù'chén.

He ignores me.

Niefuzan has thrown his head back, his body shaking with laughter. Behind him, his mó underlings cower with little chirps of fear. But it's Xisenyin's reaction that I will remember later on.

She brushes petals of Yù'chén's scorpion lilies from her dress, the red turning to white beneath her touch. When she looks up, her smile promises retribution.

"Don't you know, mortal girl?" the Higher One simpers, her gaze pinned on Yù'chén. "The reason you're alive and safe, kept in our kingdom like a precious flower in a vase?"

I stare at the sharpened points of her teeth, the way her saliva is still red from my blood when she smiles and hisses, "He *begged* for you."

Yù'chén tenses. "Enough," he says quietly, but this only encourages Xisenyin.

"Oh, *yes*." The Higher One giggles. "He begged her to spare your life. He made her an unbreakable bargain, held by the old magic of our kind." Behind her, Niefuzan's underlings titter. "You see now why mortals are weak? You see how easy it is to manipulate one at the mercy of *love*? The mó were born without this weakness, and we are all the stronger for it." She raises a hand, and ice crackles beneath her feet. "Well, Princeling—as much as I'd love to say we dropped by for a bit of fun, there is a reason we came to seek you out."

"Then spit it out and leave," Yù'chén snarls.

"Our empress has left for business in the Kingdom of Sky, but she returns tomorrow night. She has requested your presence then. And she has asked us to remind you that she will be expecting the answers you promised her."

Yù'chén falls silent.

Xisenyin smirks. "It seems you understand. Well, Princeling, if you were desperate enough to invoke the name of our empress, it seems we have overstayed our welcome. Until next time, little flower."

The air ripples with dark magic, and in a flash of frost and shadows, they're gone.

As soon as we're back in Yù'chén's chambers I pull away from him, clasping a hand over where Xisenyin licked me. The feeling of her teeth against the most vulnerable part of my throat has unmoored something inside me.

Worse, the knowledge that she holds at least one of my crescent blades—my most precious possessions and the last items Bà gifted me.

Yù'chén follows me as I rush across the chamber to where the moonlight and wind from outside spills through the open-air terrace. "Àn'yīng, wait," he calls, but I keep running.

Except I have nowhere to go. Outside, the night sky is beyond my reach with the wards over the Palace of the Aurora. And even if I return to the Kingdom of Rivers, there is no escaping this.

"Àn'yīng." Yù'chén approaches. He reaches for my neck, his fingers scraping the bleeding wound there.

"Don't touch me," I gasp. I'd tried to think of him as my one ally here, but tonight as I look at him, I can't help but remember that he, too, is one of them. The red and black scales are gone now, the crimson in his eyes faded to a faint glow, but just the same, he could command me at will. Could make me do things like slit my throat or walk off a cliff.

He draws back. "Let me heal you," he begins, but I whip out the porcelain shard from the bodice of my dress and point it at him.

Yù'chén's eyes flick down to it. He's silent for several moments. "I'm not going to hurt you," he says quietly, but makes no move to approach me again.

I don't lower the piece of porcelain. "You've hurt me enough," I choke out.

He's silent for a long time.

Then, slowly, Yù'chén tips his chin back, baring his throat to me. He takes my hand and sets it against the curve of his neck, the sharp point of the shard digging into his flesh. I can feel his pulse beneath my palm, warm and insistent.

He reaches for my neck. I shudder as his fingers slide across my skin, then as his dark magic flows, hot and intoxicating, through me. He keeps his eyes lowered the entire time, but I still catch the flare of red in his irises.

Slowly, the fog pulls back from my head. Strength flows back into my limbs, warmth into my core.

Yù'chén retracts his hand. We sit, facing each other, my porcelain shard against his throat, his gaze lowered to the grass as the crimson fades from his eyes.

"I want a weapon." My voice is too loud in the silence.

"I can't give you one," he replies.

"You can't keep me here without a means to defend myself. You saw what she—Xisenyin—almost did to me."

"She can't hurt you," Yù'chén says. "No one can—you're protected under the bargain I made with my mother."

The bargain.

He begged *for you.*

I draw a deep breath, trying to steady the tremors jittering down my body. "What is the bargain?" I ask.

A muscle tenses in his jaw. "I made a covenant with Sansiran," he says at last.

"A covenant?"

"A bond between two beings, forged by the strongest old magic of this realm. So long as one side fulfills a bargain, the other is held to their service for eternity." Yù'chén recites this mechanically. "It's how power dynamics work here. There is no trust, no loyalty—the mó thrive on power and obedience, on fear and pain."

I consider this, my eyes narrowed. "And your covenant prevents you from arming me."

"It prevents me from acting against the interests of my kingdom, so, yes, arming you when you are hostile to my realm might fall under that." He speaks with a touch of sarcasm, but he won't look at me.

"You can't keep me here without a weapon," I repeat. "I am prey, Yù'chén; I am kept in a cage, protected by your mercy."

"You are not my prisoner, Àn'yīng—"

"Then let me go."

Sorrow flickers in his eyes. "I can't do that either, Àn'yīng."

"Then why did you do it?" I ask. "Why keep me here at all? If you want me as your . . . your mortal escort, you could just drug me on oleander nectar or enchant me to do as you please—"

"I see your assumptions of me still hold," he snaps, his temper rising at last. "Àn'yīng, when have I *ever* forced you to do something? When have I ever misused my power and commanded you for my benefit?"

"My *assumptions* of you are based on when you deceived me about your true intent in the Immortality Trials, used me to find the identity of the mortal heir, and opened a gate for the Kingdom of Night to invade the Kingdom of Sky!"

The anger vanishes from Yù'chén's face, leaving behind something raw. "Àn'yīng." His voice is low, steady, when he speaks again. "I told you once, very early on, that I wanted a better life, in a better place. Do you remember that?"

I do. I remember, painfully, every word he said to me. All the lies he gave me about wishing to be mortal, about his beating, human heart.

"My tenure here demands me to act in the interests of my kingdom," he repeats. "This war—it isn't good for my realm,

Àn'yīng. The mó are beings of the night, the moon, and the stars; our energies and our lives depend solely on those. Not the flesh and blood of mortals in your realm, nor anything in the immortal realm. Each day that my mother continues these wars, lives are lost. Across my realm and across yours. And now, across the Kingdom of Sky."

I frown, trying to unpuzzle where he is going with this.

"This war is ruining my kingdom and destroying this world," Yù'chén continues. "I want to stop it."

Five words, and time comes to a halt.

Yù'chén speaks slowly, as though choosing his words carefully. "It's very hard for me to . . . influence things here. But soon, I may be able to." He inhales deeply. "I'm asking you to work with me when the time comes."

I stare at him, my heart pounding with the hidden meaning in his words. *When the time comes.*

I turn away, running my fingers over the sheer sleeves of my gown. Over the intricate patterns of swirling stars and crescent moons that Yù'chén conjured with his magic. "You really expect me to believe you? After you tricked me into giving my heart away and then used me."

"It was real for me."

Real. The word hits me like a punch to the gut. A strange, tender pain blooms in my heart when I recall the number of times he saved my life—risking his own. When he fought that mó back in my village. When he went up against Yán'lù for me. When he begged his mother for my life.

"How?" I ask at last. "How do you plan to influence things?"

Yù'chén summons a deep breath, as though steeling himself, then looks me in the eye and says, "I am heir to the mortal throne, Àn'yīng."

The dam I've built in my mind breaks. Memories of Hào'yáng flood me: his steady brown gaze and warm smile; the steel of his eyes and power of his tone as he issued commands to our villagers; the glint of sunlight on his armor as the river waters bore him like a throne; the flash of his sword as he leapt to attack Qióng'qí to buy my village time to evacuate.

The grief in his eyes whenever he thought no one was looking, grief he'd quietly held from when he was just a child and began to carry the weight of an entire kingdom upon his shoulders.

And I miss him, I miss him so much that it could carve me open.

The sunlight and waters and flowers are gone. I am once again in the darkness. Yù'chén's words ring in my ears, and the only thing I can think to say is "No."

Yù'chén draws a swift breath. He blinks quickly, then his jaw clenches.

It's a few heartbeats before he speaks, a hard edge to his voice. "Whether or not you like it, I am."

I push myself to my feet. "You will *never* be heir in the way he was."

His fingers close around my arm just as I turn to leave.

"Let go," I snap.

"No. Not until you hear me out." He spins me to face him, his other hand coming to grip my chin in a viselike hold, and I realize, truly realize, the extent of his strength, how gentle he has been with me until now. His eyes are livid with anger and something like grief as he beholds me. "Àn'yīng, I brought you here to make you a deal. Help me take the mortal throne and become emperor of the Kingdom of Rivers, and I vow to formally appoint you to a seat by my side—to help me protect it." He draws a shaky breath, and his grip loosens. "Hard as it is for you to believe, I love the mortal realm, too, and it is, in some ways, my home. I never wanted this war. Help me end it, Àn'yīng. Help me save your realm from the Kingdom of Night."

"You're mad." I snatch my hand back, but my heart is pounding. Of everything I might have imagined, this is the last thing I expected.

An alliance. A means to protect my home.

I squeeze my eyes shut, thinking of Méi'zi and Mā and Lì'líng and Tán'mù and Fú'yí, gathered in the scattered sunlight beneath the plum blossom tree. I'd sought to achieve that by seeing Hào'yáng on the throne.

The vision shifts: a throne of red scorpion lilies, night and a scythe moon, Yù'chén bearing a crown.

And the mortal realm—*home*—a world away, my loved ones safe in an eternal twilight.

My eyes fly open. The vision vanishes.

Yù'chén is gone. The shadows where he stood are still and empty.

I dig my fingernails into the sleeves of my gown. In the dark, it is easier to recall Xisenyin's hands and tongue on me. Easier to remember that I am nothing more than a bird trapped in a cage here.

Prey.

I curl my fingers into fists.

I will not be prey.

I grip the porcelain shard, thinking of the curve of my crescent blade nestled in my palm for that brief moment before Xisenyin took it again.

I'm going to steal it back from her.

Yet as I gather my dress around myself, I can't help but think of Yù'chén's words.

Help me save your realm from the Kingdom of Night.

If I can keep my loved ones and my realm safe by giving up all the values I've held close for years . . . if I can save the Kingdom of Rivers by putting one of its enemies on its throne . . . if it's the only way out, is that a trade worth making?

I sit by the crystal spring, flipping the porcelain shard between my fingers, lost in thought.

Àn'yīng

Palace of the Aurora, Kingdom of Night

He doesn't return until an entire day later—but he does send me food. Intricately planned meals on silver trays, appearing in my chamber amidst a bloom of red scorpion lilies. Most important, each tray comes with a silver-black feather: a memory of my family from his shadowcrane.

I wait for these small windows of joy. As I consume my food, I cherish the glimpses of Méi'zi and Mā's whereabouts as they settle into the Western Province. Some part of me wonders—knows—there is a purpose to these tributes; a form of bribery, a reminder that things could be good.

Help me save your realm from the Kingdom of Night.

Slowly, as I savor bright, sunlit images of my loved ones, I formulate a plan.

When Yù'chén arrives next, I'm ready.

As always, he steps out of the shadows like a houseguest

crossing through an invisible door. He looks immaculate in that same black robe swirling with dragons stitched of stars.

This time, I'm on my feet as soon as he enters.

Yù'chén takes in my proper appearance. I'm dressed—his servants have sent outfits, tailored perfectly to fit me by the magic of this realm—and I've bathed. My hair falls loose and straight over my back. The gown I've chosen is a silver one, a simple yet elegant sheath that allows for easy movement.

His eyes linger over my outfit for a heartbeat before he says, "Miss me?"

He smiles. It doesn't reach his eyes.

"Thank you," I say, approaching him, "for the food. And . . . the feathers."

Yù'chén raises an eyebrow. I notice he looks paler tonight; there are bags under his eyes. His gaze doesn't spark or tease the way it normally does.

"Where were you?" I ask.

He turns and flops onto a lacquered futon. Exhales as he brushes his fingers over his face and massages his forehead. "Nowhere important."

"I should know, if I'm to consider the terms of your bargain."

At those words, he falls very still.

I've thought about it—or, rather, I haven't been able to stop thinking about it. At first, the possibility was overshadowed by the pain of losing Hào'yáng. Of knowing that considering this means, in some way, acknowledging that he's truly, irrevocably gone.

But sitting there in the dark, with memories and enough grief to drown me, I found the answer in my boy in the jade, as I so often have in the past. I recalled a memory that Meadowsweet showed me in the moments before his death—the one of Hào'yáng, still a boy, being chastised for choosing to save me from drowning in that pond so many winters ago.

Love, family, friendship . . . you must shed everything in pursuit of your duty to your realm, to your people, and to your kingdom. My birth mother's words to him rang in my mind. *You would exist not for yourself but as a vessel to serve the Kingdom of Rivers. Can you understand that?*

It was Hào'yáng's response that changed my mind. *I can,* he said, *but, Lady, it hurts.*

The pain of having lost Hào'yáng would always be there. But I could choose to let it drown me—or I could choose to rise above it and serve my realm in a different way. I would be giving up everything I've held dear in this life for a chance to save all that I loved.

I closed my eyes and imagined Hào'yáng there by my side. *It is fruitless to live in the shadows of the dead, Àn'yīng,* he told me through his golden characters in the jade in the first days after my father died. *Look to life and do all that you can to make it better.*

Even if Hào'yáng is gone, he is, in so many ways, still with me. A part of me.

Nothing can change that.

I straighten now, hands clasped together, and I round the futon to face Yù'chén. He's slumped back with a hand draped dramatically over his face, yet as I approach, his gaze slides to me through the cracks between his fingers.

"You seemed adamant in refusing my offer last night, little scorpion. Has that changed?"

I stare at him and he stares back, neither of us relenting, neither of us able to read the other.

"I'm hungry," I say instead, and without waiting for him to reply, I turn and walk out onto the pavilion.

He trails me as I step out onto the rosewood floors, which turn to soft grass beneath my bare feet as I pass beyond the pavilion. The barren trees come to life, scorpion lilies blooming in their eerie beauty.

At the edge of a cliff, where the waterfall flows into the abyss, a stone table appears. Steam billows from platters of food laid out on it. I glance over at Yù'chén, who waits several paces behind me. In the shadows, his eyes glow crimson from the magic he used to summon our meal.

He averts them as our gazes meet.

A mat woven of tiny starflowers appears beneath my feet, tickling my toes. I sit, pick up the chopsticks, and begin helping myself to the meal. Overhead, scorpion lilies grow in clumps from tree branches, their lambent light pouring over me. They're meant to mimic lanterns so I won't have to eat in semidarkness. Though there is something uncanny about a moonlit meal beneath glimmering flowers, I understand the gesture.

After a few moments, Yù'chén approaches. He sits.

This close, I realize how astonishingly wan his skin is, how pale his lips are. My gaze slides lower, and I catch a flash of red and black scales peeking above his collar, dissolving into black veins. All indications that he is overexerting himself on magic usage.

I take a small sip of plum wine. I need the courage, but I also need my head sharp. "What happened to you?" I ask.

He leans an elbow on the table and props his chin on his palm, glancing up at me through dark lashes. "Didn't sleep well."

He's lying.

I'd normally call him out, but I need to aim for diplomacy tonight. Instead, I place a piece of braised quail on his plate. "Eat," I say, and he stares at me as though he's never seen me.

To my surprise, he picks up his chopsticks and begins to eat.

"Were you with Sansiran?" I ask. It's what I assumed, after we ran into Xisenyin last night. *She has asked us to remind you that she will be expecting the answers you promised her.*

Yù'chén reaches for his carafe of plum wine. "Yes" is all he says as he takes a swig.

His flat tone chills me. I take in his pallor, the dullness of his eyes, and something tightens in my chest.

Did she hurt you? I want to ask, but I think I know the answer already. It's a question that will get me nowhere in terms of my plans.

"What answers did she want from you?" I reach for a glutinous rice ball. Lì'líng and Fán'xuān used to bicker over these during the Immortality Trials.

Yù'chén glances at me over the rim of his porcelain carafe.

"Xisenyin said it last night," I add. I put down my chopsticks and place my hands on the stone surface of the table. "If you want me to consider your offer, you're going to have to tell me more."

He blinks slowly as he takes another sip of plum wine. "You're considering my offer," he repeats.

"I am."

"A rather drastic change in stance from yesterday's 'You will never be heir in the way he was.'" His laugh scrapes as he sets down his carafe with a thud. "Did Xisenyin frighten you so much that a monster like me is beginning to look kind in contrast? Have the atrocities of my realm whetted your appetite for a half demon on your kingdom's throne?"

He's looking at me, smiling, yet his eyes are dark with anger. An anger I've seen him use as a shield for grief.

I hurt him. I need to begin by making amends.

"I was harsh," I say steadily. I take my time with my words, for the best lies are conceived from a kernel of truth. "Because I was afraid that if I chose you, I would be abandoning Hào'yáng. That I'd be a traitor to my realm and all the promises I've made to those I love.

"But I realize that the only way for me to save them and save my kingdom is not to dwell on the past, but to look to the future." I'm convincing myself as I speak. "And the best path forward for me to keep my promises and protect my loved ones . . . is with you."

The seconds trickle past. He's staring at me, no longer smiling. "If you want me on the mortal throne," he says at last, "you'll have to help me figure out how to get it."

Everything in me stretches taut. I try to keep my voice light as I ask, "What do you mean?"

"There seems to be some ancient magic in the Kingdom of Rivers that rejects me. A connection to the land I'm missing."

My heart pounds so hard against my chest, I wonder if Yù'chén can hear it. "You tried?" I whisper. "After he—"

I can't bring myself to say it, but he seems to read it from my eyes: *After he died.*

"Yes." Yù'chén's face is as smooth as the surface of the crystal spring in the garden. "I tried to take the throne today, upon my mother's return. And nothing changed."

The mortal emperor is crowned when his blood joins with the waters of the Long River. Hào'yáng's voice rings out in my mind.

"And how," I say, trying to keep my voice calm, "did you try to take the throne?"

"I ascended it," Yù'chén replies. "I took a seat on it." His gaze is sharper than a sword. "Why, is there a different way? Some ritual I must complete?"

I'm careful to rein in any expression. "I don't know. You said nothing changed—what were you expecting?"

"It is believed that if I am crowned, the mortal realm will fall into an eternal night not unlike ours. That the wards between our realms will vanish and our peoples will be able to roam freely between. None of that has happened."

I think of the ways we clung to our shrinking hours of sunlight, of the mó we've had to fend off all these years. How I would be giving all of that up were I to accept his offer.

And yet. *Help me protect it,* he said last night.

You alone know the way to crown the mortal emperor, a small voice whispers in my head. *You alone could change the fate of the realms.*

"Say I *could* help you find the way to attain the mortal throne." I watch his expression. "What would you give me?"

"What do you want?"

"I have conditions of my own, if you'd like me to consider your offer."

He leans forward. "I'm listening."

It feels like we're playing a game of chess, like my father taught me when I was young. So I make my move. "First, I want the guaranteed position of High Advisor in your court, decreed by the laws of your realm. Then I want the war to stop as soon as you're crowned, and I want iron laws set up by you and your mother to protect mortals. Your kind must be banned from hunting them, preying on them, or any acts that harm them." I pause. My final condition is selfish, derived from that long-ago memory of plum blossoms in the sun, my family's laughter, the light lancing off my sister's braid. "And I don't want eternal night in my realm. I want there to be sunlight," I finish. "For now, those are my four conditions."

Yù'chén shrugs. "I can declare those conditions before the Court of the Aurora," he begins, but I shake my head.

"I don't want just a declaration before your court." I place my final chess piece. "I want a covenant. With you."

I've thought this through ever since he told me of the magical bargain he made with his mother, which is unbreakable for eternity.

The perfect guarantee.

Yù'chén blinks, surprise edging into his face.

Then he laughs.

"What's so funny?" I ask, narrowing my eyes.

"A covenant is for eternity. You want an eternal bond between us, little scorpion?"

I fold my arms. "How else am I to ensure you keep your word, considering your propensity for lying and betrayal?" That wipes the smirk off his face. "Can it be done, if I'm mortal?"

"I believe so. I would need to call upon the magic of my realm, but there have been cases of mortals bound to mó." Yù'chén pauses. "Even so, Àn'yīng, I cannot guarantee any influence over my mother and her decisions on ruling our realm."

"But you would be emperor of both realms. You would be the reason the two are forged together. So long as your actions do not violate the terms of your covenant with her, she cannot stop you."

And if I have a covenant with him, I hold the keys to both kingdoms, too.

"You know how she is." Yù'chén looks away, and I think of how mercilessly she hurt him back in the Temple of Dawn even as he begged her to stop.

He doesn't deserve that. No matter how much I will myself to hate his kind for what they've done to my home, I cannot bring myself to think he deserves that kind of punishment.

"We'll find a way," I say quietly, and I'm surprised by how much I mean it.

The corners of his mouth soften. "And when would we enact this bargain?"

The food before us grows cold, but my appetite's gone. I've set out upon a path of no return.

I push away from the table. "Take me to the Court of the Aurora," I say. "If I'm going to take a position in it, I need to know more about it first."

Yù'chén considers. "There is a revelry tonight," he says at last. "In the Palace of the Aurora itself. Many Higher Ones will be in attendance, along with their lower courts and subordinates. I can take you, but I'd prefer not to stay long."

I recall Xisenyin's teeth scraping against my skin. The wound at my neck gives a phantom ache of protest, but I brush it away. If I'm to remain in this world, I can't live in fear of its monsters.

"Fine," I say, glancing again at his pallor and the dark circles beneath his eyes. "Will your mother be there?"

"No. She left for other business." Yù'chén sighs and straightens, running his fingers through his hair. "Very well. If you'd like to attend a revelry at the Court of the Aurora, you must listen to the rules carefully. A revelry in my mother's court will be very different from the moonsong revelry we attended—or, indeed, any other revelries in the kingdom. This is a gathering of the most powerful mó in the kingdom. One misstep could cost everything.

"First rule: Do not eat or drink *anything*. You already know of oleander nectar. There are much worse things. Rose petals laced with poison made to cause pain worse than death in humans. Poppy milk that will induce hallucinations until your body collapses. All hold pleasurable delights for the mó yet are lethal to mortals."

I listen to Yù'chén, tamping down the combination of fear and excitement that spikes my adrenaline. I feel as though I'm finally moving forward again, and though it may not be the direction I want, it's the one my realm needs. This is my chance to learn more of the Kingdom of Night and its mechanisms, including the most formidable opponents we may face.

"Second," Yù'chén continues, interrupting my trail of thought, "in my mother's court, the only mortals present are the ones that are . . . claimed."

"Claimed?" I raise an eyebrow, but I have a horrible premonition.

"Claimed," Yù'chén confirms, "by a Higher One, or a mó of Sansiran's court. Either bound by dark magic or drunk on oleander nectar and used for entertainment and pleasure."

"Is that what I'm purportedly being kept for?" I can't help but think of Xisenyin's words: *He* begged *for you*.

Yù'chén's eyes are on the porcelain wine cup in his hands as he spins it. "It's what everyone will expect of us," he replies, and then stands. "Follow me, and . . . this will be difficult for you, but"—the corner of his lip curls—"you'll need to pretend you're infatuated with me."

I roll my eyes and grip his hand hard. "You underestimate

me," I say, and then I tip my face to him and throw him a dazzling smile. I've had half a lifetime to practice the role of the soft maiden before any mó that came across my path—right before they became very well-acquainted with my blades. "How's that?"

Yù'chén's smirk has vanished. "Disconcerting." He clears his throat, turning to lead me toward his chamber doors. "We won't be there long, so do not leave my side. Mortals who end up lost in this palace tend not to be seen again."

I can't smile anymore at that. I am walking into a tiger's lair with no blades, no weapons, nothing other than the dress I wear and my own bare hands. The darkness presses in on all sides, and the only ally I have is Yù'chén.

As I step closer to him, I find myself wondering if this is what awaits me for the rest of my life.

But I think of those feathers holding precious memories of my loved ones, healthy and safe in the sunlit dunes of the Western Province's desert—and I know I would never have it any other way. In every lifetime, I would choose to remain in the dark so that they can walk in the light.

I place my other hand on Yù'chén's chest and lift my chin.

I am not afraid.

I will not be prey.

Yù'chén's eyes are as black as moonless night; I cannot fathom the thoughts that run through his mind as his other hand comes to rest on my back. "Hold tight," he says, and around us, scorpion lilies bloom in the dark.

I lean my cheek against his chest, remembering how I once searched for his heartbeat.

Shadows from his passageway swallow us whole.

Àn'yīng

Palace of the Aurora, Kingdom of Night

Distance and space does not work in this realm as it does in mine. I hold on to Yù'chén tightly, struggling to orient myself as his passageway transports us somewhere new.

When the shadows of his passageway retreat, an explosion of music and a scene of debauchery greet us. Beneath the open night is a glade gleaming with flowers. The air is fragrant with the sweetness of their magic; colors spill from them, so that the entire place is aglow. Overhead, the dark canvas of night dances with the lights of the aurora, illuminating the abyss around us and, in the distance, the silhouettes of jagged mountains, temples, and lakes.

Here, on this island suspended in an endless night, mó are dancing in groups, gathered around tables with drinks, entwined in shadowy alcoves.

"Welcome to the Court of the Aurora," Yù'chén murmurs in my ear.

An ancient stone pái'fāng knifes toward the scythe moon. For some reason, my attention pulls to the gate, and a chill settles in my bones. Even from several steps away, I sense the magic and shadows coiled around it, invisible wards teeming with dark, demonic energies. The ground beneath it is dark with a rust color, and I can't help but think it resembles blood.

I shudder. "What's that?" I whisper.

Instead of answering, Yù'chén turns away and leads me through the throngs of revelers.

Drinks and delicacies are nestled amidst vines and flowering trees, clay cups and plates refilling magically. Fountains gush from the shadows, splashing brightly colored liquid into the open mouths of ecstatic mó, their eyes overly bright and dazed, cheeks and lips unnaturally flushed.

It doesn't take long to spot the mortals. They drift among the crowd wearing expressions of blithe joy. In my realm, they would have been lovely—but here, next to the sharp, ethereal beauty of the mó, they look plain and imperfect, their skin dull and hair lacking luster.

Claimed is the word Yù'chén used, and I finally understand his distaste. A mortal man sways upon a patch of grass, smiling vacantly as two mó circle him, examining him like a pig trussed up for slaughter. Beneath a crabapple tree, a mortal woman tips her head back as a mó presses a flower to her lips. Golden nectar drips down her chin, and she giggles as the mó sinks his teeth into her shoulder.

I jerk my gaze away, breaths coming unevenly. All my instincts war against staying here one moment longer. How can I pretend that nothing is happening? That I don't see how humans like me are being used as live feeding sacks?

Yù'chén pulls me into an alcove of wisteria. He draws me close, his hands coming to rest on the small of my back.

"You need to relax your expression or you'll give us away," he says quietly. "I'm breaking a cardinal rule by bringing an unclaimed mortal to this revelry."

"The mortals, they're defenseless," I manage. Memories of nine years past press against my eyelids, imprinted in my mind as a child and brought forth by the scenes in front of me.

Yù'chén's gaze roves my face. "We should leave," he says.

"No." Perhaps my reply comes too quickly; he raises an eyebrow, and I continue: "I need you to teach me everything about your realm."

"You're shaking." He grips my shoulder, his thumb tracing an involuntary stroke against my skin.

"I'm *fine.*" If this is truly the future I am staring down for the rest of my life, I need to face it with my eyes wide open.

Yù'chén sighs and relents, glancing over my shoulder to survey the crowd. "There is no one of import here yet," he says. "The Kingdom of Night follows a similar hierarchy as many other realms, the Kingdom of Rivers included. We have an empress; below her are the Higher Ones, the most powerful mó across these realms. Each holds a position. Niefuzan is the war general; he leads her armies based simply on brute strength. Xisenyin is one of her High Mages, specializing in winter magic. Each of the Higher Ones control a faction of the Court of the Aurora—and each one of them is sworn to my mother by covenants."

There's a lull as he considers the scene. I realize he's holding me and swaying me gently as though we are in a dance; his hand makes small, soothing circles on my back. The rhythmic motion lulls my senses, calming my body's response earlier and slowing my breaths. He is warm, the heat of his body warding off the chill from the night as I let myself lean against him.

"Why did you do it?" I finally ask the question that's been lingering in the back of my mind. "Why bind yourself to her service for the rest of your life . . . to keep me here?"

Yù'chén is silent for so long that I don't think he's going to answer me. But when he does, his words are so quiet, I nearly miss them. "It was the only way to stop her from hurting you."

I stare at him, my mind growing blank with the implications of his confession.

He begged *for you.*

It was real for me.

Gently, Yù'chén brushes a lock of my hair from my face. "You're going to give us away with that scowl." He sighs. Then he breaks into that dazzling, lopsided grin, shrugging off the weight of our conversation. "Smile for me, Àn'yīng," he says. "Pretend you're in love with me tonight."

I can't smile. I'm frozen with the knowing that this man—if he tells the truth—has traded his life away to save mine.

A flash of white over his shoulder pulls my attention.

I stiffen. Where stone pái'fāngs rise into the skies high enough to touch the aurora itself, I catch the glint of her snowy hair.

Xisenyin.

I turn sharply toward her—only to find my path blocked.

A mó stands in my way. He seems to have come from nowhere, as I'm certain he wasn't there just a second ago. His skin is the pale blue of frost, and his eyes pure black. He is slight, and though he is flanked by two taller, more muscular mó, there is something singularly terrifying about him.

Higher One, my instincts hiss.

Yù'chén's grip tightens almost imperceptibly on my waist; he shifts, drawing me closer to him, and this is how I know the danger we're in.

"Weirufeng," Yù'chén greets him. "The Wind Messenger. Did the night breeze sweep you back into this realm, or did my mother?"

I glance over Yù'chén's shoulder at where I spotted Xisenyin, but she's nowhere to be found.

The Higher One—Weirufeng—seems to shift his gaze to Yù'chén, though it's difficult to tell where he is looking, with those eyes of swirling silver. "Neither, Princeling." His voice is a whisper, like the wind he is named after. "It is your affairs that have summoned me back. Tell me, is your prize treating you well?"

"Very," Yù'chén replies, tipping my chin up and looking at me with a blithe smile. His eyes, though, are tense. His thumb trails a stroke across my cheek, a silent reassurance.

Behind him, through the crowds, comes another flash of snow-white hair in the night.

I dart another glance over his shoulder and catch the tail of Xisenyin's frost-laced gown as it slips between dancers. I think of Fleet—and perhaps my other blades—trapped in the layers of her despicable gown.

"She seems . . . distracted," comes Weirufeng's voice, and I realize I've been staring for too long.

Quickly, I school my features into some semblance of the vacant expressions I've seen the other drugged mortals in this hall wear. But the Higher One's gaze pierces me.

"After all that our princeling put on the line for you and all the resources spent on preserving your life, I would think you should show a little more gratitude," Weirufeng says, addressing me directly. *"Please him while we speak."*

His command comes out of nowhere, the dark magic sinking its claws into my skin, squeezing me tight as it attempts to bend my will with steel-like power.

Only it doesn't.

I've had time to prepare for this. After that close call with Xisenyin back at the moonsong revelry, I've spent the hours Yù'chén left me alone in the darkness re-creating the talisman my father engraved on my crescent blade Shield. It is one that blocks attacks, including magical ones. Incredibly powerful if done well, yet incredibly difficult to conjure.

Despite all my training back at Xī'lín, drawing talismans still doesn't come easily to me. I've nearly exhausted my spirit energy, yet tonight, my body bears the talisman written in blood on my stomach, my thighs, and my shoulders—the parts of me hidden under my dress. The shield talismans activate now, resisting the pull of Weirufeng's command.

I've defied the call of a regular mó back in the mortal realm; the magic of a Higher One is different. Even with five shield talismans on my body, it feels like fighting a tidal wave as Weirufeng's command closes over me. My muscles tremble and my limbs shift of their own accord as I lose ground.

But I don't need to resist this particular command. All I wanted to know was that I had a fighting chance.

As the slightest hint of suspicion tightens Weirufeng's eyes, I yield. His dark magic rushes through my veins, moving my body sharply: one single step forward to close the gap between myself and Yù'chén. My hands slip beneath his shirt to skim the hard, toned muscles of his abdomen.

He stiffens and jerks back, then grasps my wrists and pins them against my body. "She is neither your plaything nor yours to command, Weirufeng," he says irritably. "You forget the bargain my mother made with me."

"And you forget, your mother's Wind Messenger shall carry a report of her son's activities to her tonight," Weirufeng counters. "Lest you wish to impress upon me that you intend to disavow the reason we bring mortals into our realm? Or . . . worse . . ." His impenetrable silver gaze slides to me. "Do you mean to tell me you have broken a sacred rule and allowed a lucid mortal—a former enemy's ally, nonetheless—into our highest court?"

Yù'chén's fingers tighten against my wrists. "Of course not," he says after a slight pause, and his grip loosens.

Weirufeng's command surges inside me, and I let it lead me forward. I have to put on a performance to convince Weirufeng that I am claimed and drunk on oleander nectar.

I lean close to Yù'chén. His familiar scent of midnight wind and the sharp sweetness of scorpion lilies envelops me as, slowly, I press a kiss to the hollow of his throat. His skin is hot and he's tense, his grip tight on my waist as though he's preparing for a fight instead of for pleasure.

I understand: This is a game of power and humiliation. Like Niefuzan and Xisenyin the other night, Weirufeng is putting him in his place.

I suddenly wonder what else these Higher Ones have made him endure. *I'm not in the mood for games tonight, Niefuzan.* He greeted Niefuzan with cold indifference—but I recall the smirking, red-cloaked practitioner I met in the mortal realm, the nonchalance he wore like a second skin.

My touch turns gentle. I let Weirufeng's command carry me,

guided now by my own sentiments. I place my palm against Yù'chén's jaw, tracing a thumb across his cheek—a silent signal of reassurance back to him. He shifts his head slightly, his lips brushing against my fingertips. An answering signal.

I'm unprepared for how my hand tingles in response.

"Surely the empress's most esteemed Wind Messenger has better things to do tonight." Yù'chén's tone is cool, but his hands fist in the fabric of my dress, keeping my body a handbreadth from his. "Deliver your message and run back to her like the good dog you are."

Weirufeng's laugh sends a chill through my spine. "Very well. The empress returns to the Kingdom of Night tomorrow, still triumphant with the recent assassination of the mortal heir and her campaign's progress into the Kingdom of Sky."

The report is like ice in my veins.

But the Wind Messenger is not finished. "At midnight tomorrow, she requests your presence again to report on the progress for your coronation to the mortal throne. And this time, she has asked for your claimed mortal companion as well. She is to be questioned on her knowledge of the mortal throne . . . by the empress this time."

I inhale sharply. My mind is racing in a million directions, my heart slamming against my rib cage—but my body is still under Weirufeng's compulsion. As Yù'chén's grip slips from my waist, I slide my hand to his thigh and lean my hips against his.

His gaze snaps to mine. I catch a flash of panic as he tries to shift away, only there's nowhere he can go, and I'm pressed against the hard lines of his body, his desire clear.

"Tell my mother she can continue to question me." He sounds slightly out of breath. "The mortal girl knows nothing."

"The empress would like to confirm that herself, before the entire court."

"She must abide by her covenant with me."

"The covenant states that the girl shall keep her life." Weirufeng's eyes glitter.

I feel sick to my stomach—sick with the revelation that Sansiran plans to force me to reveal the secret to claiming the throne to the Kingdom of Rivers tomorrow, sick with attempting to fight Weirufeng's dark magic still twined over me . . . and sick with my body's reaction to Yù'chén's. Touching him like this is a match struck in the hollow space of my heart; where once there was only coldness and the dark, heat now sparks deep inside me.

I close my eyes as I kiss the side of Yù'chén's jaw, horrified that I no longer know where Weirufeng's command ends and my own will begins.

"You will be summoned tomorrow eve." Weirufeng's voice sounds very distant to my ears. "When the moon is highest in the midnight sky, you and your mortal claim are to present yourselves before the Court of the Aurora. Enjoy your time with your prize tonight, Your Highness."

A swirl of night wind and glittering dust, and the Higher One and his subordinates are gone. I can feel that Weirufeng's command has lifted, his dark magic faded from my veins. All that is left are the flames slowly burning through my blood, threatening to light my skin on fire.

"Àn'yīng?" Yù'chén's voice is low by my ear. His grip loosens against my waist, but he continues to hold me gently. As if he doesn't want to let go.

The worst thing is, I don't, either.

He draws back, his eyes dark as he takes me in. Pressed this close, I feel his heartbeat thundering in his chest, the tremor of his hands as he touches a thumb to my chin.

His gaze darts to my mouth as he traces a slow, careful finger across my cheek, down my jawline, stopping at the hollow crook of my neck. The nonchalance of his expression falls away to a heady, intoxicating desire that makes my head spin.

"Àn'yīng," he says again, and I suddenly realize my own face mirrors the longing on his.

I push away from him and stumble back, my cheeks burning.

Yù'chén's face is flushed. He blinks, then swallows and straightens, averting his gaze as he reaches down to rearrange his robes.

I can't look at him. We're still close enough for me to feel the heat from his body, to feel his gaze on me, to feel the hundred unspoken things burning in the air between us. I can't think like this—can't focus on what Weirufeng just revealed or how I should play my next move.

If Sansiran tortures me or uses force to draw out what I know about ascending the mortal throne, it's over. I would no longer have anything to bargain with, no reason for Yù'chén to make a covenant with me.

"Forgive me, Àn'yīng," Yù'chén says quietly.

I don't know what he's asking for my forgiveness for—the fact that his mother is forcing my hand and may very well kill me tomorrow, the fact that a member of his court just coerced me into doing things not of my own free will . . . or that the ashes of what once was possible between us are now roaring into a wildfire.

Nausea rises in my throat. How can I be feeling anything for Yù'chén, son of the tyrant who destroyed everything we fought for, whose army killed Hào'yáng?

I suddenly can't stand to look at him. "I need some air," I manage. "Alone."

Our alcove opens to a secluded balcony overlooking the edge of the glade. It's empty, concealed from the rest of the revelry by a row of purple wisteria trees. I make for this, and Yù'chén doesn't follow me. The wild, upbeat music and twirling dancers fall away, yielding to some semblance of peace.

I exhale as I lean over the stone balustrades. Clouds swirl in empty stretches of space between distant mountains, the glow of the shifting aurora overhead undulating over them.

It might have been beautiful.

I try to imagine a future here, an eternity here. I am out of time. Tomorrow, I must make a covenant with Yù'chén before we meet with Sansiran; I will secure my power in this kingdom and my influence over the policies of the mó's rule over my home. And from here, I will protect my home and those I love.

I look to the distant lights shimmering just beyond reach and imagine Hào'yáng there, his armor rendered like the sun, his eyes as steady as the earth.

I know he would want me to go on fighting.

I swipe my palms across my cheeks. I know the choice I am making as I turn to go back to Yù'chén.

But the alcove of wisteria where Yù'chén was waiting for me is gone. In its place is a row of flowering pear trees. Frost blooms at their roots, spreading across the grass, and as I watch, dozens more begin to sprout from the ground, blocking the path back. The air has turned icy, and my breath plumes in front of me.

Feminine laughter trills in the open space, which has suddenly grown eerily silent. And then a sweet voice rings out from all around:

"A little flower, drifted into my land of winter?"

Àn'yīng

Palace of the Aurora, Kingdom of Night

Xisenyin.

My heart races as I press a hand to my throat, remembering her tongue against my skin.

But this time, I am not defenseless.

I slip between two wisteria trees, their hanging flowers shielding me as I weave a talisman of concealment. Then I take out the porcelain shard hidden beneath the bodice of my gown.

I am not prey. I am a scorpion.

All I need to do is get my stinger back.

Between the branches of wisteria, I spot Xisenyin's unmissable white hair and dress as she steps out from between two of her flowering pear trees onto the balcony.

"Little flower, skin soft as petals, flesh sweet as fruit. Won't you come out so I can taste you?"

She hasn't seen me yet; my concealment talisman is working. *For now.*

I search her dress for signs of my blades, but as she moves, the snowy fabric shifts and glitters, and it's impossible to tell. She's wearing that wicked smile, prowling forward like she's hunting.

I tighten my grip on my makeshift weapon. *Not if I hunt you first*, I think.

Adrenaline surges through me, my senses sharpening as I step out and weave through the trees. Everything falls away but the chase; I could be home in the woods outside Xī'lín, stalking a deer.

I'm close enough now to see the intricate patterns in the frost lacing her dress, and I can make out a familiar moon-shaped dagger, gleaming between the folds of fabric—right where I saw it the first time.

Fleet.

My heart lifts at the sight of my crescent blade, just steps out of reach.

The Higher One moves forward—and the fabric of her dress twists to reveal two more hilts: my other crescent blades, Poison and Striker.

"Little flower, little flower, I promise to be gentle when I catch you . . . I'll peel your skin like samite, I'll weave your hair to silk . . ."

I know I am protected by Yù'chén's covenant with Sansiran, but Xisenyin's eerie song sends shivers up my spine. I dart forward silently, zigzagging between the flowering trees. Golden light spills from their petals so that it feels like I'm walking among stars in the dark. Ahead of me, Xisenyin drifts, snow falling and flowers blooming where she steps.

When I'm close enough to make out the strokes of the talisman engraved on Fleet's hilt, I act.

I dart out from the cover of trees and reach for Fleet.

The moment my fingers close around the handle, the air shifts. Frost crackles up the trees. Their petals turn sharp, the branches extending to form jagged bars of ice. I stumble back behind a tree, biting my tongue as I nearly slip on the now-frozen ground.

In my hand, gripped so hard I can feel the grooves of the engravings in the hilt digging into my palm, is Fleet.

"*As the tale goes, the fair maiden beloved by the prince was no flower . . .*" Xisenyin's voice rings out from all around, amplified and melodious. "*. . . but instead, she was . . .* a scorpion with a stinger."

Her voice hardens, suddenly coming from behind me in a puff of cold air. Too late, I spin around and look straight into a pair of white eyes.

Xisenyin's grin exposes rows of teeth, all sharpened to points. Her fingers have transformed to ice, frozen and jagged as they seize my arms in a viselike grip.

"*Be still,*" she croons, and her dark magic creeps over my body, cold threatening to sink into my bones.

I stop struggling.

Xisenyin leans into me and inhales. Out of the corner of my eye, I catch her mouth widening and her face morphing, saliva dripping down the gleaming points of her teeth . . .

She bites down, and I swallow a scream as pain sears through my shoulder. But I leverage the distraction to wrench myself free from her, my spirit energies flaring and pouring into my defensive talisman to resist her magic.

I twist and jam my porcelain shard into her eye.

Xisenyin screams, a horrid, inhuman sound, and I snatch the

hilt of my second blade from between the folds of her gown: Poison.

I fight another wave of pain as Xisenyin pulls her teeth from my shoulder. Blood splatters like rose petals on the frost-covered ground, but I follow her as she stumbles back, covering her face with her hands. Frost snakes up her pale skin, wreathing her wounded eye. The ichor leaking from it hisses, and my porcelain shard clatters to the icy ground as she begins to grow a new eye.

I leap forward and plunge Poison through her ribs, its spirit energies pulsing between my fingers.

Xisenyin lets out a snarl, and the shock wave of power that explodes from her slams me into the ground.

There's a ringing in my ears as I crawl unsteadily to my feet. But in my hand, I hold my third—and final—blade: Striker, which I snatched in the moment she was distracted by my attack.

I slip the blade into my sleeve and look up.

Xisenyin has straightened. Ichor leaks from her side, drifting upward like black smoke. Poison will be spreading through her veins now, with the jab I just gave her.

"How—" Xisenyin's face is twisted in the first genuine surprise I've seen her display as she realizes I've slipped through her magic.

I turn and sprint for the pear trees. Blood, hot and thick, wells up in the wound on my shoulder, soaking into my dress. Behind me, Xisenyin shrieks commands; her dark magic sinks into my limbs, pulling me back.

I channel more of my spirit energies into my shield talismans and barrel into the maze of pear trees standing between me and the alcove where Yù'chén should be waiting. Their lights blur as Fleet pushes me forward faster than humanly possible—yet still not fast enough. Ice crackles beneath my feet as Xisenyin's voice rings out:

"Little flower, skin soft as petals, flesh sweet as fruit . . . Won't you slow down so I can taste you?"

I run out of the maze of trees, and for a moment, I'm disoriented: Colors and lights swirl around me, movement and motion in flurries of silk and skin, music and drums thrumming through the night.

I'm not back where I left Yù'chén, I realize with horror. Xisenyin conjured a passageway of flowers and altered the path, dropping me somewhere in the middle of the revelry. As I stumble through the crowd, blood soaking my sleeve and dripping onto the ground, the mó begin to take notice of me.

I grip my blades and slow, lowering my stance into a defensive crouch. I'm growing lightheaded from blood loss, and I've exhausted all my spirit energies fighting Xisenyin.

But I have my blades, and I will go down fighting on my own two feet.

I will not be prey.

When the first mó springs at me, I'm ready. One slash of Poison opens a wound in their neck. With the next, a gash on their ribs. And a third, a stab to their shoulder.

I feel myself slowing with each strike. More come at me, crowding closer, either at the scent of blood or to watch the spectacle.

At one point, I miss. And a mó's teeth sink into my arm, bringing me to my knees.

An explosion of dark magic ripples across the glade. The mó on my back shrieks and disintegrates in a cloud of ichor.

Scorpion lilies bloom. The air fills with their petals, drifting downward to land on the ground, on my skin and in my hair—and where they touch me, I feel *his* magic. Soothing, familiar, and healing. The pain in my shoulder dulls; my heartbeat calms.

Footsteps sound, echoing in the sudden silence. Then the mó crowding me begin to scurry away. The area clears.

A long shadow falls over me. When I look up, Yù'chén is there. In his flowing black robes, his face utterly expressionless, he looks every bit the heir to the Kingdom of Night.

"This mortal is claimed by your crown prince and protected by order of your empress." Yù'chén's voice rings out, low and terrifying, across the revelry. The glade is completely quiet now, performers still. Only the aurora overhead dances, spilling an eerie green light over the scene. "Anyone who so much as lays a finger on her will be served the direst of punishments. I will see to it personally."

He bends, effortlessly graceful as he scoops me into his arms. I hold tightly to my two blades, tensed, adrenaline pulsing with every beat of my heart.

I wrap my arms around Yù'chén's neck, holding him tightly as we wind through the crowd.

The flower passage of scorpion lilies forms before us.

"One moment, Your Highness," a voice calls out.

Xisenyin appears seemingly out of nowhere. Behind her is Niefuzan, and I suddenly notice several of his subordinates scattered in the crowd. I search Xisenyin for signs of Poison's talisman working through her body but find none. The spell is probably too weak to cause any lasting damage to a Higher One.

Yù'chén's grasp tightens around me, but his expression

remains the same: cold, arrogant, his mouth twisted in disdain as he beholds the two members of his mother's court.

I raise my blades, and Xisenyin lets out a peal of laughter. "Princeling, it would seem you've been tricked," she purrs. "The little flower you chose is, instead, a scorpion with a sharp stinger."

"She is the mortal I've claimed, stinger and all," Yù'chén replies. "If there's nothing else, Xisenyin, I'll be retiring now. Count yourself lucky I won't retaliate for hurting her."

"Oh, but there *is* something else." Xisenyin's eyes flash. "Your mortal has caused harm to the Kingdom of Night and our people. She attempted to poison me; she has slain four of our court members. Punishment must be dealt."

"Her life is protected by the empress's decree," Yù'chén replies drily, turning to leave.

"We are sworn by our empress's orders not to hurt *her*. But the same does not apply to you, Princeling."

Yù'chén stops. Over his shoulder, I can make out the smile twisting Xisenyin's lips as she continues: "The laws of this court apply to you, Princeling. You have brought a mortal to a public event without the use of oleander nectar to pacify her, and in doing so, you have endangered your mother's court members."

Niefuzan speaks now as he takes a step forward. "You are familiar with the punishment for traitors and those who inflict harm upon our kingdom, Princeling. Justice must be served."

Yù'chén's gaze falls on me. Not for the first time, I cannot read his expression. "I'll be right there," he says quietly.

"No," I whisper, but behind me, the branches of the scorpion lilies are twining over my neck, my arms, my bodice, wrapping me into the passageway of flowers. I reach for him, but he pulls away. "Yù'chén—"

Flowers clamp over my lips, silencing me. Yù'chén lets me go, the flower passageway takes me in, and I'm ensconced in a gentle darkness and the soft glow of scorpion lilies.

I'm released into his chambers. When I turn around, the passageway of scorpion lilies is shrinking into his doors. I spring forward, but I'm met with hard obsidian. I call his name and pound on the doors, but there is no answer. He isn't there; he is far away, somewhere out there in the Court of the Aurora.

Being punished for my actions.

I sink against the door, holding my blades to my chest.

And I wait.

I don't know how long it is before I sense movement in the chambers. I've spent the passing time restlessly, cleaning the blood from my hair and dress, turning my crescent blades over and over between my fingers. In the dark, it is easy to summon memories: of the blankness to Yù'chén's eyes as he was whipped for stealing during the Immortality Trials; of the way he bore Sansiran's torture the night she invaded the Kingdom of Sky.

The mó thrive on fear and pain, he told me.

The slowly shifting stardust in the obsidian doors ripples suddenly, and the chamber fills with a flash of red, the thick scent of flowers—and blood.

I hear someone breathing.

I'm on my feet in an instant, blades in my hands as I approach the doors. Beyond the moonlight spilling in from the gauze curtains, I make out a crumpled form in the shadows by the farthest wall.

Only the wall is not a wall anymore but a shifting curtain of shadows and dark magic. Beyond is . . . another room. A desk, it appears, a futon . . . and a figure lying on the floor.

I step across the threshold, and I'm in an adjoining chamber, one I never knew existed until now. Compared to the decor of the Palace of the Aurora, with all its flowering trees and open skies and wilderness, this room resembles one from the mortal realm.

Bookcases line the walls, filled with gilded vellum tomes and trinkets resembling the ones from my father's study: horsetail-hair brushes and inkstones, porcelain teacups and a lacquered-wood box inlaid with mother-of-pearl. A sprig of dried peonies, a frayed tassel of blue silk.

Remnants of the mortal realm. Of Yù'chén's life when he lived in the Kingdom of Rivers as one of the emperor's bastard sons.

Yù'chén lies on the floor, halfway to the futon. Blood smears the floorboards, forming a trail from where he entered.

I kneel by him. In the near-darkness, I can only make out his back, the rise and fall of his shoulders as his breaths come fast and shallow.

This must be why the wall between our chambers yielded today—because he isn't strong enough for his dark magic to maintain it.

"Yù'chén?" I touch his arm, intending to flip him over, but he winces. When I lean over him, I see why.

His shirt is a bloody mess, shredded to strips of fabric clinging to flesh that has peeled from his body. Dark veins run through his skin as his magic works to heal him, stitching his flesh together and smoothing over the wounds until his skin glows like moonlight again, perfect and unmarred.

And I realize that Yù'chén, whose skin has always looked sculpted, does not bear any marks of his suffering. His skin will make itself over, night after night, in time for Sansiran and her court's fits of rages to split it open again and again.

He doesn't acknowledge me as I turn him onto his back. I summon my spirit energies and trace a healing talisman on his chest. My hands shake, and I press my palm to his heart as the talisman activates, my spirit energies glowing gently in the dark.

His breathing eases; his lashes flutter. "Ān'yīng?" His whisper is hoarse as his gaze settles on me. His demon's gaze, terrifying in its black and red . . . yet, now, familiar enough. I don't look away. "You shouldn't be here."

"You're hurt." My throat knots. *And it's my fault.*

"I broke a rule."

My heart clenches. He broke a rule *for me.* "How often does this happen?"

He closes his eyes. "Leave me."

"I'm not leaving," I say.

Yù'chén opens his eyes again. His gaze is very dark as he stares at me.

"Is this where you've been?" I gesture around at the chamber. It's clear to me now that this room and the one I've been staying in are all part of the same chambers—his chambers.

He nods.

"Why did you make a wall between us?"

A humorless chuckle. "You might've thrown all my teacups

at me if I hadn't, considering how much you hate me. I couldn't risk you destroying my collection."

"I don't hate you," I say.

He falls silent.

"Are these . . . from your life back in the mortal realm?" I'm struggling to make conversation, something I've never been very good at, if only to break the tension heating the air between us. In one corner is a cherrywood bathtub, perhaps enchanted to be filled with gently steaming water.

I grab one of the towels on the tray next to the tub, wet it, and turn back to Yù'chén.

He's still watching me, his expression inscrutable. "Yes."

In the half darkness, the chamber might have been one from a noble manor of the Kingdom of Rivers. I press the towel to his face, dabbing at the blood. He only blinks, his gaze unmoving from mine. "Do you miss it?"

Wordlessly, he nods. I move the towel to his throat, down to his collarbone, and then I begin to clean his chest, peeling the strips of fabric away. Beneath, his skin is already as perfect as if the wounds never existed.

Yù'chén grabs my hand, stopping me. "Don't."

The distance stretches taut between us again, unspoken words filling the silence between our heartbeats.

I set the towel down in my lap. "You've saved me more than once, yet I can't help you when you need it?"

He's staring at the ceiling, his lashes fluttering. Fighting unconsciousness. "Don't do this to me again," he mumbles, and I realize he's close to deliriousness. "Don't . . . make me think you care, give me hope, and then leave again."

"Who said I was leaving?"

"You always find a way to leave," he replies quietly. "I know you never wanted this, forced to be here with me in a land the sun never touches. So tell me you hate me, that you're only using me. Tell me I'm a monster that repulses you."

I taste each sentence he speaks on the tip of my tongue, insults I used to hurl at him without question and without remorse.

But I find, now, that they are only shadows of what once held true.

"You are my ally," I say firmly, "and I need you to be strong so we can face Sansiran together tomorrow. So let me heal you."

The expression that crosses Yù'chén's face is one I have never seen him wear.

He looks . . . afraid.

I summon my spirit energies and begin tracing the talisman for healer with my fingertips on his skin. I'm slow, steady, my eyes never leaving my work. After some time, his labored breathing eases, and then his muscles relax, and the scales, the scars, the tremors—they vanish with each stroke of my hand.

The only thing that never changes is his gaze on me, unwavering as an arrow in the dark, slowly setting fire to my veins.

19

Àn'yīng

Palace of the Aurora, Kingdom of Night

When I wake, I am in the bed. The drapes are fluttering, and across the chamber, Yù'chén is gone; he has not put up the wards to his side of the room. It must be around midday—I can now tell by the position of the moon and stars in the sky.

I recall what Yù'chén said last night about missing the sun, and I'm suddenly filled with a yearning that makes my heart ache. I can't imagine living here for a decade, half a lifetime, after having known the warmth, fires, and laughter of the mortal realm.

I make my way to the crystal spring to bathe and dress. When I return, Yù'chén is waiting for me.

He's wearing his crimson cloak again. It brings out the flush to his cheeks and his mouth, and I suddenly have the feeling I'm with that red-cloaked practitioner I first met in the bamboo forest of the mortal realm.

"Good morning," he greets me.

"Good morning," I reply after a beat, studying him.

Yù'chén clears his throat. He seems to be working up the courage to say something.

At last, he asks: "Would you have lunch with me today?"

He leads me to his part of the chambers this time. Beyond his study is a dining space overlooking his open-air pavilion. The gauze curtains have been pulled back, revealing the scythe moon and the mists rolling through the vast, empty night of this realm. I find that the sight I'd thought eerie just weeks ago feels less so now, warmed by the soft light of lamps in the study.

Yù'chén draws out an intricately carved rosewood chair—one of two placed at the matching table. I trace a finger over the patterns as I sit: dragons and phoenixes, lotuses and clouds—all emblems of the imperial family in the Kingdom of Rivers. The dishes he has had prepared are simple but plentiful, and again I spot some of my favorites from the banquets during the Immortality Trials. Egg stews steam gently from clay pots, glutinous rice balls glisten from atop spreads of bamboo leaves, and rounding out the spread of delicacies is a pot of tea and two porcelain teacups with little patterns of flora and fauna similar to the one I smashed on my first night here.

Yù'chén takes his seat across from me. There is a new, tense air of courtesy between us; neither of us has acknowledged what happened last night.

Something twists in my chest, and I blink away the image of him lying on the floor, alone and bloodied, barely breathing. "Thank you for this," I say aloud. "It reminds me of home."

The edges of Yù'chén's eyes soften, and his mouth pulls in a tentative smile. It brightens his entire face. "I'm glad. It reminds me of the mortal realm, too."

It's interesting that he has chosen this type of decor for his private chambers. The books and scrolls tucked in his bookshelves, the lacquered-wood furniture with inlaid gold and mother-of-pearl patterns, even the pale-blue sheen to the gauze drapes . . . we could be enjoying a twilight meal in the Kingdom of Rivers.

I help myself to pickled fish and steamed egg. Perhaps it is the light from the lamps hanging overhead—real candles lit within—or perhaps it is something else, but I feel warmer than I have in a long time. "You should do this more often," I say, gesturing around. "It chases away the cold and the dark."

"I didn't have a way to replace the candles after using them. The fires in my realm burn from magic, not wax, and I'm not permitted in the mortal realm without reason." Yù'chén pauses, glancing at me over the rim of his teacup. "Perhaps once I claim the mortal throne and stabilize the gateway between the two, we could have meals in the mortal realm."

Suddenly, I'm not hungry anymore.

"Àn'yīng." Yù'chén places his teacup down on the table. "I wanted to ask you about what you said last night. About our alliance."

My hands automatically go to my crescent blades. They've been strapped to the inside of my wrists ever since I rescued them from Xisenyin last night.

"Àn'yīng," Yù'chén repeats, and I look up at him. A wry smile curves his lips as he glances at my hands. "Are you wishing you stabbed me last night while you had the chance?"

My grip tightens. I must admit, last night, sitting in the dark with him wounded and weakened, it briefly occurred to me that I could overpower him and escape the Kingdom of Night.

But that thought was fleeting, born from an old instinct. I spent the rest of the night listening to make sure he was still breathing. Hoping that the healing talisman and spirit energies I poured into him were enough.

"That would have been rather foolish of me," I say, holding his gaze. "I'd have ended our alliance before it truly began."

Yù'chén falls very still. Only his finger twitches against his teacup. "Then are you officially agreeing to work with me?"

"Do I have a choice?"

"Well. You could still stab me and run for it."

"And get eaten alive by Xisenyin and your fellow mó? No, thanks." I sigh and loosen my fingers from the hilts of my blades, setting my hands on the table again. "I'm working with you only so that I can protect the Kingdom of Rivers. And if I find you're deceiving me in any way, *then* I'll stab you."

He lets out a startled chuckle and covers his mouth with his hand, but then he's leaning back against his chair and holding his stomach as he laughs.

I stare at him. "What's so funny? I meant it."

Yù'chén purses his lips. "I know," he says, and he's grinning at me. I haven't seen him smile like this in a long time—since our days in the immortal realm together. "That's why."

I roll my eyes and take a bite of a glutinous rice ball.

"I'm glad you have your stinger back, little scorpion," Yù'chén says.

I raise an eyebrow. "You mean you enjoy threats and attitude?"

His smile fades slightly. "When you first arrived, you were

a shell of yourself. I didn't know what to do, so I figured I would try to check on you, even if you hated me. Having you react angrily to me was better than having no reaction from you at all."

I draw a sharp breath. "I don't want to talk about this."

"I'm sorry." He laces his fingers together. "I'm sorry that I can't change everything, Àn'yīng. But I swear to you, I'll do everything in my power to give you what I can of the world you wanted."

"Then make the covenant with me," I say. "Before we meet Sansiran tonight. And in front of your entire court, announce the four conditions we discussed." I pause and draw a deep, swift breath before I finish. "Then I'll tell you the method to ascending the mortal throne and being accepted by the land of the Kingdom of Rivers."

Yù'chén is watching me with an intensity that burns. "So you do know the secret to claiming the throne," he says quietly.

I hold his gaze, all but confirming with my silence.

Yù'chén's gaze is brighter than I have seen in a long time. "I accept," he says softly. Starlight dances across his face as he reaches beneath the table and draws out a lacquered-wood box. "A formal token of appreciation for our alliance," he says, and there's a teasing drawl to his tone. "Let us first prepare for our appearance tonight in the Court of the Aurora. Take your time. Whenever you're ready to make the covenant, come find me outside."

Yù'chén has gifted me a gown. It's an ethereal thing: rippling fabric of shifting blues with small, glittering diamonds sewn in. It fits effortlessly over me, spilling down my curves in layers of silks and gauzes so that I look like I'm dressed in the colors of a midnight sea. Stitched throughout are cherry blossoms, and when I move, it is as though the flowers are carried by star-strewn tides.

And inside my sleeves are three slots, one for each of my remaining crescent blades.

It's so thoughtfully made that I can't help but be touched by this gesture as I step into it. A matching ribbon and a pair of silk slippers are laid neatly in the box. I braid my hair as I always have and slide on the shoes. Finally, I slip my blades into my sleeves. When I finish, I feel more like myself than I have since I arrived here.

I spend the rest of the day perfecting the defensive talismans on my body.

The moon is nearly halfway through the sky—indicating late afternoon, I've come to learn—when I'm ready. As I step toward the curtains leading to the open-air pavilion, I make out Yù'chén's silhouette. He's standing at the edge of the crystal spring, gazing out at the distant aurora. He has changed into his black cloak bearing the dragon and phoenix intertwined— imperial emblems of the Kingdom of Rivers.

As though sensing my presence, he turns. His gaze settles on me through the billowing drapes, and he goes very still.

Heat rises to my cheeks. "What?" I ask.

He blinks and looks away. The curtains between us cast shadows across his face. "Nothing," he says quickly, and then: "It's beautiful. The dress, that is. I wanted to—the water, for the Kingdom of Rivers, and the cherry blossoms—" He stops himself and draws a deep breath. "Do you like it?"

I run a finger over the intricately sewn flowers for which I'm named. "It was very thoughtful of you," I reply, and I part the curtains to cross the threshold to him. "Thank you."

Moonlight sparks in his gaze as I approach. He holds up a hand. "I have something else for you," he says. "I thought you'd like it before tonight."

My attention narrows to the shimmering black feather in his palm. I close the gap between us, my fingers brushing his as I take it.

The feather dissolves, and my family appears. Mā, sitting outside beneath a tarp, fabric and threads splayed across her lap; Méi'zi, crouched by her side. They lean together, their heads nearly touching, their fingers moving in synchrony and needles flashing as they sew. The skies beyond them are an endless azure, sunlight spilling golden over rolling sand dunes.

Méi'zi says something and Mā tips her head back to laugh, then just like that, the vision dissipates and I'm left in the dark with the image of the two people I love most in this world seared into my mind.

"They're safe, Àn'yīng."

There's a sharp heat in my eyes and on my cheeks as I nod. "Thank you," I manage.

"Can I ask you a question?" he says quietly.

I nod.

"Why did you let them leave?" He gestures at where the vision was just moments ago. "Why not go with them, or ask them to stay with you?"

I draw a shuddering breath and close my eyes. "Because sometimes, love means letting go," I whisper. "Sometimes, love means sacrificing what you want to keep them safe."

When I open my eyes again, Yù'chén's still staring at me, in a way that unsettles something deep in my chest. "I told you that I can't change everything. But I promise you, anything and everything in my power to give you, I will. I . . ." He swallows. "I hope that one day, it will be enough."

I don't know if it will ever be.

Yù'chén's breath plumes white as he tips his head back to the skies. "Our realm's lore states that the aurora is made of the energies of souls being reincarnated," he says quietly. "A divergence of fates and lifetimes. When I was young, I'd look up at the skies and wonder if, somewhere up there, I'm living a life where everything is different."

I remember his plea to me, back when we were in the Kingdom of Sky, going through the Immortality Trials. *I am a life. I, too, have a beating heart.*

I want you to look at me and see me.

"Oh?" I close the gap between us and place my hands next to his on the balustrade. "And what would you be, in this life?"

He's silent, seemingly deep in thought. Then he says, "Make me a butterfly." He's studying the scorpion lilies twining around the balustrade and between his fingers. "They're beautiful, they're beloved, and they're free."

I cant my head. *You are beautiful,* I think before I can stop myself. I barely register what I'm going to say as I draw a breath. "Mortals have a practice of palm reading to determine one's fate in each life." My voice is soft, for once. "It originated from an ancient philosophy of practitioning, that the Heavenly Order and the gods of all realms draw our destinies on our hands. Has anyone ever shown you?"

He's staring at me now, and that strange feeling in my chest returns. Wordlessly, he shakes his head.

I hold out a hand. "Want me to show you?"

He hesitates. Then, slowly, he proffers his palm to me.

I take his fingers in mine.

His palm is like nothing I have ever seen. The creases run in strange directions, few in number and some broken in the middle. I make out the heart line, second to the top, wrapping from one end to the other . . . tapering, like a story unfinished. The life line cuts across his palm—harsh and short. Too short.

"Let me guess. Mine isn't readable because I'm only half-mortal."

My head snaps up. Yù'chén watches me with that crooked smile.

"No," I lie. "It's just hard for me to see in the dark. Here—" I spin us, lifting his hand to catch the moonlight. "Better."

Gently, I press one finger to a long line I don't recognize, running from his thumb to his index finger. "This is your life line. It's long, and jagged at the start . . . but grows smooth. See?" I trace the tip of my finger across the crease, buying time as I search for my next lie.

I find a crease curving down, then slowly rising. "Your fortune and fate," I continue, and track my finger across it as I speak. "It begins low but rises." I glance up at him, and I find his gaze pinned to mine with such intensity that for a moment, I'm unable to speak.

"Go on," he says quietly.

"When we are born, we are set on a path to walk. That is our fate." The words are familiar; he once spoke them to me under the monochrome night of a distant realm. "But I've come to realize that it is how we *choose* to walk that path that becomes our destiny." I brush a thumb to the rising half of the crease. "Your fate changes because of the choices you make in this life."

His eyes roam my face, flickering with an emotion I can't quite decipher. "You've never been a very good liar, Àn'yīng." The words, spoken softly, huskily, feel more like a lover's whisper. "Tell me something true."

Again, I feel as though I am falling into a night without stars. "Your heart line," I whisper, and finally, bring my fingers to it. The one line I recognize in the utterly foreign map of his palm. "One straight, true line without an end."

The words unfurl from my lips in a plume of cold breath. The stars above us spin, the bone moon witnessing this moment that suddenly feels *real*. We stand before each other, his palm in mine, the heart line curving toward me—a single line, dividing us with the weight of realms. A lifetime of a fate missed.

Yù'chén lifts his other hand to my face. Hesitates, then touches my cheek with a single finger. "Thank you," he says quietly.

I don't move away. We remain like this in the night air, and everything stretches taut between us. Me holding his palm, him cradling my chin.

Yù'chén swallows. "Àn'yīng," he whispers, and he's silent, his chest rising and falling, as though weighing the words inside him, deciding whether to speak them out loud and break this fragile peace we seem to have reached.

Yù'chén traces my jawline with his thumb, so gently that I shiver. His palm comes to rest against my neck as he draws a deep breath. "Àn'yīng," he says again. "Can I . . . Can I kiss you?"

The blood rushes from my head. I stare at him, and everything else—the stars, the wind, the water, the ground—falls away.

But in this moment, it isn't him I see.

It is Hào'yáng. Hào'yáng, so steady, so warm, so full of life and light. The golden strokes of his brush as he wrote to me through the jade over the years, for half my lifetime. I think of him, seated at my kitchen table, the late afternoon sun painting him and my mother like a dream as he quietly confessed: *For all of nine years.*

Letting go of Hào'yáng would be akin to carving out a piece of my heart and setting it to the stars.

But I didn't realize how heavy this grief I carry in my chest is. I got so used to the pain, it numbed me and trapped me under its cold, black waters.

Perhaps I no longer want it to hurt so much. And perhaps, I think as I'm pulled back into the present, back into Yù'chén's dark, wide gaze as he awaits my answer—perhaps it's time for me to set down my grief and focus on the path forward. To be at my best and at my sharpest, to fully focus my attention on fighting for what's left of my world, I first need to stop drowning.

Maybe the answer is right in front of me.

I know what I felt in the past for Yù'chén. And I'm afraid to face it, to bring that dark thing back out into the light. Because loving him, however briefly, had cost me everything.

I wanted to hate him, because it was easier.

But if I am to be his ally, if I choose to dedicate myself to the Kingdom of Night in order to save my realm, I need to let go of the grief and anger drowning me.

Maybe, just maybe, I need to heal myself, too.

Even as I close the gap between me and Yù'chén, that ache flares in my chest. My eyes heat, and I can't stop the tears that blur my vision, spilling from that dark and drowning place inside me, as I lean forward and press my lips to his.

20

Yù'chén

Palace of the Aurora, Kingdom of Night

As her lips meet mine, she breaks my heart. Her eyes fall shut; in the moonlight, I catch the silver of her tears as they slip down her cheeks, taste the tang of salt on my tongue as she begins to cry.

Alarmed, I draw back—but her hands slide over my cheeks, tangling in my hair as she draws me to her again. Eyes still closed, she kisses me, shuddering as she weeps silently.

"Àn'yīng?" I whisper against her lips, but she captures my mouth in hers, her tongue sweeping over mine as she trails a hand down my chest—and I forget everything else. I forget about trying to hide how I feel about her, forget about the practiced nonchalance I've been wearing around her, that mask of ice I held in place when my heart felt like it was on fire whenever I was close to her.

I yield and draw her to me, my eyes falling shut as I taste her, let myself drown in the feel and smell and touch of her as I've dreamt of for so many nights. I hold her as if she is life itself, because I'm terrified that this is just another dream, that I'll wake up calling her name and reaching for her on an empty bed in the darkness again.

But as I murmur her name against her mouth, she's still here, warm and alive and in my arms.

I force myself to slow down, to let her lead. My fingers skim her back, gliding up her spine, the sharp blades of her shoulders, the soft skin of her neck and the silk of her hair.

She places her hands on my chest. I let her push me backward, stumbling over the threshold of my pavilion into my chambers, the silken drapes tangling between us briefly. She steers us to the partition in my room and pushes me down onto the futon.

"Àn'yīng?" I'm breathing hard, but her face is carved of stone, as though she's learned a new mask. It's rare that I'm not able to read her; she used to wear her emotions on her sleeves, so that with each crease of her brows or downturn of her mouth, I could tell if she was irritated or pleased.

I don't know what to make of this.

She turns to me and slides, liquid, onto my lap—and all semblance of thought scatters from my mind. My hands go to her waist, gripping her as my body reacts, desire hardening every part of me and needing her to be closer. I lift my gaze to her, drinking her in as though she is a drug, a poison, intoxicating me even as a part of me knows something is wrong.

Gods, I think, and I realize she could make me believe in such a thing again: Gods.

She's beautiful. An ache spreads in my chest as I take her in, wearing the dress I made for her with my magic. It's the colors of the ocean at midnight, the hues I remember the waves that time I took her there and she let me hold her. I wove in cherry blossoms and tiny stars, swept along by the ripples of gauzes and silks.

I wanted to make the most perfect dress for her—one that she could come to love, one that would make her feel strong and seen and empowered in this realm, in *my* realm. I wanted everything to go as well as it could tonight. If her only choice is to remain here, by my side . . . foolish as it is, I can't help but hope she might slowly come to accept it.

To accept me.

I gaze up at her, joy and disbelief as bright and sharp as a hot iron in my chest. As she presses her lips to mine again, I let myself touch her as I've wanted to for so many nights. I kiss her hard, my palms roaming up her waist to the small of her back and encircling her rib cage as I pray to whichever gods might listen to me—as I dare to begin to hope—that I can hold her like this for a lifetime.

Suddenly, Àn'yīng jerks back. She pries my fingers from her and pushes my hands off. I blink and hold my palms up as she tips her head away, breaking our kiss. Her jaw is tight, the tears on her cheeks fresh as she reaches up and wipes them away.

Confused, I reach for her, to catch her tears and hold her. She still hasn't looked at me. Her gaze is downcast, and too late now, I catch a flash of something like reluctance in her eyes.

The ache in my chest spreads. Turns to ice.

You disgust me.

Even as she takes my mouth again, the words wash over me, and suddenly, I'm shaking, my hands trembling as I lower them and spread them against the seat of the futon. My stomach twists from a burning hunger for her I have carried for so long—and now, a commingling of nausea and dread as the realization knocks all air from my lungs:

She doesn't want me.

"Àn'yīng," I gasp, breaking away from her. My voice is unsteady. Black waters at my neck, rising to my chin. Threatening to drown me. I have to know. *I have to know.* "Àn'yīng, look at me—"

Her hands are at my belt, her deft fingers undoing it, and then she eases onto me and I nearly lose control then.

I make a noise and lean into her, burying my face in the crook of her neck as sensation courses through me, my head growing light. My fingers clench against the silk of the futon as I strain to hold myself still. But as her arms encircle my shoulders and she moves against me, I yield to instinct, my hands coming to grip her hips.

I press her harder against me, gritting my teeth against the soft curve of her shoulder. In the haze of my desire, I feel her shrug me off and push me back against the futon. I let her hold me there as she shifts her hips against mine, the soft silks of the dress I made for her brushing against my thighs. Her eyes fall shut again as she kisses me, slowly now, her lips soft against mine. I'm reminded of the night we shared back in the Temple of Dawn, before everything had gone to hell: her eyes bright and liquid as she gazed up at me. *I want you*, she whispered, and it felt as though my entire life had been leading to that point, to those words from her lips.

Look at me, I want to say to her as I kiss her back, hungry and desperate and unable to help myself anymore. *Open your eyes, Àn'yīng—I'm right in front of you.*

But her eyes remain closed, her lashes fluttering like black butterflies across her cheeks as she moves against me. Her lips part and she tips her head back, and the sight nearly destroys me.

Please, I think, like a litany, a prayer. I reach for her, and this time she doesn't stop me. *Please look at me.*

My heart breaks and breaks and breaks as I hold the woman I love, the only one I have ever wanted in this lifetime, because as much as I can delude myself, I know deep inside that she never wanted this. Never wanted me. That she is here only because of circumstances, that I was never any choice for her but the last. And I know that if this is the only way I can have her, I will take it, and it will be more than I deserve.

So I love her, I love her with everything that I am and every piece of my soul, even as it breaks me and even as I know that it is all that I can give and nothing that she wants.

She clutches me, her nails digging into my neck and my back, and I let myself go, too.

Slowly, the tides ebb and my head stops spinning, enough for sensation to return to my body. I'm holding her in my arms; I feel her quiet breathing against me, the warmth of her skin and the silk of her hair, the gentle pressure of her fingertips as she presses them against my back. I lean my cheek against her shoulder, pressing a kiss to her neck.

Her cheeks glisten as she bows her head, her hands tracing the lines of my shoulder. I kiss her gently again on her cheek. *I will wait for you*, I want to tell her. *No matter how long it takes, no matter how many tears you need me to catch. I will be here.*

She stiffens. Then she begins to turn from me.

I reach for her, because now that I've held her, I can't imagine *not* holding her, and there it is again, the terror that I'll wake up in the dark again without her.

She hesitates. Her throat moves as she swallows, but then she pulls her hand back, swiping it across her face. I only feel cold again as she stands sharply; catch glimpses of the dress I made her sweeping out of my chambers. There's a splash of water as she enters the crystal spring.

Slowly, I straighten. Rearrange my shirt and robes. Fasten my belt. Then I sit and hold my head in my hands as I listen to the sounds of her washing me off her.

The pain in my chest sharpens until I can't breathe. It is as though I'm in one of my mother's rage sessions again, drowning in plain air, only this time, it's worse. I know all my mother's sessions will end at some point.

This will not.

I can't fathom an end to everything I feel for her, because that would be an end to life itself. I grew up knowing cruelty and pain in the Court of the Aurora, and then anger as my mother's scheme—and my entire *life*—fell apart in the Kingdom of Rivers. I didn't know what it felt like to live and to love until I met Àn'yīng.

A man living in eternal night who finally sees the sun could never hate it for leaving him in search of bluer skies.

I grip my chest with my hand, fingers digging in as though that will stop the pain. I finally realize that my mother was wrong. No matter how much we try, some things in life were simply never meant to belong to us.

By the time Àn'yīng returns, I've collected myself. I've rearranged my expression into the mask of nonchalance I've always worn in the Kingdom of Night, the one I've upheld before my mother and her court no matter what they did to me.

Still, I drop my gaze as she steps through the gauze curtains, the dress I made for her sweeping across the floor of my chamber.

The moon is halfway to its highest point; we have only hours before we are due in the Court of the Aurora. It's time to enact our covenant.

All the joy and hope and giddy disbelief I felt when she accepted my offer now tastes like ashes on my tongue. I recall the relief I felt when she began to yield, her anger toward me shifting to a tentative trust. The elation that surged through me when she cemented our alliance with a proposal of a covenant. The possibility of a lifetime with her, which had once felt as inconceivable as reaching for the sun, suddenly opened before me.

Now I feel only shame at shackling her to a life she never wanted.

I stand sharply to shake these thoughts from me. "Ready when you are."

The seconds trickle past; I can feel her eyes on me, can sense the thoughts running through her mind as she considers her last chance to renege on our agreement. I understand: In saving her realm this way, she is giving up on sunlight, on a life with her family. Choosing to align with me will forever be a compromise. A sacrifice, on her part.

"I'm ready," she says.

I try to meet her eyes as I offer my palm to her.

Can't.

Àn'yīng takes my hand. Her fingers curl around it—and she squeezes, just once.

I look up to find her gaze on me. Soft, open. Trusting.

I draw her gently toward me, the dark magic in my veins heating as I summon my full strength to conjure the spell.

A reverberating *gong* echoes across the night. The moon seems to brighten, the aurora shifting to crimson, then violet. On the balcony before us, red oleanders bloom and grow into an arch swirling with cold black shadows.

Sansiran.

Àn'yīng's lips part, the crease between her brows mirroring my confusion. It's still early; "when the moon is highest in the midnight sky" were Weirufeng's precise words, and we are several hours away from that.

Vines shoot out from the gateway, twining around our arms. And before either Àn'yīng or I can say a word, we are pulled into the darkness of the flower passageway.

To the Court of the Aurora.

Àn'yīng

Palace of the Aurora, Kingdom of Night

When the veil of darkness lifts, I hold tightly to Yù'chén to orient myself. The world settles: obsidian pillars, night skies, brightly colored flowers. The oleander passageway, having served its purpose, begins to fade.

We are back in the Court of the Aurora—only all signs of last night's revelry are gone. The center has been cleared to form one long aisle leading to a dais at the other end. Mó, elegant and ethereal in their black robes, line up on the sides. Tonight, there are no claimed mortals. The open-air chamber has been transformed into a proper throne room.

Sansiran's passageway has deposited us at the back. I search for the demon queen, but she is nowhere to be seen; the dais sits empty, devoid of even a throne.

Immediately, my eyes are drawn to the center of the glade, where, looming over a crystal spring, is the ancient stone pái'fāng that caught my attention at the revelry.

As I watch, the vines circling its stone columns begin to glow. Tiny aquamarine flowers bloom, and a vortex of darkness forms between the two pillars. Ghostly silhouettes move from within, then two mó step out, both clad in pale azure garments that glimmer over their bodies like spiderwebs. They round the dais and take their places amidst the rows of waiting courtiers.

The pái'fāng must be a gateway. The blue flowers crumble and disappear into the shadows, and the center of the pái'fāng clears.

I tear my eyes away to focus on my current predicament. I haven't yet made the covenant with Yù'chén. If Sansiran somehow forces the true method to claiming the mortal throne from me tonight, I will have nothing left to bargain with.

Alcoves line the walls of the throne room, overhung with curtains of flowering nightshade. I pull Yù'chén into one of them, ducking beneath the flowers and turning to lean against the wall. To anyone passing by, it will look as though their crown prince is having a moment with his claimed mortal.

I pull him to me; his hands fall to my waist as I lean forward. As I meet his gaze, though, my request dies on my lips. The mirth and nonchalance with which he regarded me over the past weeks is completely gone; the way he looks at me burns with a rawness and desperation that catches fire in my heart.

I snap my head away, my pulse racing. After last night, something fundamental has shifted between us so that I no longer know what we are. Enemies. Allies. Friends.

Lovers.

No. "Yù'chén," I begin, but he cuts across.

"You don't have to explain. I understand." His voice is even, his hand steady as he takes my chin and tips my face to his.

"You wanted to forget about him, or you simply wanted some-one to be with. I won't take it to mean anything more." He pauses. "No matter what, I'll still enter the covenant with you, Àn'yīng. I'll work with you to save the Kingdom of Rivers." His hand falls to his side. "I made you a promise."

I search his eyes, and I find that they are open to me. Raw and familiar, with the same intimacy I found in them when he held me to him earlier.

I swallow at the way my heart stutters in spite of everything I have told myself.

I'm the one to reach up and touch his cheek. "Thank you," I whisper.

He leads me out of the alcove toward the mó lining up on either side of the dais. It is easy to recognize the Higher Ones gathered closest to where the throne should sit. There is an aura of pure, unadulterated power to them, as though they are an ancient, immutable part of this world, like rivers and winds and flames.

Among them, I spot Xisenyin, with her snow-colored hair; Niefuzan, a head taller than the others; and Weirufeng, with his pale-blue skin, half hidden in the crowd.

My blades are cold against my skin, hidden in the slits of my sleeves.

Overhead, the aurora suddenly grows frenzied, turning the color of blood. A cold wind sweeps shadows in, and red olean-ders blossom on the stone pái'fāng.

From within steps the Empress of Fallen Darkness in a dress that seems cut from the sky. Her hair flows long and loose, like wisps of smoke; her lips are a slash of crimson on her pale face. The realm itself seems to shift with her every move: flowers springing up in the grass, trailing in her wake; the air and shadows curving around her; the stars brightening where she walks; the wind kissing her hair and dress.

Complete silence has fallen over the Court of the Aurora, and every crimson gaze is drawn to rest on her as though by a magnetic pull.

Sansiran, the demon queen, smiles, and she is just as alluring and terrifying as in all my memories.

She rounds the spring and stalks toward the dais. A throne rises from the ground, knitting itself out of vines and tree trunks and opening to her as she turns and sits.

"My loyal subjects." Sansiran's voice echoes across the clearing, drifting between trees. "We continue to gain ground in our war against the Kingdom of Sky. But tonight, we are gathered here to celebrate an event that will help us tip the scales of this war once and forever." She waves her hand. "Bring forth my son and the woman he claims."

The crowds part, and guards approach to escort us. My feet move of their own accord, and I'm gripping Yù'chén's hand so hard, I cannot feel my fingers as we draw close to where Sansiran sits beyond the spring. The shadow of the pái'fāng looms over her.

Yù'chén kneels. I follow.

"My *darling* son has done so much in service of our realm," Sansiran begins. Her voice reverberates across the vast hall. "Whether intentionally, that matters not. When he asked me to spare the life of the woman he loved"—by my side, Yù'chén tenses—"I made a generous decision." Sansiran pauses, and her lips curve. "But for more reasons than one.

"Tonight, my decision pays off."

Whispers of alarm tighten my chest. From around us come subtle movements as Xisenyin, Weirufeng, and Niefuzan and his underlings all emerge from the crowd to surround us from across the spring.

Yù'chén's eyes flash. He, too, has taken notice.

Suddenly, he stands.

Sansiran pauses, her lips parted, eyebrows raised, as she beholds her son.

"Your Majesty," Yù'chén says. "Before you proceed, I have conditions."

Amusement glimmers in Sansiran's eyes. "Conditions?" she repeats with a silken laugh. "What makes you believe you have the right to demand anything?"

"I exercise my rights as the prince of the Kingdom of Night and heir to the Kingdom of Rivers." Yù'chén's jaw is clenched as he stares down his mother. From this angle, I'm struck by how similar their profiles are: straight noses and sharp jaws, soft lips and raven's brows.

Similar, yet so different on the inside.

Sansiran laughs. "I see," she says, a finger stroking the armrest of her throne. A ring of oleanders grows beneath her touch, their spiky leaves glittering the color of emeralds. "Very well, then."

Yù'chén blinks—the only show of his surprise, which mirrors my own.

"I will listen to your conditions, my prince and my heir," Sansiran continues, her smile widening, "as soon as you prove yourself worthy of both titles." Her gaze cuts to the Higher Ones lurking near the dais. "Seize him and reopen the gateway to the mortal realm."

Dark magic clamps hard over my body, freezing me in place as the Higher Ones pounce.

Scorpion lilies shoot up from the ground, faster than imaginable, cocooning Yù'chén in a shield of his magic. He has drawn his sword; the garnet on the hilt flashes as he slashes through the first two of Niefuzan's underlings. They dissipate in screeches of pain, ichor gusting past him like ashes in wind.

Weirufeng's unyielding silver gaze pins me in place. He hasn't moved, he looks almost *bored*, and yet his power over me is absolute. No matter how much spirit energy I push into the talismans on my body, I cannot budge.

Xisenyin and Niefuzan clamp their power over Yù'chén. I can feel the tremor in the air and ground as they descend upon him, the resulting clash as he pushes back with all his might.

Prince he may be, but his other half is only mortal—and he is no match for a Higher One.

His knees buckle, then he's on the ground on all fours, veins darkening and eyes reddening as he fights. Scales begin to bloom on his skin, climbing up his collar and spreading across the back of his hands as he nears the limit of his power.

Niefuzan's underlings leap on him, dragging him to the center of the throne room. They fling him beneath the pái'fāng and hold him there, hunger parting their mouths as they stare at the Higher One commanding them.

Niefuzan and Xisenyin approach. The underlings peel back Yù'chén's sleeves to bare his arms.

Xisenyin makes a slashing movement with her hands, and blood sprays against the stone pillar of the ancient pái'fāng, dark red and glistening. Yù'chén makes a low sound in his throat as gashes open on his palms, on his forearms, and one at his throat. His blood forms droplets like red rubies, streaming toward the base of the pái'fāng, where the stone glows and absorbs it all.

Where Yù'chén's blood joins with the stone, the vines twined around the pillars begin to shift. Scorpion lilies bloom, and shadows pour from them, twining with his blood to darken the center of the pái'fāng.

Beyond, the night of this realm vanishes and a new scene appears: Flowing silk banners. Cherrywood pillars. A throne carved of gold. And at the end of a very long, grand hall, a sliver of blue sky.

The Kingdom of Rivers.

Home.

The gateway ripples once and settles, the scorpion lilies framing it pulsing softly with energy. With Yù'chén's lifeblood.

Throughout all this, Sansiran watches me with a small smile. As unsettling as it is that most mó cannot mimic the emotions of mortals very well, it is terrifying that hers look so natural.

"It seems you do care in some capacity for my son, then," she says softly. "I see it in your eyes. Mortal hearts are so weak, so fragile, so easily manipulated.

"Well, then, I give you a choice. Tell me what you know about ascending the mortal throne of your own volition, or wait for me to prise it from your lips."

Yù'chén's arms are held to the stone by some form of dark magic. His blood continues to stream from him into the pillar. As I watch, those black and red scales climb higher up his throat; the scene within the gateway grows clearer. His eyes are shut; his face is drawn and pale.

My gaze snaps back to Sansiran.

I find that Weirufeng's magic has released me. And I find that I do not care about the consequences of the words I speak next: "Do to me what you will, but I will not relinquish any secrets about ascending the mortal throne—not until you agree to my conditions." I look the demon queen in the eyes, and I change the entire strategy of my game. "I want you to enact a covenant with me."

I'm dimly aware of the uproar as the crowd explodes into chatter, but I don't break eye contact with Sansiran.

Her lips part with delight as she leans forward, propping her chin on her hand. "You've piqued my interest," she says, and her court falls silent again, hanging on to her every word. "And what would the details of this covenant entail?"

I blink, but otherwise, I let no signs of surprise show. Holding her gaze is as unnerving as staring into an abyss. "Should I succeed in helping your son claim the mortal throne, you will immediately stop the war upon the Kingdom of Rivers. You will set a decree that your kind—the mó—shall not, in any way, harm or frighten my kind, the mortals; any offenders of this law will be punished by death. I am to be appointed as High Advisor of the Kingdom of Rivers, with powers equal to the emperor's, and you shall not force us into a betrothal or marriage. And finally"—I draw a deep breath and turn my gaze to Yù'chén—"you will not hurt him any longer."

The throne room is so quiet I can hear my pulse roaring in my ears. Across the spring, from beneath the pái'fāng, Yù'chén lifts his face. I feel his eyes burning into me.

Then Sansiran starts to laugh. It's a deep belly laugh, one that fills the entire glade and echoes.

"Dear girl," she says coldly. "You speak as though you have

any authority over me. I birthed my son from my flesh and blood; he belongs to me in a way that you will never understand. And he has made a covenant with me." Her voice turns soft, and her smile suddenly turns sharp. "His life is mine, so long as he exists. His joys, his sorrows, his desires, and his pains—I am the one to dictate them all." She lifts her hand. "And if you care anything for him, then you'll reveal whatever secrets you know about claiming the mortal throne tonight."

Her magic slices through the air like an invisible blade. Yù'chén jerks as it hits him; his eyes squeeze shut, and his face drains of color. Red and black scales climb up his cheeks and cover his face, completing his transformation into his demon form, as he pitches over with a deep groan.

I'm running toward him before I know it. No one moves to restrain me as I barrel past the spring and up the dais to where he is bound. I slide to my knees and wrap my arms around him.

"Stop," I gasp. "*Stop—*"

"If you wish for him to stop hurting," Sansiran drawls, "you'll tell us all that your mortal heir revealed to you about becoming emperor to the Kingdom of Rivers."

Yù'chén's ears have grown long and pointed. His hands, turned to claws, dig grooves into the ground with his blackened nails. His entire body, covered in scales, is shaking from whatever she is doing to him.

I made you a promise.

"His blood must join with a river in the mortal realm." My voice sounds hollow, the words echoing in the sudden, complete silence that has befallen the throne room. "His blood must be offered to the Long River, the first river sprung from the Azure Dragon's bones."

In my arms, Yù'chén has fallen still. And though I know he despises showing his demon form, I cup his cheek and lift his face to mine. His entire face is covered in scales, and his sharpened teeth protrude past his lips. His eyes are completely black but for the crimson pupils at their center.

I stroke a thumb over his scales. "That," I finish quietly, "is how a mortal heir can lay claim to the Kingdom of Rivers, for the land to decide whether it chooses them."

Dimly, I'm aware of Sansiran's laughter ringing beneath the night skies. "How wondrous and foolish the mortal heart can be," she says. "Though . . . yours may not be purely mortal. Isn't that right, Àn'yīng?"

My head snaps up. Sansiran's watching me like a cat who's cornered a mouse, and I have a feeling everything that came before now was a foil to the true purpose of tonight's gathering.

"The night I stormed the Kingdom of Sky and met you," the demon queen continues, "I felt a power within you that I have never before seen in any mortal practitioner. One that held echoes of that female immortal I killed." At last, Sansiran cracks open the real reason she has summoned me here. "And so tonight, I will test the truth to your connection to the immortal realm."

Magic clamps down on me, pinning me to the spot. Yù'chén strains toward me, confusion clear on his face as he fights against his mother's magic.

But Niefuzan and his underlings are upon him, dragging him back. A cold energy grips me like a living thing, slithering into my veins and bones, and I'm bodily lifted into the air. I only make out Weirufeng watching me from across the crystal spring as he pulls me forward.

Sansiran's command rings across the throne room: "Drown her."

The water is cold, the silence absolute but for the fading echo of Yù'chén's yell in my ears. The moon of this realm casts a pale light upon me, and I'm reminded that white is the color of mourning in my realm.

I'm thrashing as I sink, but Weirufeng's magic holds me in a viselike grip just below the surface. Just away from air.

I've nearly drowned thrice in my life.

Once, in the half-frozen pond north of our village, when I needed to seek out light lotuses to sustain my mother's life.

Once, in the ocean between realms on my way to the Kingdom of Sky.

And once, during the third of the Immortality Trials, when I leapt into the Silver Sea.

All three times, I survived not on my own strength but by luck. Or fortune. Or destiny. Whatever it was that had tied my fate to my boy in the jade.

All three times, Hào'yáng had saved me.

I know the futility of fighting against a court of mó. Without my jade pendant and outside help, I am . . . nothing. A girl caught between greatness and the weight of realms, who has failed everyone she has loved.

Méi'zi.

Mā.

Hào'yáng.

Bà.

The names count down in my mind as the pain in my chest

tightens to an unbearable point. The world blurs in a dizzying way, my lungs at once cold and on fire. The commotion of the world above finally fades, replaced by a knifelike pain in my throat as water rushes in.

Weirufeng's magic loosens from me as I sink, farther and farther from the moonlight and shadows of this realm.

And finally, I die.

22

Àn'yīng

Between Realms

Àn'yīng.

A voice as ancient as the realms, echoing with the vastness of an ocean.

Colors weave through my consciousness, turquoise, blush, and a glint of gold . . . movement. I'm in the sea, but I can't remember how I arrived, as though I simply stepped into a dream and found myself here.

I am nothing, no one. A speck of consciousness between the currents.

Àn'yīng, that voice calls again, and something large moves behind me. I spin, but I find nothing, just ocean currents and the deep shift of aquamarines and blues fading into darkness.

In the distance, far below: a glow. It pulses, as though calling out to me in a language of its own.

I move toward it.

Its source grows clearer as I approach.

A great lotus drifts in the middle of the ocean. Its blush-colored petals are closed, pulsing like a heartbeat, cradled by the gentle currents.

I reach out, but I am formless—a wisp of a spirit, perhaps an echo of my own soul. I feel where my fingers would have brushed its petals. Feel a part of me resonate in this connection, as though . . . as though this flower is a part of *me*.

With a sigh, its petals unfurl.

Time ebbs to a stop.

He is there, lying at its heart, his white dragonhorse curled protectively around him.

Hào'yáng looks to be in a deep sleep, only his chest does not move, his lashes do not flutter. His skin is as pale as snow, his cheeks and lips are drained of blood, and his hair is now a dark shade of silver—it's as though all color and life have leached from him. Yet his body is healthy and whole, as though the lotus petals preserved him in a perfect cocoon.

Hào'yáng! I cry, but I have no voice, no body. I can't reach him, can't touch him, can't take his shoulders and shake him awake.

Meadowsweet appears to slumber with him in her dragon form. Her serpentine body is carved of ice up to her head, though rime has spread to her neck and coats her antlers and lashes.

Meadowsweet, I plead, but she is as still as stone.

They will not wake, comes that voice again, and it is as though the sea itself speaks to me. From the swirls of water and darkness comes a deep rumbling sound. The ocean floor seems to shift as something massive rises before me, like a mountain forming. Then it blinks—and I realize it is an eye, larger than that of any creature I've seen, more ancient than the echoes of this world. The pupil holds depths of unfathomable knowledge;

moss and lichen bloom at the corners, as though this being rose from the bedrock of our world itself.

Dragon.

The dragon blinks again. *Indeed*, it rumbles, and the ocean seems to shake with it.

How is this possible? I look down at the ocean currents rushing through where my body should be. *Am I dead?*

You are, and you are not. Your mortal body is dying, trapped still in the realm of demons, yet your immortal soul lives. You are in between life and death and realms.

How is it that I have come to your realm? I ask.

All bodies of water belong to the dragons, the being replies. *The sacred vessel within you preserving your life has brought your consciousness here, to where its other half resides.*

I look to the great lotus within which Hào'yáng sleeps, and it clicks. That is Lady Shī'yǎ's lotus—my lotus. It must have shattered that night not out of weakness but to preserve Hào'yáng's life. I remember how its blush glow absorbed into my skin and Hào'yáng's.

And now it has brought my spirit here . . . to where its other half remains, inside Hào'yáng.

I reach for him, a sob of relief bubbling up in my chest as I process this. Hào'yáng is here, *alive*, because my lotus saved him that night.

My fingers pass through him like air, and I remember that I am not here after all, but that this is a connection in my mind bridged by my lotus. *What's wrong with them?* I ask. *Why won't they wake?*

The dragon gives a slow blink. *They are dying. The mortal prince was so grievously wounded that even an immortal's sacred vessel cannot help him. It can only delay the process. The dragonhorse chooses to remain by his side, lending what she can of her life force to him. Yet we dragons do not possess the ability to heal or restore life. Only the immortals have such powers. Immortals, and their off-spring . . .*

Immortals and their offspring.

The dragon's gaze lingers on me. *You understand now, the role you played in saving his life . . . and that you are the only one who can bring him back—before he's gone forever.*

Tell me more, I say desperately. *Where is he? How do I save him?*

He is in the sea, at the seam between the mortal realm and that of the dragons. The great eye blinks again slowly. *The answer to your second question lies with you.* Its voice grows distant. *Make haste, daughter of immortals, for time runs out . . .*

The ocean is shifting around me, pulling back, and when I reach for Hào'yáng and the lotus, I find that my body has become corporeal again. My hands struggle against water that has suddenly grown thick, and when I look down, a pink glow radiates from my chest. Sparks dance beneath my skin, and I rise, rise . . .

When I break the surface of the water, I find my consciousness returned to the Kingdom of Night.

Everything and nothing has changed.

Power courses through my veins, soft light weaving across my eyes, illuminating the throne room—the same light and power that exploded from me when I faced Áo'yīn. I could not explain it back then, but I fully understand now. I simply do not know how it took me so long to realize this.

I am part immortal. And the dormant spirit energies of my immortal half were awakened tonight when Sansiran attempted to kill me.

I drift in the water, my world fracturing at this revelation.

I'm unable to move or fully open my eyes, but my senses are returning one by one: the cold of water sluicing against my skin, the sound of footsteps, the darkness of a shadow falling over me.

Through my lashes, I see Yù'chén's outline: hair mussed and clothing torn. Blood seeps from the wounds healing on his arms and throat as he wades through the spring to me.

His mouth falls open as he takes me in. The light of my spirit energies—of *me*—reflect on his face as realization dawns on him: of what I am, of my birthright and my true identity. He stumbles forward, shock and grief darkening his gaze as he pulls me from the spring.

Yù'chén holds me against his chest as he falls to his knees. We're crouched beneath the pái'fāng, where the gateway seems to pulse, the blue silk banners of the Kingdom of Rivers fluttering in a breeze from the other realm.

Yù'chén is breathing hard. A trickle of red drips from a cut on his lips, but he holds very still—and I see why. Surrounding us, weapons drawn and pointing in our direction, are Sansiran's Higher Ones.

"She lives," Sansiran crows. I can't see her from this angle, but from the direction of the dais, I catch the gleam of the garnets in her hair as she lifts her arms in triumph. "And therein lies the truth. This girl is no mortal but the daughter of Yǐ'lín Shī'yǎ, one of the Eight Immortals of the Kingdom of Sky. And she is to be wed to my son, cementing our claim over the three realms."

The court bursts into thunderous cheers and applause. A chant rises in the glade as the mó call out their queen's name: "Sansiran, Empress of the Three Realms . . . Sansiran, Ruler of All Kingdoms . . ."

The light from my spirit energies limns Yù'chén's face as he tips his chin up to face his mother. Rage flickers on his features. "And what if I refuse?"

The glade has fallen deadly silent. "I'm in a very good mood, my son," Sansiran says with lethal quiet. "I warn you not to ruin that. You forget, you are still bound to my will by our covenant. You will bleed into the mortal river tonight to complete your enthronement; the gateway between our realms will be made permanent. You will be wed, and our claim to the immortal realm, too, will be legitimized through her."

Yù'chén stands utterly still.

Until Sansiran's fury hits.

I sense the magic rushing toward us. Yù'chén turns, placing himself between his mother and me. Magic erupts from him, weaving a net of scorpion lilies over us. A shield of protection.

Every muscle in his body draws taut as he fights her magic with his own. Shadows bear down upon his wreaths of scorpion lilies; red and black scales again bloom on his skin, and his nails sharpen to claws.

Steps from us, the stone pái'fāng and the gateway within it ripple—as though his waning strength impacts it, too.

As I lie in his arms, my body still paralyzed and struggling to revive from drowning, I can only count the seconds before it stops.

Ten heartbeats.

Sansiran relents.

Yù'chén exhales shakily; his shield of scorpion lilies immediately vanishes. Sweat trickles down his jaw, mingling with the blood that drips from a corner of his mouth. He sways but doesn't let go of me.

He smirks as he twists his head to survey his mother. "You give yourself too much credit," he says raggedly. "You forget whose lifeblood it is that binds the mortal realm to this one."

Whose lifeblood binds the mortal realm to this one. My focus narrows to those words.

"How could I forget?" Sansiran purrs. "Every day, it haunts me that my own son's weakness has cost us permanent hold over the Kingdom of Rivers. Every day, I'm reminded that he has failed yet again to obtain the throne, that the mortal realm's lands reject him, reject his gateway, and thereby reject our kind from expanding farther in. There never comes a day that I *forget*." Her voice cracks like a whip as she slashes her hand down. And because I'm leaning against Yù'chén's chest, I catch the exact moment a red oleander flower blooms there—and spikes through his heart.

Blood pours out of him, thick and red, and into the cuplike petals of the flower. When it's full to the brim, it detaches from Yù'chén's chest and drifts into the air.

Feeling is returning to my limbs: the cold against my soaked dress, the trembling of Yù'chén's fingers as he fights to hold on to enough strength to hold me. I wriggle a toe, then test a finger, shift a hand.

Yù'chén's knees hit the floor. His shoulders cushion me as he collapses, bringing us both to the ground. His eyes, wide and unfocused, redden; veins across his face and hands darken as his magic stirs to heal him.

I act then.

I twist from his grasp, and Fleet and Poison are in my hands with a flick of my wrists. I know I have only seconds before my window of opportunity closes. Within the pái'fāng, just steps away from me, the gateway to the mortal realm flickers; beyond

the halls of its Imperial Palace are the open skies and, even farther, the vast sea.

The sea that carries Hào'yáng in its depths, life slowly ebb-
ing away from him with every second I delay.

Yù'chén's gaze follows mine, to the gateway and the halls
of the Kingdom of Rivers' Imperial Palace. Red drips down the
corners of his mouth as he reaches for me, his fingers clasping
over my wrist. "Àn'yīng?" Confusion creases his brows as he
scans my face.

He will find out, if he offers his blood to the Long River later,
that Hào'yáng is still alive; that the land will reject him. And
he will come to understand the choice I am making in this moment: to take a last chance to restore my realm to its sunlit
days, free of the grasp of the Kingdom of Night.

"I'm sorry," I whisper.

"Àn'yīng." His voice, his eyes, every part of him breaks when
he reads my intentions. Still, he holds on to me. "Stay."

My own heart is tearing. I knew this to be one of the consequences of opening myself to him again, of letting him into the
most intimate parts of my mind—this exquisite kind of pain.

Come with me, I want to say—except I could never allow that.
He is the son of my realm's greatest enemy, bound to her by an
unbreakable covenant . . . and his blood is the reason they were
able to cross the wards into my kingdom in the first place.

Now that I know Hào'yáng, the mortal heir to the Kingdom
of Rivers, lives, there is only one way this can end.

"I'm so sorry," I repeat, and then I wrench my hand from his
and turn away.

I summon my spirit energies to activate the talisman on
Fleet's hilt. Instead of a spark, a golden glow lights my chest and
dances from my fingers into the blade.

Air becomes fluid around me. Time slows as I leap forward, dodging Niefuzan's magic and Xisenyin's shield of ice. Something has changed since I emerged from the crystal spring. Spirit energies *surge* through my veins, and I feel invincible—like I can fly.

When I reach the gateway, I hesitate. Glance back.

Behind me, Sansiran has risen from her throne, her hands stretched toward me as though prepared to unleash her magic. The wrath in her blood-red gaze promises retribution, and I know this isn't the last I'll see of her.

But my attention is on Yù'chén.

He's lying where I left him, by the spring. Black veins spiral up the cords of his neck. His fingers have turned to claws, his skin to scales—the cost for his magic to heal him.

His eyes, though, have never left me. It isn't fury, or anger, or vengeance in his expression. It is heartbreak and a bleak, knowing exhaustion.

I'm sorry that I can't change everything, Àn'yīng. But I swear to you, I'll do everything in my power to give you what I can of the world you wanted.

I'll never know the extent of what he's done for me in the shadows of his realm, but I know that within the confines of his birth in this lifetime, it is more than I can ever repay.

The gateway flickers again.

I know that if I hesitate any longer, I may not have the strength to leave.

So I turn and step through.

The air of my realm greets me, the smell of pines and mountain wind and impending snow drifting through the Imperial

Palace's open doors at the far end of the hallway. It's colder here than in my village, though I don't think I've been gone long enough for the turn of a new season.

And it's dark.

I look back through the gateway into the throne room of the Kingdom of Night, bright flowers twisting around tree branches that fracture the night sky. The chamber's obsidian pillars meld into the marble and lapis of my world, and shadows drift out through the gateway.

A silhouette steps into view: Niefuzan. Dark magic explodes from him, tendrils sharper than knives reaching for me—

I fling my hands up, pushing spirit energies through my palms as I conjure the first talisman I learned from my father.

A shield blooms from my hands, blush-colored, like the warmth of spring. Niefuzan's power slams against it, and I almost expect it to shatter. Yet as his shadows refract, dissolving beneath my shield's gentle glow, I realize that the mó's magic, strong though it is, does not work the same way in my realm . . . and that the extent of my own power has grown with the awakening of my immortal half.

I turn and run, Fleet and Striker instantly in my hands. I feel it so strongly now, the hum of something new inside me, a strength both foreign and familiar that sings in my blood. The hallway of the palace blurs by, yet somehow I'm aware of every pillar, every fallen silk banner and piece of rubble strewn on the ground—all the carnage and destruction that the Kingdom of Night brought upon our palace when they poured through the gateway and launched their war against my realm.

I think of Hào'yáng, barely older than me, watching the slaughter of his family. Waiting, in the aftermath, for death to claim him as mó prowled the ruins of his beloved home.

I'm coming, Hào'yáng. The doors are in sight, flung open at the end of this grand hallway. *Don't you dare leave me behind again.*

I burst into open air and twilight skies. Ahead of me stretches a long marble walkway, cracked, and pillars crumbling from the battle that took place here a decade ago. The grand steps leading down from it are falling to ruin, but beyond that, gleaming beneath the last rays of light, is the Long River. It roars past the palace, the purest shade of turquoise, bifurcating the Imperial City that clusters around it.

This is the realm I wish to save. The realm I won't let fall into eternal night, into the power of the mó.

I take one last glance behind me. The gateway looms, as if a piece of our realm's skies has been carved away. Darkness leaks out; the Kingdom of Night's scythe moon and stars drift between clouds of the mortal realm.

My breath plumes before me as I run. It is instinct to gather spirit energies in my hands and fling them into the air. They unfurl into mist, swirling into an iridescent cloud around my feet, my legs, twining around my body. And as a wind gusts up, I am airborne. I *am* the wind and the clouds.

I am immortal.

The ground falls away beneath me as I fly, the mortal realm turned to a glittering stretch of abandoned cities and towns, and then to an expanse of red and gold pine forests. Beyond the horizon is where my realm ends and the Four Seas begin: the seam between the mortal realm and the dragon realm.

Make haste, daughter of immortals, for time runs out . . .

I travel through the night on a wisp of iridescent cloud. And at long last, when dawn tints the skies, I see it: the sapphire sea reaching all the way to the edge of the world. The rising sun paints a path of gold across the water straight to me—and somehow, I know that therein, my path awaits.

I let go of the spirit energies, my mortal body disentangling itself from the wind and the clouds.

And I fall toward the sea.

Toward Hào'yáng.

The water is cold against my skin, but I no longer feel it the way a mortal does. The light above me fades, yet . . . a glow emanates from within me. That same blush glow—like the breath of spring, the first hint of dawn, the bloom of a flower—pulses from my chest.

Growing stronger.

From the depths of the ocean comes a resounding glimmer, like a faint heartbeat.

I don't know how long I've been traveling when I spot it: the lotus from my vision in the spring, drifting in an ocean current. As I near, its light grows brighter, reflecting in my own skin—as though its magic draws out that of its other half within me.

Its petals open at my touch.

And there, lying within, is my boy in the jade.

Just as in my vision, nearly all color has leached from him; the frost has crept over his neck, framing his face and silver hair. When I press my palm to his cheeks, his skin is ice-cold.

I place my other hand over his heart.

And . . . *there.* A whisper of a flutter.

He is dying, and I know what I must do.

I close my eyes and touch my chest, searching through the woven strands of energies as Yù'chén once taught me to do. They glimmer in my vision like ten thousand magic threads of all colors and lengths.

This time, instead of searching for my life energies, I search for those threads of pure light: pink shot through with gold, resembling strands of sunlight. I gather them between my fingers, and I pull.

The lotus's essence wells up in my throat as I lower myself to my boy in the jade. His lips are like ice, yet as I exhale, the lotus's energies pour from my lips, their light dancing across his face. As they stream out into the currents, they first bloom into points, like the petals of a lotus flower. And then, slowly, the energies coalesce, shrinking into a gleaming pearl that glimmers gold and blush, the colors of a sunrise.

A pill of immortality.

I capture it in my palm and tip it into Hào'yáng's mouth.

"Hào'yáng," I whisper. My voice ripples through the water, echoing in the vast emptiness as my heart gives a responding cry. I am exhausted; my strength and energies are spent. The world begins to drift in and out of sight. And perhaps it is a dream, that light dances upon his face like the sun through water; that sparks ripple across his skin, spreading through his chest, pushing back the frost.

As darkness closes in on my vision, something strange happens.

A bright blue glow pulses through the ocean from beneath us, and the sea *opens* like a great maw or a set of heavenly gates . . . to swallow us whole.

Àn'yīng

The Four Seas, Realm of Dragons

I wake to sunlight, warm wind, and distant birdsong. I'm on a bed of soft moss in a gentle glade, the sound of rushing water threading through the canopy of leaves overhead. I have a knowing in my bones that I am somewhere else—somewhere foreign, somewhere my soul does not recognize.

When I turn to my side, I nearly stop breathing.

Lying in a pool of sunlight, bathed in gold, is Hào'yáng.

The blush has returned to his cheeks, the red to his lips, yet his hair remains the shifting silver I saw in the sea. I press a hand to his chest and nearly buckle with relief when I feel his heartbeat.

We're both dressed in white robes of silk and gauze. The frost is gone from his body, and he wears a curious new pendant around his neck: one that appears to be carved of ice yet seems to glow from within. When I press a fingertip to it, it is cold to the touch, and I think I catch a glimmer of shadows and scales stirring within.

"That is a dragon's heart," comes a familiar echoing voice.

Beyond this glade, the great camphor trees yield to a white-sand beach and a bay of clear turquoise. As I watch, the waters ripple and a shape coalesces between the currents: long and serpentine.

A dragon forms from the ocean itself. Water sluices down its body, dripping back into the sea, and the creature drifts almost lazily in the currents, watching us with eyes of the clearest blue. I recognize it: It's the same dragon that spoke to me when I was submerged in the crystal spring in the Court of the Aurora.

"She of the Moon-Frosted Sea gave most of herself to save her charge's life; only her heart remains in this world. It will be a while before she regains her form. For now, she slumbers."

My heart fills with gratitude for Meadowsweet as I give the pendant a gentle stroke. Its soft light seems to pulse in response.

"Is this . . ." I glance around me, not daring to utter the words aloud. From the ancient trees with their twisted roots to the strange, wild flowers and the ancient, echoing peace, I can only guess it's . . .

"The Realm of the Four Seas. Or what some might refer to as the Realm of Dragons."

"How?" I breathe. "Hào'yáng told me that, to enter your realm, one had to pass a test—a form of sacrifice."

"You passed it. You saved an heir of dragons and, in doing so, proved yourself worthy of entering our realm."

A slow blink, which for dragons might constitute a smile.

"Not many in this world can say the same."

I sit straighter, my hand on Hào'yáng's shoulder. I'm afraid that if I do not hold on to him, he will vanish again.

The events of last night return to me in a rush. The blood-soaked stone pái'fang bearing the gateway between the demon realm and the mortal realm. Sansiran's smile as she watched me drown. The breath leaving my lips and my immortality awakening as spirit energies illuminated my skin like the colors of sunrise.

The heartbreak in Yù'chén's eyes as he watched me slip through the gateway.

I push those images away, focusing on the dragon before me, on Hào'yáng's gentle breathing beneath my palms. Urgency shapes my voice as I ask, "How long have we been here?"

"Time does not work in this realm as it does in most others," the dragon replies. "You have entered a temporary fold between the waves of time. It has not stopped, but . . . it can slow, or speed, at your wish. For some, what feels like years here may be the blink of an eye in their realm. Others spend days here and return to find centuries gone. The only thing it cannot do is flow backward."

Time is one thing Hào'yáng and I were running short of with the Kingdom of Night's advancement into the Kingdom of Sky. I know we would both wish it to slow during our stay.

I incline my head to the dragon and say, "I seek an audience with your kind, to discuss an alliance between the mortal realm and yours."

It's impossible to glean any emotion within that ancient, noble face. "The Dragon King is willing to see you in his underwater palace."

"The Dragon King," I repeat in wonder, thinking of all the childhood stories and legends we're told of him in the mortal realm. "When? How do we get there?"

The dragon splashes a great tail as it rears up, so tall its head blocks out the sun for a moment, then dives effortlessly into the sea.

"When the time is right, the path shall reveal itself to you."

The dragon begins to dissolve back into seawater, first its scales, then its antlers and its ears, until I'm staring at nothing but the gently murmuring ocean.

Something pink materializes in the periphery of my vision. Lying in the moss by my side is a hairpin the length of my palm. A lotus flower gleams at its head, petals of soft blush shifting with the sunlight. By the spirit energies emanating from it that match my own, I know this is Lady Shǐ'yǎ's lotus—*my* lotus and vessel of power, made whole once more, now in the form of a hairpin.

I tuck it into the bodice of my gown.

A warm hand grasps my fingers, and I look up to a sight I have been dreaming of for so many days in the darkness.

Hào'yáng's eyes are open, and he is looking at me. As I meet his gaze, all the weeks we have been apart melt away, and I am back at home in Xī'lín on that sunlit afternoon, the blossoms of my flowering plum tree whispering overhead in a gentle breeze as I listened to him confess his love for me for the first time.

For all of nine years.

"Àn'yīng?" Hào'yáng murmurs huskily. "I have either died and gone beyond the Nine Fountains . . . or I am dreaming."

The dam in my chest that I built to hold back the grief of watching him slip through my fingers that night—it cracks.

Laughing and sobbing at the same time, I tackle him in a hug, and he wraps his arms tightly around me.

When I pull back, he studies me with a serious frown. "Goodness, I seem to have offended you greatly while I have been unconscious," Hào'yáng says.

It takes me a moment to realize he's teasing. "I thought you *died*," I whisper, my voice shaking again, and he sits up and gathers me to him. "I thought I'd never see you again, and I didn't even have my jade pendant to remember you by—"

"I am here," Hào'yáng says gently, tipping my chin to him. The same words he spoke to me when I first used the jade pendant and he wrote back. He trails his thumbs across my cheeks to wipe away my tears.

I drink in the sight of him, the same ink-brushed brows and straight nose, chiseled chin and intelligent, perceptive eyes. The only change is his hair, dark in certain lighting, yet shifting in mercurial silvers in others.

My boy in the jade, against all odds.

Hào'yáng cranes his neck to look around. "Speaking of 'here' . . . where are we?"

I bite back a smile. "The realm of dragons," I say, and I tell him about my encounter with the dragon just before he woke. Just beyond where we sit is a little spring, the surface of which has begun to bubble. Two teacups surface, wrought in oyster shells and filled with clear water. They drift toward us on a gentle current.

I take one and hand the other to Hào'yáng.

The instant the water touches my lips, an exhilarating rush of warmth fills me. My mind is sharper than I can remember; my body hums with energy, as though I have woken from the best sleep in years and had the most resplendent meal.

Suddenly, everything looks bright and vibrant, the world is once again filled with sunlight and hope . . . and the heir to our realm is here, alive and well.

We have a chance at restoring our kingdom. At chasing away the night and returning to days in the sun.

Unbidden, a memory resurfaces: Yù'chén lying on the ground, his grip tight around my wrist despite his wounds. The devastation to his voice as he'd said, *Àn'yīng. Stay.*

I swallow as the familiar ache flares in my heart. Choosing Hào'yáng is the only way we can banish the Kingdom of Night's hold on our home. The only way I can bring back those hazy, golden afternoons with Mā and Méi'zi beneath our plum blossom tree.

Hào'yáng catches my arm. "Àn'yīng," he says. "I made the mistake of letting you go once, and I'm not doing it again."

The air between us shifts, churning with unfinished conversations and half-answered questions. Yet as I stare back at him, he doesn't look away, doesn't evade my gaze.

"I let you fall," I whisper.

Hào'yáng takes both of my hands in his and pulls me closer. Close enough that our knees touch and I can see my reflection in his eyes.

"You saved my life," he replies. "I could feel the lotus's magic as I slipped through your grasp: the whispers of it, of *you*, twining around me and sinking into my blood and bones. When I fell, I was dying, bleeding out from the wound the hellbeast inflicted upon me. The last thing I saw before I lost consciousness was a glow, like the sun beginning to rise after a long, dark night.

"And then everything froze—as if I had entered a strange

sleep filled with dreams, a land of eternal winter. I was cold and alone in that darkness, but . . . at the end of the night, far away at the edge of the horizon, was a speck of light. I heard a voice in the wind, calling my name . . . so I kept following that light. Because I knew that if I stopped, it would vanish. *I* would vanish.

"And then, one day, in the phantom wind, I heard you calling my name. Your voice was faint, so faint, and so far away, but . . . it *was* you." His voice cracks, and I squeeze his hands. That must have been when I saw him through the spring in the Kingdom of Night. "I was so tired and so cold. But I told myself I had to hold on, just one more heartbeat, and then another . . . because you were out there, somewhere.

"Sometime later, that glow on the horizon brightened, as if the sun was rising. And then you were there, formed of the light. You held on to me, and I felt my heart begin to beat again, my blood begin to warm . . . Then I woke up here. And I'm still terrified that it was all a dream. That *this* is a dream, and that you'll vanish before my eyes."

I swallow, blinking away the sting in my eyes. "I'm here," I say, "and a part of me is terrified of the same. That I'll wake and you'll be gone."

Hào'yáng's expression grows unfathomably gentle. "I'm here," he echoes.

I tell him everything that happened in the past weeks, of my time in the Kingdom of Night, of my bargain with Yù'chén, of Sansiran's plans to marry me to her son and rule all three realms. When Hào'yáng hears the story of my drowning, fury darkens his face as I have never seen.

"I'll kill her," he says quietly.

"It awakened my . . . immortality." I stumble over the word.

"That's how I was able to escape, and that's how I was able to get to you." I run a finger over his palm. "Everything that has happened has led me back to you."

"And you chose to come back." It's a question that he doesn't ask. "After everything he did for you . . . you chose to come back."

The unspoken name lingers between us.

I trace a line on the warm sand, my fingers brushing against the little grasses and pale starflowers that grow there. I can't think of Yù'chén without that pain in my chest, and I don't know how to explain the tangle of emotions inside me just yet.

"I made my decisions when I was there because I believed it was the best way out for our realm at the time," I reply at last. "But my choice, if I'm given one, has never changed, Hào'yáng." I draw a deep, shuddering breath and lift my gaze to his. "I choose to fight to free our home from the Kingdom of Night. I choose to fight with you."

Hào'yáng's gaze sears into mine with an intensity I have never felt from him. "Thank you," he says. Then, after a pause: "I am speaking not only about kingdoms, Àn'yīng."

His words bring me back to the afternoon with Mā in my kitchen, to his confession that had changed my world.

For all of nine years.

Before I can reply, something in the currents and the air changes. On the shore, the sea begins to part, like a path forming for us.

"I believe," Hào'yáng says with a touch of wonder, "that our company is being requested." He stands. A wry grin curves his lips as he holds his hands out to me. "Our conversation can wait. The Dragon King cannot. Shall we?"

★ ★ ★

The ocean glimmers as we step onto it. Water sluices beneath our heels; curiously, our path yields no reflection of us. Sunlight appears to hit the white sand of the sea floor, and yet I have the feeling that were I to jump in, the depths of this sea would be fathomless.

Great lotuses drift past; shadows of gargantuan creatures flash beneath our feet. In the distance, clouds form, seeming to contain glints of scales and claws.

Between one step and another, a palace appears in front of us. It looks as though it's woven from the fabric of blue sky and gold sun. Pillars of mother-of-pearl and walls of the purest lapis lazuli shimmer with an ancient and timeless magic.

Ripples form on the surface of the sea as we approach the pale marble steps. Several pairs of great eyes blink at us as a dragon, then another, rises from the water, scales and teeth flashing. They watch as we climb the steps and enter the palace through golden doors.

The inside is filled with the echoes of waves. Light refracts strangely, as though we are underwater. Overhead, schools of colorful fish dart along the open-air ceilings, and crabs and lobsters cling to the pillars.

Hào'yáng leans to whisper in my ear, "Would it be a terrible time to say I'm craving seafood?"

I elbow him, holding in a laugh, but he captures my hand and slips it through his arm.

At the end of the great hall, standing before a throne resembling an oyster shell, is a man whose lower body ends in a great, serpentine dragon's tail. His face is moon-pale and elegantly beautiful, his skin aglow with the bluish light surrounding us. A smear of turquoise scales dusts his cheeks and neck, and his ears resemble fins of a fish peeking through his aquamarine hair.

"Prince of mortals." His voice stirs the waters. "Daughter of immortals."

I resist a shiver as his pale eyes fall on me. Though he wears a human face, there is nothing human in his gaze. Within is an existence that predates our knowledge of time.

Hào'yáng sinks to one knee, and I follow suit. "It is the honor of a lifetime to meet you, Dragon King of the Western Sea."

"Rise," he says, and we do. "I came as the representative of the four Dragon Kings today. Though a drop of blood of all Four Seas runs through your veins, princeling, it is my daughter who chose you as her charge at birth. Since she chose to sacrifice her fleshly body to preserve your life, it seems I must meet with you today."

Hào'yáng presses his hand to the ice pendant at his throat; the light from Meadowsweet's heart seems to pulse. "I did not deserve what she did for me," he says quietly.

"Our kind do not act upon love nor any of the moral codes upon which many beings of these realms do. We are older than this world, older than even time itself, and we will continue to exist after this world ends. Our lives are woven into the fabric of fates and destinies, spelled in the stars that only the gods can see." The Dragon King gives a slow blink. "It seems your life was an important one to save, in the piece of destiny that She of the Moon-Frosted Sea was allotted. Tell me, then, how I can help you in your quest."

"I have two asks, if I may," Hào'yáng says, and I admire his boldness in the face of a god. To my surprise, he unwinds the silver cord around his neck and cups Meadowsweet's heart in his palms. He lowers himself to both knees and bows his head as he says, "Help me save She of the Moon-Frosted Sea."

The Dragon King is silent for a long time. "A dragon takes

centuries to grow into their true form," he says at last. "She of the Moon-Frosted Sea was born in the depths of winter, when a great storm froze over the realms. She grew out of each winter's snow and the new frost of the moon throughout the years. It may be at the end of a season, it may be at the end of your life, or it may be after you are long gone when she returns."

Hào'yáng's face remains unchanged, yet I know him well enough to spot the emotion that tightens his jawline. "So long as she returns one day, even after I am gone, I will be glad for it."

Yet his words have unlocked a new, unquiet thought for me.

I clasp my hands around the front of my gown, over my heart, where my immortal powers manifested.

If I am half immortal, will I outlive Hào'yáng, and Méi'zi, and Mā? Will I watch as my loved ones grow old and vanish into the stream of time while I remain unchanged? I imagine a long existence in loneliness, with the whole world open for me to see yet no one to see it with.

"Your first ask is no ask," the Dragon King says, and the ice pendant heart of She of the Moon-Frosted Sea rises from Hào'yáng's hands and drifts toward the dais. It comes to rest on the oyster shell throne, pulsing gently. "Your second ask, then."

Hào'yáng rises, and this time, he takes my hand. I am glad for the heat of his fingers, solid and steady between my own, which have gone cold. "I ask for the allegiance of the realm of dragons in my fight to drive the Kingdom of Night out of the mortal realm."

As soon as he finishes his sentence, the waters within the palace and outside stir. Echoes of hushed, rumbling voices fill the hall as flashes of moving, serpentine forms—dragons—appear beyond the palace pillars.

The Dragon King cocks his head, his tail undulating as he

appears to listen. The dragons are speaking to each other, I realize, in a language too ancient for mortal ears. A language of oceans.

When the tides calm again and the shapes outside retreat, the Dragon King gives his response.

"Long ago, the Azure Dragon—a queen of old—crossed into the mortal realm and lay down into a long slumber. Her fleshly body became the rivers that birthed your civilization. To honor and protect humans, the dragons of the Four Seas gave a drop of blood to the first mortal emperor, thereby creating an eternal bond between the Kingdom of Rivers and the realm of dragons.

"Through the turn of dynasties and the immutable flow of time, we have watched over the land and its rulers. We are not governed by any laws of your realm nor bound by any code to do so, yet the bond between our kind and your imperial lineage has always held strong.

"And it continues to today . . . to both heirs."

Hào'yáng meets my gaze, his expression mirroring my grim understanding.

"So long as two heirs to the Kingdom of Rivers exist, the allegiance of the dragons is split." The Dragon King confirms what we've both suspected from the start. "We will not act to harm one or the other. As to what that means for you, princeling and daughter of immortals . . . I leave that to you." The Dragon King closes his eyes and inhales. "You are guests of the Dragon Kings, and so this realm is yours to enjoy. When you decide to leave, take the pearl pendants gifted to you and blow upon them, and you shall be returned to the Kingdom of Rivers."

As he speaks, the skin at my throat warms. I look down to

find a gleaming pearl strung on a silver cord resting against my collarbone. Hào'yáng, too, has one.

The waters around the Dragon King suddenly ripple. When they settle again, he, the throne, and the palace have vanished, leaving us standing on an expanse of sunlit sea.

24

Àn'yīng

The Four Seas, Realm of Dragons

Upon our return, we find that our glade has transformed. A house, its terra-cotta-tiled roof curving in a perfect replica of my home, has appeared on the white-sand beach in the shade of the great camphor trees. The wind has quieted, and the sun has shifted its angle in the hazy, dreamlike sky in a way that's reminiscent of late afternoons in Xī'lín. On the other side of the realm, stars streak the violet sky like pearl dust.

The inside of the cottage is styled with rosewood furniture and silk cushions. A grand bed with sleek turquoise sheets sits in front of a breathtaking view of the ocean, and gauze curtains hanging in the windows ripple in the warm breeze.

The beauty of this realm feels like ashes in my heart, though, with the heaviness of what we've learned.

So long as Yù'chén lives, we cannot win the war against the Kingdom of Night.

"Àn'yīng." Hào'yáng comes up behind me and turns me to face him. "Talk to me. Talk to me as you did in the days when you spoke to me through the jade pendant."

"I . . ." Words falter on my lips as I think of Yù'chén's red gaze, the crack in his voice. *I'm sorry that I can't change everything, Àn'yīng. But I swear to you, I'll do everything in my power to give you what I can of the world you wanted.*

Hào'yáng seems to sense the disquiet in my thoughts. He takes my face in his hands and says steadily, "I want to know what is in your heart, Àn'yīng, no matter what it is."

"I choose you," I whisper. "I choose peace, and I choose to fight for our realm's freedom. I choose to bring back sunlit days in my village with my family. That has never changed and never will change." I squeeze my eyes shut. "But that doesn't make this any less difficult. He saved my life. He gave me all that was within his ability, given his circumstances of birth. And . . . I loved him, Hào'yáng. I loved him, and I know what is needed to end this war, but . . ." My throat seizes. I mean to tell him that a part of me understands Yù'chén more deeply than I'll ever admit—that he was born into this life, into his bloodline and title and birthright. That he never chose to begin this war, the war that continues to rage, contingent upon his life.

"I know," Hào'yáng says softly.

"To end this war, he has to die." I force the sentence out. "Hào'yáng, Yù'chén is the reason the mó were able to break through the Kingdom of Rivers' wards in the first place. His blood ties him to that land, and they were able to create gateways in. If he is crowned emperor, it's likely those gateways will become permanent, merging the two realms together. He is the reason the dragons cannot choose a side, the reason the land cannot accept you as emperor."

There is only one way this can all end. One way we will win this war.

Yù'chén must die.

Hào'yáng tips my chin up. "We focus on the next steps for now," he says. "We haven't secured the backing of the dragons, but you still have your claim upon Lady Shī'yǎ's title and army. We make for the Kingdom of Sky next—as was our initial plan."

I recognize the way his expression shifts into one of quiet calculation. It has been weeks since the Kingdom of Night breached the Kingdom of Sky; we have no information about the state of the war and no way to contact anyone there. Returning to the immortal realm is like stepping into a tiger's lair.

"It will be difficult," Hào'yáng says. His head is tilted, his eyes have a faraway look—and I know he is contemplating strategy, running through a dozen different approaches and scenarios in his mind. "We'll need to spend tomorrow planning."

"Tomorrow," I agree.

Hào'yáng studies me for a moment. "Something else is bothering you."

I glance up sharply, surprised that he's read me so thoroughly. Survivor's instinct has trained me to hold my fears and vulnerabilities close to my heart. Sharing anything other than hard determination felt like a weakness, and yet . . . as I look up at the face of my boy in the jade, confiding in him comes to me naturally.

"When the Dragon King spoke of dragons' true forms and how it may take centuries for She of the Moon-Frosted Sea to return, I thought of myself." My voice feels tight, but I keep going. Keep pushing myself to open my heart to him, one word at a time. "Sansiran's act opened my full immortal powers. I don't know where the mortal part of me ends and the immortal part begins. I don't know if that means I have a long life ahead of me now." I swallow. "I am afraid, Hào'yáng, of being in this world once everyone I love is gone."

"Few mortals reincarnate," Hào'yáng says, "and despite being heir to our kingdom, the rules will apply to me as well. In these realms, all is ephemeral, even across an immortal lifetime. I don't know what will happen tomorrow, or if I will live past the end of the week." His gaze softens. "What I do know, Àn'yīng, is that I would spend this lifetime with you, whether as your friend or your companion or your ally or whatever you wish us to be." He smiles and tucks a strand of my hair behind my ear. "So long as I can be by your side."

I draw a deep breath. "And I think," I say steadily, "that you owe me the whole truth."

I lead him to the rosewood dining table, where a meal is set out for us. In silence, I pour tea into two cups fashioned out of seashells.

I look up at Hào'yáng expectantly.

He takes a sip from his own cup, then sets it down. "The whole truth," he says, and his face settles into that look of concentration I've seen so often on him. "Last time, I told you the story of your father pulling me from the rubble of my home and taking me to the immortal realm.

"I arrived broken, lost, a shell of who I'd been. I'd just watched my family die before my eyes, and I had failed my people and my realm. I had no idea what my future looked like—if I even had one at all. The loss and the shame of it all nearly killed me. I remember sitting down for my first meal in the Kingdom of Sky, dressed in fabric woven from the clouds and glinting with sunlight, surrounded by the immortals I had heard of in stories, beings I'd only dared hope I would glimpse once in my lifetime . . . and I wanted to disappear from this world. The real cruelty of death is the suffering it causes the living."

He stares at a spot on the table. I want to reach back out through time and hold his hand—the hand of the young heir who had lost his kingdom and the child who had lost his entire family.

"Then one day, Lady Shī'yǎ brought me something: a broken jade pendant with jagged edges. She told me that inside was a little girl who would need my help, and that I had to stay strong for her." A smile flits across Hào'yáng's lips. "I thought she was lying to me, that she had made up some silly story for my benefit—so I threw the pendant across my chambers and left it there.

"That is, until one day, I heard a voice speaking from the other side."

A shudder breaks through me. I can hear myself as though it were just yesterday; I can see the wink of my pendant in the moonlight, smell Méi'zi's hair as she dozed curled up against me, taste the fear and despair pressing against me in those early days as Mā lay unmoving on our couch. *Help me*, I whispered to the stone, because I had nothing else to hold on to and no one else to ask. *Please. Someone.*

"I picked up the pendant, certain I was hallucinating—but there you were." Hào'yáng smiles. "You were so thin, and so pale in the moonlight. You were nine or ten, just a year or so younger than me—but you looked as though you had survived a living nightmare. The way you gazed into the pendant . . . it was as though you were looking into my soul. Pleading for my help.

"I spoke to it, but I realized you couldn't hear me—so I did the only thing I could think of. I picked up my brush, and I wrote back. I wrote the first thing that came to mind."

" '*I am here,*' " I whisper.

" 'I am here,' " Hào'yáng echoes softly. "And then you continued to talk to me. I realized that, though I could see you and hear you, you could only read the words I wrote back to you.

"I felt something I hadn't in a long time: A sense of purpose. And a knowing that I was fortunate to be safe and alive and fed in a realm away from the nightmare that mine had become. That countless others—my people—were suffering and struggling to stay alive.

"You saved my life that night. I realized how much of a coward I'd been, how selfish and weak. So I began to train. I spent every waking hour training with the Kingdom of Sky disciples. I promised myself that even as a mortal, I would become the best warrior of them all."

"And you did," I say softly. "You became captain of the guard."

He doesn't match my smile. "Because of you, Ǎn'yīng. Everything I did was because of you. Because I told myself that one day, I would be strong enough to return to my kingdom, that I would find you, my girl in the jade, and I would liberate our realm."

I'm breathless with this confession. This truth, this affirmation, that I'd been seeking from him for so long.

"And somewhere along the way," Hào'yáng continues, his gaze soft, sunlit as it finds me, "I fell in love with you. From telling you how to fish and hunt to laughing when you slipped and fell in the pond . . . teaching you to spar and use your blades and draw talismans . . . I fell in love with you. With your bravery, your protectiveness, your loyalty, and your ferocity.

"When the light lotuses began to die and you were strong enough, I told you about the Immortality Trials. I was almost ready to return to the mortal realm and claim the throne by then; Lady Shī'yǎ had planned this with me early on, to save your family and enlist your help once more. But a part of me longed to see you for entirely selfish reasons, more than anything else I have ever wanted in this lifetime.

"When you fell in the ocean at the Immortals' Steps, I broke a sacred rule of the Trials and flew with Meadowsweet to save you. And when I first met you, at the edge of the Celestial Gardens, I felt as though I had been waiting for that moment for half my lifetime. I wanted to tell you everything then—all be damned, I wished to break every rule of those nonsensical trials for you. But Lady Shī'yǎ had asked me to first ensure that you *wanted* to help us. So I needed to get close to you without revealing who I was.

"But I heard the candidates speak of rumors that you had a lover among them." His gaze falls to the sand. "I also knew that the entire reason you were there, the reason your family was torn apart and you needed the pill of immortality that was the prize in the trials . . . was because of me. I had taken your place in the Kingdom of Sky, I had grown up safe and healthy while you were out there fighting for your life each day, and I realized I didn't deserve you. I told myself that so long as you were happy, you should be with whomever you wished, live your life however you wanted—and I would be content with watching you from the side, keeping you safe, and loving you in silence." Finally, he lifts his eyes again to meet mine. "And that still holds true."

The rest of the world has faded. The sun, the water, the trees, the flowers . . . nothing else exists in this moment but me and my boy in the jade.

Hào'yáng is the sun in my life. The golden strokes on my jade pendant, always there, always steady and reassuring and offering me comfort and warmth. Until the day he nearly vanished forever, I never realized how much of my life he had touched.

I hold his gaze. "I think," I begin, and he goes very still, watching me with an unwavering gaze, "that I have been searching for you my entire life."

Hào'yáng's lips part.

"And I think I realized too late," I continue, "the night I almost lost you, that I cannot bear to live in a world without you."

He exhales sharply. His eyes flicker with a torrent of emotions that I know he buries beneath that cool exterior, and I see Hào'yáng, the boy in the jade and the man I have come to love, rather than the captain or the guard or the heir.

"You saved me when I was most broken and in need of a light in the darkness," I whisper, my voice cracking now at the memory of those dark days. "All along, you were there for me, expecting nothing in return. You have been my friend, my guardian, and the one closest to my soul."

"And I always will be," Hào'yáng says, and presses something into my palm.

"My handkerchief," I breathe. The silk is soft in my hands, slightly worn, yet an inexplicable sense of comfort and hope knots in my throat. "You kept it."

"Àn'yīng." The way he speaks my name makes me look up at him. "I've never said any of this because I was afraid to put pressure on you. Afraid that it wasn't what you wanted. But today, I'm going to be a selfish man." Hào'yáng's gaze suddenly churns with the strength of an ocean, sweeping me into it without hope of resisting. "You told me the night after your first hunt, after you swapped your needles for your blades, that you'd always dreamt of seeing the ocean. Of seeing the rest of the realm and embroidering it."

I nod, my throat tight. I don't trust myself with words right now.

"I want to be the one to take you to see all the oceans. I want to be the one you see this world with. Our realm, and all the realms; what the sunrise looks like in each, what the wind feels like, and what the water tastes like." Hào'yáng cups my chin in his palm. "I never wanted to marry you simply for a political alliance. In all of nine years, the certainty has only grown clearer to me. I want to spend this lifetime with you."

Beyond our cottage, the seawater surges into a roar. Something clatters onto the table: my lotus sword, in the form of a hairpin. I last tucked it into a pocket in my bodice; I have the strangest feeling that it is no coincidence that it fell out.

I pick it up and hand it to Hào'yáng. His expression grows distant for several heartbeats as he stares at the most precious belonging of the woman who raised him.

Then he looks up at me. "May I?" he asks.

In our culture, a young woman wearing a hairpin signifies her transition from childhood into womanhood, from a girl to a married woman.

Unbidden, a memory surges in my mind again—Yù'chén, watching me with sorrow darkening his eyes right before I stepped through the gate.

I cannot live a life of what-ifs and impossibilities, of regrets and guilt. Loving him as I once did destroyed my home; allowing myself to feel anything for him was born of necessity. Caring for him danced on the edges of a most tender pain and a promised fall.

Loving Hào'yáng is like being swept forward by the currents of a river, to a destiny as clear and as bright as the sun.

I meet his gaze now.

"Marry me," I whisper. "Marry me now, under the Heavenly Order, with the skies as our witness."

Hào'yáng's eyes dart between mine. Searching. A smile spreads over his face, as slow and radiant as a sunrise. "Àn'yīng," he murmurs. "I can think of no greater joy in this life than to take you as my wife, my partner, and my other half."

The skies seem to brighten, as though the Heavens perceive us in this moment.

"And I take you," I say softly, "as my husband, my partner, and my companion in everything this lifetime has to offer."

Hào'yáng stands and rounds the table, kneeling before me. The heat of his body envelops me as he reaches over my shoulders to loosen my braid. The white ribbons I have worn for the past nine years fall to the sands as my hair sweeps over my shoulders. Hào'yáng slides the lotus hairpin into my hair.

Then he takes my hands in his. "Àn'yīng," he says. "I promise to make memories with you across each and every realm so that, even after I am gone, you have them to hold on to until you arrive at where destiny will take you next."

I don't want to imagine life without his steady warmth by my side. Was this how Lady Shī'yǎ felt when she loved my mortal father?

And yet . . . she still chose love.

Hào'yáng kisses my cheek, and then the other, heartbreakingly gentle. I close my eyes, breathing in his familiar scent, savoring this feeling of having found a home in his arms.

Then Hào'yáng's lips find mine, a soft feather's brush—and I lean forward, deepening the kiss. I sweep my tongue against his, breathing in his scent and relishing the heat of his body. Feeling as though I am at once discovering something new and also coming home.

Hào'yáng inhales deeply. His hands clench on my hips, and with a decisive move, he lifts me from my chair and carries me to the bed. He sits, shifting me onto his lap so I am flush against him.

I make a small sound of surprise, and he responds with a deep, rumbling chuckle, the corners of his mouth tugging up as he holds me tighter. As I feel him straining against me and my body responding with the same urgency, I pull back from my boy in the jade and hold his face, gazing into the eyes of the man he has become, this lover I have found in him.

I shift against him, tangling my legs in his, ablaze with sensation. The smile falls from his lips, and his face sharpens, the intensity of his eyes and desire focused on me. His hands move up my rib cage, pausing at my collarbone, lingering at the buttons of my gown.

A question.

I slide my hand beneath his. Then, slowly, one by one, I undo the buttons until I reach my waist. I twine my fingers through his and slide his palm beneath the silks.

He inhales sharply, his chest rising and falling unevenly and his pupils dilating as he watches my movement. I guide his hand down to my navel, little shivers running through me as his calluses scrape the softest parts of my skin.

I peel back my dress, baring my shoulders, then my arms, until it falls to my waist. Hào'yáng draws a deep breath, his eyes roving down every inch of my exposed body.

"Àn'yīng," he says, reaching up to touch my hair, where my hairpin gleams. "You're *radiant*." The way he says it makes me shiver with pleasure, and even more so as his mouth finds my jawline, tracing up to nip at my ear. "I don't know how many times I've imagined this."

"Oh?" I tease, drawing back and arching a brow, but my voice is slightly breathless. "The honorable heir and dutiful captain, imagining such things?"

His eyes narrow as he smiles. "I am a man, Àn'yīng" is all he says before he kisses me again, and all the clever retorts vanish from my mind. His mouth trails the curve of my neck, and I arc back as he pauses, lower, to savor me, his tongue wringing sensation from every inch of my skin. He moves to the flat planes of my stomach, and I wrap my body around his, losing myself in the heat of his muscles and the thrum of power from his core.

I tug a hand through his hair, wanting this, wanting more, wanting to be as close to him as possible.

Gently, he turns us and splays me against the bed, then his fingers are at my waist, undoing the rest of my buttons and tugging my dress off. Cool air kisses my bare skin as he draws back, his gaze roving down my body, my skin, taking in the scars, the burns from when I first learned to cook, the shape of my ribs and the flatness of my belly.

Then he brings his hand to my leg and touches me, skin and scars and all. I let him, our breaths soft and tangling in the light as he explores my every curve and dip and sharp angle.

"You're the most beautiful person I've ever met," he whispers.

I raise an eyebrow, suppressing a shiver at his words. "Even more than the immortals you've spent half your life around?" I wonder if he has had immortal lovers, wonder if he is comparing me to their perfection.

"I've only ever wanted you," he says with a sincerity that sets my stomach aflutter. "I've never . . ."

I reach up and capture his mouth with mine, pulling him down with me as my fingers work his buttons and slip off his robe. "You've never?" I tease in between kisses; feel the huff of his laugh as he draws back and flicks my nose. His grin flickers, however, when I wrap my legs around him and draw him close to me. "I want to see you lose control today," I tease, and his fingers tighten against me.

"Wicked wife of mine," he concedes, "I've never been able to control myself very well around you."

I push the hair from his face, holding his gaze as I arch into him. His breathing goes shallow and his muscles clench as he holds himself over me, his body warming mine in the cool ocean breeze. The setting sun paints his features in shades of gold and coral, his eyes in a deep, warm brown, and everything—everything—about him feels familiar and right and fills me with a feeling of safety and contentedness I haven't known in years. I wrap my arms around him as I wished to when we were children, clinging onto hope and onto comfort and onto life, and now he fills the empty spaces within me in a new way. I watch as he unravels from that cool exterior he wears as heir, captain, and guard, as his careful control finally slips and he yields completely to me. As I hold him and give myself to the tides that build and break inside me, I close my eyes and imagine his love filling me with light, and in this moment, I am the sun, I am the sea, and I am hope.

★ ★ ★

We remain tangled on the silken sheets, gazing at each other, until twilight blooms and a cool breeze pulls in from the sea, smelling of salt. In our chambers, lanterns flicker on with the magic of this realm, their warmth chasing away the shadows. Outside, the flowering trees whisper and the spring murmurs, and it feels as though the world has fallen away and it's just the two of us.

"Tell me the first moment you fell in love with me." I snuggle close to Hào'yáng, loving the heat of his body and his arms as he holds me.

Hào'yáng feeds me a piece of fruit that appeared with an entire tray of dinner upon platters made of large shells. The fruit isn't anything I've ever tasted in the mortal realm: the size of a peach, the insides soft and succulent, sweetness combined with a briny taste that renders it delicious. "Sea fruit," he says, catching my wonder, and then leans back with a grin. "What do I get for revealing my secrets?"

I eat another piece of sea fruit from his fingers. "A kiss, for every question of mine that you answer."

Hào'yáng wipes a spot of juice from my chin. "Then I'll answer your questions into eternity," he says with such innocent sincerity that I roll my eyes. "Do you remember the first day you caught a rabbit and had to butcher it? You were kneeling out in your garden with your knife and sobbing as you spoke to me through the pendant. I was glad you couldn't see me then, because I was certain you'd hate me for laughing."

I glare at him. "*That* was the moment you fell for me?"

"Or that time when you found a bush of blueberries in the

forest," he continues. "You told me you would be selfish and take just two before bringing them home: one to savor for yourself, and another so you could use its juices to draw warts on your face."

"I threatened that if you didn't show your face, I would think of you as a warty old man." I'm giggling.

"Mm," Hào'yáng says, pulling me against him. "And how do you feel about having married said warty old man and owing him two kisses now?"

I flick his forehead. "Continue."

His eyes have a faraway look, and that ghost of a smile plays on his lips. "The first day you started training again and tripped over your own feet. You sat in the dust and burst into tears."

I flip over and hide my face beneath a pillow. "Those are all such *silly* memories of me! Be glad I couldn't see you, because you probably *were* warty."

"I was handsome enough for the mortal bards to sing of me back in the days." Hào'yáng ducks as I throw the pillow at him, then captures my wrists in his hands. "Those memories of you showed me that you weren't infallible. That you, too, had your weaknesses."

I scoff. "Why do you want to remember my weaknesses?"

"Because you are brave in spite of them," he replies, and I grow still. "You didn't want to kill the rabbit, but you still did it—to make stew to feed your mother and sister. You wanted to eat the entire bush of berries, but you only took two for yourself—and brought the rest back to Xī'lín for your family and neighbors. You tripped into the dust during your training— but you got back up, Àn'yīng. When your father asked you to put away your needles and silks for your crescent blades, you did, and you never looked back." Hào'yáng's gaze burns into mine. "I love you because of that. Because of *all* that—your strengths *and* your vulnerabilities." He moves a strand of hair out of my eyes and then thumbs away the tears that have gathered at their corners. "And I'm fighting to return you to a world where you *can* cry over a rabbit, where you can eat as many berries as you like, and where you can have both your blades and your needles—whichever you please. I want you as you are now, but I also want the girl I first met, the girl who wished to sew oceans . . . should you wish to remember her."

I can't remember ever feeling this understood, feeling like someone has taken the walls *I* have spent all these years building around myself, knocked them down, and pulled out the girl I long ago buried deep inside.

"I think," I whisper, catching his hand, "that in the years I have spent shaping myself into someone . . . infallible, I left the girl who sewed oceans locked away. I didn't think this was a world where I could be both."

"I remember that girl," Hào'yáng says gently, pressing a palm to my cheek. "We can find her again once this is all over. Together."

I lean forward and press a kiss to his mouth.

Hào'yáng pulls me to him. "Now," he says, "about those kisses . . ."

25

Àn'yīng

Realm of Dragons

When the sky darkens and evening deepens into night, we rise to dine on platters of sea fruit and steamed fish and soups to replenish life energies. Then, seated at the elegant rosewood table in the living room of this house, we plan. The magic of this realm has gifted us with cups of steaming tea that refill with each sip, as well as parchment, ink, and brushes.

"The Temple of Dawn is the only part of the Kingdom of Sky where the wards will admit mortals," Hào'yáng says. He's bent over the parchment, sketching out a map of the kingdom. I lean forward, observing the fine lines on his face, the way his brows crease and his expression is wiped clear of any emotion but cool concentration. "I must enter through there."

I glance up sharply. " 'I'?"

He doesn't stop his work, his wrists flicking in elegant motions as he writes. "You're half immortal, Àn'yīng. The wards may let you through no matter where you enter."

"Or they may stop me," I counter. "I'm only half immortal. A halfling." I pause at the word, at the inevitable memory of the one it conjures. "What are you suggesting—that we split up?"

"The Temple of Dawn is the place where the Kingdom of Night first breached the Kingdom of Sky's wards. It's their stronghold in that realm. It will be the riskiest point of entry."

"And you're going to try it? By yourself, and without Meadowsweet this time?"

Hào'yáng looks at me now. "I don't see that I have much of a choice."

"Absolutely not." I hold his stare. "You're the entire reason we can still fight for our realm, Hào'yáng. Your life must be protected at all costs."

"And you are our cause's only chance to rally an army, Àn'yīng," he shoots back, and then sighs. "The point is, we do not have a choice. I failed to obtain the dragons' allegiance. I have no army, no support, and no way to get a message to my former allies. I need to do this myself."

I straighten suddenly, pressing a hand to my wrist. At first, I don't feel anything—but a moment later comes a sensation like a soft brush of fur against my skin. "We might have allies yet," I say, and I tell Hào'yáng about how Lì'líng left one of her tails with me before we parted ways.

Hào'yáng looks faintly amused. "I've heard stories of nine-tailed fox spirits leaving one of their tails behind. They say that tail always makes it back to them." He taps his brush against his chin. "If we have Lì'líng and Tán'mù and a few of the former Immortality Trials candidates, that gives us a lot more resources to leverage."

"At least a few of them would need to remain with my

family and the villagers," I say, "but even half of them would be enough for your protection."

Hào'yáng stops tapping his brush as he realizes what I'm getting at.

"Even if the wards do admit me, the warriors are mortal and can't go through them with me," I say. "You would all have to go through the Temple of Dawn, as mortals did during the Immortality Trials. Which is why I have a proposition."

A wary look crosses his face, and he resumes the tapping of his brush as he says, "Go on."

I lean forward. "I go into the Kingdom of Sky first, alone. I claim my title and army as Lady Shī'yǎ's daughter. And I bring word to your immortal allies that you're ready to fight. Meanwhile, you remain in the Kingdom of Rivers and make for the Western Province to find Lì'líng, Tán'mù, and rally our troops. Together, you travel to the Kūn'lún Mountains, where you can access the gateways to other realms to seek alliances. We all meet back in the Central Province, at Xī'lín, ready to march on the Imperial City and take it back from the mó."

We stare at each other from across the table.

"It's the most logical and efficient approach," I press.

"I understand that, Àn'yīng," Hào'yáng says calmly, "which is why I'm trying to think of a more logical and efficient approach than sending you into the tiger's lair alone."

I raise an eyebrow. A challenge. "And?"

"And you're right. This is the most logical and efficient approach."

"Then we proceed with this strategy."

He presses the tip of his brush against his lip, eyes narrowing slightly as he continues staring at me. "You," he says slowly, "have boxed me in with no way out."

"I had the impression you prioritized logic and calculation."

"When it comes to you, I can't," he replies sharply, putting down his brush and turning his face to the windows. An ocean breeze stirs the gauze drapes, spilling starlight into pools at our feet. It's several heartbeats until he speaks again, his voice quiet. "Your mother had foresight. She predicted a life like this for me: always needing to choose between kingdom and love."

"Hào'yáng," I say, and something in my tone pulls his gaze back to me. "It was never your choice. It is mine. For half my life, I've been trying to stay alive; the choices I made were all just to survive." I reach for his hand, and his grip is tight, his stare unwavering. "When I met you and Lady Shī'yǎ, a different choice opened to me. A choice to do more than just survive; a choice to *fight*. I'm choosing that today.

"I know why Lady Shī'yǎ's lotus would not answer to me before. I was afraid and uncertain. But when I watched my village burn down . . . when Mā and Méi'zi escaped the jaws of death . . . when I thought I'd lost you"—my voice breaks—"something inside me snapped. And I knew I would rather go down fighting than turn my back on this war again."

Hào'yáng's eyes soften. "Come here," he says quietly, pulling me toward him. When I round the table, he draws me into his lap. I drape my wrists over his shoulders, marveling at how I feel so at home with his touch.

His eyes rove my face, and he takes my chin in his hand. "I agree to proceed with your strategy."

I grin. "Then teach me everything I need to know about the Kingdom of Sky—about your allies and their hideaways, about how the immortals conduct their affairs and how the rules work in that realm—so I may claim my title and army."

We strategize deep into the night. He fills parchment after

parchment with maps of the Kingdom of Sky, lists of all the immortals whose support he and Lady Shǐ'yǎ gathered over the years. For his part of the plan, we sketch out maps of the mortal realm, the path to the Western Province and, deep within, the fabled Kūn'lún Mountains, said to hold gateways to so many other lands: the Realm of Phoenixes, the Realm of Flower Fairies, and more.

When the moon is high in the sky and we have recorded every last detail of our plan, he carries me to our bed. We make love to the song of the tides and the silvery glow of the moon, then lie tangled beneath the starlight and trade stories of the moments in each other's lives that we missed over the past ten years. And when we fall asleep in each other's arms, I find myself hoping fervently that we'll have a lifetime of nights like this.

At the crack of dawn, we rise. A meal sits on our dining table: sweet wine-soaked prawns and scallops, abalone soup, and braised bass, accompanied by fresh spring water. Hào'yáng and I break our fast as the sun rises over the horizon.

I left the white dress Méi'zi gifted me back in Xī'lín, but the replica that the magic of this realm conjured for me comes with fitted straps for my crescent blades—the ones that remain. Most significantly, there's a samite belt, onto which I strap my lotus sword.

The sky is waking when Hào'yáng comes to me and presses a kiss to my forehead. "Ready?" he says against my hair.

"Ready," I reply. Together, we grasp the pearl necklaces gifted to us by the Dragon King and blow on them.

A sudden wind gusts outside, stirring the blossoms and great camphors. The sound of rushing water fills the air, and ocean currents begin to seep through the cracks of the doors, pooling across our floor. As the water rises, the floorboards beneath turn to sand and kelp. I wrap my arms around Hào'yáng as the water laps over our knees, then our waists. Fish dart past our ankles, and when the waves reach our necks, we take deep breaths and let them submerge us completely.

The chambers, the furniture, the table upon which we took our meals and the bed upon which we slept—it's all gone, swept away by the rush of water. I taste salt, and when I look up, it's no longer the ceiling of our house but the distant surface of an ocean. Far away, sunlight glints.

Together we swim against the currents. When we finally break through the surface, we gulp down fresh, brine-laced air, and I can tell immediately that we have left the Realm of Dragons.

Now the water is dark, the sun is pale behind shifting clouds, and the air is cold and woven with winter's breath. Everything is a little less saturated in color, a little less radiant and perfect.

But it's home.

Here, too, it's dawn. A cliff wall rises before us, so high that it vanishes into fog. Out on the sea behind us, a series of stone pillars soar skyward, vanishing into distant clouds that loom over the horizon.

When the realization hits me, I let out a startled laugh.

"The Immortals' Steps," I say to Hào'yáng. "I crossed these to reach the Temple of Dawn for the Trials. They're also known as the Dragons' Pass." So the myths are true—they *do* lead to the Realm of Dragons. I look down at the water we tread, dark and flecked with foam, and I think I can make out a faint aquamarine glow, the glint of scales, or the flash of a golden palace deep, deep down . . .

I tear my gaze away and crane my neck up at the Immortals' Steps, then at the impossibly high cliff wreathed with fog. On the other side of that fog is Heavens' Gates, the mountain range that marks the end of the mortal realm. The one I crossed months ago to enter the Immortality Trials.

Fitting that the end should begin at the place where everything started.

I hold on tightly to Hào'yáng as he summons a great wave that lifts us upward. When we emerge from the fog, we're back in the Kingdom of Rivers.

I recognize the clifftop we alight on, the expanse of rock covered in pines. The last time I was here, the sun was shining as I turned and gazed, for the first time, at the far-off palaces of the immortal realm.

I was here with Yù'chén.

Now the distant skies roil with storm clouds; fog churns restlessly beneath us, obscuring our view of the Four Seas. I search the horizon for the silhouettes of mountains drifting in the skies, for the curving golden rooftops and pearlescent walls of the entry to the Kingdom of Sky.

I find nothing.

"The last time I was here was when I was twelve years old," Hào'yáng says quietly. He glances at me. "It was with your father."

I turn to him, hungry for any kernel of a story about my father. "You never told me this."

He searches through the thick clouds for a sign of the sun. We agreed to begin our plan after dawn, when the mó are winding down from their peak of power. "I had just lost everything and witnessed the death of my entire family. I was so, so tired, Àn'yīng . . . and when I reached Heavens' Gates and realized there was still an entire ocean to cross, I couldn't keep going. I didn't want to.

"Your father turned to me then and he said, 'You can either stop here and give up—or grit your teeth and continue on. We mortals have one chance at life, my prince. So long as you live, you are not forsaking your family and your people. One day at a time. Step by step, by putting one foot before the other.'"

My breath catches. "You said those words to me once," I whisper.

"I wanted you to hear your father's words. The words he gave me that helped me live—I wanted you to have them as well."

I hold his hands tightly, and I know from the way he grips mine that he does not want to let go.

Neither do I.

I step back and tap my wrist three times.

Hào'yáng's brows rise when the small fox tail appears like a furry white bracelet. It stirs lazily, as though emerging from a long sleep—and then gives a little wriggle in his direction, like a wave.

"Lì'líng?" Hào'yáng greets it curiously.

I give the tail a soothing stroke and then gently unwind it from my wrist. Then I press it into Hào'yáng's palm.

"Come find us soon," I whisper to it. It brushes my nose in a reassuring way, and I imagine Lì'líng's laughing amber eyes.

I really hope I see her again.

I place my palm against Hào'yáng's cheek. He wraps his arms around me and pulls me to him with a sudden, desperate ferocity. When we step apart, his face is open, emotions racing across it like a tempest.

I raise my hands, and the iridescent cloud of my spirit

energies forms. It twines around my body, then pools at my feet.

I step on.

"Àn'yīng." Hào'yáng catches my hand. We're both at a loss for words, for how can one hope to capture a lifetime of words in a single sentence? "I'll be there soon," he says, and I nod and let go.

The clifftop falls away beneath me as I rise into the air, my body reacting to every shift of the current as though I have become a part of the wind. That same rosy-gold glow dances beneath my skin, pouring out into the cloud that lifts my body as I will it.

I head down into the mist, following the shadows of the Immortals' Steps that loom out of the fog every once in a while.

It isn't long before I reach the Sea of Clouds. The skies, once clear and blue, are now a churning gray that laps at the borders of the Kingdom of Sky. Shadows swirl around me. In the absolute silence, the sounds of my breathing and my pounding heartbeat fill my ears.

A screech cuts through the clouds, followed by the sound of rapid wingbeats. I draw my lotus sword. Its glow is dim in the encroaching dark, but it brings me comfort.

Like this, I can see.

Like this, others can see *me*.

As though in answer, a gentle light pulses from somewhere ahead.

The wards.

I surge forward, and sure enough, there they are: tall and shimmering like sunlight on water. Strangely, where they used to be translucent, the other side is now dark, as though someone has pulled down the shutters on the entire realm.

Dread blooms in me. Just how far has the Kingdom of Night advanced into the immortal realm?

Nothing stirs around me as I draw up before the wards. The last time I stood this close to one was with Yù'chén. I distinctly remember those red scorpion lilies blooming, dangerously beautiful, as he opened his gates.

I draw a deep breath and plunge my hand through.

I feel only a brush of air against my skin . . . and then I'm through.

Hào'yáng was right: The wards sensed my immortal half and accepted me.

Soft light greets me as the unnatural darkness of the wards lifts and the Kingdom of Sky yawns open before me: a landscape of clouds drifting amidst floating mountains and flowering gardens. From here, the immortal realm looks as beautiful and untouched as when I left it. Curved rooftops peek out from forests of blooming wisteria; towns and villages are scattered throughout weaving bodies of water and undulating valleys suspended in the sky. The sun is hidden somewhere beyond the clouds, lending a dim golden haze to the scene.

I glance back at the wards, curious as to why they'd appeared dark from the outside—and my blood runs cold.

In the spot where I entered, the flow of the wards has frozen. Growing fast are roses as black as night, their thorny stems twisting and spreading like an ink stain on parchment.

Without warning, a vine lashes out at me, lunging for my wrist. I jerk back, but not before one of its thorns pricks my skin.

I reel through the air, my iridescent cloud shifting faster in my panic. Pain flares in my forearm. From somewhere nearby comes a monstrous shriek and the sound of rapidly approaching wingbeats.

I raise my lotus sword.

The first hellbeast shoots out of the clouds like a shadowy arrow. All I catch is a streak of darkness and blazing red eyes before it is upon me.

I swerve, swinging my sword, but it becomes clear how ill-matched I am, even with my newfound powers, against a hellbeast. My coordination of flight upon my cloud is clumsy, like learning to move with a new limb; my skills with a sword are unrefined compared to my prowess with my blades. As I miss the creature again, I'm thrown off balance. I spin through the air, barely turning in time to catch the glint of sharp teeth and razor claws.

I dodge, letting myself fall, buying myself time—and as I do, I swap my weapons. My sword shrinks into the lotus hairpin; with a flick of my wrists, the hairpin is tucked safely in my sleeves . . . and my crescent blades Fleet and Striker are in my hands.

A blur of darkness overhead, and the next moment the creature is upon me. Its wing slams me solidly in the ribs. I grit my teeth at the pain and latch onto one of its wings, Fleet propelling my movements faster than the eye can see.

I rip Fleet through its wings, satisfied when I'm rewarded with the hellbeast's earsplitting scream. Then I haul myself onto its back and plunge Striker through its head, where its core should be.

I let go as the creature begins to disintegrate into the shadows and ichor of its makeup, undone by the fatal wound I've dealt it. The last to go are its blazing red eyes and the ghost of its snarl as it fades into nothing but dust and ash.

Then there is only silence.

The second hellbeast strikes out of nowhere.

One moment, I'm in the air; the next, I'm falling, my stomach twisting with vertigo as the world turns into a blur of gray clouds and cold, sharp winds. I can smell the rotten stench of the beast's breath, see the saliva dripping down its dagger-length fangs. As the creature wraps its claws around my ribs, I yield to its embrace.

And plunge Striker between its blazing red eyes, into its core.

The creature screams—and a new, white-hot pain blazes through my forearm. My fingers spasm, and to my horror, Striker tumbles from my grasp and into the darkness below.

"*No!*" The cry wrenches from me. Overhead, the hellbeast's corporeal form disintegrates.

I twist as I fall, reaching out for Striker in the air. But my crescent blade is already gone, a speck of silver against the dark—before the shadows swallow it whole.

Another flash of pain lances through my left arm, and I find I can't move, can't breathe, as I plunge through the cloud-smothered skies of the immortal realm down, down toward certain death.

Only . . . there is a shift in the clouds around me. A great silhouette appears overhead; from the distance comes a rumble of laughter. A single white feather twirls through the sky. It stretches, and when it's as large as a hammock, it suddenly dips beneath me.

I land on fluffy white down.

The clouds part. A great crane with a red crown glides gracefully overhead, and seated on its back, grinning at me with a hand raised in greeting, is . . .

"Honorable Immortal Jǐng'xiù?" I croak in disbelief, wondering if I'm hallucinating.

The immortal gives me a cheery wave with the bejeweled

bamboo scepter he always wielded to amplify his voice as he spoke to us in the Temple of Dawn during the Immortality Trials.

The great feather soars up, depositing me on the back of his crane. "Hello again, Number Forty-Four," he booms, and then chortles at my expression. "Never thought you'd see me again? Or, rather, never *wanted* to see me again, I presume?"

He's right on both counts, but of course, I don't say that as I pull myself into a sitting position. The pain flares again in my wrist and I wince, but Jǐng'xiù appears not to notice. He looks unchanged, as all immortals are: his face handsome and ageless, long black hair and beard flowing neatly beneath his imperial cap, and official robes blazing red and gold. Legends say that he was once a mortal general distantly related to the imperial bloodline before he began cultivating his powers to cross into the immortal realm and earn eternal life.

"Thank you," I manage, but that only makes him laugh harder.

"Only you would be grappling with one of those hellbeasts and trying to stab it instead of running away, my dear," Jǐng'xiù says.

His levity irritates me, just as it did the first time I met him at the Temple of Dawn, when he tried to disqualify me for barely finishing the First Trial.

"Oh, don't look so furious, child. Be glad you're alive—unlike many others."

The solemnity of his words lowers my defenses enough to ask, "Who else is with you?"

"You'll find out soon enough." Jǐng'xiù's smile fades slightly, and his gaze slides to my left arm. The wounds where the rose thorns punctured my skin have turned black. "You're injured. Unfortunately, healing that kind of a wound goes beyond my abilities. We'll have to see what tricks Cǎi'hé has in their basket."

Slowly, the adrenaline seeps from my body, and I'm left with exhaustion and a faint, tingling pain in my arm. I nestle into the soft white feathers of the crane, its wings and the heat of its body shielding me from the cold. I hold Fleet tightly to my chest, the image of Striker plunging into the darkness fresh in my mind. And as the immortal and I soar deeper into his realm, I wonder if becoming immortal means losing more and more pieces of the human girl I once was.

26

Àn'yīng

Kingdom of Sky

As we fly, we keep to the clouds, sometimes briefly skimming between them so I'm able to catch glimpses of the realm.

I've never been far beyond the Temple of Dawn or the drifting island with the great camphor tree where Hào'yáng and I used to train. Now, as I soar deeper into the Kingdom of Sky on the back of Jǐng'xiù's crane, the immortal realm reveals its vastness to me . . . as well as the ravages inflicted upon it by the war.

Where sunlight once struck everything like molten gold, a cold shadow now lingers over the land, as though the realm is in a permanent state of twilight. We pass plumes of black smoke, delicate floating towns burnt to ashes, and flower gardens trampled to ruins. Worse are the pockets of darkness that swallow the landscape around them; we can see nothing at all of what is inside.

The red-crowned crane is careful to steer away from those areas.

"How bad is it?" I ask.

"The Kingdom of Night caught us unawares." Jǐng'xiù's tone is solemn as he follows my gaze over his realm. "More than half our armies have been lost to the war—and more troops are dying with each passing day. The mó have taken control of our wards; none may enter or leave without their knowledge, as you have just discovered. They have rounded us up like fish in a net. As the Kingdom of Night's grasp extends over both the mortal realm and this, its power grows and so, too, does that of its soldiers." He cants his head to the distant sun, almost sunken beneath clouds. "We immortals are beings of light. With the ever-growing dark, our power wanes. When our armies began to be overpowered by Sansiran's forces, most of us went into hiding."

My shiver has nothing to do with the cold.

The crane banks sharply and plunges directly into a hulking gray mass of clouds. When the clouds clear, we soar over a range of zigzagging mountains that drift through a twilight sky. A river winds through the valleys like a silver thread, and cherry blossoms, wisteria, and weeping willows dot the landscape.

As we plunge toward a waterfall, I brace myself for impact—but it doesn't come. A warm, tingling feeling envelops me as we soar right through the spirit energies of a ward.

What appeared at first to be a pitch-black cavern ripples, and the ground opens to reveal—impossibly—blue skies and green valleys.

I twist back sharply upon hearing Jǐng'xiù's amused laughter.

"Magic created jointly by the Eight Immortals," he explains

with a wave of his hand. "Only those with good intentions may pass under the waterfall—and through our wards—to find our hiding place."

Residences built of rosewood with curving eaves line the sides of the gulleys, their gardens filled with blossoming trees. Jǐng'xiù's crane flies through the fretwork windows of one, alighting inside a chamber overlooking an enormous garden. Inside, it's bright and airy, with a bed covered in soft sheets, and silk drapes to draw over the windows at night.

I step off the crane—just as that white-hot pain flares in my arm again, this time streaking up my shoulder to the back of my head.

For a moment, the world goes black. When I come to, I'm lying on the ground, my cheek pressed to the floorboards.

Overhead, a face swims into view.

"You certainly have an interesting way of making an entrance." Jǐng'xiù peers down at me, arms folded.

I glare at him and push myself up. Pause when I catch sight of my hand.

Where the thorns punctured me, a spiderweb of black tendrils snakes under my skin, pulsing in rhythm with my heartbeat.

"Curious," Jǐng'xiù says softly, following my gaze. I've never been able to read immortals, so ancient and timeless that trying to do so would be like attempting to read the clouds or the ocean.

"What's curious?" I straighten and tuck my arm behind my back. It's disturbing, the way he's staring at it.

"None who have attempted to escape through the Kingdom of Night's wards have lived to see the next sunrise. I have seen immortals a hundred times more powerful than you turn to dust and ashes upon touching those wards."

"That's comforting, thank you," I say flatly.

"You're welcome. I know someone who can help with your wound."

"Wait." I push myself to my feet, still holding my arm behind my back, as though that can stop whatever it is I contracted from the thorns. "Who else is here?"

"All of us." Jǐng'xiù pauses. "That is, the seven of us remaining."

A beat of silence falls between us as I breathe in the meaning of his words. With Lady Shī'yǎ's death, the Eight Immortals—the beings of legend, the mortals who once crossed the Endless Sea to the Kingdom of Sky and gained eternal life—are no more. What was an impossibility has become our reality: The Kingdom of Night has wrought death upon a myth.

I search Jǐng'xiù's gaze for whatever emotion passed through earlier, as ephemeral as it was, but it's gone, replaced by the indifference of an immortal.

"I shall summon Cǎi'hé," he announces loftily, returned to the persona I came to know during the Immortality Trials.

"No," I say. I'm still faint from my battle earlier, but I have to do this now. "I want to see all of them. It's very important."

Jǐng'xiù sighs and rolls his eyes toward the Heavens. "So they all say."

The only way to travel through these mountains is by flight, whether on a crane or on an iridescent cloud. This time, Jǐng'xiù's crane dives into the winding valleys, feathers skimming over the sparkling rivers. At one point, it makes a sudden left turn—and the rock before us seems to open up.

We're in a gap between two mountains. Stone walls arch upward, plants and flowering trees clinging to their sides; the mountainsides curve outward at their center to form a natural enclosed gorge. A sliver of light falls through the crack along the top, illuminating a vast arena on the ground.

An arena filled with movement.

Immortals mill about, some training, some watching, some resting. The song of clashing metal rings in the air, accompanied by flashes of gold armor as the warriors spar at speeds faster than my mortal eyes can catch.

I narrow my eyes, concentrating on opening the valve of spirit energy that now resides in my chest.

Everything slows. Brightens. Clears. The world's colors intensify, sunlight striking in sharp gold against the mountainside, and I'm aware of every movement in the parting air as the warriors spar.

My fingers skim the hilts of my crescent blades. For the first time, I feel that I stand a chance against them.

Guards at the entrance glance up as we land. Sighting Jǐng'xiù, they incline their heads to bow us through.

My feet have barely touched the ground before we're accosted by a sudden gust of wind with the fragrance of herbs and a blur of colors. The space before me shimmers, and as someone materializes, a familiar voice exclaims, "You brought her here in such a state, Jǐng'xiù?"

An immortal smiles down at me. A lovely, slim face as smooth as a gentle river, eyes crinkled in a warm smile. They hold a woven basket filled with a mixture of magical herbs.

"Honorable Immortal Cǎi'hé," I say in surprise, and their grin widens.

"Ah, I *am* glad you are alive. Your performance in the Trials was memorable."

"Certainly," booms another voice. "Memorable in surprising ways." I look up to see the leader of the Eight Immortals, Dòng'bīn, striding toward me, followed by the others. I have only ever seen them from a distance, either high up on a dais or drifting on iridescent clouds: all powerful, godlike beings a realm away from me. I remember standing beneath them at the Hall of Radiant Sun, begging for a chance at the pill of immortality that could save my mother. I remember how their eyes skimmed over me, my fate as unimportant as a roll of dice to them.

Down here, on equal footing, they look . . . smaller. More human. Though they still bear the impossible perfection of all immortals, war has taken away some of their exuberance. The disdain and loftiness to their eyes has yielded to grim acceptance of their new reality.

Their realm, too, has now fallen to the Kingdom of Night.

And all of them are looking at me as I straighten and say, "I know how to end the war."

We sit at a table made from a great teak tree beneath flowering crabapples and purple plums. In contrast to their magnificence, I am drenched in sweat and traces of battle. Beneath my long sleeves, my wounded arm throbs with pain.

I draw a deep breath and begin: "My name is Hé Àn'yīng, and I am the daughter of Yī'lín Shī'yǎ. I've come to claim her title and all the rights that come with it, in hopes of ending this war against the Kingdom of Night."

A shocked silence follows my declaration. Something in their features akin to surprise transforms to hostility—except for Cǎi'hé's, whose face radiates delight.

The immortal known as Zhōng'lì speaks first, slapping his

ostrich-feather fan down on the table. "You dare sully the memory of Yī'lín Shī'yǎ with such a baseless claim?" His thick black brows are furrowed in fury. I remember him well; he was the one who casually suggested throwing me out when I placed last during the first of the Immortality Trials.

Instead of answering him directly, I reach inside my sleeve. The lotus hairpin warms to my touch, and I set it on the table. It glints beneath the light slipping through the mountain dome overhead.

"What is the meaning of this?" demands Tiě'guǎi, the immortal I recognize from the white-flowered gourd he holds. Golden smoke from its spout twines around him, forming an aura.

I reach into my core, gathering the spirit energies inside. As they flow through to my fingertips, my skin begins to glow—as does the hairpin. A gentle blush radiance envelops it, and when it disperses, the hairpin has transformed into my—and Lady Shī'yǎ's—lotus sword.

Another stunned silence elapses. Then Zhōng'lì speaks.

"A pretty trick," he says, staring at the lotus sword. "How are we to reconcile that you entered the wards as a mortal and participated in the Immortality Trials with your claim to be Shī'yǎ's daughter?"

I lift my gaze to him. "Because my father was mortal," I say. The light of the lotus sword brightens as I look each immortal in the eye, and this time, some of them break contact first. "He was a general of the Kingdom of Rivers, and Lady Shī'yǎ's disciple in the Immortality Trials. They loved each other, once." More murmurs of shock, but I plow on: "I am her daughter by blood. She bequeathed this sword to me on her deathbed, along with the inheritance of her position. I want it announced that I am to hold her title and command her army."

My words ring out in the clearing, and I realize that the sparring warriors have stopped to watch.

None of the immortals seems to know what to say. The sudden quiet is steeped in their discomfort.

It is Dòng'bīn who breaks the silence.

"The girl speaks true." The light from my lotus sword lances off his features, somehow softening his ageless eyes as he stares at the relic. I wonder if he sees his old friend in it. I wonder if he feels anything at all. "The lotus sword is indeed Shī'yǎ's. The fact that the girl can call upon its powers and it shows its true form to her means it has accepted her status as Shī'yǎ's heir . . . and that Shī'yǎ's soul is truly gone from this world." He lifts his gaze from the sword to address me at last. "Tell us your story, Hé Àn'yīng."

I don't think I have ever heard any of them speak my name before.

So I begin. I tell them everything: the the tale of my father's journey to the Kingdom of Sky and how he fell in love with a beautiful, kind immortal. How she carried his child, and he returned with their daughter to the mortal realm, promising to see his immortal love again.

How, when he did return, it was not with their child—but with the sole surviving heir to the Kingdom of Rivers, escaping the war tearing their realm apart.

By the time I finish, a stillness has befallen the entire clearing like a spell. The immortals' gazes are pinned to me.

"Hé Àn'yīng," Dòng'bīn says, his deep voice rumbling in the

cavernous space. "Yī'lín Shī'yǎ has chosen you as her successor by gifting you her spiritual weapon. It appears that her vessel has accepted you. We respect her choice, though the matter of calling upon her army is one you must accomplish yourself. For now, we accept an alliance with you, daughter of immortals."

"The Heavenly Order does not allow for this, Dòng'bīn," Zhōng'lì interjects. His fan seems to grow in size, the silky ostrich feathers sharpening to the points of blades. "She is half mortal. Our wards allowed her into the Immortality Trials because of her mortal blood and heart."

"The Heavenly Order has never addressed this type of case, Zhōng'lì," Dòng'bīn counters steadily. "There is no precedent for a halfling assuming the title of an immortal."

"Remember your own roots, Zhōng'lì," an immortal with a melodious voice chimes in. He is beardless and carries an iridescent flute, which shimmers between his fingers. "I have composed many a tune commemorating our crossing of the Endless Sea from the mortal realm to this one. Our origins have become legends in the land of red dust; what would the Heavens say if we were to turn our backs on the beings we began life as?"

"A poet through and through, Xiāng'zǐ," cheers Cǎi'hé.

Finally, the seventh of the Eight Immortals speaks up. "The Heavens have eyes," he begins. He is the oldest among them, silver-haired and silver-bearded, with a cheerful countenance. I've noticed he tends to stare into the distance, yet now his gaze homes in on me. He holds a fish drum and taps a wooden mallet to it before he continues: "The rules of the Heavenly Order are not up to us to decide; we may attempt to interpret its meanings, yet the signs are there. Shī'yǎ's lotus sword has chosen

the girl as her successor, and we must respect that decision."
Another tap of his fish drum.

Zhōng'lì looks around the table, clearly outnumbered in his
opinion. "Fine, Guǒ'lǎo," he concedes at last, and with a snap,
shuts his feathered fan. "But I shall choose to withhold my
judgment until we have further acknowledgment of her status
from the Heavens."

With a twirl of his fan, he vanishes. Tiě'guǎi waves a hand;
the smoke wafting from his gourd intensifies, shrouding him.
When it dissipates, he, too, is gone.

Dòng'bīn turns to me. "Whether or not the Heavenly Order
has written its acceptance of you remains to be seen. But we
respect Shī'yǎ's decision, for her lotus sword—her spiritual
vessel—speaks the truth. You are free to claim her title, her position, and all the rights she held within the Kingdom of Sky."

He might have shifted the skies or moved mountains with
the words he so casually speaks. For several moments, I cannot
fathom a response that will match their weight.

I incline my head to the leader of the Eight Immortals. "Honorable Immortal Dòng'bīn, thank you for the blessings. I ask
for your help in the next stage of the war: an alliance with me
and Hào'yáng, the mortal heir to the Kingdom of Rivers, as well
as your guidance in summoning the army bound to the late
Honorable Immortal Shī'yǎ."

"Summoning an immortal army is no small feat," Dòng'bīn
replies steadily. "Those occupying positions of leadership in
our realm have legions of warriors bound to serve their causes.
Only your vessel can determine if you are worthy of this feat."

"Then please, Honorable Immortal, teach me."

All eyes go to Dòng'bīn.

He pauses before he speaks again. "The hour grows late. Let us congregate here on the morrow to hear your strategy. By then, if you are able to call upon your army with your spiritual vessel, your position and title as the Eighth Immortal will be sealed beneath the eyes of the Heavenly Order."

With that, he vanishes in a ripple of air. One by one, the others follow suit.

Somehow, with only the immortal's hint about using my vessel, I now have to learn to summon an immortal army. Hào'yáng told me of anointment ceremonies and rites in the Kingdom of Rivers, yet I suppose my situation deviates from the norm: We are in a time of war, and Lady Shī'yǎ is gone.

A chortle draws my attention. Across the table, only Cǎi'hé remains, watching me with faint amusement.

I glance down at the lotus sword. Where my fingers touch its hilt, pink light shimmers; sparks travel up my wrist, and my forearm appears aglow from the inside. "How would I know if it finds me worthy of summoning an army?"

Cǎi'hé lets out a sudden cackle. "Have you tried asking it, dear girl?" they say, not unkindly.

I stare down at the sword, taking in the jade-green hilt, the color of the lotus's stem and leaves; the blade, with shifting blush hues like the most beautiful dawn. It never occurred to me that I could communicate with it, or that the vessel would be capable of responding.

I direct my thoughts inward.

Teach me how to call upon Lady Shī'yǎ's immortal army.

The light from the sword flares for a moment—just as another streak of white-hot pain sears up my other arm. I gasp, lifting my left hand. I'd been so focused on negotiating with the Eight Immortals, I'd forgotten about my wound until now. The poison from the demonic roses' thorns has spread; black liquid now oozes from my flesh, and my veins have darkened up to my elbow. As I stare at the writhing shadows within, another blinding pain shoots through my entire body.

I recall falling and hitting the ground—and then nothing.

Àn'yīng

Kingdom of Sky

When I wake, I am back in the chamber where I first arrived. A gentle breeze gusts in from the windows, stirring the curtains to reveal a view of undulating mountains wrapped in the eerie semidarkness that has befallen this realm. My limbs are heavy, and my head is even more so; I cannot place the time or the day.

My left arm throbs. When I look down, a sprig of tiny mushrooms twines around my wrist. Their cream-colored umbrella caps rest against my skin, shimmering with energies. I can make out shadows curling just beneath my flesh, but they seem to have gone still for the moment.

"Took you long enough to come back."

I jump at the voice and turn. Cǎi'hé sits in the middle of the chamber, leaning against a flowering peach tree that seems to have sprung from nowhere. On their back is their basket of herbs, from which vines and leaves are sprouting; little puffs of clouds encircle them, and blossoms occasionally shower from the peach tree like pink rain.

I suddenly notice that little grasses, flowers, and funguses encircle my bed. The air over my body ripples with their healing energies.

"Thank you," I croak. "How long was I out?"

"Three days."

A chill besets me. Three days, when I should have been figuring out how to summon my army and forming a battle plan. I wonder if Hào'yáng has reached the borders of the Western Province, whether he and Lì'líng have found each other. Whether he has reunited with everyone—Mā and Méi'zi and all our friends.

I try to sit up, but pain shoots through my arm.

"Dear girl, are you *trying* to ruin all the work I've done over the past few days?" Cǎi'hé says, exasperated. "This is a difficult poison to counter, even for me."

I lay back down, lifting my hand to study it. "What is it?"

The immortal blinks. "Demonic poison," they say. "My magical fungus can slow its progress, but I am powerless to stop it. Only one of *them* can."

I don't need to ask whom they are referring to. A chill runs through me. I have a sense of the answer already, but I ask my next question anyway. "And what happens when it finishes spreading?"

"Unclear for an immortal or a halfling. But for a mortal . . ." Cǎi'hé's eyes flash. "Death."

The word hangs in the air between us in the silence. With this revelation, every possibility of a future I'd hoped for turns to ashes.

"How long do I have?" My voice sounds far away to my own ears.

The immortal's face is impossible to read. "Days, perhaps. Weeks at best. I do not know."

Days.

Long enough to execute my plan.

Căi'hé continues, "In the meantime, drink this and rest." With a wave of their hand, sprigs of herbs and flower petals and leaves rise from the flower basket and stream into a jade-colored calabash that appears in their other hand. With a flick of the wrist, they send the calabash toward me.

I take it with my good hand. "I need to call on my army," I say quietly. "I can't afford to lose any more time."

"Attempt more magic today and you will reverse all the work I have done," Căi'hé says, pointing an admonishing finger at me. "Calling upon your spirit energies will put them in direct conflict with the demonic energies spreading through you. That is why you fainted. Drink my herbal medicine, sleep, and your energies will stabilize tomorrow—hopefully enough for you to attempt more magic. Now I'm going to get some rest, and so are you. I shall see you in the morning."

With that, they snap their fingers, and a warm spring breeze rises through the chamber, sweeping a rain of blossoms around them. When it settles, the chamber is empty, as though the immortal was never there.

I sit alone on the bed for a long while, staring out through the shifting gauze drapes.

Death. Căi'hé's voice seems to echo in the silent chamber.

I have to find the way to call on my army, to reunite with

Hào'yáng in the mortal realm . . . and to end this war by closing the gateway from the Kingdom of Night that is swallowing the Kingdom of Rivers day by day.

A blue-tailed magpie waits patiently at my bedside—a spirit messenger that Căi'hé left with me. I tell it my message to Hào'yáng and watch it flutter away, disappearing into the falling night.

Then I drink the contents of Căi'hé's calabash in one gulp and let sleep take me.

I dream. It's the same dream I've had in the mortal realm, only this time, I am in a realm of night. The moon hangs high and round overhead, and silvergrasses and white starflowers brush against my feet as I run, chasing someone through trees. The landscape is hauntingly beautiful and almost familiar, and the wind seems to whisper a ghostly song as it rises around me.

As wisteria petals fall in a shower of violet ahead, a figure appears, turning toward me, and it's as though time has slowed.

Hair, billowing like swirls of ink.

Eyes, flashing like golden embers.

The phantom of a smile on his face as his gaze lifts to meet mine—

I wake. It is the middle of the night; shadows race across the ceiling, the clouds dancing past a hidden moon. A strong breeze lifts the gauze drapes to the pavilion outside, sweeping fallen leaves and flower petals into my chamber.

As I rise to search for shutters or doors to close, movement from the garden catches my attention.

I still, my two remaining crescent blades instantly in my

hands. I reach for the edges of the sliding rosewood doors, intending to shut them against the weather—then pause.

A single black feather drifts from the sky, landing at my feet.

I freeze, instinct kicking my adrenaline into high. And as I raise my crescent blades, a shift of the shadows pulls my gaze up.

He's there. Impossibly, he's there in my chambers: His tall, elegant form is silhouetted against the curtains, cast in monochrome by the dim moonlight. His hair and cloak are still, in spite of the wind, and I catch a flash of those crimson eyes.

For a moment, we gaze at each other, and I wonder if he, too, is thinking of when I turned back to look at him from across the gateway in the Kingdom of Night. But more than that, I'm remembering the last time we were alone like this: on his balcony beneath the stars, his hand in mine. When I traced the lines of destiny on his palms and everything between us seemed possible.

A sharp ache rises in my chest, but I tamp it down.

I angle my blades at him. "You can't be here," I say quietly.

Maybe this moment will be the one where I end it all. Maybe taking his life now to defend the safety of the immortal realm will hurt less.

"I'm not," Yù'chén replies. "I am a figment of dark magic cast from my shadowcrane. The feathers don't simply show illusions of the past, Àn'yīng."

Moonlight spills over the edges of his figure—but there is a fainter quality to the lines of his form, almost as if the night pours through him.

Despite my better judgment, I find myself approaching him. The pain in my chest tightens with each step until I'm close enough to touch him.

Yù'chén makes no move to back away. He only watches me, that red gaze burning into my heart.

"You can try to drive that blade through my throat if it pleases you," he says, "though it won't work."

Slowly, I lift Fleet to the curve of his neck. Press it forward, the tip touching his clavicle.

It falls through. He wasn't lying—he is an illusion.

As I pull my blade back, Yù'chén makes as though to grab my wrist. His fingers skim over the skin of my hand, and though I know it isn't possible, I feel a phantom twinge where we touch.

"A scorpion, through and through," he says softly.

"You knew what I was the first time we met," I reply, my voice uneven. "You deceived me, you used me, and you broke me first."

He's silent for several heartbeats. "I broke you first," he says softly, tasting the words. It's impossible to read his expression; his face is turned away from the light.

"Have you brought your army, then?" I glance out at the night beyond, so black it's impossible to make out anything. "Are you here to flaunt your victory?"

He gives a shake of his head. "Contrary to your worst assumptions of me, there is no army. No one is coming, and no one knows I'm here."

"You can't betray your kingdom. You can't defy your mother's will." I exhale sharply. "You're bound by the covenant with her."

"My mother broke her end of the covenant with me when she drowned you. Unbeknownst to her, I am no longer bound to her. She believes the covenant still holds between us because you lived—but you didn't. You were brought back to life because of the immortality in your blood. I asked her to spare your life in return for my loyalty, but she killed you that night."

I stare at him, my heartbeats growing uneven. What he is saying makes sense; I felt it that night, the cold call of death, the rushing waters of the Nine Fountains as death had tried to sweep away my soul . . . but my core had snapped, unlocking the immortal part of me inherited from my birth mother.

"How did you find me?" I ask, stalling as I think of a way I might contact the immortals. I am weakened greatly by the poison spreading through my veins, but surely if I scream, someone will come—a guard posted nearby, a soldier out on the sparring field . . .

Yù'chén's eyes lower to my left arm. "That was my spell on the wards that you triggered. My mother asked me to weave a talisman that would activate with any movement through it, meant to greatly weaken trespassers. I detected your presence and found you here."

Demonic poison, Cǎi'hé had said of the shadows that writhed just beneath my skin. My throat tightens as I realize I'm going to die by Yù'chén's hand after all.

Perhaps I deserve it. Wouldn't I do the same if I were in his shoes?

Yù'chén splays his hands, as though my poisoning is a mere inconvenience. "I told you once, Àn'yīng: The brightest and most beautiful flowers are the most poisonous."

I would have thought I would be angry—furious, even. Yet all I feel is a hollow exhaustion, a déjà vu of the irony of our fates playing out before us. "Have you come to gloat, then?" My voice is a near-rasp. "Come to tell me I chose wrong, and these are the consequences?"

That insouciant curve to his lips fades slightly. He watches me from across the chamber—across an entire realm—in silence, those black eyes gleaming with eerie shades of crimson.

"I came to give you the cure," he says simply, as though he's offering me a gourd of plum wine. "My shadowcranc can draw out the demonic energies in your veins."

My voice is a whisper when I say, "And why would you do that?"

"Don't ask questions you know the answer to, Àn'yīng."

Unspoken words linger between us, and I suddenly find it hard to breathe.

"Leave her," I hear myself saying before I can stop. It's what I should have said back in the Kingdom of Night, before I chose to step through the gateway to the mortal realm. I think back to the way he gripped my hand, the way he looked at me. *Come with me*, I wanted to say then.

Instead, he said, *Àn'yīng, stay*.

"I *have* left her before." Those aren't the words I expect from his mouth. "I've run back to the mortal realm more than once, after the emperor found out what I was and ordered me killed. I missed it so much—the blue skies and the forests, and the way the sunlight slanted through the leaves. Even if it didn't want me, it was home for me, growing up." He closes his eyes briefly. "My mother found me each time."

There it is again, that ache in my heart that seems to surface whenever I'm with him.

"So run to the ends of the realms," I whisper. "Fight her." *Come with us.*

And then what? a voice in my mind asks. As long as he lives, the Kingdom of Night's connection to the Kingdom of Rivers lives with him.

Yù'chén is watching me with that eerie stillness of the mó again. It is impossible to fathom the thoughts running through his mind in this moment. I wonder if he, too, is imagining a lifetime where he is born differently—fully mortal, in a world of sunlight instead of darkness.

At last, he smiles at me. It is gentle, tender, as though I have just confessed my love to him.

"I've thought of it, more than you could know. And I've tried, before I met you. But my mother would hunt me to the ends of every realm. I am born of her flesh and ichor; even without a covenant, she and I are bound by ancient demonic magic that cannot be broken. No matter how far I run, my path will always lead back to her." His smile grows humorless. "This is the fate I was born to walk, Àn'yīng. Now I am choosing to make a decision within its path." Yù'chén holds out a hand, long fingers splayed. "You can trust me one last time. Or you can tell me to leave and I will, and you can pretend you never saw me here. The choice is yours."

The world narrows, and I remember the first day we met in that forest clearing, his beautiful smile and the ethereal way the sun kissed the edges of his profile. I think of when he saved Méi'zi's life from sickness in my house; of when he fought off that mó, protecting me with his own body. How he was the one to pull me back, one memory-infused black feather at a time, from that endless despair I felt on waking in his realm; the pain he endured from Xisenyin and Niefuzan because I'd broken the rules.

Bà told me once when he handed me my eighth and strangest blade, Heart: *Sometimes, Àn'yīng, the heart knows before the mind.*

I'm moving toward Yù'chén before I can think, my hand outstretched toward him. He blinks, then reaches for me.

Our fingers slide through one another.

Different realms, I remember.

Yù'chén lets out a sharp breath. He flicks his wrist. Another black feather drifts down from the air, and then, with a ripple of darkness, Yù'chén's shadowcrane appears. I feel its presence as it approaches me; feel the brush of its soft feathers as it envelops my forearm with a great wing.

Yù'chén's eyes flash; the shadowcrane's orbs glow, the red intensifying as the air heats with their dark magic. The dark tendrils in my veins begin trickling toward the shadowcrane's wings. The tips of its feathers, usually a mercurial shade of silver, darken.

The pain in my bones dissolves, replaced by a blissful coolness.

When the shadowcrane removes its wings, the skin of my forearm and hand are clear.

A lightness fills me, and I suddenly find it easier to breathe.

The shadowcrane gives me one long, slow blink. Then it turns and takes wing into the night, and I'm left alone with the illusion of Yù'chén in my chamber.

He's staring at me in a way that makes me aware of my own heart pounding, of the air between us thickening with all the lines of fate we've crossed to be here tonight.

Then he says, with a sad smile, "I told you, little scorpion, you always find a way to leave."

Something unmoors within me. I recall his face as he stared up at me from the puddle of blood spreading beneath him, the utter heartbreak in his eyes as he reached for me.

"I'm sorry," I whisper, because it's all I can offer. He couldn't leave; I couldn't stay—and now, finally, this cursed dance of our destinies in this lifetime is nearing its end.

"You asked me why I came," he continues. "You've asked me, on many occasions, why I do what I do for you. The truth is, you changed my life the day I met you in that clearing, Àn'yīng. And from that day on, I became very aware of the ironic fate I was trapped in." He gives a sharp, humorless smile. "I couldn't imagine a life without you, but there was no part of you that wanted me in yours."

My heart is cracking, an old, familiar ache.

"So I've been learning to let you go," Yù'chén says steadily. "Ever since you left this realm with him that night, I told myself to let you go. I told myself that you were so happy with him, that you were smiling again, and that you were better off without me.

"But then I saw you in my mother's vision, heard her plans for you, and I couldn't do nothing. I told myself that no matter how much you hated me for it, I had to save you. As long as you were alive, it didn't matter. So I made that bargain with Sansiran—one that would bind me to her but would keep you alive. When you arrived at my side again, I knew how much you despised me, but I just couldn't help wanting you and hoping for . . . for something more, no matter what I told myself.

"I was afraid—I was *terrified*—of hoping. I wanted you to keep on hating me because the last time I hoped for something more, it broke me. It hurts more to be so close to something and have it taken away—than to never have had it at all." He closes his eyes briefly. "Despite everything I told myself, despite all the warnings I drilled into my head . . . I let myself believe.

There was a time that I thought you could want me back." He exhales long. "I suppose that's the cruelty of hope."

My own hands are trembling, the hilt of my crescent blade digging into my right palm. It's difficult to find the words, to find the voice to speak, and I don't know the point of imagining all these what-ifs and impossibilities . . . but I know I owe it to him. The truth.

"I did," I whisper. "In spite of everything, Yù'chén, I did."

He goes very still. His eyes don't leave me as I push on.

"I meant what I said to you back in the Temple of Dawn. In another lifetime, if things were different."

Yù'chén's expression is inscrutable as he slowly approaches me, each step a countdown until we are close enough to touch.

He stops an arm's length from me. A realm and a lifetime away.

"It's a date, then," he says, and his smile feels like sunrise, like heartbreak.

And for some reason, I know, we are nearing the end.

Softly, he continues: "The truth is, I also came to say goodbye, Àn'yīng. The day I met you was the day I learned what it means to be truly alive. You showed me what makes a mortal *human*, how it feels to be afraid and to be brave in spite of your fear; to want to risk everything to protect those you love." He pauses, and I swear, no one has ever held me in their eyes like he does in this instant. "The mó do not have souls, but I'd like to think if I did, mine would be carved through with memories of you."

I think of the cold and dark of the Kingdom of Night; the beings in his mother's court that thrive on cruelty and humiliation. I think of Niefuzan's words about halflings: *I would not debase my lineage by mixing my ichor with the mud of mortals.* And I understand, so much, what Yù'chén means.

I was the first to ever admit his humanity, to make him feel worthy of who he is.

I am a life, he said to me. *I, too, have a beating heart.*

I reach out, and I touch the spot where his heart might be. My fingers fall through shadows, but I look up and hold his gaze.

It's the most—and the least—I can give him.

Yù'chén lifts a hand. Presses it to my cheek. He can't touch me, yet somehow, a ghost of a chill rushes through my skin. He gazes at me wordlessly for a long time—it might have been seconds, or minutes. Or forever.

"Àn'yīng," he says, and I feel the ache of tears rising in my chest from the way he speaks my name, the way he looks at me. "Loving you in this lifetime has felt like sliding a blade into my heart, inch by inch. I don't have the strength anymore to wait for the day it stops hurting."

And then he's gone, and I am left standing alone in a chamber of phantoms stirring in the wind and shadows.

Àn'yīng

Kingdom of Sky

Goodbye, Àn'yīng.

The weight of Yù'chén's words fill every corner of my chamber, my thoughts as scattered as the blossoms in the garden outside.

He knows. He knows I'm preparing to retaliate against the Kingdom of Night. In a way, perhaps this was the kindest gift he could give me: a parting of the two people we were when we met each other in that bamboo forest at sundown . . . and a knowing that we now fully stand on opposite sides of the war, with only one way this can all end.

I gather myself, reining in the pounding of my heart and the ache deep in my chest. Then I take out the lotus hairpin from within my sleeve.

At my touch, it warms briefly and begins to glow. When its light settles, it has changed back into its true form of the lotus sword—as though it anticipates what I'm about to ask.

I glance at my hand again. The little bracelet of magical fungus that Cǎi'hé made for me gleams with strings of spiritual energies, but my skin beneath looks healthy.

I reach into my core and gather my spirit energies, watching my skin begin to glow as I channel them to my fingertips and into the lotus sword.

I need to summon my mother's army.

The thought streams from my mind into the spirit energies pouring into the sword.

The sword reacts. Where my fingertips touch the blade, the metal ripples, its light growing warm, like dawn reflected in water.

Within, silhouettes begin to take form: immortal warriors, one sweeping into the next: ageless, beautiful, and powerful, dressed in the same white-and-gold lamellar armor Hào'yáng once wore as a guard at the Temple of Dawn.

As they flicker past, a running tally of soldiers, the blade of my sword breaks apart into glowing lotus petals. Each is inscribed with golden characters spelling out a warrior's name. The petals stream out into the night, brighter than stars, scattering in all directions. And just like that, my spirit vessel has released my call to the warriors of my mother's—now my— army.

The jade-green hilt of the sword pulses softly in my palm.

I place it back on the bed by my pillow.

Then there is nothing for me to do but wait.

Before dawn, I dress in the white gown gifted to me by the Realm of Dragons. I'm armed with my last two crescent blades, Fleet and Poison, and I hold the hilt of my lotus sword. Like this, I stand at the doorway to the pavilion outside my chamber. Waiting.

They arrive one by one, at first light—my mother's battalion of immortal warriors, led by several dozen generals whom I identify by the emblems on their helmets. Hào'yáng prepared me for this during our time together in the Dragon Realm: He taught me their names, their functions, the units they command, and each unit's specialties.

With each new arrival, a lotus petal returns to me, fitting itself to the hilt of my sword until the blade is whole again. Spirit energies roll off the warriors and their weapons like sunlight, and they look every bit the legendary immortals from the storybooks and myths I grew up with—ones I never thought I would set eyes upon, let alone find myself having to command.

You fought and clawed your way here, comes a voice in my mind. *You have the secret to victory. Do not diminish the strength of your heart.*

My lotus sword pulses in my hands. When I look down at the blade, I have to blink several times before I believe what I'm seeing.

Lady Shī'yǎ's face gazes out at me, her eyes gentle and soft, exuding an ageless wisdom. By her side, smiling up at me with the black eyes and sharp, strong features I inherited . . . is my father.

The blade shimmers gently, and again, a voice—a mixture of their voices—speaks in my mind.

You began on the path we set out for you, yet you have accomplished and become so much more. Walk your own path, Àn'yīng, and remember that we are always with you in your heart.

With another ripple, they vanish, and I'm left staring at my own reflection.

I lower the sword and lift my gaze to my mother's battalion.
My battalion.

And I hold up a hand.

The warriors fall silent, hundreds of sets of eyes coming to focus on me. I draw a deep breath.

"Warriors of the Kingdom of Sky," I begin. "My name is Hé Àn'yīng. I am the daughter of the immortal Yǐ'lín Shī'yǎ and the mortal general Hé Zhàn."

A murmur of interest—and confusion—rises in the battalion of immortals.

"My birth parents are dead, killed in the war that the Kingdom of Night inflicted first upon the mortal realm and now upon yours. Lady Shī'yǎ bequeathed her title, position, and spirit weapon to me before departing our world." I sweep my gaze across the crowd as I lift my lotus sword as proof. More chatter hums through the crowd. "And today, I am calling for your help to retaliate in the war against the Kingdom of Night by allying with the Kingdom of Rivers, whose heir Hào'yáng, the son of the late emperor and empress and prince to the mortal throne, awaits us with an army of his own in the mortal realm.

"For ten years, the mó have been gaining ground and gaining power with the gateway they opened into the Kingdom of Rivers. They leach the life energies from my realm, pulling it into night. This fuels their strength, enabling them to progress farther into the Kingdom of Sky with every passing day.

"I know how to stop them." I tighten my grip on the hilt of my sword. "I know the source of the gateway the mó use to keep their grasp on the mortal realm. And I know how to break it. The key to doing so lies in the mortal realm's Imperial City, where a gateway can be opened to connect the Kingdom of Rivers to the Kingdom of Night. This gateway can only be created by a halfling born of the last mortal emperor and the demon queen. The blood that flows through his veins can join the two realms together permanently." My hands are fisted. "We kill him and we sever the gateway once and for all, crippling the Kingdom of Night's power."

A stillness has befallen my audience. Every eye is on me, every face focused with rapt attention.

Emboldened, I step up onto a table fashioned from an old tree trunk in the front of the open-air pavilion. "But the Kingdom of Night now controls your wards. The only way out from here is through the Temple of Dawn." I straighten slightly, glancing down at the flat of my blade where Bà's face appeared to me only moments ago. "My father was a general of the Kingdom of Rivers' armies before he died in the war. My strategy follows a principle of war he once taught me: *Lure the tiger away from the mountain and strike.*

"We gather all our forces for a battle at the Temple of Dawn. We force the Kingdom of Night to summon all their forces to this battle, weakening their guard back in the Imperial City.

"That is where I will go with Prince Hào'yáng and his army to sever the Kingdom of Night's gateway.

"When that is complete, Prince Hào'yáng will ascend the mortal throne to claim his rightful title as emperor. We will have the allegiance of the dragon realm, and the mortal army will join forces with yours to finish this war."

I end my speech, and a long silence stretches out. In the distance, the clouds stir, covering the sun.

"How do we know your words are to be trusted?" a general asks, her voice slicing through the air like a sword. I recognize her as General Shè'shēng, commander of the Song

Shooters—legendary archers whose arrows travel faster than sound and song.

I'm not certain how to answer, for the truth is, I have no proof of what I've said. No proof that I am Lady Shī'yǎ's daughter but for the lotus sword in my hand.

"Because we of the Eight Immortals stand with her and testify that she speaks true," comes a familiar voice that rumbles like a thunderclap. A sharp wind rises, and in the next moment, Dòng'bīn alights on a wisp of iridescent cloud, his somber scholar's robes billowing, his red-tasseled sword hanging by his waist.

"Because Honorable Immortal Shī'yǎ's vessel has accepted her and summoned you to follow her in this war," says Cǎi'hé, appearing in a flourish of peach blossoms by my side. They throw me a wink.

"And because Hé Àn'yīng has rightfully ascended to the position of the Eighth Immortal," says Jǐng'xiù, who alights from his red-crowned crane, bamboo scepter magically amplifying his lofty announcer's voice. "And today, those of us gathered here pledge our allegiance to her." He gives me a raised-eyebrow look, as though to say, *Surprised?*

That would be an understatement.

Xiāng'zǐ follows with a trill of his magic flute; last to arrive is Guǒ'lǎo, with light taps of his fish drum. Missing are Zhōng'lí and Tiě'guǎi, whose stances against my claiming my title seem not to have changed.

Yet as five of the Eight come to stand by my side, a rush of gratitude sweeps through me. Though none but Cǎi'hé show any trace of friendliness, their support has made allies of us, and we are united in our respect for Lady Shī'yǎ and our common goal in this war.

I turn to them and incline my head.

And before the eyes of hundreds of immortal generals and warriors, Dòng'bīn meets my gaze and bows back.

Dòng'bīn, Jǐng'xiù, Cǎi'hé, Xiāng'zǐ, and Guǒ'lǎo have summoned their own armies. The clearing beneath the mountain dome is teeming with activity, training, and sparring when we arrive with my army.

"I need to send word to the other realms," I declare. "I'd like to tell them that the Kingdom of Sky backs Hào'yáng and is ready to fight against the Kingdom of Night within the next day. Anyone willing and able to support us in the war should join us at the Imperial City, where the mortal heir awaits them."

"An allegiance of realms," Jǐng'xiù says grandly, raising his bamboo scepter to the skies. Jade-green light spirals upward in the form of vines, leaves unfurling as it climbs.

"I like the sound of it," Cǎi'hé cackles. They reach into their basket and fling a handful of herbs into the air, which flow up to join Jǐng'xiù's gently spiraling green vines.

Xiāng'zǐ and Guǒ'lǎo contribute their own spirit energies, a trill of lovely, winding flute music and the beat of a fish drum. And at last, Dòng'bīn lifts his red-tasseled sword.

"Lady Hé," the leader of the Eight Immortals says. "Your vessel."

I lift my lotus sword, feeling foolish as I mimic them. But as my spirit energies flow through my veins and bones, my sword gives a responding pulse as the vessel's spirit responds to my will.

Before my eyes, it disintegrates.

A gentle blush glow envelops the clearing. The warriors

around us pause to exclaim in wonder as the mountain dome fills with light.

Then it fades. In its place, a hundred butterflies flutter in the air, their pearlescent wings gleaming. As we watch, they take wing and spiral up, up, and out through the crack in the mountain gorge, into the endless skies.

We spend the rest of the morning drawing up battle plans. When the sun hangs high in the sky, we make our move.

I clamber onto the back of Jǐng'xiù's great white crane. I'm to fly with him and Dòng'bīn, along with the Dark Spears, the stealth unit of soldiers specializing in assassinations and covert missions. Following right behind us will be the Iron Swords, the strongest unit of warriors, adept at swordplay and hand-to-hand combat; as well as the Flying Daggers, the cavalry fighters whose spirit weapons manifest as powerful steeds. Bringing up the rear will be the Song Shooters.

With my lotus sword gone to carry my message across the realms, I palm Fleet and Poison. I have the strangest feeling that I have returned to where I began, and yet everything has changed. I turn around to look at the legendary warriors, the generals, and at last, the Eight Immortals. I wonder briefly if this is the last I'll see of them.

I hope it isn't.

Cǎi'hé gives me a cheery wave from where they sit on a great leaf pad hovering just above the ground. Xiāng'zǐ twirls his flute in his hand, and Guǒ'lǎo sits peacefully atop a little white donkey, eyes closed as he taps his fish drum to an unheard melody.

Dòng'bīn gives the command, and we're off.

Jǐng'xiù has bespelled his crane to camouflage itself, its feathers shifting hues to match the color of the cloud masses we soar into. Soon, it feels as though we are alone again, wind whistling in my ears, the cloud mass shifting with shadows and smoke as we plunge through them in silence. To my left and right, though, I make out the gleam of a blade, the whip of a cloak. The Dark Spears, it seems, are living up to their name.

As we approach the back of the Temple of Dawn, there is a colder bite to the air. Darkness thickens until it feels as though we are soaring into a falling twilight.

The first hellbeast swerves at us out of nowhere. It shoots out from a cloud, red eyes blazing and fanged teeth bared. Astride the crane, I lift Fleet, preparing to greet it—

—only for a shadow to flit across my vision, quicker than the blink of an eye. The hellbeast's shriek echoes as a Dark Spear drives their blade into its core; my stomach drops as Jǐng'xiù's crane plunges suddenly to avoid the dissolving tendrils of ichor the hellbeast has become.

Suddenly, we're out from the bottom of the clouds, in clear skies, the immortal realm unfurling beneath us in a constellation of floating mountains and twining rivers. And there, right ahead, is the Temple of Dawn.

Only, I barely recognize it from the gleaming palace of pearl-white walls and golden-tiled roofs it once was.

Now the curved eaves are a glistening black, shadows writhing from it. The pillars and walls have turned fog-gray. Darkness yawns from its steps as we approach it from the back. Wards rise high into the skies beyond it, denoting the end of the immortal realm and the beginning of the mortal realm.

The second hellbeast lunges at us from above. Dòng'bīn vanquishes it with a powerful swing of his sword—but not before it lets out a ghastly, bloodcurdling scream.

And then they're on us, swarms of winged hellbeasts, their

skeletal torsos made of writhing shadows, fanged maws agape as they descend. I raise my crescent blades to defend myself.

A sharp jerk on my wrist pulls me back down. I look up, and Jǐng'xiù is calmly shaking his head at me. "This is our battle," he says majestically, lifting his bamboo scepter. "Yours lies ahead of you."

The scepter's gemstones catch a glint of light. There's a burst of unfathomably strong spirit energies, and at once, the air fills with dazzling light and colors that form a shield, dissolving all the hellbeasts that attack us.

Yet as we draw closer to the Temple of Dawn, I catch sight of something that chills my blood.

Mó. An entire army is lined up at the back of the Temple of Dawn and in the Celestial Gardens. They stand as still as statues, only their glinting red eyes showing signs of life.

Before them, in a neat row awaiting us, are Higher Ones. Their court attire stirs in the wind, and even from here, the air trembles from the magic that springs from their palms.

"How irksome," Jǐng'xiù mutters under his breath. He grips his scepter tighter, but the flow of colors shielding us is beginning to dull. "Dòng'bīn, brother," he calls. "A little help here would be appreciated."

Out of nowhere, lightning strikes, spearing through two of the hellbeasts pursuing us. Then Dòng'bīn is at our side. With each slash of his blade, streaks of lightning burn through the hellbeasts before us, accompanied by deafening rumbles of thunder.

"Dark Spears!" Jǐng'xiù shouts, his voice magnified by his scepter. "First line of attack!"

The shadows coalesce, and suddenly, the Dark Spears

materialize before us, their weapons raised as they approach the demonic army. The remainder of the immortal forces let out battle cries.

With a blinding flash of lightning and another earth-shattering boom of thunder, the immortal and demonic armies collide.

Spirit energies and demonic energies tear through the air as the temple fills with the clash of steel and the screams of battle.

Jǐng'xiù's crane swerves to a side of the courtyard at the back of the Hall of Radiant Sun. "Go, Àn'yīng," the immortal urges me, and then a touch of humor quirks his lips. "Ironic, isn't it, that you once fought so hard to get through those doors into the Temple of Dawn . . . and now you must fight to get out?" He winks. "Though you of all immortals should know the way back to the mortal realm from here." He raises his scepter, and the shield of flowing colors shifts around us to stretch into a protective tunnel leading into the Hall of Radiant Sun.

I leap off the crane, Fleet and Poison raised before me. Ahead, Jǐng'xiù's path leads to the back doors of the hall—and is swallowed by the darkness within

I glance back, about to thank Jǐng'xiù, when the Higher One comes out of nowhere.

One moment, the immortal is flashing his lopsided grin at me. The next, sharp-leafed purple flowers sprout from his chest and his mouth, now open wide in surprise.

A Higher One lifts her crimson gaze to mine from over Jǐng'xiù's shoulder. She has one arm wrapped around his throat; the other is plunged straight through his chest.

Jǐng'xiù sighs, then his form scatters into iridescent dust, disintegrating before me.

"No!" The cry tears from my throat. I leap forward, fury pulsing through my veins—

Lightning blinds me, and I'm thrown back by a surge of spirit energies. When the flare dims, the Higher One is nowhere to be seen.

Dòng'bīn straightens, lowering his sword. For a moment, he stares at the spot on the ground where Jǐng'xiù stood just seconds ago—when I'd been about to tell him thank you for saving my life, for proving me wrong about how immortals could be.

The leader of the Eight Immortals raises his gaze to me. His eyes could be made of stone. "Go, Àn'yīng," he says. "If you don't succeed, more of us will be gone."

He casts a final glance at the place where his friend and brother of thousands of years last stood.

Then he lifts his sword and leaps—toward the onslaught of mó.

I turn to the back of the Hall of Radiant Sun. At the other end of the hall are the gilded temple doors opening to the mortal realm. I remember first setting foot through them, a mortal girl a long way from home, searching for a pill of immortality for her mother.

I have come so far from that.

The inside of the hall has gone dark. There are mó within, awaiting me. But I am no longer prey.

I take off at a sprint, flaring my spirit energies. My senses heighten, and as my vision adapts to the darkness, I spot the line of mó guarding the temple doors at the end of the hall.

I'm on the first two before they even see me, my crescent blades flashing as I plunge them through their cores: Fleet for a quick kill, and Poison for a slow death. I take down four, five, six more; a final burst of speed, and I'm through.

I burst through the golden doors that once allowed me entry into the Kingdom of Sky; now they open toward home. The light of the mortal realm envelops me, warm and scented with an ocean breeze. The Immortals' Steps rise from the sea before me, leading home.

Leading to Hào'yáng.

I glance back at the Hall of Radiant Sun one more time, recalling the drowning relief and desperation I felt the first time I set eyes upon it. I thought that the immortals and their kingdom were a place of unbreachable safety and power; that no matter what transpired across the realms, they would be constant, immutable.

I once stood below them, begging for a chance to save my mother's life. Powerless and terrified.

Now, I am their only chance at winning this war.

I turn and make for Heavens' Gates as swiftly as my feet will carry me.

29

Àn'yīng

The Imperial City, Kingdom of Rivers

The distraction we've set up has worked. While the Eight Immortals' army engages the Kingdom of Night in battle at the Temple of Dawn, no one follows me as I make my way down the Immortals' Steps. The stone steps vanish into the clouds, and soon, I'm surrounded by a mass of swirling gray and shadows again, with only the sounds of my own breathing and pounding heart to accompany me. I focus on my footwork, boots landing sturdily against moss-slicked stone.

The clouds begin to diverge from the steps as I reach the mountains of the mortal realm. Here, the skies are overcast, and raindrops soak me as I draw closer to the Heavens' Gates.

When I'm far enough away not to be seen by any mó from the Temple of Dawn, I flare my spirit energies and summon an iridescent cloud.

I race through the skies of the mortal lands. The rain whips in my face, and the wind tears at my cloud. As I near the Central Province, an unnatural cold sinks into my bones, and the shadows begin to stretch longer. Here and there, I catch glimpses of the land: bamboo forests, once-brilliant emerald leaves now dim and gray; undulating mountains wreathed in darkness.

I descend. It feels like instinct, finding the way back to my village.

But nothing prepares me for the sight of it.

Between the red and gold treetops and the muted darkness, a clearing opens with the bones of my home.

Xī'lín is in ruins. Charred remnants of our cheerful houses sit, desolate, in the downpour, burned to nothing but jagged wooden pillars. I recognize the places where I used to play with the neighbors' children before they moved away; the street corner where an old willow used to grow and we'd sit beneath it for shade in the summers; the carpenter's house, where I'd admire his craft and, after the realm fell, I'd visit his daughter to ask for help with thatching our roof.

I soar around the most familiar corner in the village, where the plum blossom tree once stood, and my heart breaks. My house is gone; on the flattened ground are wood scraps and torn pieces of the curtains Mā and Méi'zi sewed, the bright colors of the floral patterns trampled into the mud.

From the ruins, a figure steps out. Gold lamellar armor gleaming wet with rain, the blade of a sword glowing with turquoise light. Through the pouring rain and wind, Hào'yáng's eyes meet mine—and I realize I would cross realms again and again to find him.

He reaches out as I land, and he folds me into his arms. I hold him like it's the end of the world, because part of mine has ended here along with the home I swore to protect.

But I hold Hào'yáng, and he anchors me in this storm, and I know I will see the sun again.

Hào'yáng draws back, his hands cupping my face. "The last time I was this afraid," he says, "I was twelve years old and the war had just begun. As heir to the mortal realm, it is my duty to put kingdom above all—but I don't know that I can make that same choice again when it comes to you, Àn'yīng."

"Once the war is over, you won't have to," I tell him fiercely. "Once the war is over, we'll rebuild. Xī'lín, the Imperial Palace, every single village they took and home they destroyed, we'll rebuild it all from the ground up."

Hào'yáng presses a kiss to my forehead. "Together," he vows. Then he slides his fingers through mine and says, "I received your message."

He reaches into the silk pouch at his belt. When he unfurls his palm, a tiny pink butterfly flutters out. It lands on the hilt of my sword and transforms into a lotus petal, joining back with my vessel.

A shout rends the air, and I turn.

"Àn'yīng!"

A small white blur darts through the rain to me, and the next moment, I'm laughing and crying as I greet my assailant in a tight hug.

Lì'líng draws back, amber eyes bright like the sun, hair still done up in two buns. She beams at me and then waves to someone behind her.

Tán'mù emerges, tall and dashing in her black cloak and boots. She nods at me in greeting, and though her expression is as neutral as ever, I think I catch the hint of a smile curving the edges of her lips.

Behind her, several other former candidates of the Immortality Trials trickle out. I count eight of us in total.

"The others chose to stay behind with the villagers," Lì'líng informs me. "But a makeshift army of volunteer fighters has gathered from across the provinces in Hào'yáng's name." Her eyes twinkle. "They arrived here not too long ago."

Dozens of figures emerge from the edge of the forest, led by someone very familiar.

Fú'yí's hair is done up in a graying bun, her eyes fierce as she gives me that fiery grin. She is dressed in blue battle robes, lamellar armor glinting with every shift of her strong, wiry frame. She was a martial artist and practitioner, I knew, but she didn't go to war after the first invasion, as she was pregnant at the time. When her husband died, she lost their unborn son as well.

"Oh, my girl," she says as I throw my arms around her. She strokes the back of my head and whispers, "I am *so* proud of you. Today, we show those bastards from the Kingdom of Night just how strong we are." She draws back and squeezes my hand. "Your mother and Méi'zi say hello. They asked me to bring you this." She presses something soft into my hands.

It is a handkerchief, intricately embroidered with golden threads unique to the desert silkworms in the Western Province. I recognize Mā's and Méi'zi's handiwork in the stitches, Mā's coming a little neater and Méi'zi's a little wilder. They've sewn me a portrait of the three of us seated beneath the plum blossom tree of our house. The sun spills across the scene like honey; the world is bright and clear, like the air after a storm. It is as though they have peered into the dream I hold on to and stitched it into this handkerchief.

"Thank you, Fú'yí," I whisper.

Her eyes soften. "They are safe, in a sunny village, far from the mó. They asked me to send all their love, and they can't wait to reunite with you."

An ache rises in my throat as I think of all those feathers Yù'chén brought me, allowing me to glimpse my family for a few moments each day.

It was real.

"Your summons reached quite far and wide," Hào'yáng says, and cants his head to the skies.

A great bird's cry echoes through the storm, powerful and melodic, like an ancient song across time and worlds.

Nine brilliant phoenixes soar through the rainclouds, their wings and crowns trailing flames, their feathers shimmering with iridescence. They land before us on the clifftop, each the size of a horse. With a great sweep of their wings, the pink butter-flies that had borne my message to them release into the air and return to my sword.

"The Nine Sunbirds of the Western Province," Hào'yáng tells me. "As creatures of fire and heat, they are threatened by the eternal night, too."

The myth of Hòu'yì, the divine archer, is one we in the mortal realm grew up with. Legend has it that the mortal realm once had ten suns, which dried up the land and the rivers. Hòu'yì shot down nine of them, and they turned into golden sunbirds that remained in the mortal realm. It is said that they reside in the mystical Kūn'lún Mountains of the Western Province, where the great deserts are warmed by the magic of their bodies and they, in turn, can continue inhabiting a land of fire and heat.

"I also present to you," Lì'líng says proudly, "the nine-tailed fox spirits of the Kingdom of Green Hills."

Through the trees, a dozen or so pale silhouettes emerge: foxes the size of tigers and the color of snow, eyes a brilliant carmine. Their nine tails fan out behind them, the tips pluming into the same red as their eyes. In the downpour, their fur remains sleek and dry as they watch me with calm elegance.

Then, behind them, more figures step out from the shadows. They resemble us in appearance, yet there is *something* inhuman to each of them, marking them as different: a horn here, a tail there, a flash of canines or a growth of flowers on their cheeks.

Yāo'jīng.

Tán'mù steps closer to them. "There is a resurgence of hope throughout the mortal realm," she says. "These yāo'jīng have gathered from the mountains and forests to support us in this war."

Traditionally, yāo'jīng have been feared across our realm, with tales of them luring mortals into traps and stealing babies in the night. But after I met Lì'líng and Tán'mù, I'd realized the stories were just stories.

I incline my head deeply to both the fox spirits and the yāo'jīng. They mirror me, releasing their pink butterflies back to me as well.

"Like Hào'yáng said, your word has spread far and wide across the realms," Lì'líng says. "The fox spirits tell me they have heard talk of the return of the mortal crown prince; that other realms are speaking of the mortal heir and a Lotus Immortal who are fighting against the Kingdom of Night."

Hào'yáng turns to me. The light of the sunbirds dances over

his face. "Less than a day's journey to the Imperial City," he says, looking westward, in its direction. "Are you ready?"

I don't know that I'll ever be ready for what must come next. But I do know that I need this war to end.

I raise my palm to the skies and send a spark of my spirit energy to the Heavens. There's a flash of corals and a brief illusion of a sunrise through the storm clouds.

Then, through the darkness, hundreds of sparks illuminate the skies. They swirl from the clouds, funneling toward me: butterflies—fragments of my lotus sword—returning to me from having relayed my summons message.

They gather between my fingers, and my lotus sword reappears, jade-green hilt and soft pink blade bright in the rain.

I lift it to the skies. "We fight," I declare, and amidst the crowd of mortal warriors, sunbirds, fox spirits, and yāo'jīng gathered, I meet Fú'yí's gaze. "Today, we show the Kingdom of Night that we are still here. We are still alive. And we are ready to take back our realm."

While I lead on my iridescent cloud, Hào'yáng and our army travel by sunbird and nine-tailed fox, which can cross the mortal realm to the center of the Kingdom of Rivers within a matter of hours. I imagine that the sunbirds' trails of fire will be seen across the mortal villages as a sign heralding the return of the mortal heir.

A harbinger that the sun is returning to our lands that have long been falling into night.

At noon, when the sun should be highest in the skies, a chill falls upon us. The air shifts, the light dims, and a preternatural cold sinks into my bones.

We descend swiftly into night. Below us, the curve of the Long River vanishes into a swathe of shadows and the skyline of the Imperial City rises, as though out of a different realm.

The nine-tailed foxes land and move in uniformity through the trees, ghostly streaks barely visible from afar.

The sunbirds alight in the trees just before the ancient walls of the city, and I follow on my cloud. Behind us, the nine-tailed foxes slip out from the trees as the rest of our army dismounts.

"It looks empty," Hào'yáng says quietly, scanning the crenellated walls.

The sunbird carrying Hào'yáng turns to him, and her voice rings out, melodious and deep: "The city is warded in a magic of darkness and shadows, mortal prince. We cannot pass without a fight."

Hào'yáng slides off the sunbird and draws his sword in a flash of turquoise. "Then we fight," he says. "We make for the gates and focus our attack on a single point. You all know the plan: Help Àn'yīng and me get through so we can defeat their halfling crown prince and break their connection with our realm once and for all."

An insidious whispering draws our attention, like the rush of phantom voices on the wind. On the walls, shadows peel out from the night; hundreds of pinpricks of red suddenly flare to life—demonic crimson eyes, all trained upon us.

Mó guards.

Tán'mù starts forward. Her human shape ripples, peeling apart as she steps into the skin of the monster. Sharp gray scales like sword metal coat her exterior; veined wings unfurl from her body, which has elongated into a serpent's tail. She looks to the Heavens and lets out a long, inhuman cry. By her side is Lǐ'líng, shoulders tensed, knees bent in a defensive stance, a corner of her lips lifted to reveal sharpened canines. The other yāo'jīng follow suit, their human appearances rippling as they transform into their true spirit forms.

The mó descend upon us like a vicious black cloud of teeth and talons. There are at least a hundred of them, more than we anticipated, and as Tán'mù and the others leap forward to meet them, I know our numbers won't be enough.

I lift my sword and cut down one; Fleet finds another, and I hear a resounding shriek from behind me as Hào'yáng plunges his blade through one. We are back to back, falling into the rhythm familiar from when he trained me to spar during the Immortality Trials.

"There are too many," he shouts, his voice strained as he cuts through another mó. I dodge to avoid the splash of ichor as it dissolves. "We won't be able to clear the path to the palace."

I look up at the steps, darkened now with mó in their black uniforms, colorful magic and flowers twisting in the air as they fight. Tán'mù holds her own; I spot Lì'líng, a small speck of white, darting between two enemies. The sunbirds have taken to the air, scorching enemy forces with bright bursts of flame. The nine-tailed foxes pounce on the mó, ripping and tearing with their powerful claws and teeth. And our mortal warriors are engaged in battle, weapons flashing, robes whirling.

They're opening a path for Hào'yáng and me to get to the Imperial Palace—and it's working.

A crackling sound comes from the ground. When I look down, frost is spreading across the paving stones, freezing the grass and choking the life from everything it touches.

I know who is responsible before I set eyes on her.

Xisenyin stares down at me from where she's standing on

the city walls, long white hair whipping in a rising wind. The Higher One holds no visible weapon; she has no need for one. She twirls an elegant hand and a spike of ice explodes from the ground, spearing through two of Tán'mù's warriors. The tang of blood is thick in the air, and the rime-covered stones redden.

By Xisenyin's side, a second Higher One appears out of the night—a mó with skin shimmering purple and horns protruding from his forehead. He holds in each hand two silver rings, gleaming as though wrought of starlight, and begins to spin them.

The air vibrates with a thrum that drills into my head like the sound of a thousand screams. All around me, our armies stagger, holding their hands to their heads, some falling to the ground. Xisenyin's ice continues to spread, freezing victims as it finds them in its path.

"Tricking the tiger to leave its lair unguarded?" Xisenyin's voice rings across the night to me. "That only works when your forces are evenly matched. My army will cut through yours in no time." She speaks the words in a mocking sneer. "You had your chance to join the winning side, *Lotus Immortal*. And no doubt our pathetic halfling prince would welcome you back with open arms here and now should you decide to." She cracks her knuckles, and four more mortal soldiers' cries are cut short as her ice spears impale them. "Say the word, and we can still curb the bloodshed today."

Hào'yáng's hand closes over mine. He is bleeding through a gash on his arm, but he meets my gaze with one of silent resolve as he hoists his sword higher.

"If I didn't know better, Xisenyin, I'd think you were anxious that we got this close." I step forward, my lotus sword flaring in the night. "I think you're afraid of facing your queen's wrath at such a slipup. And I think you're terrified at the prospect of what'll happen to you when you lose."

Xisenyin's lip curls. "Very well, then, Lotus Immortal. May you be known as the one who led her army to death."

She lifts a hand.

Suddenly, a bright light cleaves the sky. Feathers begin to drift downward like snow, increasing in speed and turning into sharp blades—making for Xisenyin.

The Higher One pivots with a hastily-raised shield, snarling as the magical blades rain down around her.

"Perhaps, then, we can make our forces more evenly matched," comes a voice from above.

More feathers spiral from the skies in a torrent and coalesce into a human shape: the immortal Zhōng'lì, striding elegantly toward the battle on a wisp of cloud. Behind him, Tiě'guǎi appears with his white-flowered gourd. Smoke spills from it, drifting down to the wounded and dying. Where it touches, their injuries seem to shrink and their breaths grow steady. All the legends say that Tiě'guǎi is famed for his healing powers, and that he once traveled the mortal realms as a benevolent physician. Today, I'm glad they hold true.

Xisenyin wears a very ugly look on her face. "Alert the empress," she snarls at one of her subordinates, who vanishes in a swirl of night.

I curse under my breath. If we can't penetrate the Imperial City's walls before Sansiran knows we're here and sends reinforcements, our plan may fail.

"Leave this to us," Zhōng'lì says to me.

I'm not certain I know how to react to this change of heart from an immortal who has scoffed at my presence since the very first time we met, who consistently spoke out against me during the Immortality Trials.

Zhōng'lì seems to sense my hesitation. Eyes still on the enemy ahead, he continues: "This is the battle we should have fought eleven years ago instead of turning our backs on the realm we were born in."

The feather tips of his fan grow sharp, their shafts taking on a steely quality. By his side, Tiě'guǎi raises his gourd, its smoke pouring out thicker as his spirit energies build.

"Thank you for coming," I say to the two immortals, and when I bow deeply to them, I am thinking, too, of Jǐng'xiù.

Without another word, they leap forward to greet the two Higher Ones in battle.

Hào'yáng turns to me as a gap opens in the mó's guard— a chance we may not have again. I raise my sword and, side by side, we plunge through the gates into the heart of the fallen Imperial City.

Àn'yīng

Imperial Palace, Kingdom of Rivers

Silence and shadows wrap around us, thick and oppressive, as we draw away from the main scene of battle. Hào'yáng conjures a concealment talisman similar to the one my lost blade Shadow had.

With the majority of the Kingdom of Night's forces occupied in the battles at the Temple of Dawn and outside the Imperial City's gates, the streets of their stronghold in the mortal realm are now eerily empty.

We keep beneath the houses' curved eaves. Broken doors and torn paper windows gape at us; here and there, I spot signs that mortals—families—once inhabited this place. Children's zodiac figurines line a windowsill; an open door shows a meal set upon an elegant table, the porcelain now coated in dust, untouched for a decade. Unbidden, a dozen different scenes play out in my mind as I imagine the fate of the family who prepared the meal.

Hào'yáng, too, takes this all in, his eyes raking across the devastation left of his home city by the Kingdom of Night. "I can hear them still," he says quietly. "From the day this city fell."

"You did the only thing you could that day, the only thing that would give our kingdom any hope of fighting back as we are now," I tell him. "You lived."

"Sometimes, I wonder—why me? Why my life? I'm worth no more than any of the people who died here."

I consider him, and I think of another who asked me the same question, with the same pain and grief raw in his crimson eyes.

"But isn't that the greatest burden of all to bear?" I say softly. "The knowledge that others died while you lived?" I take Hào'yáng's hand, forcing him to look at me. "When we are born," I continue, "we are set on a path to walk. That is our fate. But how we *choose* to walk it—that becomes our destiny. I don't think we should question why we are given the lives we are but, rather, how we should live them."

"*How . . . romantic.*"

The words ring out in the night, echoing across the streets as a surge of demonic energies hits us: wrath incarnate, laced through with centuries of hatred.

Sansiran.

I step forward, sword raised, shielding Hào'yáng behind me as we both turn to face the source of her voice: the Imperial Palace itself.

I can make out the marble steps leading up to the palace doors, which is writhing with shadows; the golden roofs and vermillion pillars, the jade-green and mother-of-pearl signs cast in night. A familiar scythe moon hangs over it inside a vortex of black.

The gateway.

It seems to have expanded since I escaped a few days ago. Now it has widened beyond the palace, spilling down toward the city crouched in its shadows.

My chest tightens as I think of what it takes to maintain that gateway—of whose blood wet the stones at the base of the pái'fāng, of the resignation on his face as he was forced to his knees. Of the blankness to his eyes as they cut him up like livestock.

I need to know that he's all right, that he's not hurting. Even if I know the ending to our tale, I don't want him to be in pain any longer.

"Come greet me face to face, Crown Prince." Sansiran speaks as though right next to us, her voice resonating through every street and alley, the sheer power of her energies shuddering through the derelict buildings all around. *"Let me see what it is that rendered you the chosen one."*

Hào'yáng makes to move forward, but I catch his arm, tugging him back into the shadows of the house beneath which we are hiding.

"Don't," I whisper. "It's a trap."

His gaze lingers on my face. "There is no way around it," he replies quietly.

"Hào'yáng, wait—"

"Ān'yīng, you must be the one to close the gateway." Hào'yáng lifts his gaze to the city walls, where bursts of light and the clamor of battle fill the air. His expression hardens. "While I engage her in battle, you need to find Yù'chén and end this once and for all."

A violent wind stirs, whipping past us—a wind laced with shadows of the Kingdom of Night.

"Together, then," I say to Hào'yáng, and I summon my spirit energies. An iridescent cloud forms at my feet, and I rise as Hào'yáng kicks off with a burst of qīng'gōng that sends him vaulting onto the rooftops.

The demon queen stands at the top of the marble steps, framed by the palace doors and exuding darkness as though the night warps around her.

Hào'yáng and I alight across from her on the open marble walkway. Lining the sides of the walkway are alabaster pillars with carvings of golden dragons twined around them: the symbol of the Kingdom of Rivers' imperial lineage and a commemoration of the Azure Dragon, who gave life to this realm.

Sansiran tips her head to watch us, the garnets flashing in her hair. "At last, Crown Prince," she croons, "we meet face to face."

Hào'yáng grips the hilt of Azure Tide. Power rolls off him, beneath which flows a decade-long current of anger. "You may have forgotten my face, but I haven't forgotten yours, Demon Queen."

Sansiran gives a delighted laugh. "Ah, yes. Nearly ten years ago, was it, mortal prince, when I killed your family?"

I shift my sword in my hands. My spirit energies burn, their lights writhing like flames beneath my skin.

Hào'yáng's voice, however, is steady. "Your memory is as good as mine, Demon Queen. But you made the mistake of leaving me alive. From a single seed, a forest springs." His mouth curves in a triumphant smile.

"Yes, and now I've come to clean up the petulant little seed that has slipped through our fingers all these years," Sansiran says, narrowing her gaze. "You've been quite the annoyance, Crown Prince. With you still alive, the throne remains contested and my son unable to secure his position in this realm." As sudden as an arrow, her stare pins me. "And now the mortal girl turned immortal; the halfling with a claim on both realms. I admit, you have some value yet to me, for the sole reason that you could offer my son a link to the Kingdom of Sky *and* the Kingdom of Rivers . . . and my son—my foolish, stupid son—for whatever unfathomable reason, believes himself in love with you still."

The air shifts and the shadows move behind Sansiran.

He emerges, standing tall behind his mother. His face, once so expressive with that wicked grin, is devoid of emotion; his eyes, once dancing with delight and so alive, are vacant. Yù'chén stares down at me, looking every bit the heir to the Kingdom of Night.

"If the Crown Prince wishes to face me, then I shall end his life by my own hands," Sansiran purrs. "My son will deal with you as he sees fit, immortal halfling." Her gaze snaps to Yù'chén, her voice suddenly as sharp as a blade. "Capture her. If you fail to bind her to you again, I *will* kill her this time."

Yù'chén moves—so quickly that even with my enhanced senses, I fail to catch him. One moment, he's at the palace entrance behind Sansiran; the next, he is at my side. His sword plunges toward me in a flash of crimson, and I lift mine to block, barely in time. The strength of his blow rattles my teeth and bones. I stumble away inelegantly and catch myself—just as his second attack comes.

I dive to one side as his sword comes down. With a crack like a whip, the marble walkway splits beneath the force of his blade; stone flies through the air, raining down around us.

Out of the corner of my eye, I catch Hào'yáng moving toward me.

Sansiran strikes.

Hào'yáng leaps back as the force of Sansiran's power hits where he stood half a heartbeat ago. Rubble erupts from the spot; when the dust clears, the marble is black, as though burned.

A trickle of blood winds down Hào'yáng's temple. His sword radiates a turquoise glow that seems to light the skin of his hands and face.

As Sansiran closes in on him from the front, there comes movement to his *sides*.

Two massive shadows peel off from the pillars. At first, I have the illusion that the dragon statues are moving—but when I make out the figures, my stomach sinks with cold fear.

Two of the Four Perils emerge, one on each side of Hào'yáng. I recognize them: Qióng'qí and Táo'wú, the very hellbeasts that destroyed Xī'lín.

I move toward him—

Yù'chén steps in my way. The garnet on the hilt of his sword flashes the color of blood; his expression is as cold and unfeeling as death as he stares at me. For the first time since I've known him, I see him—truly see him—as what he is.

A demon.

There is nothing left of the man I knew.

I raise my sword again. "Finally showing your true colors?" I'm slightly out of breath.

He says nothing.

As the hellbeasts and Sansiran spring their attack on Hào'yáng, I summon my spirit energies. I surge forward on my iridescent cloud—

—only to ram into a wall of darkness.

I tumble back, barely catching myself as I land on the ground again. Yù'chén's eyes glow crimson as dark magic flows from his palms, forming the shields behind him. Cutting me off from Hào'yáng.

At the same time, we thrust our palms out. Spirit energies explode from me, as bright as the sun against his magic of night. The resulting clash flings me backward in the direction of the palace doors.

Pain lances through my back as I slam into the ground. The world splinters with the acute pain of my ribs cracking. When I come to, it is to a bright-blue light streaking through the dark. Like a shooting star, it arcs across the eastern sky . . . straight toward us.

Snow falls from its tail—gentle, beautiful flakes of snow, drifting down toward us.

The light slows as it descends over the palace roofs, and I make out a shape within, serpentine and scaled and utterly familiar:

She of the Moon-Frosted Sea.

The dragon soars past me, making straight for where Hào'yáng faces off against Sansiran and the two Perils.

It has been a while, Lotus Immortal. Her voice, sweet and ancient, rings out in my mind. *I come of my own volition, not as a representative of the dragons of the Four Seas. Our realm cannot declare an alliance with one of the two heirs to the Kingdom of Rivers— yet as Hào'yáng's chosen companion since birth, I have the right to participate by my choice.*

Outwardly, she utters a sound between a shrill cry and a melodic song. Qióng'qí and Táo'wù look up as her power hits them; even Sansiran pauses.

Hào'yáng, blood dripping down his arm, hefts his sword

upright—and plunges it straight into Táo'wù's core as She of the Moon-Frosted Sea descends upon the demon queen.

I push myself to my feet, spitting out blood. I'm shaking, my entire being aglow in the soft blush of my spirit energies as they rush to heal my broken bones. My vision slides in and out of focus.

A shadow falls across the floor. When I look up, Yù'chén is standing over me.

He reaches out with his magic: shadows forming vines, blooming with bright, beautiful scorpion lilies. I expect pain, a dagger in my back or thorns from his magic to pierce my heart.

But there is none of that. The darkness is almost gentle as Yù'chén lifts me into the air, high enough for me to glimpse the other side of this battle, for Sansiran to glance over and see me. The palace steps blur as we ascend.

Dimly, I feel myself being deposited on the floor. Something soft brushes my cheek; when I open my eyes, frayed blue carpets come into focus, threaded through with golden dragons. Dust tickles my nose.

Footsteps, sharp and clinical.

Then Yù'chén steps through the double doors, his shields of darkness expanding behind him.

Trapping me inside the palace.

31

Àn'yīng

Imperial Palace, Kingdom of Rivers

Cold. Black. Sinking into my bones with a frightening familiarity as my spirit energies resume healing me and my senses slowly return. I'm lying in the middle of the long hallway leading to the dais, where the throne of the Kingdom of Rivers rests, unoccupied for over a decade. On either side of me are the tatters of silk banners that once hung with the insignia of our kingdom: a golden circle with a river of lapis lazuli. The air is as still as death.

All but for the shifting, swirling gateway open behind the throne.

The gateway that I need to destroy—by ending Yù'chén's life.

I clench my teeth, and with enormous effort, I heave myself onto my feet, dragging my lotus sword with me.

Yù'chén stands against the great mahogany doors of the palace, watching me in silence. Neither of us moves—him, sharp and clear as steel; me, wounded and swaying, the soft blush of my energies pooling at my feet as my body desperately tries to heal itself.

Panting, I point my sword at him.

He blinks once, glancing at the blade, then looks back at my face. "You've figured it out, then," he says.

I'm too tired to speak, but I need to stall, at least until my wounds are healed. Warmth seeps back into my limbs, the pain dulling as my bones and tendons mend themselves back together. "Figured what out?"

"The secret to the gateway. Why it remains open, decades later. How Sansiran managed to create one in the first place."

"It's you," I whisper. "You are the key to keeping that gateway open."

Somehow, he looks pleased. "Well done. You're right. It's me, Àn'yīng—it's been me from the very start. My blood, my life, is what ties my realm to yours; how the gateway remains open, expanding into the Kingdom of Rivers. Without me, the Kingdom of Night cannot maintain this gateway." A humorless smile curves his lips. "You figured that out the night Sansiran spilled my blood, didn't you?"

I grip Fleet and my lotus sword tighter. "I did."

His laugh is humorless. "Is that why you're here, Àn'yīng? So you can kill me and close the Kingdom of Night's way into the mortal realm once and for all? So Hào'yáng can finally be crowned emperor of the Kingdom of Rivers and everyone can have their happy ending?"

I search his features for the man I have come to know—the man I loved in spite of realms colliding and the fates dissenting. I know he must be in there, somewhere. I know it was real.

"I never wanted this," I say softly.

Yù'chén is quiet for several heartbeats. I can't read the thoughts behind those fathomless black eyes, as dark as the ocean at midnight.

He gives a tiny shake of his head. "It's never about what we want, Àn'yīng," he replies. "In the end, in spite of all the palm readings and prayers to the stars, this is what our fates have led us to, isn't it?" That same, humorless smile lingers around his mouth—but when he glances away briefly, there is something like shattered glass to his gaze. "My blood was made to destroy your world; my very existence has been to help my realm take yours. No matter how you look at it, I was made to be your monster in this lifetime." Yù'chén lifts his sword. "So let me be your monster until the very end, Àn'yīng."

Without warning, he charges at me.

I raise my own blade, my body protesting in pain as I retaliate. But Yù'chén is too strong, too fast, too powerful. His first blow knocks me back several steps; I've barely reoriented myself before he's on me again, sword flashing, the air parting before him as he cuts through with the grace of a blade's edge. Again and again, I trade blows with him, each of my parries growing weaker and slower, even with Fleet's talisman pouring energies into me, even with my spirit energies sparking at my fingertips like guttering candle flames.

I realize, now, that Yù'chén has never used this side of him against me. I've seen him tear down enemies without batting an eye; I've witnessed the terrifying demonic powers he holds. But in all those times, he has used them to protect me.

He has never unleashed them upon me.

My lotus sword flies from my grasp, clanging onto the ground somewhere beyond my reach in the darkness. All I'm left with is Fleet. I'm gasping in breaths, a sharp ache has bloomed near my ribs, yet miraculously, I've sustained no flesh wounds.

Yù'chén lands, again blocking the doors. Sometime in the course of our fight, they have cracked open. A sliver of the outside yields glimpses of the battle: flashes of icy white and turquoise—She of the Moon-Frosted Sea facing down the two Perils, and Hào'yáng still holding ground against Sansiran.

Yet more movement catches my attention. Through the darkened streets and alleys of the Imperial City come moving pinpricks of . . . light. Flame. *Torches.*

A shout goes up as mortal warriors spill out from the streets and abandoned houses, gathering at the palace steps. And then they're charging up, and I think I see Fú'yí at the front, long-sword flashing as she runs. Soaring overhead on wisps of clouds are Zhōng'lì and Tiě'guǎi . . . and, farther behind them in the skies . . . specks of white and gold, winking like stars.

Growing closer.

I hardly believe my eyes as uniformed immortal warriors materialize, descending upon iridescent clouds, weapons out and energies blazing.

The immortal armies are here.

We won, I think in disbelief. *We beat the mó in the Temple of Dawn.*

Yet they're not the only ones who have arrived.

All across the palace grounds, from the white marble walkway to the steps, the air is shifting. A darkness blots out the fading sun like a storm cloud.

Mó—an entire army of them, some riding hellbeasts, others on foot. They descend like flocks of birds from the skies, gathering behind where Sansiran battles.

With a flick of his wrist, Yù'chén slams the palace doors closed again with his dark magic and turns to me. His face is in shadow; I cannot make out his expression, but I speak first this time.

"The immortal army is here," I tell him. "Even if you kill me, they won't spare you."

"Kill you?" He raises an eyebrow. "Again, assuming the worst of me, little scorpion."

I blink at the familiar nickname.

Yù'chén lowers his sword. Beyond the gateway, in the Kingdom of Night, comes movement. Silhouettes emerge: more mó warriors, dressed for battle, gathering in the Palace of the Aurora to cross over into this realm.

"The entire mó army in the Kingdom of Night is coming through this gateway for this war." Yù'chén's words confirm my worst nightmare. "It won't be an even fight, Àn'yīng."

I'm kneeling on the ground, too drained to stand. Sparks of my spirit energies flutter weakly at my wrist and on my skin, like embers of a dying flame. My lotus sword lies somewhere out of reach.

"Àn'yīng."

I glance up sharply. Yù'chén's tone has changed. It's softer, gentle, the way he would call my name when we were still candidates in the Immortality Trials; when we were in the Kingdom of Night together.

When things between us were real.

"Àn'yīng," Yù'chén repeats, raising his sword again. "I promise, you'll be safe."

Safe, like a bird in a cage. Safe, like those claimed mortals relying on the whims of their mó masters. Safe, while his realm ravages mine.

I'd rather die than let that happen. And if this is how it comes to an end, then I'm going to take him with me.

Yù'chén leaps through the air toward me. Too high, too fast, and his cloak whips back behind him, revealing the glint of something familiar.

Something that falls, arcing like a crescent moon.

Right toward me.

Heart.

The blade I left with him back in the Kingdom of Sky. The one with the strangest talisman: a talisman that listens only to the intent of one's heart.

I'm on my feet. My hand darts out; my fingers close around my blade's familiar hilt, the touch of my energies activating the talisman engraved there by my father.

I pray for the talisman to work this time.

For my heart to guide me true.

Yù'chén lands before me. One step, two, and he's within arm's reach, his sword flashing as he thrusts it toward me.

I surge forward to meet him, arm outstretched, Heart gleaming in my hand.

I plunge the crescent blade toward his chest, where his demon's core and his mortal heart sit. A move that will end with me on his sword, and him on my blade.

We collide.

Resistance. The sound of metal slicing through flesh. Liquid heat, spilling down my sword hand.

We are caught in an embrace: Yù'chén's arm encircles my back, holding me to him, my hands fisted against his chest. The hilt of my dagger in my palm.

The blade buried in his heart.

The seconds pass by; the pain I'm waiting for doesn't come.

Then, dimly, I hear the sound of a sword clattering to the ground.

Yù'chén slumps against me. His breaths heave against the crook of my neck as he lifts his sword hand and places it on the back of my head. He turns his cheek to me as he strokes my hair, once, infinitely gentle.

A stillness falls. The air that was, moments ago, charged with energies and motion has fallen still and silent.

I can't move, can't think, can't process anything but for the ridges of Heart's hilt in my palms, pressed against the warmth of his chest; the gleam of his own blade, discarded at his feet.

Yù'chén's body seizes against me; his fingers dig into my back as a tremor passes through him.

I gasp and wrench myself from his grasp. He stands there, swaying, the hilt of Heart protruding from his chest. His head is bent; his hands are open. One is outstretched, as though reaching for someone or something. Suddenly, I'm reminded of that day back in the Immortality Trials when he was punished by the immortals for stealing a sewing kit—a sewing kit that he gifted me—and no one came to his aid.

Slow and steady comes the drip, drip, drip of his blood, seeping into the blue carpet and its gold dragons beneath us.

Over the throne, beyond the dais, the gateway gives a palpable shudder, like a ripple running across the surface of a lake.

Yù'chén falls to the floor. He is very still but for his chest, rising and falling in shallow breaths. The cold light of the moon from his realm beyond the gateway spills over his figure as his veins darken and scales spread across his skin. His demon's form, revealed as his demonic magic works desperately to heal him.

I kneel before him. His clawed hands grip the hilt of Heart;

his terrifying demon's eyes, black with pinpricks of red, are focused on a spot on the floor.

Blood pools beneath his chest, and black ichor leaks from his wound, dissipating like smoke. The surface of the gateway shudders again.

Gently, I touch my fingers to Yù'chén's cheeks. He flinches and closes his eyes, bringing an arm up to cover his face. "Don't," he rasps.

"You . . ." I don't have the words. My voice catches; my throat is too tight.

"Àn'yīng," he pants. "Please. Grant me . . . some dignity."

But I reach for his scaled shoulders. Pull his arm from his face. Take in every darkened vein running across his skin, the curve of his fangs, the length of his claws. The demon's form that he has been so reviled for.

"Tell me this isn't real," I whisper. I'm cold all over, shaking; I keep looking to the hilt of Heart in his chest, the blood flowing from his wound that isn't slowing.

The corner of his lip curves. When he speaks, his words are so faint, I barely catch them. "It's real."

The ichor leaking from his chest begins to slow. The dark veins on his skin are fading, the scales and claws and fangs retracting. And then I'm looking into a most beautiful human face—one that captured my heart once upon a time in the woods of the mortal realm.

Yù'chén's chest rises and falls as his breathing grows labored. His lips are pale when he says, touching a finger to Heart's hilt, "You meant it this time."

The first time I tried using Heart against him, my own traitorous will stayed my hand. He lived and kept Heart with him.

"Did you know I would?" I whisper.

He blinks, then gives a single, slow nod.

"Then why?" My voice cracks. Somewhere outside, beyond these doors, freedom for the mortal realm is spreading its wings—but instead of victory, I feel in this moment as though I have lost everything.

"I promised you," Yù'chén mumbles, "that I'd do everything in my power to give you what I can of the world you wanted."

Warmth slides down my cheeks. I feel cheated: I thought our farewell in the immortal realm meant severing whatever we once felt for each other. That we'd both chosen our families and our kingdoms over each other.

Knowing he is choosing me after all feels like a betrayal. A debt I'll never be able to repay.

"I'll admit, I thought of doing the worst things you assumed of me," Yù'chén continues. "I thought of taking you away and making you mine. But you taught me that selfishness isn't love; that true love is selfless. That our fates can change because of the choices we make in our lives." His lashes flutter. "Those nights you spent in the Palace of the Aurora, I heard you dreaming of afternoons beneath your plum tree with your mother and Méi'zi. I wanted to gift you that. And I realized there was only one way I could. Because . . . because sometimes, love means letting go."

Words I once spoke to him beneath the stars of his realm. Words that are now breaking my heart.

Yù'chén lifts a hand and touches my cheek. Drops of my tears cling to his fingers when he pulls away.

"Thank you," he murmurs. He blinks rapidly, his chest rising and falling fast. Too fast. "Stay," he says suddenly, reaching for my hand. "Stay this time. Please."

"I'm here, Yù'chén."

His eyes search mine.

"I keep having a dream," he whispers. "The same dream. I'm in a forest, and I've been searching my entire life for something, but I don't know what it is. Then I hear someone say my name, and suddenly, I know in my soul that I've found what I'm looking for."

I stare at him, my heart pounding. *The same dream.*

He stands in the clearing, turning toward me as though time has slowed—a painting in the rising dawn.

Hair, billowing like swirls of ink.

Eyes, flashing like golden embers.

The phantom of a smile on his face as his gaze lifts to meet mine—

Impossible.

"Àn'yīng." Yù'chén speaks my name with infinite gentleness. His lashes flutter, yet he gazes at me with something nearing serenity. "Can I . . . ask for one thing?"

I nod, not trusting myself to speak.

He tries to lift a hand to touch my cheek. Can't. It falls to his side. "Will you smile for me?" he asks.

I realize I have never smiled at him, not truly. I've regarded him with caution, suspicion, sorrow, and hatred . . . I've kissed him and desired him. I've loved him.

But I've never smiled at him.

It feels monumental, in this moment, to lift my head beyond the sorrow in my lungs. But I somehow do. I hold his gaze and pull my lips into a smile, even as my tears fall on his cheeks, his neck, his lips.

Yù'chén breathes in deeply. A glow seems to emanate from his skin, warm as dawn, as the throne room around us fills with a great rushing sound. Shadows dance on the walls, tendrils of darkness curling through the air, pulling gently toward the open gateway. Red scorpion lilies bloom and fade against its opening, as though time is unwinding before our eyes. The blues and golds of the carpet gleam, the marble walls and lapis patterns brighten, and suddenly, the night begins to lift.

The gateway behind me is collapsing. The edges dissolve like smoke, the red scorpion lilies braid in on themselves, as though stitching a broken seam between realms. As the ground and the air tremble around us, I gather Yù'chén in my arms. His head falls against my shoulder, his lashes casting perfect crescents against his cheeks. Like this, he could be asleep.

The gateway gives one last shudder. A great, sourceless wind blasts through the palace, shattering windows and breaking open doors. I close my eyes, curling my body over Yù'chén's as sand and rubble from the ruins blow over us.

Then: nothing.

I open my eyes. The palace doors are open. Sunlight spills through, bright, clear, and golden, pooling on the floors and warming the air. Outside, the sky is the most brilliant shade of azure. A winter-tinged wind kisses my cheeks, blowing flower petals from the gardens inside. They drift toward the back of the room, onto a gleaming gilded throne framed against a great painting of the Kingdom of Rivers: white clouds and green pines, lakes and mountains, all drenched in the gold of the sun.

I look down, and there I find the greatest mystery of all.

Where Yù'chén's body was is now a scattering of red scorpion lilies, petals bright and gleaming. They face the sun, and as

I watch, a butterfly lands on a petal. Its wings, patterned in the most remarkable swirls of black and crimson, open and close. It rests for several heartbeats, then takes off, circling once over my head before flitting outside and vanishing into the endless blue skies.

32

Àn'yīng

Kingdom of Rivers

I follow the butterfly.

Outside, the sun is too bright, too warm, as it caresses my skin. I close my eyes, and when I reopen them, the colors of my realm are effervescent. Everything is drenched in a gleaming golden haze, the realm at long last awakened from an eternal night.

I heard you dreaming of afternoons beneath your plum tree with your mother and Méi'zi. I wanted to gift you that.

I turn back to the throne room, convinced for a moment that I'll see him there, red cloak stirring in the wind, smile curving his lips, as beautiful as the first time I met him.

But the hall is empty, the gateway gone.

I sweep a last glance across the chamber. Then I wipe my sleeves across my cheeks, turn, and step outside.

The liberation of the Imperial City turns the tides of the battle. Everywhere I look, mó are backing down, their powers waning beneath the energies of the sun. The immortals' power, on the other hand, grows, the air filling with their spirit energies.

I charge through the battleground, lotus sword in hand, Fleet granting me speed. My spirit energies are buoyed by the presence of the sun, and on my chest, where my jade pendant once rested, I feel a tug in my heart drawing me forward.

He's there. White-and-gold lamellar armor glinting, blue sword flashing, he fights astride She of the Moon-Frosted Sea. Somehow, across the entire battlefield, Hào'yáng's gaze finds mine.

He flies to me, She of the Moon-Frosted Sea weaving gracefully through the battle, and leaps off when he reaches for me.

Gently, he tips my chin toward him, eyes searching mine, brows furrowed.

My eyes burn even as I whisper, "It's done."

Hào'yáng draws me into his arms and simply holds me, his heartbeat against mine. I don't know how to explain to him that what should be a moment of victory has turned, instead, to one of grief. That I love him so endlessly and brilliantly as the sky loves the sun—but beneath, now, the shadow of another is carved into my soul.

But I don't have to.

Hào'yáng places his palms on my cheeks and wipes the tears away. "I understand," he says quietly, and that is all I need to hear.

We mount She of the Moon-Frosted Sea, who shoots up into the skies. Wind whistles past us as we soar beyond the raging battle, the walls of the Imperial Palace . . . to the glittering river encircling the city. The dragonhorse's scales reflect on the water's surface as we descend.

I squeeze Hào'yáng's hand. "Go," I urge him.

The waves of the river rise to meet him as he slides off his dragonhorse's back. Hào'yáng steps into the tide, and the water wreathes him like a robe, lowering him to the surface of the river.

Then he sinks.

A tremor goes through the earth. Quietly, subtly, like the soft tap of a finger against a sheepskin drum. Only those paying attention will notice how the surface of the river quakes, waters breaking into thousands of little ripples; how the leaves in the surrounding trees quiver in unison. How even the clouds seem to pause.

A second tremor runs through the land, and this time, it is unmistakable: a shiver, as if the ground itself is waking.

And then the river begins to undulate, rippling across its aquamarine waters, and in the center, a vortex forms.

The waters part for Hào'yáng as he emerges, armor glinting as though it holds the sun within. The river wraps around him, giving the impression that he glides toward us on the backs of two cerulean dragons.

As he approaches, She of the Moon-Frosted Sea does something I have never seen. She dips her head, bending her forelegs as though in a deep bow.

That's when I know.

Hào'yáng's smile is radiant as he holds both hands out to me. I take them as I step off the dragonhorse, and then I'm standing on the backs of the waves in his arms, embracing him tightly.

They are coming, She of the Moon-Frosted Sea announces in our minds. *The dragons are coming.*

I follow her gaze to the distant east—the direction of the Four Seas. At first, I mistake them for undulating clouds. Yet as they draw closer, I catch the gleam of scales. The flash of talons.

They are coming to support the crowning of the emperor.

Hào'yáng and I turn to face them. In his other hand, Azure Tide's glow pulses, growing stronger and brighter like a heartbeat, a silent call. And answering that call is the light radiating from the dozens of dragons approaching us.

They soar through the skies, scales shimmering in jewel tones of sapphire and amber, cinnabar and amethyst and jade, forming a line like a gleaming rainbow. Where they go, the air ripples, the clouds part, and plants grow from the soil, leaves turning from jade to a rich gold-red of late autumn beneath their serpentine shadows.

Hào'yáng takes my hand as we mount She of the Moon-Frosted Sea again. The dragonhorse takes off joyfully into the air, and soon, we're flying amidst dragons, some as tall as mountains or as long as rivers, others the size of hills and streams.

In that moment, astride a dragonhorse with my boy in the jade, I am a little girl again. I am the Àn'yīng of Xī'lín, needle and thread in hand, dreaming of seeing the ocean. Believing in fairy tales and the myths of old. I am her, and yet I am also the Àn'yīng of now: the warrior, the fighter, provider for her family and Lotus Immortal.

On the ground, the mó army is retreating at the sight of the dragons. Throughout the battlefield, they open passageways back to their own realm—passageways that, now, can never be reopened from their side of the Kingdom of Night. Those lucky enough to escape the clutches of the immortal army and the dragons flee through them, vanishing forever from our realm.

We alight before the steps of the palace. There, still engaged in battle with several of the Eight Immortals, is Sansiran. The power emanating from her crackles like a storm, and even Dòng'bīn is no match for her.

Hào'yáng steps forward, the sea-blue glow of Azure Tide flowing across the palace walls and grounds. Sansiran looks up—and stills.

"Demon Queen Sansiran," Hào'yáng begins. "You have defied the Heavenly Order and waged war across the realms. Your insatiable greed has caused the suffering of so many, including your own.

"Today, the Heavens speak back. The dragons of old are here to declare their alliance with me. The gateway between our realms has closed, freeing my city of your grasp. Now I intend to take back the Kingdom of Rivers to return peace and prosperity to its peoples and its lands. Surrender and swear never again to wage war upon our realms, and we grant you amnesty and return to the Kingdom of Night. But continue . . ." Hào'yáng's sword pulses with a sudden, fierce light. "Continue, and we will have no mercy."

For the first time ever, Sansiran's expression shows an inkling of fear. It yields quickly to fury as she bares her teeth in a snarl. *"Yù'chén, come,"* she calls, the power of her command ripping through the air.

But there is no one to answer.

I think of the scorpion lilies, bright and red in the sunlight; of the butterfly soaring out into blue skies.

"Yù'chén, come to me," Sansiran repeats, her voice rising to a near-scream, perhaps to mask the fear slowly sinking into her expression. Her dark magic crashes through the crowd and surges into every corner of the Imperial Palace.

When she receives no answer from her son, realization twists the demon queen's expression. Fury darkens the air around her like a storm, shadows whipping in an invisible wind as she rises from the ground, flanked by her two Perils.

Sansiran lashes out with her powers: a bolt of black lightning, aimed straight for Hào'yáng.

Hào'yáng raises Azure Tide, and around us, magic fills the air. The dragons begin to glow, their energies pouring toward Hào'yáng. The air thrums with the vastness of oceans; the churning of tides; the shift of seasons, the turn of realms and lives across time. Power more ancient than this world, coalescing around us.

Hào'yáng steps forward, sword raised, an aurora of light splintering through Sansiran's shadows. Azure Tide arcs through the air, sending the combined powers of the dragons tearing through the demon queen.

Sansiran's mouth remains open in that furious shriek. As a blinding nexus of light explodes over her, the last I see is her face, distorted in hatred until the very end.

When the light fades, the marble steps are empty. Nothing remains in the spot where Sansiran and her Perils stood, not even a trace of shadows or a single petal of her red oleander. The sun gleams over us, and the Imperial Palace sparkles with remnants of the dragons' magic.

Slowly, immortals, mortals, and halflings alike gather around us, forming a circle. Some are wounded and bloodied, some in disbelief at the sudden end to the battle—yet as they turn their gazes to their heir and rightful emperor, their expressions transform to reverence.

One by one, they kneel. Even the immortals follow suit, heads bowed in deference. A chant rises, soft at first but growing stronger: *"Emperor . . . Emperor . . . Emperor . . ."*

Hào'yáng's eyes, however, remain only on mine as, before

all his subjects and allies, he, too, lowers himself to one knee and inclines his head.

Toward me.

"Hé Àn'yīng," he says, his voice ringing across the grounds. "Honorable Lotus Immortal. Without you, my life would be forfeit. It is you who pulled me from the gates of the Nine Fountains, who breathed life into me again. It is you who turned the tides of this war by destroying the gateway to the Kingdom of Night, which the mó used to feed on the energy and life of our realm. And it is you who secured the alliance with the Kingdom of Sky." Hào'yáng's gaze meets mine, and I find that I cannot breathe. "The honor of winning this war, therefore, belongs to you."

Murmurs ripple through the crowd, and I feel it, the moment their attention shifts to me. Then, one by one, the warriors turn to me, heads bent, as they chant my name. Behind me, the dragons rise into the skies, sunlight refracting off their colorful scales. The air fills with their ancient, echoing song until they blend into the brilliant blue of the distant horizon, disappearing into the folds of another realm.

33

Àn'yīng

Kingdom of Rivers

The soft dawn light coats the blossom in hues of gold. My breath plumes before me as I brush aside a dusting of snow and bend to examine the flower.

It's a red scorpion lily. The petals taper to sharp edges, unfurling like a crimson star and gleaming like a ruby in the snow.

A beautiful flower for a beautiful maiden.

A flower foretelling a tragic fate? You can keep it.

I blink, glancing around me, half expecting to find him there before me, dressed in his bright red cloak and wearing that wicked smile. Yet as the ghosts of voices past fade, I find that there is no one else in this section of the Imperial Palace gardens. No one and nothing but me, the blossoms, and my footprints in the freshly fallen first snows.

It's been one month since the Battle of the Imperial City. The palace is being rebuilt, much like the rest of our kingdom.

Hào'yáng summoned our remaining mortal practitioners to journey with him throughout the realm, repairing the wards the Kingdom of Night broke past over a decade ago. Word of our victory has spread throughout the Kingdom of Rivers, spinning it into tales and legends of the crown prince and the Lotus Immortal; of the Day the Dragons Danced, heralding a long and prosperous reign for the new emperor of the Kingdom of Rivers.

The immortals, too, have reclaimed their realm since the mó were driven out. Shortly after the battle, I bid farewell to the Eight Immortals who stood with us. We are soon to be reunited when I attend a ceremony before the High Court of the Kingdom of Sky to officially seal my title and position among them.

All is well; the valiant warriors have been honored, the fallen soldiers paid their due respect.

Except for one.

I kneel before the scorpion lily. I had another dream last night—the same one, in the forest, where I search for something. For someone.

Dark magic leaves signs behind, he once told me. *Unnatural growths of flowers, birds, and animals that don't belong . . .*

As his voice echoes in my mind, I catch movement in my peripheral vision.

A butterfly, flitting between the branches of snow-kissed plum blossoms. Its wings catch the early morning sunlight, reflecting patterns of red and black. It flies toward me, circling the scorpion lily.

In disbelief, I hold out a hand. Chest tight, hope drumming a wild heartbeat inside me, I can't help but wonder . . .

"Àn'yīng!"

A cheerful shriek pierces the peaceful silence. I turn as a whizzing pink blur rams into me, tackling me onto the snow. Méi'zi is cackling as she draws back. Her cheeks are flushed, her eyes bright; her chin is tucked into the thick fur of her new winter cloak. By her side, a familiar little white fox with amber eyes and a bushy tail yips in what sounds like laughter.

"We're finally doing it!" Méi'zi squeals, clasping my hand as I right myself, brushing snow from my hair and shoulders. "Mā and I are packed, and our carriages are arriving this afternoon!"

I can't help grinning. As soon as Mā and Méi'zi arrived from the Western Province, they enlisted in the recovery efforts across the kingdom. As seamstresses, they will travel the realm, distributing blankets to those in need ahead of winter, helping patch up broken paper windows and curtains, and sewing sheets and pillowcases for bedding. The sun and the wind were good for my mother, who returned from her journey stronger. She is now able to spend most of her day on her feet—and most importantly, that spark to her eyes is back, as though traveling healed her body and soul.

I ruffle Méi'zi's hair. "Make sure to send word every day. Who knows, I may join you should our paths cross."

Méi'zi taps the plum blossom hairpin clasped over her braids; its bright fuchsia gemstones glint in the sunlight. In my own hair, I wear a matching cherry blossom hairpin. With some help from Hào'yáng, we enchanted these with the same talismans my father used on the pair of jade pendants. Now Méi'zi need only speak my name into hers for me to hear her and respond.

A yip catches our attention. With a swirl of snow, the little white fox waiting at our feet vanishes and Lì'líng returns to her human form, wide-eyed and dressed in a cream-colored winter coat. She stretches, yawning in a manner extremely reminiscent of her animal form. "I'm hungry! Let's go have breakfast. Tán'mù and your mother are waiting for us; I asked the kitchens if they had any lotus-wrapped glutinous rice." She bares all her teeth in a wide grin. "They do."

"Race you!" Méi'zi squeals, and she takes off, dashing through the snow, Lì'líng streaking by her side in her fox form again. Their laughter echoes through the palace gardens.

I'm smiling as I watch them round a pavilion, where I make out two figures seated at a table laden with food. Mā waves to me, then laughs as Méi'zi flings her arms around her shoulders, shrieking that she's won. Leaning against a pillar, Tán'mù watches this with the slightest curve to her lips. Lì'líng bounds up to her and leaps into her lap, transforming into her human form. She's giggling as she pecks a kiss on Tán'mù's cheek. Sunlight spills golden and crisp upon them, and all around us, the plum trees in the garden are blossoming beneath the snow.

I look down at the scorpion lily. The butterfly is gone.

I heard you dreaming of afternoons beneath your plum tree with your mother and Méi'zi. I wanted to gift you that.

I press a finger to the petal of the scorpion lily. Perhaps there are traces of magic that linger on this earth, but wherever he is, I hope he is happy, and I hope he is free. I hope he has found the life he so wished for, beyond the Nine Fountains.

I hope he knows that in the end, his choice not only defined his life; it changed the world.

My fingers brush against the scorpion lily's petals—but unlike in the myths, they do not cut me. They are gentle, soft velvet.

"Àn'yīng."

I turn, my heart and spirit lifting at the sound of that voice—one I've been waiting to hear for weeks.

Hào'yáng leans against one of the mahogany pillars of the walkway leading from inside the palace. He's dressed in a long brocade gown the blue of rivers, woven with patterns of golden scales. Silver lamellar armor pads his body, and at his waist is Azure Tide. In the sunlight, his hair shifts colors, ink-black to mercurial grays, like liquid starlight.

I'm on my feet, running to him, and then in his arms, my face buried in the crook of his neck, in his familiar scent of oceans and sword metal. "I missed you unbearably," I say, and kiss him.

"As I did you," he murmurs. "I came for you as soon as I returned."

I draw back, only long enough to say, "Never leave me for so long again."

He captures my lips again, grinning this time. "Is that an order, Empress?"

Empress. By the end of the week, we are to complete our coronation ceremony, where we will also be married—not just beneath the Heavenly Order but also by the laws of the Kingdom of Rivers. Ambassadors from all provinces—East, West, North, and South—will be present as we reestablish the government. Villages have been asked to nominate their representatives, who will cast their votes for regional officials.

Then Hào'yáng and I will embark on a tour of the kingdom, enacting policies across the land as the kingdom rebuilds.

One policy I will be leading has to do with the acceptance of halflings. Under a new law, we will abolish the presence of yāo'jīng slave pens like those where Lì'líng, Tán'mù, and so many others were held. And slowly, we will reeducate the kingdom on the topic of halflings . . . beginning with me.

I search Hào'yáng's face. His eyes are bright as he gazes at me, but the shadows beneath reveal his exhaustion.

"The wards?" I ask.

"Strong enough for now. We'll keep mending them—and teaching future generations how to preserve them." He smiles at me and kisses my hand. "There is so much I wish to do, Àn'yīng. I want to bring back schools of practitioning. I want to reopen exchanges between our realm and the Kingdom of Sky, bringing the Immortality Trials back to what they were meant to be when they were first established." Hào'yáng cups his palm to my cheeks, his face open with joy. "I want to do it all; I want to see this world and rebuild it, with you by my side."

I gaze into the eyes of my boy in the jade, and in that moment, I myself feel nothing but hope. There are nights when I still wake with a gasp, certain a mó lurks outside my windows or terrified that Mā is slipping away from me. But those nights, the bad nights, are beginning to fade. With time, the good days will triumph.

For once, with Mā and Méi'zi off on their own callings, the future lies wide open before me. No more family to protect. No more duties to fulfill.

My life and destiny as bright as silk waiting to be woven.

I understand the words my mother and sister once said to me: that I've lived my entire life chasing the shadows of the past and fulfilling Bà's wishes. But now it is as Mā said: I must look to the future and choose how I wish to shape it.

I lean forward and kiss Hào'yáng again, slowly and softly. "I wish to see the oceans with you," I tell him. "I want to see all the realms, everything this world has to offer, by your side."

Hào'yáng reaches into his storage pouch. "I brought back gifts for you," he says, and presses something into my palms.

It's a lacquered sewing box, decorated with fine golden patterns: dragons and oceans, mountains and forests, and a great river winding through it all. When I open it, I gasp in delight.

Threads of every color lay nestled within: rolls and rolls, gleaming like rows of jewels. As I press the tips of my fingers to them, I can tell that they are no ordinary threads.

I look up at Hào'yáng. "These are . . ."

"Silk threads spun with the magic of different provinces, realms, and beings," he says. He points to one that shimmers like strands of light caught beneath the ocean. "That was gifted by the Dragon King of the Western Sea. This," he continues, indicating one with the luster of sun-kissed sands, "by the tribes of the Golden Desert known for raising sand silkworms. This one"—like clouds racing across an azure sky—"from our immortal friends. This"—he points to a thread lit with the flicker of flames—"from the empress of the Realm of Phoenixes."

I listen to him name the allies we've made, beings from realms I'd once only known from storybooks and myths, back before everything happened, when I thought I was destined to be a local seamstress of the Central Province.

"Àn'yīng." Hào'yáng takes my hand and presses a kiss to it. "You deserve these tributes, and more. You've irrevocably shaped lives and realms and the fate of the world we live in. That, as someone very wise once told me, is destiny." From his sleeve pocket, he draws out my half-sewn handkerchief. The ocean and the glinting dragon scales gleam beneath the sun as he hands it to me. "Now, your own destiny awaits you. Perhaps it simply starts with finishing this piece of sewing; or perhaps you'd like to start a new piece." He meets my gaze, eyes as brown and as steady as the earth. "No matter what you choose, I will be there with you through all of it."

I smile as I take the handkerchief, the landscape around us blurring into a golden haze of warmth, snow, and blossoms. A laugh bubbles from my lips. "Why choose?" I say. "Come with me as I sew them all. From every realm, every corner of this world. Together, in this lifetime."

The years rushed by like the currents of a great river. Some were gentler waters, years of peace and calm and love; some were torrential and imbued with major events. There were years of rainfall and years of sunshine; times of sorrow and times of joy. And all of it, I experienced knowing that this was mortal life in the realm of red dust. Knowing that one day, I would turn to the path my birth mother had walked, gazing from the skies into the warm fires of a past life. When that time came, I knew I wished to face it with only joy.

I experienced all of it with Hào'yáng: the blissful love of raising a family, the trials and tribulations of running a kingdom . . . and the world, the entirety of the vast, endless world we lived in, with realms enough for many lifetimes. I did not age as they did. When Méi'zi wed a yāo'jīng ambassador of the Northern Province and began her family, when Mā's hair grew white and her skin wrinkled, when my children grew past my mortal age—I held the same countenance of the young woman I had been the night my immortality was unsealed.

And, inevitably, when all those I loved in my mortal lifetime were swept away by the currents of time into the gentle after of the Nine Fountains, I remained. When spring rains melted the winter snows and the earth bloomed with orchids; when cicadas sang in the lush greens of summer; when autumn burnished the larches in fiery bronzes and golds; and when the silent goose-feather snows of winter returned the world to slumber . . . I remained.

I chose to wander the realms, making good on my first promise to myself, to the young girl I had once been. The one who had wished to see the world. I was searching for something— though I didn't know what it was.

And one day, a day as ordinary as any other, I found it.

Dawn has swept a soft radiance over the cathaya forest. Mists pull in from the nearby seas, gently dressing the trees and blanketing the soil in a shifting haze that catches the faint golds of a rising sun. That light reflects on the glint of my crescent blades.

Today, I am searching. I woke to find a silver-tailed fĕi'fĕi watching me, a mythological creature the size of a cat, with a mane and tail as white as if dusted with snow. Its countenance reminded me of an old friend, and I set off in its direction, determined to find it and capture its likeness in my sewing.

My storage pouch swings from the belt at my hips, carrying within a curious variety of items for an immortal: sewing kits, threads, and handkerchiefs bearing carefully stitched designs of oceans, flower fields, and the portrait of a family sitting beneath a sunlit plum blossom tree. Keepsakes from a past life many centuries ago. The only other items on me, apart from my pale silk dress and my blades, are two hairpins: one bearing a lotus, and another a cherry blossom.

I crouch, sweeping a hand over the fallen leaves and flower petals. There, a single, tiny paw print, delineated by drops of dew.

I grin, following the track farther along—and that's when something catches my eye. A vivid streak of color, jarring and bright against the tranquil corals of the forest at dawn.

A red scorpion lily.

For several moments, I forget to breathe. I'm aware only of the pounding of my heart against my chest, the surge of hope and the inevitable letdown that always follows. In the centuries since the Battle of the Imperial City, I have learned to stop looking for these flowers. They appeared to me after his death, and always in the accompaniment of a red-and-black-winged butterfly, in the Imperial Palace gardens, and at times when I was traveling the realms alone. As though a part of him had never left, and what remained of his soul was returning to the mortal realm to see me. As the years passed, as the trauma of the war and all that had happened in that time faded from me, so, too, did the red scorpion lilies.

Until now.

Hardly daring to draw breath, I approach it. My steps are velvet against the soil, my movements cautious in the way I would approach a small animal, afraid of startling it.

But the flower does not vanish. As I come to a stop before it, I search for a butterfly perched on its petals, as it so often had presented to me in those early days.

I find none.

I let out a long breath. Perhaps loneliness has addled my mind; perhaps the knowledge that my story with him never truly ended has led me to hope in ways beyond all possibility.

Perhaps this is just a regular scorpion lily, blooming from the red dust of our realm.

I crouch by the flower, a faint smile curving my lips even as a familiar ache rises deep in my throat. Foolish, for I had thought that after all these centuries, my once-fiery heart would have frosted over and my emotions would no longer be stirred by such nostalgia.

I touch a finger to stroke a petal of the scorpion lily—just as a voice rings out through the trees.

Someone is laughing. Deep and melodious laughter, heart-felt and genuine . . . one I know like the echoes of a dream.

I stand. Sunlight drips through the canopy in pools of gold, yet through it all, I catch sight of a glade just several dozen steps away. I make out the curved eaves of a moss-colored temple, mahogany pillars blending into the surrounding foliage. A wooden plaque announces in elegant gold lettering that it is a practitioning temple—perhaps one of the many Hào'yáng and I reestablished across the kingdom during our reign. Smoke plumes from its open doors, and wind chimes before its paper windows tinkle in the breeze.

In the clearing, two men are in conversation. Their swords catch the glint of light. One, dressed in a deep-blue shift, turns away and walks into the temple.

I shift my grip on my crescent blades. Their talismans have been aglow with my spirit energies, Fleet lending me speed and Heart pointing me toward what I'd thought was the fěi'fěi.

In a single leap, I'm at the edge of the clearing. My head is light; my limbs are like air; my heart is in my throat.

The man sheathes his longsword and reaches for his cloak, slung on a nearby tree branch. As he tosses it over his shoulders, its rich red hue flares beneath the rising sun, and that is the moment I'm certain.

I keep having a dream, he told me. *The same dream. I'm in a forest, and I've been searching my entire life for something, but I don't know what it is.*

A sudden wind sweeps through the trees, stirring jade-green leaves and peach blossoms into the air. Overhead, the clouds shift, and the sun seems to grow brighter, so that everything is rendered in a golden haze.

I take a step forward, and I dare myself to call out to him.

He pauses. His back is to me, his crimson cloak shifting with the breeze. Then he turns toward me as though time has slowed—a painting in the rising dawn.

Hair, billowing like swirls of ink.

Eyes, flashing like golden embers.

The phantom of a smile on his face as his eyes lift to meet mine.

Then I hear someone say my name, and suddenly, I know in my soul that I've found what I'm looking for.

His lips part, eyes widening as he takes me in. And suddenly, it is as though time flows backward, as though all the years between us vanish within that single heartbeat of our eyes meeting, and we are once again in that same forest in a lifetime long past: me a mortal and him a demon, beholding each other for the very first time.

But this is a different life, in a time centuries later. There is no recognition on his face. Yet his gaze roves me as though he is searching for something; and when he meets my eyes again, his eyes crease in puzzled warmth—perhaps because a memory lingers in his soul, flitting just out of reach of his conscious mind.

He cocks his head, a smile spreading over his face, and it is like watching the sun rising after a long, dark night. His voice is as deep and smooth as the night—exactly the same as I remember it—when he speaks those same first words to me as when we met a lifetime ago.

"Do I know you?"

ACKNOWLEDGMENTS

Having reached the end of my seventh book, I find that my gratitude only continues to grow for those who still stick by my side on these long, sometimes-grueling yet always-magical journeys with me. First and foremost, to my phenomenal editor, Krista Marino: You are the best of the best, and I thank the gods/dragons/Heavenly Order that I get to work with you. You have come a long way from "Let's cut this kiss scene" to, now, "She needs to see his *manly form*." You are so special, hilarious, and wonderful in all ways. And of course, we all live for the travel stories. Peter Knapp, my super-agent from day one and the first person to open the doors of publishing to me: Thank you for your tireless spirit even when I feel fatigued, your endless enthusiasm when I lack the confidence, and the hundreds of things you do to champion my work. I couldn't have found a better partner than you in this industry, which sometimes seems to serve its own Trials!

To the team at Random House Children's Books: It truly takes a village to make a book, and I have landed in the best one (confirmed: no hellbeasts here—though plenty of hot demons). Josh Redlich and Cynthia Lliguichuzhca, my utmost gratitude for all that you do to promote my books and keep my scheduling straight when I can't even do so myself. My thanks to Candice Gianetti and Colleen Fellingham, extraordinary copy editors who seem to know my work better than I and catch my various (often directionally challenged) logistical plot holes and also make fantastic plot point suggestions. To Emma Leynse, who keeps me organized and on top of things, and has done so much in moving this book from a pile of words into an actual book. To Liz Dresner for the beyond-stunning cover design and Danzhu Hu for the breathtaking illustrations of my dreams—thank you for creating a beautiful package for this story. And to Sveta Dorosheva, who illustrated the gorgeous map of the realms for this series. My gratitude to Julie Wilson and Annie Q, who have once again brought Àn'yīng's story to life in the gorgeous audiobook rendering. Thanks to Andrea Baird, Stephania Villar, and the entire GetUnderlined team for all the fantastic, clever, and creative marketing ideas for this book (hot demons forever); Michelle Campbell and the School and Library Marketing team; and, of course, Wendy Loggia and Mallory Loehr for helming the Delacorte Press and RHCB ships. As well, my gratitude to Beverly Horowitz and Barbara Marcus for their support throughout my career.

To the incredible team at PF&B, I couldn't have landed a better home. Thank you to Stuti Telidevara and Danielle Barthel for ensuring I met all the deadlines and logistical dates of publication; Andrea Mai and Emily Sweet for shepherding my books through the marketing and publicity gamut; Kat Toolan for taking my stories to foreign languages; Ben Kaslow-Zieve and Angela Lee for the tax and international rights support.

To my UK team, thank you to Claire Wilson for continuing to champion my stories across the pond. Thank you to the HarperVoyager UK team for all the care you have put into publishing my stories: Natasha Bardon, Ajebowale Roberts,

Catherine Perks, Robyn Watts, and Chloe Gough. Sarah Foster, for the most perfect cover designs, and Dong Qiu, for once again illustrating covers (the standard and FairyLoot editions!) that feel like you've taken the essence of the book and rendered them in art form.

Thank you to the teams at FairyLoot and Illumicrate for their life-changing support of my novels. Anissa and Daphne, you are truly two of the best in the publishing world. Thank you, thank you for putting my stories into so many more readers' hands.

Thank you, once again, to Jennifer Zhang for helping me brainstorm the perfect Chinese title (and for being an encyclopedia of C-dramas and 内娱). Thank you to my friends both in and outside of publishing for their unending enthusiasm over my books, for shouting me out or reading my stories or being excited over my book news/updates.

To my family, I am so lucky to have one as wonderful as you. 妈妈，爸爸：感谢你们一直以来给我的支持以及丰富的文化教育，还有我们从小快乐的成长环境，培养了我的想象力与对世界的认知，给了我充实的灵感来写今天的小说。Arielle, I'm glad we still share the same love of stories and shows/movies; thanks for all the fun sister time. Mom and Dad Sin：谢谢你们的支持；加入你们的家庭算是我一生的大福！And of course, Clement—my Pewp and other half, I couldn't be luckier to share this life with you. Thanks for entertaining and loving all my shenanigans, and for wholeheartedly supporting me and my dreams. I'm glad it didn't take a multirealm war and another reincarnation for me to have found you (though I suppose we'd never know). Now we have GTS2PM, and the family continues to grow.

Finally, to my readers: my stories and I would not be here without your support. Whether you found me through this series or whether you've been reading me since my debut, thank you from the bottom of my heart for sharing in this magic with me.

ABOUT THE AUTHOR

Amélie Wen Zhao is the *New York Times*, No.1 *Sunday Times*, and internationally bestselling author of The Three Realms duology: *The Scorpion and the Night Blossom* and *The Dragon and the Sun Lotus*; the Song of the Last Kingdom duology: *Song of Silver, Flame Like Night* and *Dark Star Burning, Ash Falls White*; and The Blood Heir trilogy: *Blood Heir, Red Tigress,* and *Crimson Reign*. She was born in Paris and grew up in Beijing, where she spent her days reenacting tales of legendary heroes, ancient kingdoms, and lost magic at her grandmother's courtyard house. She attended college in the United States and now resides in New York City, working as a finance professional by day and fantasy author by night. In her spare time, she loves to travel with her family in China, where she's determined to walk the rivers and lakes of old just like the practitioners in her novels.

ameliezhao.com